IMMUNE

The characters and events portrayed in this book are fictitious. Any similarity to real persons, living or dead, is coincidental and not intended by the author.

Published by 47North
P.O. Box 400818
Las Vegas, NV 89140

ISBN-13: 9781612184944
ISBN-10: 1612184944

IMMUNE

BOOK TWO OF THE RHO AGENDA

RICHARD
PHILLIPS

47NORTH

ACKNOWLEDGMENTS

I would like to thank my lovely wife, Carol, for her support, encouragement, and feedback throughout the telling of this tale. Many thanks to Alan Werner for the long hours he spent going over the story line and providing me his fresh perspective. I also want to express my appreciation to my agent, Paul Lucas, and to the fine 47North team for all of their efforts to bring the Rho Agenda trilogy to a broader audience. Finally, I want to thank Jeff VanderMeer for the wonderful work he did to refine the Rho Agenda novels. It has been a pleasure working with a master of the craft.

CHAPTER 1

The naked teenage boy lay flat, suspended in the air as if he rested upon an invisible examination table.

If he could have blinked his eyes, he would have. But that was not possible. The stasis field that held him suspended four feet above the floor permitted no such movement. Instead, his eyes stared upward, unable to close, unable to blink, his movements now subject to a will other than his own.

Gray light from the conduits that snaked overhead illuminated the jumble of machinery crowding the room. The teen's ears thrummed with the low, throbbing pulse that surrounded him. He wasn't sure how long he had lain there. Except for the thrumming, his only full-time companion was pain. He dared not think about his other visitor.

A subtle current in the air wafted around his body, a passing coolness that gently brushed the hairs on his arms and alerted him to the visitor's arrival before the other man passed into his peripheral vision. The arrival confirmed only one thing: God had abandoned him. A lifetime of belief had been stripped away; the awful truth lay bare. No loving God would allow his child to endure this. Not this.

The face of Dr. Donald Stephenson, deputy director of Los Alamos National Laboratory, swam into the boy's view. The scientist's eyes swept him as clinically as a medical examiner's studying a corpse. An apparatus the size of a small screwdriver dangled from Stephenson's fingertips. From one end, a bundle of hair-thin wires extended for an inch and a half; the other end terminated in an odd-shaped lens that swiveled about on a pivot. Leaning in close, Dr. Stephenson held the device to the teen's face, reaching out with his left hand to touch the skin that covered the orbital socket of the boy's right eye. Satisfied, the deputy director set the device to one side and pulled on a pair of latex gloves.

Stephenson's hawkish face leaned in once more.

"Good morning, Raul. Shall we begin?"

Clamped within the grasp of the invisible lines of force that draped his body, Raul's mouth could not even twitch to release a scream as the scalpel removed his right eyelid, then scooped deeply into the socket. A single spurt of blood splattered Raul's face before his nanite-infested bloodstream could stem the flow. Moving faster than Raul's healing process, Dr. Stephenson thrust the end of the lens device into the empty socket, sending the hair-like wires squirming into Raul's head, burrowing deep into the exposed optic nerve.

Having abandoned his prayers for death, Raul hurled his mental curses at the God who had abandoned his son to an altogether more horrifying crucifixion.

CHAPTER 2

School had been out less than a week. Heather should have started feeling that wonderful sense of relaxation that comes from getting used to the idea that there isn't any homework due. Instead, a growing sense of foreboding plagued her.

She had been dreaming again. Those strange dreams, which she couldn't quite remember when she awoke at odd hours of the night, left her skin damp with sweat. Neither Mark nor Jennifer had mentioned nightmares, leaving Heather the only one of the three who wasn't sleeping peacefully and looking rested.

That she couldn't remember the dreams was strange in itself. After all, she remembered everything else. All three of them could play back anything they saw, the images as clear on the theater screens of their minds as if they were seeing it anew. But not these dreams. She actually dreaded going to sleep for fear of what the dreams contained, although that made even less sense.

What sleep she had been getting came toward dawn, marring her pattern of being an early riser.

This morning, a bright sliver of sunlight made its way through the branches of the tree outside her window and into her room. As the branches swayed in the gentle morning breeze, the annoying sunbeam repeatedly stabbed at her eyes, like the glint from a cavalry trooper's signaling mirror in an old Western movie.

"OK. OK. I'm getting up!"

In addition to her not feeling rested, this morning her head hurt. Griping at sunbeams wouldn't help, but somehow it made her feel just a little bit better to vent her annoyance to the universe.

Heather debated just throwing on her robe and going downstairs for a cup of hot tea. But a hot shower called to her. She breathed in the steam as she stood beneath the pulsing jet from the massage nozzle, the temperature set just cool enough to avoid raising blisters on her skin. She gave thanks for old houses built before flow restrictors reduced the available water pressure to an impotent trickle. It was one of the many things about her house that she loved.

By the time she dressed and made her way downstairs to the kitchen, Heather felt almost human. The television news blared from the living room, indicating the location of her parents, but she bypassed it, blocking out the breathless voices of reporters in Breaking Story mode as she homed in on the bin with the tea bags.

"Good morning, Mom, Dad," she called out over her shoulder as she slid the cup into the microwave to heat the water.

The lack of response to her greeting struck her as curious. Perhaps her parents had gone outside without bothering to turn off the TV. She'd switch it off and join them as soon as her tea was ready.

Thinking of the TV focused her attention in that direction, finally allowing the words of the news report to filter into her consciousness.

"...at his home just outside of Fort Meade, Maryland, this morning. In what police are calling a tragic case of murder-suicide, the FBI discovered the bodies of NSA director Jonathan Riles and senior NSA computer scientist Dr. David Kurtz at the Riles residence this morning.

"Although the investigation is ongoing, high-level sources inside the administration tell CNN that FBI agents were in the process of executing a search of the Riles home, pursuant to a search warrant, when they discovered the two bodies in Admiral Riles's private office.

"We have also received word that Admiral Riles may have been despondent over an FBI investigation into illegal activities being conducted by the NSA, activities that Riles had authorized without the knowledge or approval of the president.

"...Hold on. We are just getting word that the vice president, a longtime friend and college roommate of Admiral Riles at the Naval Academy, is about to issue a short statement. We go now to the vice president..."

Heather didn't remember leaving the kitchen and making her way into the living room, but she now found herself standing behind the couch where her mom and dad sat riveted to the television screen. Vice President Gordon stared somberly into the television camera from behind his desk at the White House.

"My fellow Americans. It is with the deepest sadness that I address you this morning. I have taken this unusual step because I cannot bear the thought of how my good friend may be portrayed in coming days. With that in mind, I think it is important to let you, the American people, know a little of what I know about the man and the situation that led to this tragic outcome.

"I have known Jonathan Riles since we were roommates together at Annapolis. I played alongside him on the Navy football team. I studied at a desk across the room from him as he qualified for selection as a Rhodes scholar. And I served with and under him as he rose to the rank of vice admiral in the United States Navy.

"Never have I met a braver man or one who cared more about his country than Jonny Riles. He was a man's man, a man from a different age. He cut his teeth in the historic struggle of the Cold War. That struggle against the Soviet Empire molded his belief set, and in the end, I believe that it was that belief set that destroyed him.

"All of you are aware of the tremendous implications of the president's public announcement of the existence of the Rho Ship, along with his plan for a phased release into the public domain of the beneficial technologies your government has been able to unravel to this point.

"You are also, no doubt, aware that there has been a tremendous ongoing debate, both inside and outside the administration, about the wisdom of making that information public. Our president took the courageous and, I believe, correct step in putting the good of our planet ahead of selfish national interest by releasing that information.

"Unfortunately, despite all of his years of exceptional service to our country, my oldest friend could not bring himself to accept that decision. In recent days, it has come to our attention that Admiral Riles was misusing his position at the National Security Agency in an attempt to discredit the ongoing work being done by the fine scientists on the Rho Project. In doing so, he hoped to prevent the release of technologies that Admiral Riles felt were best kept secret and used solely in the interest of the United States.

"Once he became aware that his unauthorized criminal activities had been discovered, Admiral Riles killed Dr. David Kurtz, the man whom he believed to be a government informant, and then turned his gun upon himself."

The vice president paused momentarily, his eyes shining with moisture.

"People often speak of the fog of war. Well, there is another type of fog that can obscure the vision of those who have risen to a position of power through a lifetime of service to their country. It is the fog of personal beliefs. Sometimes that fog can become so thick that it obscures the one thing that serves as a constant beacon, leading our ships safely into port. That one thing is the Constitution of the United States of America.

"I close now, hoping that I have given you some sense of the man I knew. A good man, a brave and honorable American, an old Navy hand who lost his way in the fog and allowed himself to lose sight of the beacon that could have guided him safely through.

"May God provide his mercy and forgiveness to my oldest friend. May God be with his family in these terrible times. May God be with us all."

As the image of the vice president disappeared, replaced with one of the myriad of TV analysts, Heather found tears rolling down her cheeks. She had never even heard of Jonathan Riles but, almost, she felt that she knew the man. The sense of foreboding that had been growing in her mind these last few days now had substance. Apparently, their attempts to stop the Rho Project had failed.

From the kitchen, the periodic "food ready" beep of the microwave continued, unnoticed.

CHAPTER 3

Those eyes.

They were a part of the Ripper's legend: the way the light refracted in his oddly shaped pupils whenever he was angry, so that they seemed to burn with an inner flame. Those who had seen that red glint and lived to tell about it thought that it was like peering into the depths of hellfire itself. The flames behind those pupils leaped and danced, as if to a tune that only Beelzebub and Jack Gregory could play.

But Janet knew. Lucifer might rule in hell, but here on planet Earth, Jack Gregory was the reigning killer angel.

As she looked into Jack's face, a chill ran up Janet's spine all the way to her scalp, leaving in its wake a tingle reminiscent of the aftereffects of a jolt from a Taser. Amazing. There was no thrill on earth quite like what she got from staring into those eyes. God, it made her hungry. It made her want to wrap her legs around him and dig her long fingernails into the skin of his bare back. But that would have to wait.

Jack was planning something big, so they were gathered around a table in a safe house just north of Santa Fe to work out the final details.

"So we have confirmation?" Jack asked.

Janet nodded. "Yes. The refrigerated truck will depart the special medical lab at Kirtland Air Force Base at midnight, get up on I-25, and head directly back to Santa Fe before turning off toward Los Alamos. It looks like they are going to turn the body over to Dr. Stephenson at Rho Division sometime before dawn, right back here at the Los Alamos National Laboratory."

Raymond Bronson leaned forward, placing both elbows on the table. "It sure didn't take long after Riles's death for the powers that be to get Priest's corpse transferred to the control of the Rho Project team."

Jack shrugged. "They are in full-blown cleanup mode. That's why tonight we are going to dirty things up for them."

Bronson frowned. "Jack, you know I never question your judgment. But don't you think we are really stepping out on the ragged edge on this one?" Janet noted Bronson's caution without surprise, his nature serving as a valuable foil to Jack's studied recklessness.

"No more than we already are. We are completely out in the cold now. All our government contacts are cut, and we have to make damn sure to keep it that way. Somehow, Jonathan Riles managed to limit knowledge of our involvement to a group that apparently only included himself and David Kurtz.

"If that knowledge hadn't died with the two of them, you can be very sure we would have already had to deal with people sent to make us just as dead. Whoever betrayed Jonathan has to know that Riles had a special field team deployed, but they will assume the team will be doing its best to disappear."

Bronson shook his head. "Which sounds like a damn good plan to me."

"Maybe so, but we aren't going to be that cooperative."

Bobby Daniels, a tall, lanky man with a head as bald as a cue ball, stepped out of the shadows near the window. "I'm game, Jack. Can't live forever."

Janet smiled. Same old Bobby.

Seeing Jack staring at him, Bronson shrugged. "Of course I'm with you. Just thought I'd offer you one last chance to take the easy way out."

"I'd rather be the hunter than the hunted," Jack said. "And I want that body."

Leaning over the table with the one-to-fifty-thousand-scale military maps of the target area spread across it, Jack stuck a pin in a spot on the highway, sticking two others in locations where the terrain contours indicated that line of sight back to the first point terminated.

"Bobby, you'll wait right here, just at this bend in the highway, about a half mile before the ambush point. Bronson, you'll take the other spot, blocking the highway approach from the opposite side. Remember, when Bobby gives the signal, it'll take between thirty and forty-five seconds before the truck reaches me and you hear me take it down. There shouldn't be much traffic there that time of night, but if there is, you get it stopped."

"And if a car is too tight to the truck and makes it through before I can get the police detour set up?" Bobby asked.

"I'll deal with that on my end. Let's hope it doesn't come to that, though."

Then Jack turned to her. "How's the Abdul Aziz recording coming, Janet?"

Janet felt a jolt of adrenaline just hearing Jack say her name. "I've still got about an hour's work left to do. I have the available recordings of his voice, and I'm using as many of his natural phrasings as possible. But for part of it I have to synthesize the vocal patterns in order to create the extra words we need and to keep a natural-sounding sequence. By the time I route it through the disposable cell phone, the best analysts in the business won't be able to say for sure whether or not it was manipulated."

"That's good, because even the local nine-one-one operations record everything. And we damn sure want the call recorded."

"And the chopper?" Bobby asked.

"I'll be appropriating one of the forest service birds from the site just outside Taos. Janet and I will be in it. You two get your hands on a couple of fast dirt bikes.

"Remember, you are going to keep the road blocked for exactly five minutes while Janet and I deal with the truck and its contents. After that, haul ass along this dirt road to the rendezvous point. Dump the bikes into the canyon. We'll be waiting with the chopper in this clearing right here."

Jack straightened up, handing a marked copy of the map to each of them. "Any questions?"

"Just the usual." Bronson's cocky grin had returned. "How'd I get so good-looking?"

"Just don't be late," said Jack. "We'll give you fifteen minutes to reach us before we leave."

"Wouldn't think of it," said Bronson as he and Bobby turned to the door.

As soon as the other two had left the house, Jack walked to the closet and retrieved a large box full of personal effects and other items of interest that they had purloined from Carlton "Priest" Williams's house. Two large files of information on Jack and Janet

Johnson were among the contents, but it was not these that had attracted Jack's attention.

Finding what he was looking for, Jack held up a skull-shaped key ring.

"I think it's time we paid one more visit to Priest's old haunt."

Janet nodded. Just the two of them, alone together. Like always.

Her right hand subconsciously checked the Heckler & Koch 9mm Compact strapped beneath her left armpit. The Los Alamos high country was about to heat up.

CHAPTER 4

Jennifer didn't like lying, especially to Mark and Heather. But there was no way she could tell them that she had not been sleeping at all. Not without revealing the reason for her sleepless nights. And that knowledge would freak them out enough to put them both into low earth orbit.

Jennifer paused, her gaze sweeping out over the near-perfect darkness of the canyon and then up to the night sky above. There was no moon tonight to dull her view of the stars and planets that swarmed above her.

The night skies of the high desert of New Mexico were one of the most awesome sights on the planet. The large stretches of open country with no human habitation and the thin air and low humidity of the high altitudes combined to reveal a view that few on the planet had ever seen: a sky so full of stars and planets that it was hard to find gaps between them.

Jennifer loved looking at that sky. She often lay outside, gazing upward, imagining that the sky was below her and that she was glued to the ground, gazing downward at the stars. If she were to come unstuck, then she would fall, down and down, past the planets, to the very stars themselves. She pulled her thoughts back from the heavens to gaze down the steep slope.

Her theory had proven correct. The only thing that limited the effects of the neural enhancements each of the three of them had received on their first visit to the Second Ship was their self-image, but that limitation could be overcome by need. Her need had finally driven Jennifer to overcome at least some of her self-imposed limitations.

Only that need had driven her to believe that she could run as she now could. Not as fast or as powerfully as Mark, but fast enough and without tiring. Only that need had let her cast off her glasses and develop her eyesight so that she could now see in the dark almost as well as a cat. Only that need had driven her to lie to her friends and family so that she could sneak out on these nightly runs.

She knew she was risking discovery, should anyone check closely enough to discover the pillows stuffed under the covers on her bed. But her need drove her beyond the timidity that, only weeks before, would have left her a nervous wreck had she even contemplated doing what she now did. She was through playing the meek geek, through playing second fiddle to Mark and Heather.

Jennifer moved down the steep wall of the canyon, passing silently through the brush before turning left along an invisible but thoroughly familiar path. The soft magenta light of the ship cavern enfolded her, the warm glow gentle enough that it did not blind her, despite the darkness from which she had just come.

Ducking under the smooth curves of the ship where it touched the wall, Jennifer moved directly to the spot where the alien weapon had punched a hole cleanly through all the decks of the Second Ship, the edges of the hole so smooth that it looked as if the deck and hull had been made that way. Without pause, Jennifer leaped up to catch the edge of the first deck, swinging her body smoothly up and in.

Continuing onward, she rapidly ascended to the room where the four headsets lay along the curving desktop, each positioned directly in front of one of the chairs that rode the narrow track in front of that table. Jennifer glanced down at the delicate, flexible bands with the small bubble at each end. It was odd, really, the way she, Mark, and Heather always left those headsets in almost the exact position in which they had originally found them. Anything else just didn't feel right.

Jennifer picked up the first of the translucent bands, sliding it over her temples, pausing only momentarily as the feeling of relaxation swept through her body, like a shiver from a cool breeze. Then, once again, she began climbing up through the hole to the decks above.

Even before she had settled into one of the three swivel couches, the imagery that dissolved the smoothly flowing ceiling, walls, and floor of the command deck left her wrapped in the vastness of space itself. It was only a recorded section of this ship's vast travels, but Jennifer loved it.

However, tonight she allowed herself only a brief glance at the wondrous view, shifting her attention to the data banks provided by the ship's onboard library. It was the discovery she had kept secret from the others, telling herself that once she understood how to better access and understand the information it contained, she would reveal the treasure trove to her brother and best friend. And she still intended to do that. Just not yet.

After all, she had only just begun to scratch the surface. With each visit to the ship, Jennifer managed to solve more of the puzzle, each attempt uncovering some little clue that allowed her to delve a little deeper into the ship's data banks. Not deep enough to uncover anything of great importance, but the progress kept her going, feeding her thirst for knowledge. Not enough to quench it. It merely stoked the fire of her need.

And as Jennifer lay back, engulfed by the alien couch, swimming in a sea of data, that fire burned white-hot.

CHAPTER 5

It had been in the rugged mountains due north of Chitral, across the Kunar River, high up along that narrow strip of Afghan land that separated Pakistan from Tajikistan, that Jack had last worn full Arab garb and carried an AK-47 rifle. Now, as Jack crouched in the darkness overlooking New Mexico Highway 502, just west of the intersection where Highway 30 curled away toward the sleepy town of Española, a whisper of déjà vu caressed the nape of his neck.

The Arab clothing, the AK-47, and the weapons selected for this raid had all come from the special locker Jack had uncovered at the remote hideaway, which had formerly been used by one Carlton "Priest" Williams. That weapons locker had been one of many unusual discoveries Jack had made upon tracking down the site the day after he had killed Priest.

Priest had always been overconfident. It was one of many unprofessional aspects of the ex–Delta Force commando that Jack had despised upon first meeting the man. That overconfidence produced sloppiness, which had resulted in the insurance form Jack had found in the glove box of Priest's truck. That form had revealed the truck had been stolen from a man named Delbert Graves. A quick check of public records revealed that Graves was a hermit survivalist who owned a small ranch deep in the high country northeast of Los Alamos along the boundary of the Santa Clara Indian Reservation.

How many months it had been since Priest Williams had killed Delbert Graves and appropriated the man's property as his hideout, Jack could not determine exactly. By the state of decay of the corpses Jack had found in the dry well near the main house, Priest must have been using it off and on for almost a year. There was little doubt that Priest had kept the place secret from everyone, including his unknown employer.

In addition to a collection of women's bodies, there were two male corpses. One of these was probably that of the unfortunate Delbert Graves. Jack had recognized the other male corpse, despite the rot. Now he knew what had become of the assassin Abdul Aziz, for whom numerous agencies of the US government were still searching.

Here tonight, Jack's earlier decision to avoid relaying the information of Priest's hideaway to the people at the NSA was about to pay dividends.

Jack glanced down at the dimly illuminated display of his watch: 1:03 a.m. The drive from Kirtland Air Force Base to Los Alamos took an hour and a half under normal circumstances. The refrigerated truck carrying Priest's corpse would be traveling the speed limit on roads that had little traffic at this hour. That meant that it would be turning off Highway 84 onto Highway 502 right about now.

Pulling a small infrared flashlight from his belt, Jack flashed it twice, signaling Janet to begin the cell phone transmission. Then, slipping his goggles into place and adjusting the infrared laser sniper-sight, Jack settled deeper into his hide position to wait.

The wait would not be a long one.

CHAPTER 6

Yolanda Martinez was tired. It was never easy being a 911 operator, even in a small town like Española, New Mexico, but working the night shift was the worst. On weekends and paydays, the call volume built steadily as last call at the bars drew nearer. Drunk-and-disorderlies were the most common calls, although stabbings and shootings happened often enough. Then there were the alcohol-related accidents and the late-night angry spousal confrontations.

But tonight was Monday night. Actually, it was now Tuesday morning, and it was most certainly nobody's payday. It was one of those nights when even the lowriders who liked to cruise town in their hydraulically enhanced hopping cars could not find the energy to stay out past midnight. Out in front of the police station, where the Los Alamos Highway met up with Paseo de Oñate, only an occasional vehicle rumbled past to break the silence. The place was dead.

That should have been a good thing. But Yolanda's daughter had stayed home sick from school, and Yolanda had been forced to take care of her until her husband, Roberto, had gotten home from work. She had barely had time to get ready for her shift, grabbing a microwave burrito at the Quick Stop on her way to the police station. Sleep was a distant memory. In the absence of things to do, drowsiness tugged at Yolanda's eyelids as she sipped at another mug of burned coffee. It didn't help that Sergeant Billy Collins was fast asleep a dozen feet away from her, his booted feet propped on the desk at an angle that threatened to send a stack of unfinished police reports fluttering toward the floor. At least he didn't snore.

As long as she could remember, it had been like this. Some nights so busy and disturbing that she wanted to cry, some nights so dismally boring that she wanted to go start trouble herself, just so someone would call.

When the 911 line rang, it startled her so badly that she jumped. Shaking her head to clear the grogginess, Yolanda answered it before it could ring again.

"Española Police Department. What is your emergency?"

The voice that answered her was so heavily accented that it took her several seconds to understand the import of what she was hearing.

"Listen carefully. Do not interrupt me, because I will not say this twice and I will not be on the line long enough for you to trace this call. My name is Abdul Aziz. I am the one your government has been hunting with such utter futility. On this night, only a few minutes from now, I will take something that America, the Great Satan, has been hiding from the rest of humanity under the name of the Rho Project. Are you listening to me?"

There was a pause on the line as Yolanda struggled to simultaneously answer and throw a pencil at Sergeant Collins.

"Yes. I am listening."

The pause at the other end of the line dragged on for several more seconds before the man continued.

"If you hurry, it is possible that you might get some of your mobile police cruisers to the intersection of Highway 30 and Highway 502 before I have finished my business and departed, but I doubt it. There will be dead bodies, so be prepared. If you are wise, you will have the officers take some blood samples that they do not turn over to your military.

"*Insha'Allah*, even godless swine like you may yet be enlightened. Hurry now. Do not delay."

"Wait."

But the phone line went dead as the word left Yolanda's lips.

"What have you got?" Sergeant Collins's voice at her shoulder startled her again. Apparently, the man had not been as deeply asleep as she had thought.

By the time she had played back the recording, Billy Collins was already removing a twelve-gauge shotgun from the rack and heading toward the door. He paused to yell back over his shoulder, "Get on the horn to Fred and Enrique. They're the closest cruiser, so get them rolling. I'll meet them on the way. After that, round up every other squad car we have out there and get them all moving that way."

"What about the state police?"

"Let them know as soon as you have our folks moving, and put in a call to the sheriff. I won't wait for them, though."

The door slammed behind Billy Collins as Yolanda pressed the switch that activated the radio microphone. As she began speaking, the thought that she might never see Billy alive again tickled the back of her mind.

CHAPTER 7

The sensation of the stock of the AK-47 against his cheek felt good. Something about the solid feel of a Kalashnikov made it obvious why this was the most popular assault rifle in the world. The weapon felt like what it was: reliable.

Jack Gregory thumbed the infrared laser's power on and peered out through the scope, which made the targeting dot visible. This was a sniper modification he had added to the rifle to fit this particular purpose, one that he had zeroed in exactly four hours before.

Jack had handloaded a hundred rounds of ammunition using the press and loading die he had found in Priest's basement. He always loaded his own ammunition if given the opportunity. A bullet's trajectory brings it out of the barrel of a rifle up through the sight line, continuing to rise several inches for the next hundred-plus meters. Then the round begins to drop, passing back down through the line of sight before running out of energy. Only by loading the exact measure of gunpowder into each round and by using the same weight and shape of slug can a shooter know precisely where the round will hit.

Priest had never bothered with such details. Jack did.

A three-burst crackle of static on the small radio at his side let him know that the truck had just rolled past Bronson's position and was rounding the curve that would shortly bring it into Jack's sight line. Jack had picked this spot so that the first shot would take the driver while the truck was still on the curve, causing it to veer off the road at that point. That would force the man riding shotgun to reach for the wheel, exposing him for the second shot.

As the twin high beams of the refrigerated truck swept around the bend, the driver's face swam into view, illuminated in the infrared scope by the lights from the truck dashboard. The laser dot steadied on the driver's mouth. At this range, the bullet would strike an inch above the dot. Jack's gloved finger squeezed the trigger smoothly, his shoulder kicking back with the recoil as the sound of the weapon split the night air like thunder.

The truck swerved and then straightened as the other man in the truck grabbed the steering wheel. Jack let the natural resistance of his body rock him forward again as smoothly as if he were on springs, his aim-point steadying as his finger squeezed off the second round.

The sound of screeching metal mingled with the echoes of the second gunshot as the truck veered off the road and plowed into the rocks and trees on the far side. The trailer jackknifed past the truck cab, twisting and flipping over as it came to a sudden halt.

Jack was already halfway across the highway by the time the trailer rocked to a stop. A quick glance to his left revealed Janet lying prone a few feet off the road, her rifle leveled and ready to provide covering fire.

Jack reached the far side of the highway and plunged down the slight embankment. The cab of the truck had sandwiched itself around the thick trunk of a pine tree, the lower branches of which were illuminated by a headlight that had somehow survived the impact, although it now pointed skyward. A strong scent of diesel hung in the air.

Jumping up on what was left of the driver's side running board, Jack tugged at the door, which yielded reluctantly to his second effort. The inside of the cab was a ruin of shattered glass, crumpled metal, and blood. The driver's head was wedged between the spokes of the steering wheel, a large chunk of the rear and top of the skull blown away by the exiting bullet.

Jack cut the seat belt strap and heaved the body out of the cab and onto the ground below. As Jack climbed farther inside so that he could cut the seat belt off the guard, the man's head turned, revealing a perfectly round hole just above the junction of the man's eyebrows. The eyes fluttered open.

Jack cut the strap, grabbed the guard's shoulders, and pulled hard, sliding the body across the wrecked cab and out to fall beside the body of the driver. Jack jumped down, landing just beyond the two men.

If he hadn't already watched the miraculous healing powers displayed by the nanites that had infested Priest Williams's blood, the sight of the bodies of two men who should already be very dead trying to repair themselves would have shocked him to his core. Already, the wound at the back of the driver's skull had begun to knit itself closed, although the damage was so severe that the operation would take some time, assuming the nanites could overcome the loss of brain tissue.

But the slug that had passed through the head of the guard had not created such a large exit wound. The man was beginning to show signs of recovered voluntary movement; his eyes followed every motion as Jack bent down, grabbed the driver's body, and turned it over so that it knelt, face to the ground, toward the west.

Jack repeated the process, positioning the guard's body next to that of the driver. Then, he drew the long, curved Saracen sword from the sash that bound it to his waist and prodded the sharp point into the small of the guard's back. The body arched involuntarily, trying to move away from the poking blade, and as it did, the fellow's neck rose, raising his head with it.

In a motion so swift that the eye could barely follow, Jack brought the Arabic weapon around in an arc that swept the guard's head from his shoulders. The head rolled across the ground, chased by a large arterial spray of blood as the body collapsed forward once more.

Jack moved to the driver, once again prodding hard into the man's back with the tip of the sword. However, this time the body failed to respond. Apparently, even nanites had their healing limitations, at least within the amount of time he had allowed them. Jack repositioned the driver slightly so that he could place a foot on his back. Then, grabbing a handful of hair, Jack simultaneously lifted and chopped. It took three short strokes with the sword before the head came free.

When a person is beheaded, blood does not gush or flow; it spurts forth, powered by the rapidly dying pump of the heart. And it is not brain or nerve death that kills the heart. It is the lack of sufficient fluid to fill the chambers.

Jack had been eight years old when he had seen his first man beheaded. It had been in the central square of Riyadh, Saudi Arabia, a place known by the foreigners in the Saudi capital as

Chop-Chop Square. Jack had watched as the man had been forced to kneel so that he leaned over the chopping block.

At the last instant, a second Saudi had jabbed the kneeling man in the back with the tip of a knife. The involuntary reaction was automatic; the man arched away from the knifepoint, the movement extending his neck. And the mighty sword had descended, sending the man's head tumbling into the basket that waited below. The heart of the dead man pumped the lifeblood from his body in one great pulse, followed by another much weaker jet, before extinguishing itself in a final set of small spasms.

Jack had watched it all from the front row of the gathered crowd, he and his mother guests of honor. The man had been his father.

Draped in the shadows produced by the headlight-illuminated branches above, Jack moved quickly to reposition the bodies in the kneeling position in which he had first placed them. The heads he placed two strides to the west facing back toward their respective bodies.

Then, retrieving a small plastic bag from a pouch at his side, Jack extracted from it a section of fingernail and two hairs.

Hair and nails continued to grow long after a corpse was dead. Jack had taken these particular strands of hair and the accompanying piece of a fingernail from the corpse of Abdul Aziz after pulling the body from Priest's well earlier in the day. They would now serve a higher calling than they would have achieved had they remained attached to their previous owner.

With a quick scratching motion, Jack embedded the fingernail fragment beneath the skin of the driver's right wrist. He then dropped the two hairs onto the man's blood-soaked shirt, letting them attach themselves to the sticky garment.

Done with this portion of the crime scene setup, Jack glanced at his watch: 1:13 a.m. The cyan digital numbers winked up at him, as if urging Jack to move faster.

A handful of powerful strides carried him around the jack-knifed rig to a spot at the rear of the trailer. It lay on its side, the silver metal warped and twisted but intact.

As Jack had expected, the rear doors were closed and secured with a high-grade lock. Not that it mattered. C4 had a way of dealing with locking mechanisms that was nothing short of spectacular. In this case, Jack used a foot-long strand of det cord, wrapping it through and around the locking mechanism before attaching the detonator.

Unreeling a strand of paired wires, Jack backed around the side of the trailer, securing the wire ends to a small green device with a handle. A quick twist of that handle sent another loud explosion echoing through the night, a sound that would cue Janet to abandon the overwatch position and move back to the helicopter.

The blast had torn open the lower door of the overturned trailer, allowing the refrigerated air to flow out, forming a slow-moving river of condensing fog. Jack switched on his flashlight and stepped inside.

It did not take him long to find what he was looking for. Priest's frozen corpse had been wrapped in a body bag and encased in a thick plastic box. Having been thrown open by the force of the impact, the case had spilled the body onto the overturned equipment that lined the wall of the refrigerated truck, a wall that now formed the floor.

Jack unzipped the bag, scanning the contents with his flashlight just long enough to satisfy himself that it contained the autopsied corpse and severed head of Carlton "Priest" Williams before zipping it closed once more.

Tugging the body bag clear of the wreckage, Jack checked his watch: 1:18. Time enough for one last task before departure.

Jack withdrew a needle from his robes as he moved back to where he had positioned the corpse of the driver and the guard. Then, attaching first one Pyrex tube and then a second, Jack extracted a vial of blood from each of the two corpses.

Making one final circuit of the area to ensure he had not overlooked anything, Jack returned the sword to its spot at his waist and tossed the body bag containing Priest's body over his shoulder. By the time he made his way back to retrieve the AK-47 rifle, Jack could hear the helicopter engine winding up on the ridge above the highway.

High above, stars spilled across the moonless night sky, the Milky Way pointing a trail back toward the waiting chopper. With a deep breath, Jack hitched the corpse higher on his shoulder, then moved out, his powerful legs propelling him up the steep slope and into the darkness beyond.

CHAPTER 8

For every one of his forty-seven years, Tribal Police Sergeant Jim "Tall Bear" Pino had lived here on the Santa Clara Indian Reservation. For more than half of that time he had been a tribal policeman.

It was hardly normal procedure for nontribal police departments to call Indian police on things that were not considered Indian affairs. But Yolanda Martinez, a 911 operator for the Española police, was his third cousin by marriage, and she had sounded spooked.

Always, when they were children, Yolanda had come to Tall Bear whenever she needed help or reassurance. He had been the big brother she never had. While the years had sent them their own families and their own paths to travel, Yolanda and Tall Bear had remained close. Tonight, a dread premonition had made Yolanda call him and play the 911 recording over the line.

Although the Española Police had several squad cars on the way, Tall Bear was on duty and he was closer to the intersection described in the call. Tall Bear's tribal police cruiser was a Jeep Cherokee that had traveled country that most people thought only a man on a horse could reach. While he would never win any road races in the vehicle, it allowed him to use roads across tribal lands, which shortened the distance to his desired destination.

Crossing one last cattle guard, the Cherokee's wheels spewed a cloud of dust as Tall Bear left the dirt road to climb up onto the pavement of Highway 30. There was no traffic tonight, and he did not switch on the police light bar atop the vehicle. No use broadcasting his imminent arrival.

As he rounded the bend in the highway from which the junction of Highway 30 and Highway 502 was visible, Tall Bear discovered the reason for the complete lack of traffic. A small line of cars and trucks was stopped at a roadblock just west of the road junction.

Switching on his flashing police lights, Tall Bear maneuvered the Cherokee around the waiting traffic, through the Y intersection, and west along Highway 502. The roadblock consisted of a couple of unmanned construction barriers with blinking orange lights. Perhaps a hundred yards beyond the barrier, at a bend in the road, the lights of a police vehicle cascaded through the woods.

Odd. Even the local police departments never set up haphazard roadblocks such as this. There should at least be one deputy manning the point where traffic was blocked.

Tall Bear eased the Cherokee off the highway, around the barriers, and then back onto the pavement again, moving the vehicle forward much more slowly now. If his black hair had not hung to his waist, it would certainly have been standing straight up on his head. He was close enough now to see the flashing police light bar in the woods to the side of the highway clearly, but he could see no other vehicle lights.

Why didn't the police car have on its headlights and parking lights?

As he angled the Cherokee toward the spot, Tall Bear got the answer to his question. There was no police car. The flashing police light bar had been connected to an automobile battery and hung from a tree branch to make it appear that a police car had pulled into the wood line.

Suddenly, the night air seemed to take on a chill that had not been present moments before. The 911 message had said there would be death here. As he stared at the flashing light bar in the tree, Tall Bear believed.

Leaving his own police lights flashing, Tall Bear grabbed the heavy flashlight from the floorboard, touched the handle of the forty-five-caliber revolver that hung in its holster strapped to his side, and moved into the woods. Within seconds, he was away from the lights, moving west, parallel to the highway, a shadow among the shadows.

As a small boy, Tall Bear had worshipped his grandfather. The old man had taught him to hunt and fish, not with rifle and pole, but in the old ways of their people. His grandfather had instructed him to read trail sign, to understand what the earth said with each bent blade of grass, with the sudden silence of the insects, with the faint smells that hung on the breeze.

So few of the young people cared to learn the old ways now. They had been seduced by the call of the white man's world, lulled by the lethargic drone of the television, hunting only on an Xbox. But Tall Bear had stayed true to his ancestors, passing the old knowledge to his own sons. Here in the dark woods, as he moved silently among the trees, the voices of the ancients whispered to him.

The curve in the highway swept Tall Bear beyond sight of the roadblock, although a flicker of police lights lit the tips of the tallest trees. As he continued westward, the smell of cordite brought him to a halt. Someone had been blasting, although this smell was different from the dynamite used by road crews. It wasn't gunpowder either.

He was close now. The scent of spilled diesel told him that much. From high up on the ridge above, the sound of a helicopter rose in volume as it passed overhead before banking away to the north.

Tall Bear stepped to the edge of the road, trying to catch sight of it, but if it was up there, it must have been flying without lights.

Now that he had stepped out of the wood line, Tall Bear could see a light shining up into the trees from the far side of the road, no more than a hundred feet from where he now stood. It was a headlight.

Crossing the highway, Tall Bear moved more quickly now. Whatever the danger, there had been a wreck, and the possibility that someone lay injured in the wreckage pulled him forward.

As he got closer, the extent of the accident became clear. A truck had left the highway at high speed, its momentum wrapping the cab around a tree, sending the overturned trailer sliding past the cab in a motion that had almost ripped it free of its moorings.

In the indirect lighting provided by the one surviving headlight, Tall Bear saw two people, kneeling facedown to the ground, less than twenty feet from the mangled cab of the truck. They were not moving.

"Hey, are you hurt?" Tall Bear yelled as he ran toward them, flipping on his flashlight as he ran.

Two faces stared back at him, eyes reflecting in the moving beam of the flashlight, a sight that brought him to a stop, weapon drawn. The heads sat side by side, at least five feet separating them from the kneeling bodies.

The silence of the night draped him like a blanket. Tall Bear did not bother to switch off the flashlight. If this had been a trap, he would already have been dead. No. Not a trap. This was a message.

His pulse still pounding from the initial shock of the scene, Tall Bear tried to reassert his self-control. It wasn't that he hadn't seen dead people before—he had—but there was a coldness here that was…different.

Moving forward once again, Tall Bear allowed the flashlight beam to sweep the bodies before returning to the two heads, each of which had a bullet wound in the forehead. As he passed the bodies, he stepped around the large pool of blood that had spread out from the twin torsos of the murder victims. The initial spurt of blood had spewed out several feet, but the heads themselves sat on the ground beyond the farthest extent of the splatter.

Moving methodically now, Tall Bear noted the small details: The bodies were in military uniforms, both wearing sidearms, military-issue nine-millimeter Beretta pistols. The torsos had been ritualistically positioned so that they knelt in the manner of Muslims at prayer oriented due west instead of east, heads facing back to the east, five feet past the bodies.

A bullet had passed through each forehead and out the back of the head, although one of the exit wounds was much more massive, having blown out a significant portion of the skull.

What bothered Tall Bear had nothing to do with the way the corpses had been arranged. It had to do with where they had died. It was all wrong.

Moving back to the cab of the truck, Tall Bear climbed up onto what was left of the running board and leaned inside. The force of impact had shattered the windshield. Shining his flashlight around the back of the truck's cab, Tall Bear found what he was looking for. Blood and bits of brain matter splattered the seats and rear wall. Within seconds, he located the holes where the rifle slugs had punched their way out of the cab after exiting the heads of the victims.

The sense of wrongness now had a reason. Both men had been shot in the head, right here in the cab of the truck, shot in the head by a high-powered rifle that had splattered parts of their brains around the truck's interior. How then, when they had been pulled out of the truck after it wrecked, had their hearts still been beating powerfully enough to provide full arterial spray when they were beheaded?

The chill bumps that rose along Tall Bear's arms and neck had nothing to do with the temperature of the night air. What was it that the Arabic-sounding voice on the 911 tape had said? Something about making sure to take a blood sample of the dead men before the federal authorities arrived on the crime scene.

The sound of police sirens snapped Tall Bear out of his thoughts. That would be the boys from Española. If he was going to do something, it had to be now.

Jumping down from the truck cab, Tall Bear pulled a small, round can of Copenhagen tobacco from his pocket, suffering a momentary pang of regret as he dumped the contents of the nearly full can on the ground. Then he strode back to the spot where the corpses had spewed their lifeblood into the dirt. Ignoring the Navajo aversion to touching a corpse, he scooped some of the blood into the can, then replaced the lid and slid the can back into his pocket.

As he stood up and turned to walk back toward the highway, Tall Bear stepped on the small spot where he had scraped up some of the blood, leaving a bloody boot print in its place.

Since he was about to be kicked off a crime scene that was outside of tribal jurisdiction, it bothered him very little to have disturbed such a small amount of evidence. No doubt the Española Police would find some satisfaction in noting that the Indian cop had screwed up.

As Tall Bear reached the highway, the leading police car screeched to a stop beside him. Feeling the Copenhagen can in his pocket, Tall Bear had the uneasy premonition that he had just involved himself in something that felt like very bad medicine. It was going to take a powerful Ghost Sing to clear his mind to the point where sleep once again came easy.

CHAPTER 9

"Hello?" Heather's head poked through the open front door of the Smythe house.

"Hi, Heather," said Mrs. Smythe from the living room. "Mark and Jennifer are in the garage."

"Thanks."

As she stepped into the garage, Heather spotted Mark and Jennifer huddled together in the workshop area, peering intently at the cold-fusion apparatus.

Mark spotted her first. "Hey, Heather. Get over here and take a look at these readings."

"Why? Is something wrong?" Concern colored Heather's voice as she moved around the workbench that held the tank.

Peering over Jennifer's shoulder at the laptop's flat-panel display, Heather's concern faded away. "It looks good to me," she said.

"That's just it," said Jennifer, her fingers flying over the keyboard, bringing up a scrolling display of recorded data. "It might be a little too good. The national science contest is next week, and I'm afraid this project is going to stand out as something a group of high-school kids might not have been able to pull off."

Mark rolled his eyes. "In other words, Jennifer's worrying about nothing again."

Ever since they had each tried on one of the four headsets they had found on the alien ship, the three friends had experienced radical changes. Somehow, the metallic rings had formed a connection between their minds and the ship's computer, activating portions of their brains that had previously been dormant. And those changes to their brains and neuromuscular systems had remained, even after the headsets had been removed.

For Heather, the most pronounced effect had been her savant-like mathematical abilities. She could glance at a pebble and know that its volume was 4.3583 cubic centimeters. The same applied to her ability to manipulate the most complex mathematical equations. The answers were just there. It was nothing short of magical.

Heather shook her head. "Jen, this time I have to agree with Mark. Yes, the control systems are allowing the tank to generate a level of energy that is above the norm. But we've toned down our output to a level that is below that produced by several scientific teams."

"I don't know," said Jennifer. "Those research teams are made up of graduate students or professional physicists."

Heather patted Jennifer's shoulder and smiled down at her friend. "Did you see last year's National High School Science Competition winning entry? The kid made a working microscale model of a wind tunnel, instrumented and calibrated accurately enough to provide test results comparable to much larger, professional systems."

"Maybe."

"Jen, there's no 'maybe' to it. If Rain Girl here says it's so, then that's the way it is."

Heather ran her hand along the tank, feeling the warmth that radiated out through the shielding. When they had first tested the thing, it had put off so much heat that a person could burn herself by touching it, and the whistle given off by the steam-powered generator had been teakettle loud.

Their mechanical improvements had resolved these problems, and the power produced by the apparatus had completely eliminated the Smythe electric bill. Best of all, they had finished their project paper, except for one more proofreading pass.

"By the way, you sure took your sweet time getting over here this morning," said Mark, a broad grin spreading across his face. "What did you do? Have a sleep-in this morning?"

Heather slapped her hand to her forehead. "Oh crap. I almost forgot what I wanted to talk to you guys about. Did you watch the news?"

"News? No. We've been in here working on this damn science project since seven a.m., like we all said we would be. Or maybe you forgot that we need this finished to cover our collective asses. Besides, our TV's been on the fritz since the day before yesterday. Dad says the power supply is shot. He's going to rebuild it this weekend."

Noticing that Jennifer was paying no attention, Heather tapped her on the shoulder. "Jen. Pull your head out of the computer for a second. You'll want to hear this too."

When Jennifer didn't respond, Mark rolled his eyes, reached over, and smacked his twin on the top of the head.

"Ow! What is wrong with you?"

"Just trying to bring you back into the real world for a little bit. Heather's been trying to get your attention for five minutes."

"Mark, I have not. It's only been about thirty seconds."

"Whatever."

Jennifer's scowl indicated that it didn't matter greatly whether it was five minutes or five hours. "Well, you've got it. What's the big emergency?"

Mark raised his eyebrows. "Whoa. What's up with the attitude?"

"Attitude? I'll give you some attitude if you slap me on the head again while I'm working on something. You'd be a little angry if I did something like that to you."

A little exasperated that she was apparently the only one paying attention to any news, Heather interrupted.

"Much as I hate to break up the brother-sister lovefest," said Heather, "I do have something important to tell you guys. I was late getting over here this morning because of the news. There was a terrorist attack last night, right here on the highway between Pojoaque and Los Alamos."

Jennifer's eyes widened. "You're kidding."

"No, I'm not. The government had Highway 502 closed for more than eight hours. It was a giant mess for all the people trying to get into town from Santa Fe this morning."

Mark leaned forward, his attention suddenly fully focused on what Heather had to say. "The *government*? What happened?

"A truck was ambushed on the highway and two people killed. It was a big mess. They said the truck contained sensitive US government equipment. The military kicked the local cops off the site and took control of the whole area."

"They kicked the local cops off the crime scene?" Jennifer asked.

"Yes."

"I bet they were mad as hell," Mark laughed.

"They didn't say so, but the policeman being interviewed didn't look happy about it. The FBI agent wasn't looking too pleased either."

Mark looked puzzled. "You mean they even had the FBI blocked? I didn't think that was possible."

Heather shrugged. "It sure had the press spun up. The only thing they could get out of the military spokesman was the same line about the classified cargo on the truck requiring special security measures. But there was something else."

Heather paused, rewarded almost immediately with a look of annoyance on Mark's face.

"Which was? Christ, Heather, if I'm going to have to pull the story out of you piece by piece, this is going to take all day."

"Someone in the Española Police Department leaked the nine-one-one tape to the media. They played it on the air. Talk about creepy. It was that terrorist, Abdul Aziz, the one who killed that Los Alamos scientist's family last fall. On the tape, Abdul Aziz mentioned that he was going to steal something from the Rho Project."

A gasp from Jennifer reminded Heather of the other twin's presence.

"And," Heather continued, "he said that the police should collect blood samples from the dead men. Aziz warned them not to share the samples with the government."

Mark, whose mouth had fallen open, closed it with a snap. "Holy crap. Aziz must know about the nanites. Did they say any more about the blood or what was on the truck?"

"The government spokesman just said that this was typical terrorist propaganda, lies designed to fool the Muslim faithful into believing wild conspiracy theories."

Mark had begun pacing back and forth beside the cold-fusion tank. "But how could Aziz know that the Rho Project is working with alien nanotechnology? His people couldn't have intercepted one of our messages. We put those directly onto the NSA SIPRNet using the subspace transmitter."

"They must have an agent inside the NSA," said Heather.

"Oh, that is just great," said Jennifer. "The NSA director and his top computer scientist are dead, and now you think there may be a double agent on the team?"

Heather was surprised to see that her own hands were shaking. She clasped them together, hoping that Mark hadn't noticed.

"I don't know." The probabilities that cascaded through her mind for each of the possibilities were small. "Something doesn't add up. I just can't put my finger on what's wrong."

Mark stopped pacing, turning to stare directly into Heather's eyes. "What about the quantum twin bug I put into Janet's laptop? Those two are bound to know something. I think it's time we checked it out."

Jennifer rose to her feet so rapidly that she almost knocked over her chair. "Are you insane? Jack and Janet won't be able to detect a transmission, but that doesn't mean they can't detect the fact that files on the computer have been accessed."

Sometimes Heather thought she'd never understand Jennifer. Sometimes she was devil-may-care, sometimes too cautious. Lately her friend had seemed to veer even more to extremes.

Mark sighed. "That's exactly why we have a computer whiz like you. Figure something out."

"I've already figured it out. It's OK for us to passively monitor what they're doing on that computer, but there's no way we can remotely browse the files on that system without leaving behind some evidence that it's been accessed. That's all there is to it."

Mark refused to be cowed. "Fine then. So they might be able to tell that someone browsed their system. They can't trace it, so what's the problem?"

Jennifer's forehead furrowed in frustration. "You don't get it. If they notice the system has been tapped, they'll tear it apart. When they do, they'll find the little QT microchip. Even though they won't be able to determine what it does, they'll know that it was put there by someone who was in their house. Even you, maybe."

"I'm a senior in high school."

"Yeah, whose dad works on the Rho Project." Jennifer's lower jaw jutted out like an English bulldog's. Heather interrupted the argument. "Mark, I agree with Jennifer on this one."

"What a shock."

The unfairness of Mark's statement slapped her in the face. "Hey, I back you up too, when I think you're right."

"Oh yeah? And when was the last time that happened?"

"When we decided to explore the inside of the Second Ship, for one."

"Hell, that was almost a year ago."

Heather, her own anger rising, took a deep breath. "All I'm saying is that Jack and Janet scare me. Even if they're the good guys, they're too dangerous to take unnecessary chances with…"

Jennifer nodded. "Please, Mark. Just go along with us on this one."

Mark looked from Heather to Jennifer, his eyes locking with those of his twin. "OK, Jen. I'll go along with you, for now. But since you don't like my idea, you two need to figure out another way for us to find out what's happening. I have a bad feeling about this."

Heather watched as Mark turned and stalked out of the garage, leaving her and Jennifer staring after him. Something in her unremembered dreams tugged at the corner of Heather's mind as she watched the door close behind him.

Like Mark, Heather had acquired a very bad feeling.

CHAPTER 10

From the entryway, the Black Forest cuckoo clock squawked its 4:00 a.m. call, a sound that barely registered to Mark.

His breakthrough had come at 10:13 the night before, and he had been unable to stop reading since then. For Mark to be engrossed in a book was almost unheard of. He had never really had the interest it required to make his way through one.

Then, two weeks ago, he had seen a commercial advertising a new speed-reading course. The idea had hit him like a bucket of bricks. If he could learn to read as fast as the people in that commercial, he could knock out his studies in a heartbeat, leaving plenty of time for the things he loved doing. Plus he would have a secret advantage over Jen and Heather. That would be really nice for a change.

True, he already had a perfect photographic memory. But scanning the pages of a book into memory was unsatisfying.

Mark still had to go back in his mind and read through the material to find the information he needed. It was like buying a book for your library but never reading it.

That is why he had paid the $350 with his own money, waiting impatiently for its arrival by UPS. That wait had ended two days ago, and Mark had been there to meet the delivery man, spiriting the package off to his room without telling anyone else, especially Jennifer.

It had taken only a few minutes for him to scan the entire set of course workbooks into memory. The books themselves had gone under his bed, no longer needed.

After spending four hours that evening mentally practicing the exercises, Mark had given up in disgust. The big problem was subvocalization, or the sounding out of words in his mind as he read them. He couldn't seem to squelch the need to hear the words as he read.

That problem was complicated by Mark's ability to memorize a page by glancing at it. In an odd way, that ability made his mind lazy, reluctant to take the step that would allow him to understand phrases of text at a glance. Mark had gone reluctantly to bed, where he tossed and turned for the remainder of the night.

Yesterday had started with similar results, but Mark kept at it, devoting every private moment to practice. Then, late in the evening, just as he was about to admit defeat, he stumbled upon a technique that worked.

He began focusing on small phrases, allowing pictures to form in his mind as he looked at them. After his first few successes, he began working at seeing larger passages, letting his mind deliver pictures instead of the sounds. It was as if he had rubbed a magic lamp or whispered the magic words. All at once, he understood everything. And as he practiced, his speed increased. By 3:30 a.m. he had read every book in his room.

His excitement drove him downstairs to the bookshelves in the living room. Propped in his father's easy chair, with a pile of books on the end table beside him, Mark immersed himself. He could read each page almost as fast as he could scan it. It was like watching incredibly detailed movies unfold in his mind. Fascinating.

The front door opened, startling him out of his concentration. Jennifer slipped inside, taking great care to close the door silently behind her. Her clothes gave him another surprise. Jennifer was wearing a sweat suit and running shoes. As she turned toward the stairs, she spotted him, and a small gasp of surprise escaped her lips.

"Mark. You startled me."

"I startled you? What were you doing out there?"

Jennifer bit her lower lip. "If I tell you, promise me you won't breathe a word to anyone else."

Mark set down the book and stood up. "What is it?"

"Promise."

"OK, I promise." Mark folded his arms expectantly.

Jennifer paused before answering. "I've been out jogging."

Mark's snort of laughter brought an angry look to his twin's face.

"I have been," Jennifer snapped.

"Really? You've never jogged a day in your life, much less in the middle of the night."

"I'm worried about my figure?"

"You're kidding, right?"

Jennifer's scowl deepened. "Mark, you better not laugh. Is it that unbelievable?"

"Well, besides the fact you have never cared about boys, you're already skinny."

"That's just it. I don't want to be skinny. I want my legs to look a little more defined. Like Heather's."

Jennifer could not have surprised Mark more if she had slapped him in the face.

"Like Heather? Since when have you wanted to look like Heather?"

"I didn't say I wanted to look like her. I just want to look a little better."

"Whatever you say."

"You'll remember your promise?"

"My lips are sealed. After all, how would it look if it got out that my sister is normal?"

The scowl faded from Jennifer's face. "Thanks."

As she made her way up the stairs, Mark marveled at the fact that she had not noticed his late-night reading binge. Oh well. They'd all been acting a bit strangely lately. If his sister had decided to start exercising, it was hardly weirder than Mark becoming a speed-reader.

Heather was the one who had been worrying him. Her claim that she couldn't remember her dreams bothered him. Mark didn't believe that for a second. Heather didn't want to remember them. Something about the dreams was scaring her so badly that she was suppressing them.

Mark's heart ached at the thought of all that Heather had recently been through. As badly as he wanted to protect her, to make her feel safe, this was something that was beyond him. Since they had found the Second Ship, her premonitions had been uncannily accurate. The thought that these dreams might be another premonition scared the crap out of him.

Ignoring the sudden chill that had crept into the room with Jennifer, Mark resumed his seat in his father's chair. But it was a long while before he regained his former concentration.

CHAPTER 11

"Sergeant Pino?" The redheaded FBI man wound his way through the metal-legged tables in the Pueblo Diner, careful to avoid brushing his dark slacks against the table edges, as if he feared what Rosita might have missed with the wipe-down rag.

Sergeant Jim "Tall Bear" Pino leaned back from the counter, ignoring the proffered hand. His eyes swept over the federal agent in a manner that communicated his annoyance. The agent wore shiny black shoes, somewhat dulled by a thin coating of parking lot dust, dark suit pants, but no jacket. His white shirt had sleeves rolled up to the elbows, intended to show he was willing to get his hands dirty. Tall Bear had seen the type before. An asshole.

"My name is Special Agent Sullivan," the agent said, awkwardly withdrawing his hand and sliding onto a stool at the counter next to Tall Bear.

Tall Bear took a sip of coffee, noting that it was well past time for Rosita to brew a new pot, the dark contents having taken on the awful burned flavor so adored by all those white yuppies in their latte joints.

"That's nice."

Agent Sullivan's fake smile melted from his face. "I want to ask you some questions."

"Fire away."

"Can we go somewhere more private?"

Tall Bear glanced around the nearly empty diner, shrugged, then reached into his pocket for change. Tossing seventy-five cents on the counter, he led the way out the door, his worn cowboy boots leaving clear imprints in the dust of the parking lot.

Walking around the side of the diner, Tall Bear stopped by his battered Jeep Cherokee squad car. He reached into his hip pocket and pulled out a small can of Copenhagen. Tapping it twice against his wrist to settle the tobacco, he twisted off the lid and was rewarded with the familiar pungent smell.

Only when he had finished packing a large pinch firmly into his cheek did he glance up at the FBI man. The sight of the fading wrinkle of repulsion on Agent Sullivan's face gave Tall Bear his first enjoyable moment of the day.

"Well, here we are," Tall Bear said, indicating that the empty dirt parking lot was as private as it was going to get.

Agent Sullivan's eyes acquired an angry glint. "Fine. I'll get started then."

"Please do."

"I'm here to find out what you were doing at the murder scene on Highway 502 before the proper authorities arrived."

Tall Bear adjusted the brim of his hat, enjoying the fact that the New Mexico sun had already brought a sheen of sweat to the face and neck of the federal agent. The tribal policeman had been anticipating a visit like this since the night of the murders.

The only odd thing was that he hadn't already been visited by New Mexico state authorities. If there was one thing that pissed off the New Mexico attorney general's office, it was tribal policemen getting involved with anything on public highways, even if they passed through tribal lands.

Tall Bear spat a thin jet of tobacco between his teeth, hitting the dust close enough to Agent Sullivan's feet to cause the man to glance down. A splatter check.

"Just looking for survivors."

"You know you're required to wait for official permission before getting involved in a crime scene outside your jurisdiction."

"I thought it was an accident scene."

Agent Sullivan frowned, wiping sweat from his brow with a handkerchief. Already, twin damp spots darkened the white shirt at his underarms.

"You didn't call when you saw the murder victims?"

"I told you. I was looking for survivors."

"They had their heads cut off."

"Yeah. But there might have been others."

"Bullshit. You should have made a call as soon as you saw what went down."

"Look, I'm just a tribal cop. We don't get the big-city training."

Agent Sullivan's Irish face had taken on a shade of red too deep to be attributable solely to the high desert sun. He leaned in close.

"Don't screw with me, Sergeant Pino. This case is under federal jurisdiction, and if I want to, I can get a search warrant that will let me tear your tribal police station apart, along with your house."

Tall Bear spit again, this time sending the brown stream much closer to the FBI agent's foot. "You mean my hogan."

Agent Sullivan nodded. "One way or another, you will cooperate."

As the agent turned and walked angrily away, Sergeant Pino called after him. "Bring a four-wheel drive. It's a ways back on the res."

CHAPTER 12

Vice President Gordon didn't like Garfield Kromly. The old CIA trainer was a uniquely dislikable man, which was precisely the reason Kromly had been put in charge of new field operatives instead of rising through the ranks. Unlike the military, the CIA had a place for people who would rise no higher than their current station. Kromly might suck at kissing ass, but he was very, very good at everything else.

Besides Kromly, two others sat at the briefing table across from the vice president: Bert Paralto and Bridget Dunn, both senior NSA staffers who had worked closely with Jonathan Riles.

George Gordon leaned back in his chair. "OK, Kromly. Let's see what you've got."

Kromly clicked a button on the remote control, and a list of names appeared on the flat-panel display at the end of the table.

"As you requested, sir, this is a list of all the operatives capable of pulling off the Los Alamos truck hit. On the left is a list of contract mercenaries who could have been in the service of Jonathan Riles before his unfortunate demise."

"In other words, you haven't been able to track down those people's recent activities," said Gordon.

"Precisely."

"And the right column?"

"That's a list of field operatives who were reported killed in the last five years but we don't have a body for."

"Show them to us."

Kromly pressed another button on the remote, and the photograph of a man replaced the list on-screen. For the next hour and a half, he presented the photographs, accompanied by a brief biographical description of each. And after each photograph, the two NSA people would shake their heads. They had never seen a single person on the live list.

The dead list presented problems. The files of several people on that list contained no photographs.

Having exhausted their usefulness, the vice president released the NSA staffers before turning his attention back to Kromly.

"I want pictures of everyone."

"We have people working on it."

George Gordon rose to leave, then looked back at Kromly.

"Jonathan Riles was the best I ever knew at picking his team. Worst-case scenario, who on that list would give us the most trouble?"

Kromly hesitated briefly but did not glance at the list to answer. "No question. That would be the Ripper."

"I don't recall that name on the list."

"Real name's Jack Gregory. Killed in Calcutta three years ago."

"You know that for sure?"

"We don't have his body."

"I want a picture."

As the vice president turned back toward the door, Kromly's voice stopped him.

"Sir, I hope your intuition is wrong."

"And why is that?"

"Best to let the nightmare sleep."

CHAPTER 13

Freddy Hagerman stared out his second-floor window, in what should have been his spare bedroom but was now his home office, watching the first drops from the approaching storm splatter on his driveway. Christ, what a dump. Well, what could he expect? He was a forty-six-year-old three-time divorcé, an ex–*New York Times* reporter who now tried to meet his alimony, child support, and rent digging up gossip for the *Kansas City Star*. Funny how the dreams of his youth had faded. And as much as he loved New York, the cost of living had driven him to the Midwest.

Why they called this the Midwest was a mystery. Mid-dead-center would have been more appropriate since the exact center of the country lay near Salina, Kansas, a good couple of hours to the west of where he now stood. Didn't really matter. The Mid-frickin-west was where he was stuck.

When the UPS truck pulled into his driveway, Freddy almost didn't answer the door. Anything someone thought important enough to send to him via a special carrier meant trouble. No doubt one of his ex-wives' attorneys had found some way to dig deeper into Freddy's pockets. Legal paperwork was something he expected, things being the way they were.

There was no avoiding it, though. If he didn't answer the door today, they would just come back the next day and the next, finally resorting to delivery by an officer of the law. Best to just get it over with.

As he opened the door, the UPS man handed him a package roughly the size of a shoe box before having him sign his name on the computerized clipboard, which would immediately uplink the delivery status to the World Wide Web. The damn attorneys would probably be smiling before the truck was out of his driveway. Wasn't technology grand?

Freddy tossed the box on the coffee table in preparation for making his way back upstairs, but it missed. The package caught the edge of the table and then tumbled to the floor. Freddy paused. The sound it made as it bounced off the floor wasn't right. Certainly not a sound you would expect from a box stuffed with legal forms and documents. And despite that he had been demoted to the role of backwater gossip columnist, Freddy had once been an investigative reporter with instincts second to none. The only thing that had kept him from the acclaim he had thought himself destined to receive was his piss-poor judgment in women. Thrust a couple of nice tits in his face and he thought he was in love. He should have been an ass man.

When he bent down to retrieve the package, Freddy felt the contents shift. Definitely not packed by any legal office. Eschewing the couch, Freddy moved to the kitchen table, where the lighting was better. The box was wrapped in plain brown paper. The

"From" label on the shipping slip was so sloppily printed that he couldn't make it out, although his name and address on the "To" label were clearly legible.

Freddy turned the box over, carefully examining every crease and fold in the wrapping. Absolutely nothing unusual about it. So why was he suddenly as nervous as a kitten?

Taking out his pocketknife, Freddy slipped the blade under a fold, slicing a straight, clean cut along the corners of the paper that covered the box. As he pulled the wrapping away, he saw that it did indeed cover a shoe box. Nike. With another couple quick slices, he severed the tape that secured the lid to the shoe box.

The reason for the rattle became immediately apparent as he lifted the lid. The box contained a sealed envelope and a small locked jewelry box. The packing around the jewelry box was insufficient to keep it from sliding back and forth in the shoe box, at least if dropped on the floor.

Freddy Hagerman rubbed his chin. Damn odd. The envelope was a white velum of intermediate quality, the type used for thank-you cards. Across the seal, two capital letters had been printed: *AA*. Freddy slit the envelope along the upper edge, extracting the folded card with two fingers. The preprinted "thank you" was the only writing on the outside of the card.

His first glance inside startled him so badly that he almost dropped the card. The note was short:

> Dear Mr. Hagerman. My name is Abdul Aziz. Since you have received this package, I am already dead.
>
> This means I have failed to deliver my message to the world, so I must rely on you, postmortem. I picked you because you are too talented and have access to too many unusual resources to be where you are today. I need your desperation.

> As you are no doubt aware, I have come into some information about the Rho Project. Unfortunately, if I told you what I have learned, you would be obliged to immediately hand over the classified information to your government. Instead, I will provide clues that should allow you to discover the story for yourself.
>
> In the small jewelry case I have placed two items and an address. The first of these items is a specimen slide. Take it to a medical examiner you can trust.
>
> The second item was in the possession of one of the Rho Project's experimental subjects, a man who called himself Priest Williams. The effects of the Rho Experiment on his mind will become self-evident. Go to the address. There you will find the answers to all your questions. There you will find your Pulitzer Prize. Insha'Allah.

At the bottom of the note, a small key was taped to the card. Freddy stared down at the key, his eyes moving to the locked jewelry box, which now sat on the kitchen table. The whole thing was probably a hoax, something designed to humiliate him. Perhaps one of the enemies he had made from his gossip column had come up with an ingenious way for him to make a fool of himself. Of course, he couldn't really make that judgment unless he looked in the jewelry box, now could he?

Removing the tape that held the key, Freddy slid the key into the small lock and twisted. The catch released with a click. For a moment, he considered the possibility that the box might contain a bomb. But that made no sense. If the sender had wanted to kill him, he could have done so when Freddy opened the outer box. And why take the trouble to write the note?

Despite the logic of the thought, Freddy found his hands shaking as he raised the jewelry box lid. Inside, a scrap of yellow paper wrapped a microscope slide, held in place with a red rubber band. Unwrapping the paper, he noted that it contained a New Mexico address and a set of latitude and longitude coordinates. Although he did not have a microscope to examine the contents, Freddy held the glass slide up to the kitchen light. A thin slice of translucent red material lay sandwiched between the plates.

Disappointed, Freddy turned his attention to the last item in the jewelry case, a black plastic bag, the top tied into a knot. Since the knot seemed unlikely to yield to gentler measures, he grabbed the sides of the plastic bag and pulled, spilling the contents out onto the tabletop as the bag ripped open.

Freddy scrambled backward, knocking over his chair in his sudden panic. There on his kitchen table, sprawled across his white tablecloth, lay a necklace of severed female fingers, the nails all neatly polished red.

CHAPTER 14

"Mr. Vice President. There's something on CNN you will want to see."

Carl Palmer's voice caused George Gordon to glance up from the intelligence briefing papers. His chief of staff rarely interrupted him. The fact that Carl did so now meant George probably wasn't going to like what he was about to see.

As the flat-panel television came to life, the voice of CNN's Robert Collins provided the running commentary, but the pictures alone were enough to confirm the vice president's premonition. A large crowd of Native Americans had gathered around the front of a small building and appeared to be in an ugly mood. Working to keep them back, a group of FBI agents in stenciled Windbreakers blocked the entrance. As Robert Collins continued his report, the reason for the demonstration became clear. The

FBI was in the process of searching the Santa Clara Tribal Police headquarters pursuant to a federal search warrant.

At the moment, Collins was in the midst of an interview with Tribal Police Sergeant Pino.

"Officer Pino, is it true that this raid is related to the fact that you were the first person on the scene of the terrorist attack that took the lives of two Los Alamos Security people two weeks ago?"

The Indian policeman was striking, both in appearance and demeanor. He was dressed in a manner common to local police in the southwestern United States: black, broad-brimmed cowboy hat, police uniform, and cowboy boots. His long, straight black hair hung almost to his belt, framing a rugged face worn by years spent outdoors. Pino's black eyes flashed with a thinly controlled anger.

"I was the first on the scene."

"But is this raid connected to that incident?"

"The FBI is here for only one reason. I'm a Navajo cop."

"So you are saying it has nothing to do with the recent terrorist attack along the Los Alamos Highway?"

Sergeant Pino pointed to the surrounding crowd and the FBI agents gathered outside the modest building that contained the Tribal Police headquarters. "Oh, it's connected to the incident. But ask yourself one thing. Would the federal government have come into any nonnative police station in this manner?"

A loud chorus of agreement from jostling bystanders momentarily drowned out Collins's attempts at further questions.

"But why the search warrant? The FBI must suspect you of something."

"Ask them."

"I did. They refused to comment about an ongoing investigation."

"And I'm sure they wouldn't want me commenting either, so I will. An FBI agent showed up here a few days ago, asking me questions that implied I screwed up the crime scene. I took offense at his tone and sent him on his way. This search warrant sends a message. I'll let you and your audience decide what it means."

As the interview continued, Vice President Gordon's alarm grew. Not only did the tribal policeman make a damn good case that the FBI had overstepped its bounds with its heavy-handed intimidation tactics, but the man was a dynamic television personality. There he stood, tall, proud, and indignant, his long black hair blowing out around his shoulders in the stiff breeze. And all the while, the camera drank him in.

Great. With the backdrop of the increasingly agitated and growing Native American crowd, the situation appeared to be rapidly spiraling out of control.

"Goddamn it, Carl!" Gordon's voice was loud enough to echo down the hallway outside his office. "Get me the FBI director. I want him on the phone now!"

Carl Palmer stepped out of the office without closing the door. In less than a minute, he returned. "He's on the line now, sir."

The vice president picked up the phone. "Bill, what the hell is going on in New Mexico?"

"Mr. Vice President, I'm looking into that right now," Bill Hammond responded.

"You'd better get a handle on this quick. When the president sees this, he is going to have someone's ass."

The pause before the FBI director answered made it clear he knew whose ass George Gordon was talking about. "As I said, I'm looking into the matter now."

"Well you'd better do more than look. You know what this looks like? It looks like another government cover-up of something related to the Rho Project. That's not exactly the type of press coverage the old man wants right now."

"Mr. Vice President, I know my job." Hammond's voice cracked with indignation.

Vice President Gordon smiled to himself. Now he had the man's attention. "Which is why I called you, Bill. I didn't want you to be blindsided when you get the call from the president."

"I appreciate that. Now, if you don't mind, I have some calls to make before that happens."

As he hung up the phone, George Gordon glanced up at his chief of staff, who stood awaiting the instructions he knew would follow.

"Carl, give Andy a buzz. The president probably already knows, but his chief is going to want to orchestrate the White House response to this incident."

Watching his chief of staff disappear down the hall, George Gordon shook his head. The moron who came up with the brilliant notion of rousting the Indian police was probably some FBI regional office director. Well, whoever it was would soon find him- or herself in charge of the most out-of-the-way shit-hole Bill Hammond could come up with. Of that, the vice president had no doubt.

CHAPTER 15

Freddy Hagerman lurched in his seat, praying that the rusty undercarriage of his Subaru wouldn't fall out on the rutted dirt road. It would make for one hell of a long walk back to the highway. But the old girl hadn't let him down yet. It was why he had nicknamed her the African Queen, after the boat in one of his favorite old Bogart movies.

In an odd way, he felt like Bogey right now, lurching along this rough New Mexico dirt road as the sun sank toward the western horizon. He hadn't seen any rattlesnakes yet, but surely they were out there waiting for him, coiled under bushes and rocks, every bit as menacing as the leeches that had awaited Bogey in that African river. His sense of isolation was heightened because Freddy hadn't seen a house, car, or person since he had left the county road an hour ago. And Freddy didn't even have a bossy Katharine Hepburn to keep him company.

The thought of bossy women reminded him of his ex-wives. Maybe solitude wasn't that bad after all.

He glanced over at his satchel, sitting on the passenger seat beside him. Inside it, along with his Nikon camera, rolls of film, and tape recorder, was the letter that had sent him scurrying to New Mexico as fast as the old car could carry him. Two days of hard driving had brought him to Taos. From there, it had taken a number of stops at courthouses to find the exact location of the spot he was looking for. Even with the GPS device, his one surrender to modern digital technology, it had taken most of the rest of the day to find the right set of barbed wire gates to get this far.

The letter had come via overnight mail. In all the years he had known the retired New York City medical examiner, Freddy had never gotten anything from Benny Marucci that hadn't been sent at the cheapest postal rate possible. Yet there it was: an overnight registered letter, with its Little Italy postmark.

Benny was one of the few old Italians left in what had once been the heart of Italian New York City. Now, for all intents and purposes, it was a part of Chinatown. Most of the Italian families had long since departed, including Benny's. But not Benny Marucci.

His father had been a mob boss. His three brothers had risen through the ranks of the family business from low-level enforcers to high-ranking crime figures. Two of them had died under a hail of bullets in Morris Park, and the other had died in prison. But somehow Benny had served thirty years as a New York City ME while eating Thanksgiving and Christmas dinners with the mob. Having survived numerous investigations by Internal Affairs and a couple of hit attempts, Benny had just kept on working until he hit the mandatory retirement age.

Benny Marucci was a bulldog of a man, even now, late into his seventies.

The letter had confirmed that the fingers strung onto the necklace had been cut from the female victims while they were still alive with a guillotine-style cigar cutter. The fingers were from five different women, each of whom had been reported missing in northern New Mexico in the last year. Benny had included pictures and short bios of each. Each of them was in her twenties, beautiful, and rich.

But it was the contents of the microscope-slide specimen that had caused Benny to send the response with such urgency.

It was a razor-thin slice of human heart tissue. By calling in a few old debts, Benny had gained access to the DNA record of one Carlton "Priest" Williams and had verified that the sample was, in fact, his. The man's records after he joined the military were only partially available, indicative of a highly classified position. His discharge under other-than-honorable conditions did not elaborate on the reasons.

What made the sliver of heart pressed between the glass slides so astounding was the blood. It was infested by something that Benny could not identify, other than to say that it contained a high concentration of microscopic machines of unknown manufacture and purpose. Benny had never seen anything like it and didn't seem to think anyone else had either.

The letter had ended with just three words. "Be careful, *paesano*."

Unfortunately, careful wouldn't get it done for Freddy. These last few years had been filled with a growing sense that he was buried under circumstances beyond his control, doomed to a life of mediocrity in Hicksville, USA. Now he had been handed a chance to dig himself out, and he wasn't going to give that up in the name of caution.

As the Subaru crested a steep rise, he saw it: an odd little ranch house nestled in a draw, so run-down its rusty tin roof drooped like the brim of a wet cowboy hat. Several wooden outbuildings sat off to one side, the barn so poorly maintained that the back third had fallen down. The entire compound was surrounded by a barbed wire fence, the gate of which lay open, its supporting post having rotted off near the ground.

As Freddy pulled up in front of the house and killed the engine, the sun finished sinking behind the western hills, painting the sky with scarlet. An old windmill stood silhouetted against the red skyline, several of its blades missing. Freddy was fairly sure that *blades* was not the correct term for them, but what the hell. Windmills, or any of this farmer shit, weren't exactly his specialty. Still, something about the sight of the tall structure with its missing appendages, backdropped by the red sky, sent a shiver down his back.

Freddy reached across the seat, grabbed his camera and an old metal flashlight, and slammed the car door. He started to lock it, then stopped. If someone came by and stole the old clunker all the way out in this godforsaken spot, he just wasn't meant to have the damn thing.

Turning toward the old house, Freddy flipped on the flashlight. At first it failed to respond, but after a couple of thumps, the batteries engaged the contacts, bathing the ground in front of him in a yellowish beam. The twilight sky still held enough light that he didn't really need the extra light, but the shadows from the overhanging porch made him skittish.

Three concrete steps led up onto the porch. It wasn't much, just a dozen feet of poured cement under a six-foot overhang. A rocker that looked nearly as old as the house sat to the left of the front door. It probably gave an excellent view of the broken windmill and crumbling barn. All that was missing was some mangy old mutt humping his leg and he'd be in redneck heaven.

The screen door didn't squeak when he opened it. Odd. A quick examination of the hinges showed the first sign of recent maintenance that he'd seen in a dozen miles. They were brass and had been recently installed, so someone had been living here. Somehow, Freddy doubted that someone was Old Man Graves.

From what he had been able to discover of the old hermit, Delbert Graves hardly ever came to town, a fact that didn't break too many hearts. He was reputed to be an old survivalist, mean as a snake and stupid as a fence post. The man didn't like anyone, and they returned the favor. His taxes were paid up for two years in advance, so nobody bothered him.

And from the look of the place, Delbert didn't seem like the type who would have bothered putting new hinges on the screen door. But the squeaking had bothered someone enough to do it.

Freddy expected the front door to be locked, but it wasn't. The door swung inward into the kitchen. On impulse, Freddy reached over and flipped the light switch. Nothing. The whole house probably ran on generator power, and he wasn't about to go around looking for that. Shit, he probably wouldn't know how to start the thing if he found it.

Sweeping the yellow beam around the small room, Freddy stepped all the way inside, closing the door behind him. A small rectangular table with a single chair sat against the window. An old wood-burning stove stood beside the sink. The only electrical appliance was the refrigerator. He opened it just long enough to confirm that the generator had been off for quite some time. What might have been food several weeks ago had been reduced to a foul-smelling mess.

A narrow opening led out of the kitchen into the living room. Lovely. One overstuffed chair in front of the fireplace. If it had faced the window, someone could have sat there and watched the weeds grow.

Freddy moved across to the bedroom and its adjoining bathroom, the last of the rooms in the small house. Here he paused, letting the flashlight play across the walls and furniture. The darkness inside was nearly complete. Considering the tiny dimensions of the rest of the house, the bedroom appeared disproportionately large. A king-size bed, complete with log headboard, occupied the far wall, while a dresser and a small closet took up most of the wall to Freddy's right. A single nightstand occupied a spot next to the right side of the bed. Other than the ceiling light, currently useless, there were no other lamps. Evidently, neither Delbert nor the house's more recent occupant was a big reader.

Just as Freddy was about to move toward the bathroom, he spotted the rug. It was a six-by-eight-foot rectangle of Indian design and looked out of place in the otherwise undecorated house. Freddy moved closer, bending down to examine the stitching. It was handwoven, obviously authentic and expensive.

Freddy had always had a reporter's nose. That, along with his annoying habit of putting it into everyone else's business, was what had made him one of the best. Something about this rug just smelled wrong.

A soft creaking sound caused him to swing the flashlight back toward the doorway. Just as he was about to lay it off to his imagination, he heard it again. It sounded like a loose board moving under weight.

Freddy straightened and moved back to the door into the living room. There was no use sneaking. If someone was there and hadn't seen his flashlight, they were blind. The living room was empty, as was the kitchen beyond that. Once again, Freddy paused to listen. There it was again, along with another sound: the wind.

Freddy shook his head. It was only the wind picking up as the temperature dropped that was causing the old structure to shift and complain. Jesus H. Christ. He was getting jumpy as an old woman. But then Benny Marucci had never before warned him to be careful.

Freddy moved back into the bedroom and resumed his examination of the Indian rug. Why was it here?

Unslinging the Nikon and checking the flash, Freddy began snapping pictures in rapid sequence and from a variety of angles. Sometimes just looking at the film as it developed in his darkroom revealed some little detail he missed while on location. Although this room appeared benign enough, something about that rug gave him the creeps.

Satisfied that he had captured everything, Freddy knelt down and gently pulled the rug to one side. No attempt had been made to conceal the trapdoor beneath it except for the rug covering, which stood out like a sign along an empty highway. A simple handle with a sliding dead bolt secured the thing. There was no lock.

The dead bolt opened easily, another unusually well-maintained piece of this run-down property. Well, the people he'd talked to at the courthouse had said that Delbert Graves was a survivalist. You'd expect some sort of underground bunker on his place. How else would he survive the nuclear war?

Somehow, Freddy doubted that fear of impending nuclear attack was the cause for the well-oiled latch. Well, he wasn't going to find any answers just staring at the closed trapdoor. Inhaling deeply, Freddy lifted it open.

He played the beam around the opening, leaning forward to look down into the hole. Iron rungs had been set into the concrete wall about a foot apart. The narrow opening continued downward for a few feet before opening into a room further down. Beyond that, the flashlight's yellow beam was too dim to provide detail.

"Anyone down there?" The echo of his voice startled him, making Freddy feel even stupider than when he'd yelled out the question.

Looping the camera strap back over his shoulder, he swung his legs into the dark opening, gently lowering himself until his foot found a rung. It seemed solid. With the flashlight angled downward, he began climbing down, almost immediately enveloped by a coolness common to poorly insulated underground spaces. The place probably felt great in the heat of a New Mexico summer day, even at this high altitude. But with the arrival of night and the rapidly dropping temperature, he had become chilled.

Hell. That was probably why his hands were shaking.

At the bottom of the ladder, Freddy paused, shining the flashlight around the room. It was about ten feet across and of a similar width, and constructed of unpainted concrete blocks. The ceiling was a dozen feet above his head. As he shone the flashlight around the room, Freddy wondered if the beam was getting dimmer. It was probably just his imagination. He was pretty sure he'd changed out the D cell batteries not long ago.

A steel door in the far wall was closed with yet another dead bolt. To his left, a large metal closet jutted outward into the room. Beside it, a long workbench contained an odd-looking assortment of tools and equipment. It took Freddy a couple of moments to realize what he was looking at. It was an ammunition-reloading workbench, complete with gunpowder scale, reloading dies, and other unfamiliar tools.

He opened the metal closet doors.

Holy shit. The bastard had been preparing for World War III. At least a dozen rifles and handguns hung in mounts along the back wall of the gun closet, although several of the racks were now empty.

Freddy moved to the closed steel door in the far wall. As he got close, he saw that the dead bolt had not been engaged and that the door was open a crack. As he touched the handle, he paused, listening. Nothing. Down here in the concrete underground bunker, the silence was nearly perfect. Even the roar of the wind outside and the creaking of the old house had been completely damped out.

He tugged. Damn, the door was heavy, a blast door. God, it must have been a bitch getting the damn thing down here. It must have been lowered before the ceiling had been constructed.

Freddy edged inside, directing the flashlight beam at the ground before his feet. The cement floor looked cold, and indeed the chill in this room was worse than in the adjacent one. As it swept the room, the yellow beam of the flashlight revealed walls lined with red candles, a sink, a toilet, and a double bed. There was no other exit and only a six-inch air shaft in the ceiling provided ventilation.

Ahead, the sink looked filthy. As Freddy moved closer, the reason for the mess became clear. It and the floor around it were splattered with dried blood—lots of it.

Freddy swung the flashlight toward the bed. The blankets and sheets lay wadded at the end of the stained mattress. A set of chains and cuffs dangled from the steel frame. But it was the sight of the pillow and its pink pillowcase that brought moisture to his eyes. The pillowcase was covered with faint tearstains.

He moved back over to the sink, looking closely at the splatter pattern on the wall and on the floor. Strange that the blood trail did not extend more than a few feet from this spot. There was no sign that the sick bastard who had done this had bothered to clean it up.

Once again, Freddy began snapping pictures, pointing the camera by instinct as the bright flashing torched his night vision. Except for his own labored breathing, the only other sound to break the cellar's stillness was the whine of the Nikon's auto-winder.

He changed film rolls twice. Then, deciding that he had recorded the scene from every angle, Freddy exited the room. As he readied his camera to capture the details of the weapons room, he froze.

There on the workbench beside the reloading press lay a journal, the corner of the book jutting out beyond the edge of the bench. Freddy knew he had been a bit distracted, but he was a reporter, a damn good one too. There was no doubt in his mind. That damn book had not been there ten minutes ago.

CHAPTER 16

Heather awoke with a start. In the darkness that surrounded her, the room seemed vaguely unfamiliar. For several seconds she struggled to recognize where she was, her fading dreams tugging at the corners of her consciousness. This was her bedroom. The dim outline of her dresser and her small desk were separated by a yawning darkness that had to be her closet.

There it was again—the distant buzzing in her head, vaguely familiar, although she couldn't quite place it. The harder she thought about it, the more it retreated from her observation until it disappeared. Now there was only stillness.

That in itself was odd. Normally there was some sound in the old house, even if she woke in the middle of the night. Perhaps she was still asleep. Dreams of awakening had plagued her in the past, so perhaps this was one of them. Equations cascaded through her mind, resolving to a probability so close to zero that it was negligible. Something about the way the numbers made sense to her savant brain reassured her amid the surrounding strangeness.

As Heather thought about walking down the hallway and checking on her mom and dad, the buzzing returned, growing stronger as she focused her thoughts. Despite her growing unease, Heather followed this train of thought, letting herself visualize her parents' bedroom, imagining them both sleeping soundly in their king-size bed.

The buzzing became a vibration reminiscent of when she had first tried on the alien headset in the starship, filled with a confusing blitz of sounds, imagery, and feelings, so rapid and distorted that a wave of dizziness assailed her. Then it was gone, like a dropped signal on a cell phone.

Heather waited, a slow dread that the buzzing would start up once again making her pull her covers up under her chin. Gradually, as the minutes passed with no recurrence, the dread and the accompanying feeling of strangeness dissipated, leaving her feeling relieved and more than a little ridiculous. Talk about overreacting. She had even considered turning on her bedroom lights to check the closet.

Rolling onto her side, Heather curled back into her blankets, but sleep was a long while coming. Something was still wrong. Bad things were happening, and there was nothing she could do about it...yet.

CHAPTER 17

"Shut the door behind you."

From his seat at the head of the table in the National Security Agency conference room, Vice President Gordon watched as the handful of NSA senior staffers filed out. They looked tired. Hell, it wasn't all that long ago that George Gordon would have felt exhausted himself. The meeting hadn't even started until 10:00 p.m. Not that he felt bad about having them recalled from home for a late-evening session. That thought never even crossed the vice president's mind.

He had called them back into the black glass structure nicknamed Crypto City because he had just received the picture of Jack Gregory, and he needed to know whether he was the same person these people had seen meeting with Jonathan Riles. And even though the picture was terrible, having been taken at the church hospital in India where Gregory had reportedly died, the staffers had still been able to recognize his face.

Having dismissed all of the NSA people, Gordon stared across the room at Garfield Kromly. The old CIA trainer had been the only person, other than the vice president's driver and Secret Service team, to accompany him on this nighttime jaunt from DC up to Fort Meade. Now the man sat as he had throughout the meeting, his face an unreadable mask as his eyes watched Gordon's every move.

The vice president leaned back in his chair. "We've got our man."

"I'll want to pick the team," Kromly said.

"Bullshit. The FBI will handle this by the book."

"I don't recommend that."

Gordon smiled. "And I don't care. You just take care of briefing the operations folks over at FBI headquarters. I want every member of Gregory's team ID'd before they move, and I want you to personally let me know when they're ready."

"And the president?"

"I'll have the FBI director brief him. Like I said, by the book."

"This one is going to get bloody."

"That's OK. We can handle a few dead rogue operatives."

"That's not what I meant. The press secretary better be ready to explain a lot of dead FBI agents."

The vice president leaned forward once again. It was amazing how the CIA man could irritate him. "You just take care of your part. I'm sure the FBI special units can handle Gregory." He started to rise and then stopped. "Why 'the Ripper'?"

Kromly raised an eyebrow. "Pardon?"

"I want to know about Gregory's nickname."

"Three years ago, Jack was attacked by a group of six men in a Calcutta alley. Jack killed them all, but he suffered some serious knife wounds. By the time he was taken into a Catholic missionary clinic, he had lost so much blood that he died on the operating table. At least that's according to the doctor who signed his death certificate."

Kromly paused. "The old nun that found Jack stayed behind to clean up the mess before wheeling his body out. She claimed she was bending over Jack when he awakened. Apparently, the shock of what she saw in his eyes as he came back from the dead drove her mad. After that, she kept repeating a single phrase over and over."

"Which was?"

"Dear Lord, the Ripper walks the earth."

Vice President Gordon laughed. "And you believe that?"

"I went to see her, just before she died, at a small convent outside London. By then, Sister Mary Judith was almost catatonic, but every once in a while, she would still mutter the phrase."

Once again, Gordon chuckled. "The Ripper, my ass."

The older CIA man's eyes narrowed momentarily, then he shrugged and walked from the room. As hard as it was to believe, George Gordon thought he had just glimpsed something he had never expected to see in Garfield Kromly's eyes: fear.

CHAPTER 18

Freddy Hagerman held his breath, every bit of his concentration focused on listening. Nothing. Not a goddamn sound.

But somebody else had just been in here, and he had made sure Freddy found the journal. As his eyes once again locked on the book, Freddy remembered to breathe. After all, he was still alive. Somehow, he thought that if the ghost wanted him dead, he already would be.

Steadying the camera, Freddy began to capture the room. He was sorry he hadn't done this the first time he had come through here, just in case something else had been moved since then. Oh well, he'd spot it anyway when he got a chance to spend some time with the film.

Satisfied, he moved over to the bench where the journal rested. It was a nicely bound book with a soft gray hardback binding. Not wanting to have his own fingerprints disturb any potential evidence, Freddy extracted a kerchief from his pocket. Luckily, he hadn't gotten around to using it yet. This New Mexico desert didn't have the Kansas plants that set off his allergies.

He grasped the journal by the edge of the cover and carefully opened it. The first page had a spot for the owner to fill in his name and personal information. In stylized handwriting that filled the block, someone had written two words:

"The Priest."

Freddy snapped a picture. For the next hour, he stood there, carefully turning page after page, reading and then photographing each one. What began as fascination quickly gave way to shock and then disgust. Within half an hour, Freddy thought he would become physically sick, but he kept at it, changing film rolls as needed, until he was finished.

Straightening, he wiped his damp brow on a sleeve. If he hadn't already seen the other room and gotten Benny's report, he would have thought he was being had, that this was some sort of sick joke. This guy Priest had been compulsive in his journal entries, but not in the sense of a normal diary. The journal had started less than a year ago and only covered events that Priest regarded as exciting. The first entry was the strangest.

Priest had apparently been an unwilling participant in an experiment conducted by none other than Dr. Donald Stephenson, the deputy director of Los Alamos National Laboratory, and Dr. Ernesto Rodriguez. They had injected Priest with some gray fluid, the pain of the process so great that he had regarded it as a quasi-religious experience. The gray goo had given him tremendous healing powers.

The remainder of the journal had described the killing of Abdul Aziz and the capture, torture, and killing of Priest's female "guests," all of whom had been dumped down a shallow well on the property.

One thing was very clear to Freddy: the experiment conducted on Priest by Dr. Stephenson had not been an officially sanctioned one. He had been trying to test something derived from his study of the Rho Ship, but that test had gone horribly wrong. The same fluid that had given Priest such unbelievable healing powers had apparently rendered him violently insane, setting loose the darkest desires hidden deep in his psyche, accompanied by feelings of invincibility that led him to act out those desires.

With the handkerchief, Freddy picked up the journal, moved back to the ladder, and began climbing back up. For a moment, the thought that he would find the trapdoor closed brought on a brief bout of claustrophobic panic. But it was still open, exactly as he had left it.

By the time he climbed out into the bedroom, it was clear that the flashlight batteries were dying. It was now hard to see more than a couple of feet to either side of the beam's central bright spot. Well, that was OK. Only one more thing to check out, and then he'd be out of here.

Freddy exited the house, walked out to his car, and gently placed the journal into his satchel along with the used rolls of film. Then, grabbing a couple of fresh rolls, he began walking toward the spot where the decaying outbuildings stood. A crescent moon had risen and gave forth just enough light that he could make out the dark outline of the barn and what must have been a couple of storage sheds. Next to one of them, Freddy remembered seeing an old well.

As he got closer, he found he didn't need to be able to see it. The smell led him to it. In the dying light of the flashlight, Freddy could see the circular outline of the rock structure. The beam, which had once supported a pulley, rope, and bucket, lay to one side of the hole. The rope and bucket lay alongside it, the bottom of the latter having long since fallen out.

Freddy leaned over the opening and shone the flashlight down. Shit. People should have been able to smell it all the way from Taos. The darkness swallowed the weak beam of light so that he could only see down the rough rock wall for about a dozen feet.

He picked up a small rock and dropped it down, rewarded with the sound of it striking solid ground not far below. The thing couldn't have been more than about thirty feet deep and, from the sound the stone had made, must have been dry for a long time now. These shallow wells usually relied on tapping into an underground aquifer that came close to the surface. Apparently, this one had changed course or died altogether.

In his satchel back in the car, Freddy kept a small bottle of melaleuca oil. It was a great natural treatment for cuts, scratches, and bugbites, but it smelled like you had dunked your head in a Mentholatum jar. He walked back and retrieved it, swabbing some of the liquid just inside each nostril. Jesus. That would clear his sinuses. But he'd rather smell that than what was down at the bottom of the well.

Making his way back to the well, Freddy bent down and began examining the old rope, finding it surprisingly strong. Although the beam supports had broken, the old log itself seemed stout enough. Securing one end of the rope to the log with an end-of-the-line bowline knot, he heaved it up so that it straddled the well. With his pocketknife, he cut the other end of the rope free from the bucket handle and tossed the rope into the well.

"Here goes nothing," he mumbled as he swung his legs over the side, taking a single wrap of the rope before swinging down, sliding into the blackness hand over hand.

The thought occurred to him that he already had plenty for his story, more than enough to win a Pulitzer. Shit, if his story stopped what was going on at the Rho Project, he should get a goddamn Nobel Prize. But Freddy was a reporter to his core. There was no way he could not look at and record what awaited him at the bottom of this hole, any more than he could hold his breath until he passed out.

Except for one tense moment when the log shifted, his descent into the well was uneventful. The darkness pressed in around him like the stench. He could practically see the foul smell in the dim yellow beam of his flashlight. At a depth of twenty-five feet, he hit bottom, shuddering as he struggled to find a spot for his feet that didn't involve stepping on a corpse.

As dim as the light had become, he almost wished he didn't have it. It soon became clear that most of the people had died because of the fall into this well, something that matched the journal's descriptions. However, bloody marks high up along the walls indicated that one of the women had tried to climb out. As he examined the rough stone, Freddy determined that such a climb should have been possible, if she had still had fingers.

Freddy bent to examine the corpses more closely. The fresher of the two male corpses must have been that of Abdul Aziz, although it was so badly decayed as to be unrecognizable. As he moved to the corpses of the women, he stopped. Shit. He had wondered why the blood pattern around the sink in the basement hadn't trailed out across the room and up through the house. Priest had tied them up, snipped their fingers in the sink, and then wrapped the stumps of their hands with Ziploc bags and rubber bands before carrying them out.

He had seen enough. Freddy began working his camera, forcing himself to remain in the hole until he could no longer stand it. Then, using his best high-school rope-climbing technique, he started the climb back toward the top. By tomorrow morning, he would be in Santa Fe, having already finished typing out the story on his old manual typewriter that waited in the trunk. Then a couple of faxes to people who still remembered his name at the *New York Times* and he would be back in the business for real.

There would be no more Kansas shit-kicking for Freddy Hagerman.

CHAPTER 19

By the time the president's staff moved into action, every major news network was running with the story—hard. The look on the president's face as he stared across his desk at the chief of staff was not a happy one.

"Damn it, Andy. What the hell is going on? I thought the FBI had this thing under control."

"Yes, sir, that's what the director said."

President Harris pointed at the flat-panel television screen. "Does that look like things are under control? Get him on the phone."

"Yes, sir." The chief of staff turned and disappeared through the doorway.

Within a minute, he returned. "Director Hammond is on the line now, sir."

President Harris picked up the handset. "Bill, didn't you just brief me yesterday morning that you would soon have the Los Alamos situation back under control?"

"Yes, Mr. President. We're not sure that this news story is related to Jonathan Riles's rogue team that is still out there—"

"Horseshit! That man Gregory has been orchestrating things since Admiral Riles committed suicide. He did the hit on the truck. Now he's led a reporter to something that's going to give us trouble."

"I just don't think we can leap to that conclusion."

The president's voice hardened. "Bill, you're out of time. I want the rogue agents taken down. Now. Are the plans in place?"

"Yes, sir. We identified Gregory's last three team members last night. We already have a joint FBI and ATF task force in place."

"Good. As soon as they're ready, do it. I want to be watching the evening news tonight and see the story of the takedown. Maybe it'll get some of this other stuff off the air for a while."

"Yes, sir, Mr. President. I'll take care of it."

As soon as the FBI director had hung up, President Harris buzzed his secretary. "James, get Dr. Stephenson from Los Alamos National Laboratory on the phone. Tell him to make himself available by phone for my nine a.m. cabinet meeting. And yes, I know what time it is in New Mexico. Get him out of bed if you have to."

"Yes, sir."

Setting the phone back in its cradle, the president grabbed the remote control and turned up the volume on the news. He wanted to hear it all. In his experience, the old saying was dead on. Bad news certainly didn't improve with age.

CHAPTER 20

Jack glanced in his rearview mirror. Traffic looked normal, but it felt wrong.

As he swept both sides of the street, he began picking them out, perfectly normal-looking people in perfectly normal-looking postures. But they weren't normal. They were part of an ongoing operation. He had been expecting this day for a long time now, and here it was.

Jack hit speed dial on his cell phone. Out of service. He switched to walkie-talkie mode, but again got nothing. Someone was jamming him. Sloppy. If he hadn't already known the take-down was in progress, this would have confirmed it.

Jack pressed a specialized button on his cell phone, sending out a cross-frequency squelch signal. He paused, then pressed it three more times in quick succession. The signal wouldn't have much range, but Janet would get it. The rest of the team would have to rely on themselves.

Ahead, on his left, was Fuller Lodge, the parking lot filled with cars. Jack gunned the engine, whipped the wheel hard, and tapped the brakes, sending the Audi sliding into a sideways skid, which ended as he floored the gas pedal once again. The car shot through a gap in traffic and into the Fuller Lodge driveway, leaving a smoking trail of rubber in its wake.

Swerving left once more, Jack sent the car crashing through the front entryway, scattering glass and debris into the wedding crowd gathered inside. As people screamed, struggling to scramble out of the way, Jack brought the car to a sliding halt.

He opened the car door and stepped out. Immediately, the handful of people in the crowd who had already recovered from the initial shock began moving angrily toward him. Three quick shots over their heads from his Beretta sent everyone scrambling away once again. He didn't want to kill them, but he needed their panic.

Jack moved around to the trunk, popping it open to reach inside, grabbing a long case and the Kalashnikov rifle. He slung the rifle over his shoulder and moved to the stairs leading up to the loft, a mental count running through his head as he walked. If the team outside was Delta, he would have less than a minute before the lead elements of the assault team hit the entrances, perhaps as little as thirty seconds if they were really, really good. They wouldn't want to let him get temporal separation.

Reaching the loft, Jack slapped a clip in the AK-47, partially snapped open a window, and secured the weapon to the frame with the strap so that it pointed down toward the edge of the parking lot. Working quickly, he flipped open the case, extracting a small device that looked like two opposing C-clamps.

He picked up the remote control and pressed the button, and the small device expanded slightly, pushing the ends farther apart and then letting them pop back together. Satisfied, Jack popped the thing over the Kalashnikov's trigger. Grabbing the case, Jack paused at the door and pressed the button again. The noise of the AK-47 firing shook the room. Not only was the weapon reliable, it was very loud, and right now he wanted that volume.

On his way back to the first floor, Jack remotely fired the rifle two more times. It didn't matter that it wasn't aimed at anything in particular. The firing would draw his enemies like moths to a flame.

As he moved down the stairs, Jack extracted the pieces of the sniper rifle from the long case, snapping them together in rapid sequence. By the time he reached the bottom of the stairs, the assembly was complete and he flung the empty case to the side.

He squeezed the remote control three more times, sending the booming echo of gunfire cascading across the parking lot. This time it was answered by a staccato smattering of gunfire that quickly died out.

Jack shook his head. That wasn't Delta out there. It was someone more concerned about limiting civilian casualties than with immediately taking him down, no matter the cost. Well, it had forced his hand. Squeezing off two more rounds from the weapon upstairs, he moved back toward the people huddled at the far corner of the hall.

His voice thundered through the large room. "Everyone! Get out of here and into the parking lot. Now!"

With no need for additional encouragement, the panicked crowd raced toward the front exit. As they did, Jack slid unnoticed out the back.

CHAPTER 21

Janet walked to the flashing alarm, reached out, and switched it off. OK. So it all came down to now. That was Jack's signal, the thing they'd been awaiting for weeks.

She walked into the kitchen, opened the freezer, and extracted two plastic Baggies, one filled with one-inch meatballs and the other holding three frozen syringes of blood. Making her way around the corner and up the stairs, Janet pulled the cord hanging from the hallway ceiling and climbed the steps into the attic. The computers and SATCOM equipment sat where they had since Admiral Riles had been killed, unused since the team had been cut off from any external support. Moving rapidly from system to system, Janet removed the hard disks and memory units, setting them in a pile around a pre-wired detonation device attached to a white phosphorous grenade. She smiled. Good old Willy Pete, as they had called it before her day, back in Vietnam. It burned so hot that almost nothing could put it out.

Within a minute, she was done and moving back down the steps to the second floor. In the office, she retrieved the ultrathin laptop and placed it in her backpack along with the two freezer Baggies. Then she opened the locker, grabbed the bulletproof vest and an M95 military protective mask, and slid into both.

Next she retrieved a pair of green M57 firing devices, more commonly known as clackers because of the sound they made when squeezed. These babies would produce the electrical signals that would set off the No. 2 blasting caps on the Claymore mines. And each of those lads held seven hundred little ten-and-a-half-grain steel spheres backed by a pound and a half of C4 plastic explosive. Soon enough, like the ancient Scottish broadsword from which they drew their name, the two Claymores downstairs and the daisy chain of four out back would cut her a path out of here.

Having completed these preparations, she retrieved one last toy, the Israeli Uzi nine-millimeter submachine gun, stuffing several ammunition clips into her backpack. The Uzi wasn't a Jack type of weapon, but she loved it. It was light, compact, and packed a hell of a punch. Somehow, cradled in her arms, it just felt right.

Janet walked to the inside corner of the room and slid down the wall until she was seated with her back pressed up against the corner. Her fingers found the twin pairs of wires that had been secured to the wall along the baseboard with a staple gun. A quick tug popped enough of the staples to give her the slack she needed. Then, a couple of quick twists of the bare leads fastened them to the connectors on each clacker.

Settling back, she could feel the click of the valve in the filter canister as she breathed in and out through the mask. It felt a bit claustrophobic, but she had felt that before. She just had to slow her breathing and follow the plan that Jack had laid out. The hit team would expect her to run if she was warned. If she didn't run, they would assume she could be taken by surprise. She just had to wait for them to come to her. And that probably wouldn't happen until they thought they already had Jack under control.

And so she sat there, grasping the clackers and her Uzi, waiting for the reckoning that was coming. If they thought they had Jack, they were in for an unpleasant surprise. Inside the clear faceplate of her gas mask, Janet smiled.

CHAPTER 22

"You've lost containment. Shut the operation down now."

Darnell Freeman spun to face Garfield Kromly. "Shut your ass up. This is an FBI operation, and I will be making all the operational decisions."

But Kromly persisted. "Look, Freeman, just have your team back off temporarily to regroup. We want Jack, but only on our terms."

"We have him cornered now, and I am damn sure not backing off just because he started running before he got all the way to the preplanned kill zone. In a few more minutes, the task force will have moved to surround Fuller Lodge. In the meantime, he is pinned down on the second floor, shooting wildly."

Kromly stepped in close, his eyes ablaze. "Listen to me, for God's sake. Gregory doesn't shoot wildly. Something is drastically wrong in there."

Freeman turned his back on Kromly, facing toward the situational displays and communications equipment that filled one corner of the task force command center. He keyed the mike on the command radio.

"Gibson. What's your ETA?"

The speakers crackled. "We should have everyone in position in about two more minutes."

"Good. As soon as you do, have Alpha team sweep around the left flank and cover the back side of the lodge. Let Bravo and Charlie teams cover the front and right."

There was a pause on the other end of the radio.

Freeman keyed the mike again. "Gibson, did you copy that last transmission?"

"Shit. Something new is happening. I have a couple hundred civilians running out the front door."

"Goddamn it. He'll be mixed in with them. Get them directed to a holding area."

"No way. We're still taking fire from the second floor window. All the civvies are scattering like wild rabbits. I think a couple of them are down."

Freeman cursed, then keyed the mike again. "If he's firing, then he's on the second floor. Put some suppressive fire into that room."

"What if he has hostages up there?"

"Goddamn it, Gibson! He's shooting into a crowd of people. Put some suppressive fire up there and then take him down as soon as you have all the teams in position."

"Roger."

Freeman slammed down the microphone to stare at the situational displays. The green dots indicated the GPS position of every member of the task force. The last of Charlie team had just made their way into position for the assault, having had the farthest to travel from where they had been prepositioned at the planned takedown location.

The other radios in the room were filled with chatter, monitoring the interteam tactical communications from Fuller Lodge. Now they had new problems. A host of squad cars from the Los Alamos Police Department had arrived on the scene, and Freeman's teams were having to expend resources to keep them out of the way. Although advance coordination had been made with the local authorities, it had not included this unexpected detour into a wedding ceremony at Fuller Lodge.

A quick glance at his watch told Freeman more than he wanted to know about how things were going. They were almost eight minutes into the operation and still hadn't really gotten things started. Jesus, what a cluster. The thought of what Kromly had said crossed his mind, but he angrily dismissed it a second time. Too late for that now.

The CIA man now stood off to one side, slowly shaking his head. *Well, screw him*, thought Freeman. They still had plenty of firepower to get the job done, and the last thing he needed now was more advice.

Finally, the little dots on the screen were moving out toward their designated assault positions. But something about Alpha team looked wrong. Two of the lead dots had stopped moving before reaching their assigned locations. Suddenly the radios were alive with chatter.

"Two officers down. Christ. Someone just killed Jonesy and Christopher." The sound of automatic weapon fire drowned out the remainder of his words.

Gibson's voice broke in. "Bravo Team. Where the hell is the suppressive fire onto that second floor?"

Another radio squawked. "Damn it, we're pounding the hell out of it. We've launched five gas grenades in there too."

Gibson's excited voice shifted to the other channel. "Alpha team? Where is the fire coming from?"

This time a different voice answered. "Shit. Get us some backup. We've got two more down over here. I can't tell where the hell the fire is coming from."

"Bill, can you get to your wounded?"

The other man's breathing was coming in ragged gasps. "We don't have any wounded. The bastard is shooting everyone in the head. Get us some goddamn help over here or there won't be anybody left."

"Bravo, move over to support Alpha," Gibson's voice cracked with stress.

Suddenly, Freeman felt Kromly's hand grip his arm. He swung his eyes to meet those of the old CIA trainer.

"You don't have much time," said Kromly in a voice devoid of emotion. "Jack is on their flank, rolling them up like ducks in a shooting gallery."

"That was before we got the gas into the building."

"Goddamn it, Freeman, you stupid asshole. Don't you get it? Jack isn't in the building. He's out there somewhere among your men, and he's hunting. Don't send more of them to him."

"Kromly, you're not telling me something. Why all the head shots?"

Suddenly, the Bravo team radios began to chatter. One of their men was down, but it was unclear where the shot had come from.

As much as it galled him and despite the fact that he knew this meant the end of his career, Darnell Freeman knew where his duty lay. It lay with those men out there, who put their lives on the line for their country every day of the week, those men who were getting butchered by the abomination called Jack Gregory. He picked up the microphone.

"Gibson, this is Freeman. Pull Bravo team back now."

"Sir?"

"You heard me. We've lost containment on Gregory. Get your men back to where they can establish a defensible perimeter and await further instructions. And keep those Los Alamos cops out of there too."

Having finished with Gibson, Freeman switched to another frequency. They may have lost Gregory for the moment, but taking down the other three members of his team would help take some of the sting out of it. He would, no doubt, be fired tomorrow, but that man had killed some good agents, some of them men he had known personally. It was now time to close the other two traps and bring home some of the vengeance that the FBI was owed.

He picked up the SATCOM radio handset and spoke the words that would set the other two parts of the task force into motion. Fifty miles away in Santa Fe and just a few miles down the road in Los Alamos, two other special assault units moved into action.

CHAPTER 23

The tear-gas canisters crashed through the windows of the house in volleys, rapidly filling every room with a noxious cloud.

In the second-floor office, Janet leaned back against the corner, breathing slowly in and out through her M95 protective mask, holding the Uzi and twin green clackers. She waited. It wouldn't be long now. A matter of seconds.

The sound of imploding glass downstairs signaled the arrival of the special weapons assault team into the Johnson house. Janet squeezed the handle on one of the clackers, sending an electrical signal down the line to the Claymore antipersonnel mines positioned behind the couch and in the pantry downstairs. The shock wave lifted the floor beneath her, signaling that the thousands of small ball bearings had introduced themselves to her attackers, blowing what was left of them back out through the doors and windows they had just crashed through.

Before the second floor of the house could quit vibrating, Janet was on her feet, pressing the handle of the second of the twin green clackers. This one shook the house from the outside as a long daisy chain of Claymores cleared a path from the back door into the canyon behind the house and set off the thermite grenade in the attic.

She moved through the smoke-filled hallway and down the fractured remains of the stairway by feel, since smoke rendered visual cues nonexistent. In the kitchen Janet paused just long enough to orient herself to the doorway before launching herself into a dead run down the line that had been cleared through the SWAT perimeter by the four daisy-chained Claymores.

Before the first layer of smoke had begun to clear, she was already in the steep wooded canyon, moving toward the distant rally point where she would meet up with Jack. Behind her, the sound of gunfire directed into the roaring inferno gave ample evidence that the SWAT team did not yet have a good idea of what had just happened.

The *whup-whup* of a helicopter moving out over the canyon indicated that this situation was changing. Yells from above her to her left and right indicated that the leader of this assault team knew what he was doing. He had been surprised by the Claymores and had lost several men, but he was now getting things put together. He had sent men racing out on two sides in an attempt to cut off escape along the line cut through his perimeter by the daisy chain of Claymores. Clearly she had not been seen, but the man was making all the right assumptions.

Job one was to get rid of the chopper; then she could worry about slowing the pursuit. Janet pulled off her protective mask, stuffing it into the backpack, and raised the Uzi into firing position. From where she knelt, deep in a thicket, she could judge the direction from which the helicopter was approaching. As the sound grew louder, she waited, her finger gradually tightening on the trigger.

Janet shifted position, clearing her line of sight to the chopper, which was now almost directly overhead. Leading it by a half hand, Janet squeezed the trigger, cutting a lazy S-pattern along the helicopter's line of flight, letting it fly into the spray of nine-millimeter slugs.

The pilot banked hard to the right, but that only helped her, providing a moment when the entire body of the aircraft aligned itself with her firing line. The Uzi slugs chewed into it, rupturing the fuel tank. The helicopter spun, and struggled back up toward the rim in a desperate attempt to set down before it lost the capacity for controlled flight.

Once again, Janet was moving. The helicopter had cost her precious seconds, and during that time, the FBI assault team had been busy. The sound of rolling rocks to her right indicated that the lead elements on that side had almost reached a point even with her.

Janet turned right, moving toward them in a running crouch that kept her in the midst of the thorn brush, accepting the small rips it inflicted on her clothes and skin in payment for the concealment it provided. Reaching a small rocky outcropping, Janet dropped to her belly, wiggling into a slot between boulders, which gave her a view up the canyon. Almost immediately, she spotted them, three men scrambling down the steep slope, trying to get ahead of her. She slapped a new clip in the Uzi, aimed, and fired.

The short-barreled weapon had limited accuracy at this range, but one of the men stumbled forward and the other two dived for cover, sending a volley of return fire into the rocks. Janet ducked down the back side of the outcropping and resumed her former path down a sheltered draw into the depths of the canyon. She didn't know how long her pursuers would pause before figuring out that she had gone on, but they would certainly proceed with more caution. And that would let her build her lead.

Something slapped Janet's left thigh hard enough to send her rolling down the slope to crash into the thick branches of a juniper tree. The echo of the shot followed her down. Pain exploded in her brain, shock narrowing her vision...and it kept narrowing as she fought to remain conscious. When she could see again, a quick glance at the rapidly expanding red wetness along her pant leg meant she didn't have long. But before she could deal with that, she had to get some separation.

She aimed the Uzi up the slope in the general direction of the shot and emptied an entire clip. Slapping in a replacement, she forced herself to move, although the pain almost made her scream. Reaching back inside the backpack, she extracted another of the white phosphorous grenades, pulled the pin, and tossed it into the thick, dry brush above her.

As she struggled down the slope and into the defile of a narrow ravine, she could feel the heat of the blaze on her back. Within seconds, the inferno spread to the tinder-dry surrounding brush. Fed by the wind that funneled up through the canyon, the fire began to climb upward, throwing off a thick cloud of smoke and burning embers.

Janet continued to move down until she found a long line of brush that let her turn right. Already blood loss was weakening her, but she needed to get outside of the direct line the two pursuit teams were taking. If she didn't get the bleeding in her thigh stopped, she wasn't going to be alive for them to catch.

She slumped to the ground with her back against a jutting rock ledge and slit open her left pant leg above the knee. The bullet had entered the outside of her thigh and punched a clean hole out the top, barely missing the bone. Janet ripped the bottom of her pant leg free, cutting it into long strips. Then, grabbing the small military first-aid pouch from her bag, she wadded the gauze into twin lumps, which she pressed into both sides of the wound and bound tight to form a pressure bandage.

It wasn't great, but it had slowed the bleeding to a mere trickle. It would have to do.

Janet forced herself to get up and moving again. On the hillside above, the fire had become an angry orange storm, generating its own local updrafts that drove it all the harder. And with every fresh bit of dry brush that it consumed, the smoke and flying embers became denser. Already the entire upper part of the canyon was masked behind a dark haze.

She focused her attention on the task ahead. The rally point Jack had designated lay three miles to the southwest, separated from her current location by incredibly rough terrain. No use thinking about that now. No matter how badly she hurt, it all boiled down to putting one foot in front of another and repeating that process over and over.

She reached the canyon bottom and paused. The FBI might be delayed, but soon it would recover, and when it got back on the trail it would use dogs. Janet reached into her backpack and extracted the bag with the balls of strychnine-laced hamburger meat, sprinkling a handful of the doggy treats along and to either side of her trail. The remainder she put back into the backpack for use farther down her trail.

She began moving forward again, rounding a bend in the canyon and moving up along a winding arroyo on the far side, letting the natural folds in the land and the periodic dense vegetation hide her movements. Her leg was tightening up more with each stride so that now she was almost dragging the left leg behind her.

Her thoughts flashed back to Dahlonega, Georgia, and the Camp Merrill Mountain Ranger Camp. She had been the first woman to successfully complete Army Ranger training. Even though hers had been an unofficial class, it had been the real thing, conducted by real ranger instructors, or RIs, as they were known to the current crop of students. Nine weeks of hell began at Fort Benning, made its way into the mountains of Georgia, and eventually culminated in the swamps of northwestern Florida.

Twenty-three of the ninety-seven members of her special CIA class had been women. Of those, she had been the only woman to graduate, along with forty-two of her male classmates. The only sign she had noticed that was different from that given to the graduating men was a half nod from one of the ranger instructors as she received her ranger tab. It had been the slightest of movements, but one that had meant the world to her at the time, something that said, "You did good, Ranger."

Putting one foot in front of the other was what being a ranger was all about. When everyone else quit, they didn't. They didn't at Pointe du Hoc in World War II and hadn't from then through Somalia to now. And although she would never be a part of a real ranger unit, Janet wasn't about to let mere pain and fatigue drive her to quit either. She would never have a uniform to wear it on, but that ranger tab felt as if it had been branded onto her left shoulder, and the force of that brand pulled her onward toward the rally point and Jack.

As night descended, Janet dispersed the rest of the doggy meatballs, unconsciously dropping the bag that had contained them along the trail. She was no longer sure how much farther she needed to go. Sickness had leached its way into her very soul, a weakness that spread to her uninjured limbs, making her feel weak as a kitten.

Exactly when she had stopped walking and started crawling, Janet could not recall. But with each lurch forward it became clearer that she was not going to make it. Still she could not quit.

She was going to die, but she would die trying to get to the place Jack had told her to go.

It seemed that she had merely blinked her eyes, but then she found herself staring up at the star-filled sky. Somehow she had rolled over onto her back and passed out. For several seconds Janet struggled to rise. She barely managed to raise her head before collapsing back to the ground.

Suddenly he was there. Jack's face was illuminated in the red glow of his hooded flashlight as he examined her body. A sharp pain surged through her injured thigh, Jack replacing her pressure bandage. Then his face was back, leaning in close.

"Stay awake until I get back. Don't you go to sleep on me. Got it?"

Janet did her best to smile up at him. "Got it."

As he stared down at her, she saw it: the red flicker of flame that leaped from deep within his pupils.

Then Jack turned to look toward her pursuers. As he disappeared along her back trail, Janet finally managed that smile. Her hunters had just become the hunted. In the midst of the dark night, a deeper darkness was coming for them—and they didn't even know it.

CHAPTER 24

Jim "Tall Bear" Pino hadn't been back up this way in a long, long time. As the bottom of the Jeep Cherokee dragged over the rocks, he remembered why. What qualified as roads up on this corner of the reservation would have been proud to be called goat trails in other parts of the world. Last monsoon season's rains hadn't improved them. The only reason he was here now was the dream.

Last night his grandmother had walked with him in his dream, and it was into this steep canyon country that she had led him. She had not spoken a word, and as Tall Bear watched her move through the canyon, her long gray hair hanging over ceremonial buckskin garments, a great feeling of dread had consumed him.

Suddenly the old woman had stopped, her arm sweeping out before her. Everywhere he had looked, the Navajo people he had known all his life lay naked, their hands and feet staked to the ground atop massive ant mounds. But the things that had crawled over their bodies and into long cuts that had been opened in their flesh weren't ants. They were something else, something that swarmed into the cuts by the thousands. And as those tiny things had burrowed deep inside their bodies, his people had screamed their lungs out.

Tall Bear had awakened soaked in sweat. He had little doubt about the nature of what he had seen in the dream. Those tiny crawling machines were the same things that his friend Dr. Eddy Oneta had showed him under the microscope when he had examined the Copenhagen can full of blood from the truck murder scene.

Most people would have thought the dream was only the result of that shocking revelation combined with news of the botched FBI raids yesterday in Los Alamos, but not Tall Bear. Over the years he had been subjected to only a handful of such incredibly detailed dreams, and in every case the special dream had presaged some terrible event. He no longer ignored their warnings.

In the dream, his grandmother had been pointing to something in the distance beyond the screaming Navajos. He had awakened before he could identify what she was trying to show him, but the answer was out here in these rugged canyons. Of that he was certain.

Across the distant hills to the southwest of the reservation, a huge plume of smoke rose up into the sky, the result of the forest fire that raged in the canyons near Los Alamos. Damn. Whoever the FBI had been after in Los Alamos had kicked its ass—big-time.

CNN had run with the story around the clock, calling it the worst disaster in FBI history. By the end of the night, the extent of the damage had become all too clear. A total of twenty-two FBI and ATF agents had been killed with several others injured.

A number of civilians had also been injured during the running gun battles that had started near Fuller Lodge and soon spread to the canyons beyond town. To top off the disaster, a major forest fire had been started intentionally by the fugitives during their escape.

Worse, from the FBI perspective, the killers had escaped, although one of them, a woman, had apparently been injured. Now the largest domestic manhunt in US history was being seriously hampered by the rapidly spreading forest fire, which also posed a serious threat to the towns of Los Alamos and White Rock. The only law-enforcement bright spot had been the success of the raid in Santa Fe, which had killed two more members of what was being called a team of rogue mercenary agents affiliated with the deceased former NSA director, Admiral Jonathan Riles.

As the Cherokee lurched around a bend in the steep trail, Tall Bear brought the vehicle to a complete stop. Ahead, a rockslide had obliterated the narrow track, making further progress by vehicle impossible. Oh well, he was going to have to walk sooner or later anyway. At its best, the jeep trail would have only taken him partway into the backcountry into which he was heading.

Killing the engine, Tall Bear climbed out, letting his ears accustom themselves to the sounds of his surroundings. Without the engine noise, the canyons almost seemed silent. It just took a while to purge his senses of the roaring machine noises, which had masked all other sounds.

The wind was up this morning and bound to get worse as the day progressed, bad news for the firefighters around Los Alamos. It was going to be a hot day too, with temperatures expected to rise into the nineties even above seven thousand feet. Tall Bear reached across the seat, grabbed his Winchester 30-30 rifle and canteen, set the parking brake, and slammed the door.

If his intuition was right, the rifle wasn't going to do him much good. It was a saddle gun, not a very accurate long-range weapon. But it was easy to carry, and he had a certain fondness for the way it rested across the crook of his arm.

Tall Bear moved off the trail, taking a more direct route through the rough country toward his destination than would have been possible in the vehicle, even if the jeep trail had been passable. Even taking this shortcut, he had a little over five miles to travel. And that just brought him to the dream spot. After that, who knew where the trail might take him.

The silent ease with which Tall Bear passed through the rough terrain seemed unnatural in a big man, even for a Navajo. It certainly wasn't a natural trait associated with his race. These days most of his people made enough noise hiking to startle a stampeding buffalo herd. But Tall Bear had spent a significant portion of his life learning the old ways, working to carry forward the knowledge of the elders. Now it was just second nature.

Out here he was at home, many miles from the nearest human, only the plants and animals for company. And it wasn't just that this was reservation land that kept it free from people. This was New Mexico, a place where vast stretches of land were still free of paved highways and population. Even the massive manhunt had not made its way in this direction, focused instead toward the Bandelier National Monument in the rugged country southwest of Los Alamos and White Rock. After all, that had been the direction in which the killer called Jack Gregory had been heading when the feds lost the trail.

Tall Bear shook his head. Lost the trail indeed. From what he had heard, it sounded more as if Jack Gregory had spent the night hunting federal agents and shooting them in the head. One reporter had said that things had gotten so bad that the search had been called off some time after midnight so that the FBI could establish a defensive perimeter to avoid losing more agents in the dark. They had made matters worse by cordoning off the area and refusing to allow firefighters in to battle the blaze until it had gotten so large it could not be contained.

Something about the whole situation stank of cover-up.

According to a government spokesman, Jack Gregory had set up a team of operatives in the Los Alamos area several months ago and had been trying to gain access to information that could be used to disrupt the governmental release of Rho Ship technologies. Gregory and his team had worked for Admiral Riles, forming a group that believed the Rho Project technologies should be kept solely for use by the US military and intelligence communities. Over time, that small group had become a rabidly violent militia, bent on the overthrow of the government. Yesterday, Gregory had gone on a killing rampage, shooting federal agents in the head, one after the other.

Tall Bear thought back on the truck ambush where he had been first on the scene. Those men had been shot in the head, then dragged from the truck cab and decapitated. But the blood spatter at the spot of decapitation meant they had still been alive when their heads were severed, despite having parts of their brains splattered around the inside of the truck.

And then there was the blood he had scooped into that Copenhagen can, the blood that had been laced with tiny machines he had seen through Dr. Oneta's microscope. There were other things too. The original 911 tape that Yolanda Martinez had played for him had implied that there was something about the blood that the federal government was hiding.

Combined with the recent news about the serial killings, Tall Bear had arrived at a much more troubling conclusion. Something was going on at the Los Alamos National Laboratory that had driven a highly trained team of US operatives to commit treason to try to stop it. And from Admiral Riles on down, those operatives were now being purged. Could he prove it? No, but it seemed right.

The canyon wall pivoted, a long jagged crack etching its way into the edge of the high mesa to the west. Into this monstrous crack Tall Bear's silent footsteps carried him, moving him across the spot he had walked in last night's dream. He almost expected to see his grandmother walking along before him, beckoning him to follow.

Already the sun had moved well past its zenith so that shadows walked outward from the high rock walls and jagged spires. The shade should have been welcome, but the reaching darkness seemed deeper than that of normal shadows. Tall Bear's eyes swept the high cliffs along both sides of the rift, finally settling on the spot ahead where the trail flattened out and the canyon widened. No staked-out, screaming natives. But there was another presence out there somewhere, just beyond his senses.

As Tall Bear moved out into the wider portion of the canyon, he almost missed it. He was about to bypass a thick stand of juniper when he saw the blood. It was just a dollop on the needles at the end of a small branch, making them look almost like a paintbrush that had been dabbed with color from a painter's palette. The blood had not been there more than a couple of hours.

Tall Bear moved in a slow spiral out from the spot, and as his eyes read the trail sign, the story it told sent a shiver up his back. A man had passed this way carrying someone. Had it not been for that extra weight, Tall Bear doubted that he could have seen any sign at all that anyone had passed this way. As it was, only the slightest of disturbances to the rocks and plants were evident between the occasional spots of blood. Whoever this was, it was someone who moved like nobody Tall Bear had ever seen.

The ghost trail led him up away from the bottom into the roughest part of the canyon, giving indications that the person had been moving quickly. The increase in blood sign told him why. The one being carried was in serious trouble.

Suddenly Tall Bear froze, every sense attuned to his surroundings. Although he couldn't see or hear anything, someone was out there, very close now.

Straightening, Tall Bear spoke in a voice that was clear and loud.

"Either squeeze that trigger, or step out and talk to me."

CHAPTER 25

Wind stirred the juniper branches, momentarily bringing them across his sight line, obscuring the point at which the scope's crosshairs tracked his target. The man moved along the slope with a steady purpose, head bent, occasionally stooping to examine trail sign. He was a Native American, obviously a tribal policeman. Whoever he was, he was good. Damn good.

Jack doubted that even Harry could have tracked him like that. But Harry was dead, a victim of the one who had called himself the Rag Man. Now, except for Janet, the other members of Jack's team were also dead, and if he didn't get lucky very soon, deadly little Janet was going to join them.

Jack's attention returned to the Indian cop who moved steadily along his back trail. Why was the man out here alone? If someone had found his trail, he would have expected choppers and an army of special ops folks trying to cut him off. Well, Jack didn't have time to get curious. In a few seconds, the man would step out of the thick brush into which he had disappeared, and then he would meet his ancestors.

The tribal cop emerged into the clearing. Jack let the cross-hairs settle on the man's throat. It was a downhill shot of about a hundred and fifty meters. The trajectory of the bullet would put it three and a half inches above the aim point at this angle and range, just above the bridge of his nose. Just as he was about to tighten the muscles in his trigger finger, the Indian straightened, looking up the hill directly toward Jack's hide position.

"Either squeeze that trigger, or step out and talk to me."

The man just stood there, his long, straight black hair hanging down over his shoulders—tall, unafraid. Incredible.

Jack rose to his feet and stepped out into the open, his long stride taking him quickly down the slope toward the man who awaited his arrival. As he got within a dozen yards of the Indian, he recognized him. It was the cop he had seen on the news, the one who had been the first on the scene at the truck ambush, the one who had given the FBI so much trouble when they tried to intimidate him into cooperation.

"Jack Gregory, I presume." The tribal cop spat a thin stream of tobacco.

"That's right," said Jack. "And you are?"

"Sergeant Jim Pino."

"Ah yes, I saw you on TV."

"You've been generating some press coverage yourself."

"And you still thought it was a good idea to follow me by yourself?"

"Let's cut the crap. I'm here because of what I found at the truck murder scene."

"And what did you find?"

"What you wanted someone to find."

"That's why the FBI came down so hard on you? To see if you'd discovered something you hadn't reported?"

"Nah. They did that because I'm Navajo. Gotta keep the red man in his place."

"And that place doesn't include federal crime scenes?" A thin smile creased Jack's lips.

"They didn't seem to think so."

"What if I don't like Indian cops either?"

"Doesn't matter. You know something that makes the government want you very dead. From what I saw in the blood of those truck guards, I think I better know it too."

Jack paused. The man standing before him knew he was as good as dead, but he had the gall to press Jack for information.

Pino spat again. "Where's the girl? Dead?"

So the tribal cop had read the meaning of the blood on the trail. A hundred feet above Jack's original hide position, Janet struggled for life. Why was it he felt compelled to waste the time required for this conversation? Perhaps he just wanted a few extra moments of delay before he was forced to make the choice, a choice as unpleasant as any Jack could remember.

"She will be soon if I keep standing here talking with you."

"I know a place near here, an old cave hidden back in the cliffs. You're going to need a place to hide and someone trustworthy to bring you some supplies."

Jack laughed, his weapon rising to point at Jim Pino's chest. "And if I let you take me there and let you go, you'll take care of us?"

Pino's black eyes locked with his. "Do what feels right."

Jack's voice hardened. "Well, Jim—"

"My friends call me Tall Bear."

"Well, Jim," Jack continued, "it took balls tracking me like this, and you got my attention about the guards' blood. Doesn't mean I trust you."

"OK."

Jack hesitated a moment more. Some part of him still just wanted to shoot Pino. But every once in a while you had to take a chance...

"Tell you what. Bring some supplies back here tomorrow evening, just before dark. I'll consider your offer."

"What about the information I need?"

Jack motioned with the barrel of his weapon. "Tomorrow."

With a shrug, Jim Pino turned, walking away without a backward glance. Jack watched him until he had disappeared around a bend in the canyon. Then Jack began the climb back up the steep slope to the spot where he had left Janet.

She hadn't moved. As Jack bent to examine her, the sound of her breathing hurt his ears. No longer was her chest rising and falling with a weak regular rhythm as her breath sighed out. Now her breathing rattled deep in her chest. He touched her cheek with his fingertips, an action that left pale indentations that refused to pink out again.

Jack moved to Janet's pack, rummaging around inside until he found three syringes and a needle. Although he didn't care to think about what he was going to try, he had made his decision. It might kill her, or he might have to kill her even if it worked, but Jack wasn't going to let her lie there drowning in her own fluids.

The vials were labeled with a blue alcohol marker. Priest. Driver. Guard. The blood inside had long since thawed. Three different vials. Probably three different blood types. Each one massively infested with the Rho Project nanites.

Most likely the nanites had long since become inoperative, the blood in the vials rancid. Even if this worked, the stuff would probably leave Janet as insane as Priest had been. As Jack attached the needle to the first of the three vials and slid it into a vein in Janet's arm, he took a deep breath. It didn't matter. He would give her this one last chance at life.

CHAPTER 26

The night after the report about the FBI's massive failure, Jennifer was where she spent most of her nights, now: in the starship cavern.

A dull throbbing pulsed through the cave, accentuated by the changing intensity of the magenta glow from the alien ship. Reclined on one of the command deck couches, completely immersed in the holographic experience as her mind probed the onboard computer systems, Jennifer didn't notice the change. Neither did she notice when she rose from the couch and began climbing down through the hole between decks.

Reaching the room she thought of as the medical lab, Jennifer moved directly across to the door that blocked access to the inner part of the ship, the door they had never discovered how to open.

Jennifer stopped, her unseeing eyes staring straight ahead, her arms hanging limply at her sides, her head tilting slightly to the left, as if some part of her subconscious was aware of the problem the door presented. Suddenly, she stepped forward again, passing through the wall as if it had no more substance than the holographic field that cloaked the cave entrance.

The room was smaller than the medical lab, crowded with glowing transparent tubes of varying thickness, like the tentacles of some psychedelic sea anemone. Each of the tubes pulsed with flowing multicolored globules of light. Thousands of the plasma globules climbed and danced atop each other where the tubes connected together, like a great hive of bees rubbing together in a dance of communication.

Amid the forest of plasma tubes, a lone central couch, a larger replica of the tentacle couch in the medical lab, awaited. Jennifer moved forward, settling into the couch as easily as if she were sliding into her own bed. And as she settled in, tiny tendrils sprouted from the surrounding tubes, each feeling its way across her body toward the desired nerve ending that would form its connection. The tendrils continued to multiply until there were thousands of them, millions, each lit with its own internal light.

As the last of these came to rest, a new pulse rippled through the room, the light rising in intensity to several orders of magnitude brighter than before. Deep within the confines of the couch, Jennifer's small body convulsed.

Ten miles away, stretched out in their own beds, Heather's and Mark's bodies shook their bed frames hard enough to rattle the floor. But not hard enough to dispel the dream.

CHAPTER 27

Dr. Stephenson might have been brilliant, but his skills as a surgeon were rudimentary at best. It was now clear why he didn't attempt surgery directly on the brain. Even with his knowledge of the alien technology, he needed nerve endings that did not require superior surgical technique to reach. Because the nanites that infested Raul's body prevented painkillers or other drugs from having much effect, Stephenson hadn't bothered to administer them. Either that or he just didn't give a damn what Raul felt. And while they didn't help with his pain, the nanomachines had kept him alive.

As Raul stared down at the tangled mess of connecting alien tubes and conduits, a sharp pang of regret pounded his brain like a five-pound sledgehammer. Stephenson had removed his legs at the hip, leaving him connected to the alien wiring harness in such a way that he could only squirm along the floor on his belly, hunching himself forward with his hands and arms, the bundle of tubes dragging along behind.

Not that it mattered. Raul only had a couple dozen meters of slack in the tubes that formed his wormy rear end. He could slither back and forth through that amount of open space before their connection to the great central machinery brought him up short.

It allowed him to travel far enough to reach the corner where Stephenson had stacked his supplies. There were enough cases of the military meals ready to eat to feed him for a year, along with a matching quantity of gallon-sized plastic water jugs. In addition, his space had the luxury of a camper's portable toilet, little more than a folding chair with a toilet seat and plastic bags that attached to catch your business. Then it was just a matter of dumping the bags into the machine he thought of as the *garbage disposal*. In reality, it was a matter reprocessor that separated its contents into their elemental components, then transferred that matter to the ship's fuel storage for later conversion into raw energy. Nothing was wasted. Everything became fuel: trash, human waste, everything.

Considering Raul's physical limitations, that was a blessing.

At least he still had his upper appendages. Why the good doctor hadn't yet taken his arms, Raul didn't know. The mere thought of the loss of his remaining ability to move about horrified him more than the pain and deformities he had already endured.

Raul didn't yet know precisely what Dr. Stephenson hoped to accomplish by connecting more and more of the alien machinery to new nerve endings in his body, but he was starting to get an inkling. Stephenson was attempting to create an advanced interface to the damaged shipboard computing systems.

At first, not counting the pain, Raul had experienced no response to the wiring that had been inserted into his eye socket.

It was only after several hours, when the screaming in his head had quieted, that he had observed the anomaly. He almost thought he had imagined it, that it was a by-product of the madness into which he felt himself sinking.

It was only a shadow of movement at the edge of his vision, an alien something that dissipated as he attempted to focus on it. Then it reappeared, gradually approaching more closely, as if it gained confidence as it probed, skittering around the dark recesses of his mind, refusing to submit to direct observation.

But it had not been until after the amputation of his legs that the dreams had started. Vivid didn't even begin to describe them. They made no sense; they were merely a sequence of incredibly vivid shapes in colorless grayscale. Raul could feel the scenes, almost as if they were extensions of his own body. Sometimes the dreams continued after he had awakened, their weird images and feelings blending with his surrounding reality.

Perhaps madness had already claimed him. But if that was the case, why did Dr. Stephenson seem so pleased with his progress?

Raul pulled himself to the end of his tether, feeling the tension in his arm muscles as he lifted his torso up off the floor. They were getting stronger. At least the confining stasis field was gone. He paused for several seconds, then turned, his arms propelling him back in the other direction like a misshapen lion pacing slowly back and forth in its cage.

Stasis field or not, Raul wasn't going anywhere.

CHAPTER 28

All the way back to New York, Freddy had been filled with anticipation. And that anticipation had been fulfilled, the biggest story of his life having landed him a big job at the *New York Times*.

Now this!

Freddy Hagerman kicked the chrome trash can hard enough to send it spinning end over end, spewing its contents across the kitchen and into the living room of his East River apartment. He hadn't wanted to kick the garbage can. He had wanted to kick the flat-panel TV set. But even with his newfound notoriety, he couldn't afford to be doing that.

Shit. Now he'd have to clean up the mess.

His gaze returned to the television screen as the president continued his press conference. Freddy watched as the man worked his way through his talking points and then began taking questions. Unbelievable. After the press feeding frenzy that had engulfed the White House these three weeks, you would think the entire executive branch would be making plans for life after a failed and foreshortened presidency.

After all, Freddy's story had nailed their collective asses to the wall, exposing the ill-conceived and illegal testing being conducted on the alien nanotechnology. Then the botched FBI raid in Los Alamos had produced the single worst day in FBI history. Although they had managed to kill several of the rogue agents, the leader of the group and his female accomplice had disappeared. Although the FBI director had endured an unusually strong public rebuke, the president's already battered image had deteriorated, something that didn't break Freddy's heart, not one little bit.

Freddy shook his head. He should have known some shit like this was bound to happen. Everything had been going a little too perfectly. Stepping over a trail of coffee grounds, Freddy picked up his cell phone and pressed five on his speed dial.

His boss's high voice sounded smug. "Hello, Freddy. I guess you've got your TV on."

"Yeah, Charlotte, I'm watching it."

"Sort of throws the conclusion from your big story into question."

"Not at all. I know bullshit when I smell it. This is a cover-up."

"Really?"

"Yes, really. The president's people have cooked this whole thing up."

"Good luck proving it."

"I'll be needing travel authorization." Freddy ignored the editor's annoying chuckle. "I'll be leaving tomorrow for California. I want to take a look into that clinic in Santa Barbara. After that I'll be heading back to Los Alamos."

The silence from the far end of the line lingered, but Freddy waited. He knew this power trip. First one to speak loses.

Charlotte's voice broke the tension. "OK, Freddy. But I stuck my neck out giving you this job ahead of some damn fine reporters. If you don't come up with something good, don't bother coming back."

The line went dead before he could respond. The bitch.

Stepping across the refuse trail, Freddy paused just long enough to give the garbage can one more good kick, then walked into the bedroom to pack his suitcase.

CHAPTER 29

By the time Heather finished breakfast, finished picking up her room to her mom's satisfaction, and made her way to the Smythes', the morning was halfway gone. It really was absurd that she found herself annoyed by the delay. Her mother did so much for her daily; it was only right that Heather pitch in and help a little. But today she just couldn't help feeling put out.

Mark opened the door with a look of surprise on his square face. "Well, I thought you blew us off."

Heather shrugged. "Housecleaning."

"You?" Mark's laugh only added to her annoyance.

"Where's Jen?"

"Garage. She got tired of waiting. Said she wanted to make some final system checks before we take it apart and crate it."

Heather nodded as she headed for the kitchen and the door that opened from there into the Smythe garage. This was the weekend when they had to have everything crated for shipment to Denver, the site of the final competition for the National High School Science Competition. Their cold-fusion entry had breezed through the regional competition. Now it was on to the big show.

Heather had read all the write-ups about the other finalists and their projects. From what she had seen, none of them could hold a candle to what Mark, Jennifer, and she had done. Not only did their project work spectacularly, their report was first-rate. As far as Heather was concerned, victory was in the bag. Just so long as they didn't screw it up.

As expected, Heather found Jennifer sitting at the terminal, her fingers flying across the keyboard, her face lit by the twinkle of multicolored LED light, completely oblivious to Heather's entry into the garage. It was amazing. Jen no longer glanced at the laptop display, instead focusing her gaze upon her custom-made LED board attached to the lead side of the cold-fusion tank, the colors showing the internal contents of the registers. She was thinking in hexadecimal.

"Earth to Doc." Mark's loud voice brought Jennifer's face around, a look of annoyance tightening the corners of her mouth. Despite her best efforts, Heather laughed out loud.

"What?"

Heather shrugged. "Jen, I'm sorry Mark interrupted you so crudely."

"Uh-huh."

"And I'm sorry I laughed," Heather continued. "It's just that Mark provokes you into some pretty funny expressions."

Mark leaned in, a sly grin on his face. "And I'm just as sorry as Heather is."

Heather's elbow caught him in the stomach before he had a chance to tighten it, producing an audible exhalation of air, a sound that finally brought a smile to Jennifer's lips.

"Since you're finally here, come over and take a look at these readouts."

Heather walked around the equipment to stand behind Jennifer's swivel chair. Her eyes swept the numbers that filled the spreadsheet on the laptop screen. Now here was something with which she was completely comfortable. The equipment was performing far better than would normally be expected. Between Heather's slight modifications to the theoretical equations and Jennifer's magical command of computers, their final touches looked complete.

Heather straightened. "Looks great."

Mark raised his hands in a hallelujah salute. "Good. Let's bag it and tag it."

Jennifer nodded in agreement.

The rest of the day passed in a flurry of activity. Every piece of the apparatus had to be carefully tagged with a number and listed on diagrams before disassembly. Then, carefully packaged, the parts were placed in a set of crates. By the time a copy of the diagrams and inventory list had been placed in the last of the crates and Mark had nailed the lid closed, Heather was exhausted.

"My God," Heather gasped. "Are we really done?"

"Oh, shit, we left something out." A look of horror spread across Mark's face.

As Jennifer and Heather's panicked gazes swept the room for what they had missed, a chuckle brought their heads back around.

Mark's grin was ear to ear. "Oh, your faces are priceless."

This time Mark was ready, moving aside just in time to dodge Heather's elbow. Unfortunately, his side step exposed his upper arm to Jennifer's flying fist.

"Ow! That hurt."

"Serves you right." Jennifer's angry gaze showed no sign of softening.

Heather clenched her teeth. "Mark, sometimes you're not nearly as funny as you think you are. That was just mean."

Before Mark could respond, Jennifer stormed from the garage. Mark glanced down at his arm, raising his short sleeve to examine it. Seeing his look of amazement, Heather leaned in for a look.

As incredible as it seemed, Jennifer's punch was raising a deep blue bruise in the hard muscle of Mark's neurally enhanced shoulder. The surprise Heather felt at seeing the result of that punch left her shaking her head. Apparently, Mark wasn't the only one getting stronger.

CHAPTER 30

"Peaches. You OK in there, Peaches? Such a pretty bird. My Peachy, Peachy, Peachy."

Freddy Hagerman glared at the woman across the airplane's central aisle as she stared into the multicolored bird-carrying travel bag on her lap. Jesus H. Christ. If the idiotic woman's cooing wasn't bad enough, now the damn thing was squawking. He'd been hoping to get some sleep on the flight to LA.

Three quick presses of the call button brought the head flight attendant, an aging blonde who could have passed for a storm trooper, beelining toward him.

"Sir, one press of the button is quite enough. May I help you?"

Just then the bird squawked again, this one an earsplitting screech highlighted by the laughter of several people in nearby rows. Freddy stared at the flight attendant, his raised eyebrows leaving no doubt as to what he regarded as the problem.

The flight attendant turned her attention to the woman. The bird woman was an older lady, probably in her mid- to late sixties, her attention so focused inside the mesh of the travel cage that she had failed to notice either Freddy's annoyance or the flight attendant's arrival.

The flight attendant leaned in closer. "Ma'am. Excuse me, but I'm going to have to ask you to put the case under the seat."

The look on the woman's face could not have been more horrified if the flight attendant had just told her the bird would now be served as lunch. A heated discussion ensued, only abating when it became clear that the chief flight attendant, whom Freddy had begun to think of as Mein Frau, would not be cowed.

With the bird case safely settled beneath the seat, the squawking miraculously subsided. Then Freddy discovered that because he was in front of an exit row, his seat would not recline. For the next four hours of sleepless hell, he was forced to endure his head nodding forward hard enough to cramp his neck and a panic from bird woman as Peaches discovered how to unzip its case. This time the old lady refused to be mollified until a frantic search turned up enough tape to secure the zipper.

LAX, perhaps the most crowded and uncomfortable airport in the continental US, had never been something Freddy looked forward to walking into, until now. By the time the plane rolled to a stop at the gate and Freddy rose to retrieve his carry-on from the overhead storage compartment, he was ready to wade through hell itself if it got him off that plane.

Bird woman leaned down and retrieved the case from its resting place, cooing out a string of "Peachy, Peachy, Peachys" before setting it on her seat. Something in Freddy's face must have given her the impression that he wanted to hear a detailed explanation of why she had been so concerned about the damn bird, because she immediately turned toward him and began imparting a detailed breakdown of the events. As if he hadn't been a firsthand witness.

As her voice droned on, the bird case on the seat behind her tumbled to the floor with a small thud that sent the woman spinning in that direction, a squeal of horror issuing from her lips. "Peaches!"

As Freddy disengaged himself to follow other passengers off the aircraft, a grin split his face. Perhaps there was a God after all.

His newly acquired good mood failed to last. Arriving at the rental car terminal, Freddy failed to find his name on the Gold Club reservation board, something that resulted in an hour-long delay while the attendant placed repeated calls to the office, trying to locate his reservation.

As he pulled onto Airport Boulevard, Freddy glanced at his watch: 4:30 p.m. LA traffic at rush hour. Lovely. He could only hope this trip wasn't a harbinger of things to come.

It was just before 11:15 p.m. when Freddy finally pulled into the Motel 6 just off El Camino Real in Santa Barbara. As he stumbled into the office to check in, his gaze fell on a sign printed with the slogan "Welcome to the American Riviera."

"Yeah, right," Freddy mumbled to himself as he dropped his bag and banged on the bell.

One thing he had to admit: although the attendant was away from the desk, they had left the light on for him.

After dropping his bag in the room, he made his way across the street to the beckoning diner, where a Denny's Grand Slam breakfast slid down his gullet, chased down by half a pot of coffee, hot, strong, and black. It was 11:53 p.m., but he needed it—all of it and more. Freddy surveyed the front page of the *Santa Barbara News-Press*, settling on the headline story, a follow-up to yesterday's presidential press conference. Since the president had focused a large portion of his comments on the Rondham Institute for Medical Research, located right here in Santa Barbara, almost the entire front page had been devoted to the story.

As much as Freddy hated to admit it, it sure looked as if the entire thrust of his big Pulitzer Prize story about the out-of-control government nanite program was dead wrong. Unless he could find something wrong with the information the president had presented, he was screwed. But that was all right. Finding stuff that was wrong with something was what Freddy did. In the divorce papers, Dalia, his latest ex-wife, had claimed it was his sole defining trait.

Even though he now knew it by heart, Freddy studied every detail of the story. In his press conference, the president had admitted that the second alien technology involved an injected form of medical nanotechnology. He had even admitted that a rogue scientist at the Los Alamos National Laboratory, a certain Dr. Rodriguez, had abused the national trust, conducting his own illicit nanotechnology experiments outside the secure confines of the laboratory. Although the man had enjoyed a top security clearance, the terminal brain cancer of Dr. Rodriguez's son had caused him to try to accelerate his own research, violating all accepted scientific protocols. That illegal research had involved experimentation on the maniac who called himself Priest Williams, something that had contributed to the man's sense of invincibility and thus to his homicidal rampage.

As the string of presidential admissions had continued, the assembled press lay in wait, expecting anything from a presidential apology to a presidential resignation. But neither had happened. In a single move that would have brought a smile to Machiavelli's corpse, the man had transformed from commander in chief to caregiver in chief.

The Rodriguez security lapses and their associated consequences had been quite dire and had merited a detailed investigation. According to the president, he had waited more than a week after Freddy's big news story had broken to hold this press conference in order to give the investigators the time they required to conduct a detailed review of every aspect of the alien nanotechnology research. That review was now complete.

Initial experiments using the technology on animals at the Los Alamos National Laboratory had produced such impressive results that several months ago the US government had commissioned an independent study of the technology that was conducted at the Rondham Institute for Medical Research in Santa Barbara, California.

The study involved the injection of a serum of tiny microscopic machines, called nanites, into the bloodstreams of children in the final stage of terminal cancer, children for whom all other treatments had failed.

The nanites were really quite simple machines and had only two functions: they would read the DNA of the person into whom they were injected, and they would attempt to aid the body in correcting any problems.

At first, the results of the study were so amazing that everyone involved assumed something was wrong with the data. A new round of testing with new patients was overseen by experts from around the world, and again the results were the same. Every patient experienced a complete recovery from his or her cancer within days of being injected with the nanite serum.

Again, the study was expanded, this time to include children with other fatal conditions, including AIDS and heart, lung, or liver failure, and again the results were the same. One hundred percent of the patients experienced complete recovery. Not remission. Not some sort of immune response. The nanite-assisted healing process made it as if the conditions had never existed.

The government had been on the verge of announcing the experimental results and releasing the nanotechnology for public trials around the globe when Freddy's story broke, forcing several weeks of delay while another thorough review of the program was conducted. That review was now complete. The original test results had been thoroughly validated.

The president had paused to read a statement signed by a host of internationally acclaimed medical research scientists and doctors who had participated in the final review, among them several Nobel laureates. Their report left no doubt. Every day of delay in the release of this incredibly beneficial technology meant that thousands of people across the planet would die unnecessarily, people who could now be saved.

Freddy shook his head. The slick bastard had gutted him like a carp on a fishwife's chopping block. Although the president hadn't specifically said it, the implication was clear. Freddy's horrifying nanite story had caused a huge delay that had killed thousands of innocent kids. Kids! Shit. Why couldn't they have been experimenting on some old geezers nobody gave a damn about?

Tucking the paper under his arm and rising, Freddy took one more pull on his now-lukewarm coffee, tossed a buck on the table, and headed toward the register. It was about time to introduce himself to the good people at the Rondham Institute for Medical Research.

CHAPTER 31

The excitement of the trip to Denver for the finals of the National High School Science Competition should not have overcome Heather's horror at the president's announcement that the alien nanotechnology was on track for public release. But somehow, as she stood in the midst of the exhibit level of the Colorado Convention Center, it did. No matter how self-centered and shallow it seemed, she just couldn't help herself. They had done it. Their cold-fusion project was right up there on the national stage.

As for the other thing, she would just have to have some faith that the US government knew what it was doing.

Heather had ridden up to Denver in the backseat of the family car, cheered by her mom and dad's excited chatter as they drove. Mark and Jennifer had traveled with their own parents, but they had all linked up at the Country Inns and Suites where they were staying. This quick trip over to the convention center was merely to allow them all to get a look at where they would be setting up tomorrow, in preparation for the Saturday event. As she stood here on a Thursday night, despite a number of other students scoping out their assigned spots, the exhibit hall felt like a tomb. Something about a huge hall before it filled with people, equipment, and noise just felt hollow.

"Dad, Mom, I'm going to grab Mark and Jen and check this place out."

Gil McFarland smiled. "OK, but let's meet back here in a half hour. Everyone's starting to get hungry, and tomorrow's going to be a long day of setup and preparation. I want you to be in bed early."

"Got it."

Heather found Mark and Jennifer already heading toward her from the Fourteenth Street lobby.

"I see you're the early bird, as usual," said Mark.

"My dad just drives faster than yours."

"No joke."

Jennifer looked around. "Have you found our designated spot yet?"

"Yes. They marked areas for each entry. We'll be setting up right over there near the partition between exhibit halls A and F." Heather pointed across the floor. "They said we'd get more instructions in the morning when we sign in."

Something about Jennifer caused Heather to look at her more closely. She seemed nervous, her small hands clenching and unclenching as she moved around. "What's up, Jen?"

Jennifer looked at her curiously. "What do you mean?"

"I don't know. You just seem a little wired."

Mark nodded. "Yeah, she's been like that all evening."

"I guess I'm just nervous about being out in front of all these people."

Mark laughed. "We're hardly in front of anybody. There must be spots for a hundred finalists."

"Fifty-four," Heather corrected. "One from each state, one from the District of Colombia, Puerto Rico, the US Virgin Islands, and Guam."

"Well, let's take a look around. What do you say we start from the outside and work our way in?"

"Lead on," Heather said, falling in beside him. Jennifer followed a couple paces back, something that, again, struck Heather as odd. When she got a chance to chat with her friend privately, sans Mark, she'd dig a little deeper into what was going on with her.

The circuit around the building only reinforced her first impression. It was beautiful, all modern angles and glass, designed to bring the beauty of the Western skies inside. From the outside, the evening reflections in the glass were simply gorgeous.

Fourteenth Street, Champa Street, Speer Boulevard, Welton Street, and then back to Fourteenth Street. Each side of the convention center featured its own lobby, although the two largest were off Speer and Fourteenth, since the parking areas occupied most of the space on the other two streets. The net effect on a small-town girl was breathtaking.

As they walked back into the Fourteenth Street lobby, Mark clapped his hands together, rubbing them briskly. "OK, I'm ready to kick a little booty."

Heather laughed. "OK, Coach. You know it's not a sporting event, right?"

"Competition's competition."

"Whatever. We'd better link back up with our folks. I told Dad we'd be back fifteen minutes ago."

Mark shook his head. "By now I'm sure he's learned to mentally adjust for your time estimates. After all, you are a girl."

"Ha ha. You're so funny."

As they reached their parents, Jennifer bent to tie a loose shoelace. Seeing his chance, Mark leaned in close to Heather and whispered.

"I need to talk to you privately." As he pulled back, a slight nod toward his sister indicated the subject of the desired conversation.

Just then, Anna McFarland interrupted. "Enough chitchat. We're all starving, and you kids need to get some sleep tonight. Everyone back to the cars."

By the time they finished eating dinner at the restaurant and made their way back to the hotel, it was after ten. As much as Heather wanted to meet with Mark, she was desperate to talk to Jennifer first. Since Jennifer was rooming with Heather, leaving Mark a solo room, the choice was easy. She'd catch up with Mark tomorrow.

When Heather stepped into her room and flipped on the light switch, she spotted Jennifer sitting on one of the double beds. As she started to say hi, the word froze in her throat. Jennifer sat fully clothed in the center of the bed, her arms hugging her knees tightly to her chest, slowly rocking herself backward and forward. And as she rocked, completely oblivious to Heather's presence, her eyes stared off into the distance, focused on something that only she could see.

Heather turned to go get help, but Jennifer's soft voice stopped her.

"Heather, wait."

Heather turned back toward Jennifer, and as her eyes locked with her friend's, a sudden calmness draped her like a blanket. Somehow, as she stared into those strangely active pupils, all her worries slowly melted away.

CHAPTER 32

"You're looking perky this morning," Mark said, pouring a plastic cup of waffle mix onto the waffle iron.

Heather smiled. "I haven't slept that well in I don't remember when."

Mark closed the waffle iron, rotating the handle into the upside-down position and setting the timer. Grabbing an apple from a bowl on the breakfast bar, a hotel perk he planned on taking full advantage of, he slid into a chair beside Heather. As he studied her face, he smiled back. She did look good, damn good. All traces of the worry lines on her forehead from this last week had been erased as if they had never existed.

Well, he wasn't about to spoil things for her this morning by bringing up his own concerns. The Jennifer conversation would just have to wait until after this weekend. So would his other proposal. It would do them all good to lose themselves in the hustle and bustle of the science competition for a couple of days.

A loud buzz from the waffle iron brought him to his feet just as Jennifer strolled into the breakfast nook. Mark froze in his tracks.

Jennifer had done something to her hair, brushed it out or blow-dried it or something. And she was wearing makeup, not too much either. Mark hadn't ever seen her in the little knit top and snug jeans either. She had even lost the horn-rimmed glasses. Damn, Jennifer didn't look anything like the person he'd grown up with.

"Wow, Jen! You look fantastic." Heather's exclamation woke him from his trance.

A broad grin spread across Jennifer's face as she moved past Mark to grab a glass of orange juice.

"Thanks. Mom took me out shopping the other day. I thought I'd try out a new look."

"Well, you can quit trying. This is it."

"What do you think, Mark?" Jennifer's laughing eyes locked with his.

"Uh…Yeah. I mean, you look good."

Those eyes. Something about the way Jennifer's gaze held him made it hard for him to break the lock. Never in his life had he seen, in his sister, anything close to the confidence that shone in those eyes, a glow that seemed to illuminate her whole face. Hell, it shone from her entire body. Coming from little Jennifer, it gave him the creeps.

Before he could ask the question that rose to his lips, Mrs. McFarland popped around the corner.

"For heaven's sake! Do you kids have any concept of time? We've been waiting in the cars for ten minutes."

"Oh my God," said Heather. "We just got to talking. Sorry, Mom."

"Hmm. Finish off whatever you have left. We barely have time to get over to the convention center for the start of orientation." Without waiting for a response, Mrs. McFarland vanished back around the same corner.

Mark folded his waffle into a taco, poured on a dollop of syrup, and began eating as he walked toward the door.

"Disgusting," Heather laughed.

"Hey, it works."

By the time they arrived at the convention center and made their way inside the lobby, a large crowd had already gathered around the in-processing and registration tables. The excited babble of voices grew as they worked their way into the room, rising to a buzz that made Mark think of the sound that must be present within a hive as the workers struggled to please their queen. Only here, the buzz was all about personal glory. No matter what anyone might say, as he looked around, he could feel it: that growing sense of the glory that awaited the winning team, that sense that, in the matter of intellectual prowess, one team would be acknowledged as superior. And just like those around him, Mark wanted it.

He glanced over at Heather, noticing the proud way her delicate chin tilted upward, her eyes misted with a wet sheen of excitement. God, she was beautiful.

This was it. This was their time. It didn't matter that they had the extra advantage provided by the neural enhancement they had received from the Second Ship. After all, that had merely released the potential that had always existed within them. Now it was time for Mark, Jennifer, and Heather to put the world on notice. The future was now.

His musings were interrupted by their arrival at the front of the registration table and the menial task of filling out the forms that presented themselves. Before he knew it, he was back in the exhibition hall, this time one of hundreds working to prepare their stations for the judges. Minutes became hours as their project reassembled itself, his fingers tuning and adjusting each piece of the apparatus, guided by the steady drone of feedback from his sister as she brought more and more of the computer-controlled instrumentation online.

And always at the periphery of his consciousness, Heather hovered, her gaze staring outward into a numeric dreamland that only she could see, her musical voice chiming in from time to time with special optimization instructions.

Evening came so suddenly that it was not until they were in the restaurant adjacent to their hotel that Mark remembered he hadn't eaten lunch. Dinner passed through his lips and into his stomach with a rapidity that caused his mother to raise a disapproving eyebrow. However, it was Heather's grin that made him aware he'd dribbled barbecue sauce from the baby back ribs onto his shirt.

"Sorry. Guess I was pigging out."

Jennifer shook her head. "There's not much guessing about it. No use bothering with a napkin."

Just as he was about to deliver an angry retort, Mark felt Heather's hand slide up onto his arm. Something about the gentle squeeze of her hand drained the anger from his soul. Her eyes caught him, pulling him deeply into their gentle brown depths. That gaze took his breath, causing his heart to thunder in his chest so that a wave of dizziness threatened to sweep him away.

Then the moment was gone, swept away by the arrival of the waitress bringing the check. Before he knew what had happened, Mark found himself back at the hotel, alone in his room.

And, tired as he was, sleep was no longer an option.

CHAPTER 33

Raul's harness dangled from his buttocks as he swung himself up along the wall of alien machinery to which the far ends of the cables were attached. The knotted muscles in his arms seemed ready to burst through the thin layer of skin that covered them. In his concentration, he hardly noticed the minor amount of effort the climb required.

Dr. Stephenson had been encouraging him to explore his connections to the ship's machinery, only the good doctor had no idea how successful that exploration had become. With every attempt, Raul's access to the ship's neural network got better, despite the severe damage the ship's systems had suffered. Like him, she had been horribly injured, but she was a survivor.

Crude as they were, the connections Dr. Stephenson had made between the machines and Raul's amputation-exposed nerve bundles had been effective. It had taken a while to make sense of the wild sensory data that bled into him through his optical nerve and through the cables he now thought of as his tail. At first, he had thought the strange sensations were only pain-induced hallucinations. How wrong he had been.

His nanite-infested bloodstream had worked miracles, accepting the attachments as if he were a hybrid plant with some new genetic sprigs grafted to its trunk. New skin had grown up around them in a way that just seemed right. Even better, the physical connections to his nervous system were getting better. Yes, the nanites had been one busy little colony, always analyzing his health, always seeking ways to fix imperfections. And while they could not regenerate lost limbs, they were very good at keeping him alive and incorporating usable new parts.

What Raul had initially thought were hallucinations were his first feeble attempts to deal with the data coming from the ship's damaged neural network, a magnificently capable system that his consciousness roamed at will. It was incredible. Now, when he thought about something, he not only thought about it with the neurons in his own brain, he thought about it with all the functioning neural pathways in the ship.

Unfortunately, only a very small portion of the original neural net was currently functional. The molecular data storage banks were the most heavily damaged, although he worked steadily to repair them. He had the feeling that if he could just reach a critical mass here, he would attain access to knowledge that would enable him to understand how to bring more of the power systems back online. And with more power, he could bring the main computers back to life.

In the meantime, he had made a glorious breakthrough. He had managed to tap the Internet remotely. Raul still didn't quite understand how he had achieved it. He had been wishing that he could access data from the outside world, and somehow the ship had brought a connection online. It wasn't a physical connection like a cable line or an uplink to a satellite. Somehow, the ship just managed to make it happen.

But that connection was spotty and limited, the result of damage to a set of components that were the object of Raul's current repair efforts. Clinging with one hand to a set of conduits, Raul unfastened the casings, his artificial right eye seeing the activity in those circuits in a way that no human eye could. As he observed the dataflow, his brain, augmented by the shipboard neural net, understood exactly what was wrong. He might never again leave this craft, but that didn't mean he couldn't touch the outside world.

A broad smile crawled across Raul's face. Perhaps his suffering had not been in vain. Maybe God wasn't done with him after all.

CHAPTER 34

The process had been grueling, and they'd seen a lot of great projects, but now all of that was over and it was time to find out who had won. It was the reason they'd all gathered in the auditorium. Heather's chest felt as if someone had wrapped it in steel bands, the kind used to strap up wooden shipping crates.

"And now, ladies and gentlemen, I have the great pleasure of announcing the winning entry of the National High School Science Competition." Dr. Laura Brannigan, professor emeritus at the University of California, Berkeley, the chairperson of the judging committee, paused as she held aloft a sealed envelope.

As much as Heather had tried to tell herself that it didn't really matter if they lost, as the third- and second-place awards had been announced, she had come to realize what a mental liar she was. It did matter to her. It mattered a lot. Pressed close against either side, she could feel Jennifer and Mark gripping her hands.

Dr. Brannigan slid a letter opener along the seam of the envelope, extracting a single folded sheet of paper. She scanned the page and then, with a broad smile, she read it aloud.

"The winner of this year's National High School Science Competition is the team from Los Alamos High School..."

Heather's scream was matched by Jennifer's and Mark's yells of joy, mingled with those of their parents and a good number of supporters who had made their way from Los Alamos. Amid the hugs and tears, somehow Heather found herself ushered up onto the podium beside Mark and Jennifer. As she looked out over the crowd, it looked like a sea of flashbulbs, reminding her of the lights reflected from one of those spinning disco balls. She wiped at her eyes with the back of her left hand, then stepped forward with Jennifer and Mark for the picture of the three of them holding the plaque, and then for several more official photographs with Dr. Brannigan and Dr. Zumwalt, their own Los Alamos High School principal.

By the time the congratulations were over and Heather found herself back at the hotel hugging Mark and Jen and kissing her parents good night, she felt completely wrung out. Beating Jennifer to the bath, Heather let herself sink beneath the hot water, allowing her head to slip all the way below the surface so that the ceiling appeared to ripple above her.

My God, they had really done it. Popping back above the surface, she ran both hands over her hair, squeezing the water from it before leaning back and settling down once again.

A gentle knocking finally roused her. "Heather? Are you alive in there?"

"Sorry, Jen," she said, stepping out and grabbing a towel. "I'll be right out."

"OK. I was starting to wonder if I was going to get my turn." Jennifer's laugh sounded good. It had been a while since Heather had heard that laugh from her friend.

As Heather slid into her pajamas and crawled into bed, the thought of that warm laughter followed her gently into the land of dreams. She never felt Jennifer crawl in beside her.

Morning broke bright and clear, but the sense of unreality lingered, adding a rosy tinge to everything. Having the winning entry did not relieve them of the necessity of disassembling and packing up their project for return shipping. Heather found that several hours of hard work had the effect of restoring some of the feeling of normalcy to her life. By the time they turned the crates over to the shippers and headed out on the drive back to New Mexico, the only thing she felt was tired.

It was well past midnight by the time the Smythe and McFarland convoy rolled into their respective driveways in White Rock. When she had been a little girl, Heather's dad had picked her up out of the backseat, draping her over his strong shoulder, and carried her to her room on late nights like this. Tonight she really, really missed that. Still, tired as she was, a deep inner sense of satisfaction enveloped her. Her dad and Mr. Smythe might not have PhDs, but their kids could still kick a little ass in this intellectual snobfest capital of the planet.

"Heather. Time for breakfast." Her mother's voice was like a distant beacon, calling her out of the fog.

"Mmm. Sure, Mom. Give me a minute."

"That's what you said ten minutes ago. You've got to get up if you're going to make the ceremony."

Heather sat up in her bed. "What ceremony?"

Anna McFarland smiled down at her. "The town is having a big ceremony over at the high school to congratulate the three of you on your award. The mayors of Los Alamos and White Rock will be there along with the press. Even a TV crew from Santa Fe is supposed to be there. You three are going to be famous."

Heather stretched her arms out over her head. "Well then, I guess I better not keep my adoring fans waiting."

Mrs. McFarland's laugh followed her from the room. "At least you should get some breakfast before starting your big day."

The ceremony at the high school was a surprise. Heather wasn't sure how the community could have organized it on such short notice. Apparently, Principal Zumwalt had anticipated a respectable finish for their project, although even he probably had not expected a first-place finish. Perhaps it was the perfection of the event that injected a note of concern into her consciousness, although it was more likely the presence of the stern-looking man she noticed standing against the back wall of the gymnasium. Whatever the cause, by the time the ceremony reached its conclusion, a low-grade dread had settled firmly onto Heather's shoulders.

As the crowd filed out, Heather noticed the stranger move up to whisper in Principal Zumwalt's ear, an action that immediately preceded the two of them walking briskly from the gymnasium. As the principal passed through the double doors, he glanced back, his gaze momentarily locking with hers. Something in that look confirmed her very worst fears. Equations filled her head, all of them resolving to the same solution. Something was horribly wrong.

Despite the tables full of refreshments and the dozens of people who came up to her to offer their congratulations, the sense of impending doom continued to deepen. Before she got a chance to discuss her fears with Mark or Jennifer, Principal Zumwalt reentered the gymnasium, walking directly up to the spot where Heather stood beside her mom and dad.

"Mr. and Mrs. McFarland, if you would be so kind, please bring Heather to my office. An urgent matter has just come to my attention."

Gil McFarland set his soda on the table and raised a questioning eyebrow. "What's this all about?"

"I'm sorry, but I only want to go through this once, and the Smythes need to be present as well. Please wait for me in my office while I go find them."

Gil McFarland nodded. "Come on, Anna, Heather. Let's go find out what this is about."

When they reached the principal's office, Heather saw that the slender man with the stern face she had seen earlier was already present, shuffling through a briefcase that lay open on the corner of the principal's desk. Before he had finished arranging a stack of papers, Principal Zumwalt arrived, leading the Smythes into the room.

"I apologize for this..." Dr. Zumwalt momentarily stumbled over his words, something that Heather could never remember him doing. "This gentleman is Dr. Caldwell, one of the judges of the National High School Science Competition. He has just informed me of some very disturbing news, which I will now ask Dr. Caldwell to elaborate on."

Dr. Caldwell straightened, the act exaggerating his thinness so that it seemed that every fold in his brown suit had become a wrinkle that matched the skin that draped his bones. He stepped forward so that he stood even with the front of the desk, turning the stack of papers with a bony finger.

His gray eyes swept the room. "Unfortunately, Dr. Brannigan had already flown back to California when this matter came to our attention. Therefore, she could not be present to deal with the situation. I am here in her stead.

"As you are no doubt aware, we at the National Science Foundation have no tolerance for plagiarism. And while I regret that we did not find it earlier, so that we could have avoided all the embarrassment that this will cause, our duty is clear. We are stripping your team of its award."

"What?" Gil McFarland's exclamation was accompanied by those of the other parents. "I don't understand. What are you talking about?"

Dr. Caldwell picked up the stack of papers and began spreading them out on the coffee table that sat between the principal's desk and the three overstuffed chairs on the opposite wall.

"It was very subtle. It was almost a surprise that we found it. If it hadn't been for the elegance of the equations in this section of the report, we would never have looked this closely at it. But that, in itself, attracted attention." Dr. Caldwell paused for effect.

"You see this section right here?" His hand swept a page from the team's report. "This particular derivation of the quantum equations governing the cold-fusion reactions matches that produced by a team at the Fermi Laboratory, a team of physicists that only recently published their paper on the subject. We were seriously surprised that a group of high-school students had even managed to make sense of it."

Again, Dr. Caldwell paused, his eyes scanning them sadly. "It's a shame, really. If you had only documented the source of these derivations instead of trying to take credit for them as your own, you would have still been the runaway winners of the contest. Unfortunately, cheating demeans you all and leaves us no choice but to strip you of the award."

"But that's not right. We didn't cheat!" Mark's fists knotted so tightly, the veins along the backs stood out in purple spiderwebs.

"Really?" the sympathetic look faded from Dr. Caldwell's face. "Then maybe you would consider explaining how a group of three high-school students came up with such a complex set of equations—so complex that the feat has been achieved by only one other team of physicists on the planet?"

Heather's head felt as if it would explode, a clear set of visualizations flooding through her brain in a manner that left the outcome clear. There was no way the committee was going to believe that she had derived the equations on her own. The only way they could explain themselves would be to reveal the existence of the Second Ship. Feeling sick at her stomach, Heather stepped forward.

"I'm Heather McFarland. I believe I can explain."

"Well?"

The faces stared back at her. Dr. Caldwell, Dr. Zumwalt, Mr. Smythe, and even her own father looked at her with a mixture of disbelief and dismay.

"It was my fault," Heather said, unable to keep her hands from shaking. "I was so excited when I read the Fermi paper that I used its equations in our report."

"But that fails to explain why you didn't document your source." Dr. Caldwell's face grew even more severe.

A small sob escaped Heather's lips before she could stifle it. "I know. I was responsible for that section of the paper. I never meant to cheat. I must have gotten sloppy in our rush to the finish."

"Sloppy?" Dr. Caldwell took a step toward her. "That is something I cannot believe. Everything about your team's report is first class, all meticulously assembled and documented. But you tell me that you got sloppy with your attribution? Ridiculous. If there is one thing I can tolerate even less than plagiarism, it is a lie. And you, young lady, are a liar."

"Now see here," Gil McFarland sputtered.

"You take that back!" Something about the tone of Jennifer's voice caused all eyes to settle on her. Her delicate features had warped into a mask of anger, her forehead creased in concentration, her eyes alive with something that seemed vaguely familiar to Heather.

Jennifer stepped closer to the startled professor, her eyes locking his gaze. "Apologize. Now!"

For several seconds, everyone stood frozen in place, awed by the surrealistic confrontation. Suddenly Dr. Caldwell bowed his head, both hands rising to rub his temples.

When he raised his head again, the harsh look of moments before was gone.

"Odd. I don't normally allow myself to become emotional. My response was entirely inappropriate. I apologize to you all, especially to you, Heather. I had no business questioning your veracity. Unfortunately, that does not alter the sanctions that the judging committee has decided to impose.

"Your award has been stripped and will be presented to the runner-up team. As for your cold-fusion apparatus, you have a choice."

Heather felt the constriction in her chest increase. "What choice?"

"The committee has decided, due to your age, to allow you the possibility of partial redemption. If you choose to donate your apparatus to the National Science Foundation, signing over all rights to the ingenious design, we will refrain from issuing a formal report on your disqualification. Otherwise, you can keep your device and we will issue a formal report, something that will go into your academic record to be considered by future college admissions boards."

Mr. Smythe interrupted. "That's not a choice. Even if your report is not formalized, the plagiarism story will still be out there in the press. These kids will be humiliated."

"I'm afraid we cannot help that. All we can offer is to mitigate the long-term impact of this situation."

Dr. Caldwell picked up his satchel and turned back toward Principal Zumwalt, indicating the papers on the table.

"That is your copy of our report."

As he made his way to the door, Dr. Caldwell paused to survey the three shocked students one last time.

"Think it over."

Then he was gone, the depression left in his wake blurring Heather's vision so that she could barely see Mark and Jennifer. But even through her watery eyes, she could tell that the twins also struggled for self-control. It was a struggle Heather was determined not to lose…not until she was shut inside the car for the long ride home.

CHAPTER 35

Freddy Hagerman was used to cold trails, but this one had gone cold as a penguin's ass. If it wasn't for pure stubbornness, he would have given up a long time ago. Of course, knowing that he wouldn't have a job to go back to if he didn't come up with something had added a little extra motivation. Even so, amid all the glowing interviews with the Rondham Institute staff and follow-ups with the cancer survivors, he had almost missed it.

Of the thirty-eight experimental subjects, he had tracked down all but one, a fourteen-year-old boy named Billy Randall. By all reports, Billy had been every bit as successful in his recovery as any of the other patients. But tragically, he and his entire family had been killed in an automobile accident on their drive back to Arizona, after his release from the institute. The horror of the news had shaken the small community of Wickenburg, Arizona, to its core.

The entire town had planned a welcome-home celebration, complete with banners and a parade. Instead, the collision between the family Taurus and a semitruck just outside Barstow, California, had left the bodies so disfigured that the people of Wickenburg were left to bury three sealed caskets.

The thing that had attracted Freddy's attention was the Barstow medical examiner's report. Containing a detailed description of the fatal injuries suffered by each member of the Randall family, the report was well ordered and typical. It had taken Freddy three passes through it before he could place a cause for the feeling of wrongness.

All three family members had suffered fatal head injuries as several pipes from the semi's load had penetrated the car's passenger compartment. Everything was thoroughly described in the report. There was absolutely nothing unusual about it.

There was only one problem with that. The car had been carrying one very unusual young man who had been injected with nanites derived from Rho Project research. Freddy had read Priest Williams's journal, had seen the evidence of what those nanites could do. And even if those people should have been killed instantly, those microscopic machines didn't just give up without trying to repair broken bodies. There should have been signs of unnatural healing on Billy's corpse, even if that healing had not saved his life. But the report contained no mention of anything unusual about the boy's mortal wounds.

Freddy straightened his aching back and looked up. It was unbelievable how many stars you could see at 2:00 a.m. in the high desert of Arizona, especially on a night with no moon. Well, staring at the stars wasn't going to give him his answers.

Freddy stomped down, driving the shovel deep into the soft dirt. There was no way around it. He was going to have to see Billy Randall for himself.

CHAPTER 36

"You've hardly touched your breakfast."

"Sorry, Mom. Guess I'm just not that hungry this morning." Heather couldn't bring herself to look into her mother's eyes. The air was thick with her parents' distress at her situation, a mixture of sympathy, worry, and disappointment. She hated not being able to tell them that she hadn't plagiarized anything, no matter what she had been forced to admit to.

Her father's gentle voice caused her to look up from her eggs. "Heather, tough as this situation is, it will pass. In the meantime, you just have to press on with your normal routine."

"And not eating won't help," her mother continued.

"I know, Mom."

When she didn't move to put more food in her mouth, her mother shrugged in defeat.

"Oh well, I guess you can be excused. Maybe visiting with Mark and Jennifer will help more than breakfast."

"Thanks," Heather said, rinsing her plate and sliding it into the dishwasher.

The problem, she thought, was that too much had happened all at once. It wasn't just the plagiarism thing, though that stung. Last night, she had had the Rag Man dream again. The same crude letters traced on the outside of her window: "I know what you are." And when she'd gone to the window, she'd seen they were written in the frost. Out in the yard, standing in the snow: the Rag Man, his long, greasy blond hair and the mouthful of bad teeth in his grinning face immediately recognizable. His eyes, though. Where were his eyes?

It was becoming all too familiar to her. As before, she had grabbed a long butcher knife from the block on the countertop and stepped out into the predawn darkness, only to have the Rag Man slip back into the trees. As before, she lunged after him, but he was gone, leaving only footprints. She followed them, screaming after him, "What do you want from me?"

And then, from behind her, so close she could feel the hot breath puff against the back of her neck, could smell the rot in those decaying teeth: "I know what you are becoming."

But even if this dream, and others she couldn't remember, had gotten worse, her waking hallucinations had them beat. Heather had quit seeing numbers in her mind, and for three weeks she had been seeing visions instead. As scared as she had been during her original savant experience, this new phase horrified her beyond belief.

Several times she had caught herself briefly lapsing into a sequence of visions, each producing a variation on something she had been observing, each vision ending with a different predicted outcome. The visions had become so real that she had difficulty bringing herself back into the present. Anything might trigger them.

Yesterday, Heather's mom had bumped into the back of a chair, triggering a sequence of visions of her mom falling and catching herself on the table, or tipping over the flowerpot, or cutting her arm on the vase. Always the visions converged into a single projected outcome, but for that brief instant in time, while under the influence of her waking dreams, Heather remained frozen, unable to move or respond.

Heather had once read about people—the institutionalized insane—who experienced fugues, trancelike states in which they lost touch with reality. If this continued, it was only a matter of time until others began to notice. And it was getting worse.

It was all she could do to force all of this into the back of her mind as she stepped up onto the Smythe front porch and Mark opened the door.

"Hi."

Something about seeing him standing there in the doorway waiting for her, his chiseled face filled with protective concern, pulled down all her defenses. Without warning, sobs wracked her body. Then he was there, his arms enfolding her in bands of steel as she buried her face in his chest, and somehow, for the first time in days, Heather felt truly safe.

When she finally managed to push herself away and stand erect, she thought she saw a strange light sparkling in his eyes. Then again, why wouldn't there be? Christ. She'd been bawling like a baby.

"Sorry."

"Why?"

"Hey, what's going on out here?" Jennifer asked, poking her head out the door. Seeing Heather's red eyes, Jennifer turned toward Mark, punching him hard on the arm. "Mark! What did you say to her?"

"Ow. Crap! What is it with you and those fists?"

An involuntary chuckle escaped Heather's lips. Then, unable to contain herself, she burst into laughter. No matter how bad things got, the Smythe twins were the cure. God, how she loved these two.

Seeing the puzzled look on Jennifer's face, Heather managed to establish some semblance of control over her emotions. "It's OK, Jen. Mark was actually being really nice."

"Mark? Really?"

"Hey, I can be nice."

"Humph," Jennifer snorted. "Anyway, I knew the TV coverage would upset you."

It was Heather's turn to look puzzled. "What TV coverage?"

Mark rolled his eyes at his sister. "Open mouth, insert foot."

A look of horror spread across Jennifer's face. "Oh, Heather. I'm so sorry. I thought that was what had upset you."

"Now you're scaring me," Heather said, stepping inside the Smythes' front door. "Is it still on?"

Mark followed on her heels. "Still on? They won't get off it. You'd think nothing this big had happened in Los Alamos in years."

Without waiting for her friends to slow her forward progress, Heather walked into the Smythe living room, sliding onto the couch directly across from the television, thankful that there was no sign of Mr. or Mrs. Smythe.

Sure enough, there was Maria Sandoval, news anchor for KOAT, Action 7 News, her face a picture of surprise and disapproval at the story of how three Los Alamos High School students had been caught cheating at the National High School Science Competition.

"...And although only one member of the Los Alamos team has admitted to plagiarism, a young lady by the name of Heather McFarland, her actions have embarrassed her team, her school, the communities of Los Alamos and White Rock, even New Mexico as a whole. Unfortunately, the review board of judges did not spot the attempt to take credit for someone else's work before the Los Alamos team had been announced as the winner."

Maria paused and turned to Barry Jenson, her co-anchor. Barry shook his blond head slowly for the benefit of the camera. "That is unbelievable."

The camera shifted back to Maria. "That isn't the worst of it. The communities of Los Alamos and White Rock had already welcomed home their winning team with a big celebration at the Los Alamos High School, complete with the mayors, school staff, and a large crowd of townspeople."

The camera panned to Barry. "I can only imagine how betrayed the good people of those towns are feeling right now."

As the camera zoomed out to catch a shot of both anchors, Maria raised her left eyebrow in a manner that indicated that the biggest news was yet to come. "If you think it couldn't get worse, you're wrong. It turns out that another member of the team was Los Alamos High School's pride and joy, all-star, all-state basketball point guard Mark Smythe."

"I'll tell you, Maria. If I hadn't seen the reports myself, I would think you were making this up."

"And I wouldn't blame you."

The camera shifted back to Barry's handsome face one last time. "Well I'm sure that all our viewers out there are as shocked by this as Maria and I. You can bet we haven't heard the last of this one." Barry leaned back and shuffled the papers on the news desk. "That's all for this morning. Maria and I will be right back here tomorrow morning, bringing you the latest from Action 7 News."

The impact of the story left Heather numb. "Oh God. We're…"

Mark nodded. "We're screwed." But Heather only heard Mark's voice as if from a great distance. For a moment, she'd been elsewhere. She shook her head to clear away the sequence of clear visions within which she had been wandering, each of them playing out different outcomes of their current situation. As her eyes refocused on Mark and then Jennifer—how long had she been out? It didn't look as if they had noticed—there was no doubt in her mind what they had to do. They had to take action and soon. She flipped off the television.

"Where's the cell phone number of that contest judge? Never mind, I remember it."

"Dr. Caldwell?" Jennifer asked. "Why?"

"Because we're going to call him right now and cut a deal."

Mark stepped closer. "Are you out of your mind? He wants us to give away our cold-fusion device."

"It can't be helped. We have to get this damped down or we'll have mobs camped on our doorstep."

Mark shook his head. "No way. Without the cold-fusion device, we can't run our subspace transmitter. We won't be able to hack into secure networks anymore."

"Mark's right," Jennifer chimed in. "We'll be completely blind. And right now, I get a very bad feeling about that."

"Look," said Heather, "I know it's bad, but I don't see any other way out. Even if we didn't worry about getting into college, I think the press will start following us. Think about it. We'll be watched twenty-four seven."

For several seconds silence filled the room.

Finally Mark looked up from his study of his hands. "I'll go along with this on one condition."

"What's that?"

"You let me try to contact Jack Johnson using the quantum twin device I implanted in Janet's laptop."

"Jesus, Mark! How's that going to make things better?" Jennifer asked.

"You know Jack and Janet are on the run or dead," Heather added. "Even if they're alive, they probably scrapped the laptop."

"Then it won't hurt to try. Anyway, that's my offer. If we don't all sign the release papers, then Dr. Caldwell isn't going to agree to the deal."

"But how can it work out?" Jennifer continued. "The last thing we need is Jack finding out about us. At this point he's a hunted terrorist."

"I don't believe Jack's a terrorist and neither do you. We won't let him know who we are, just that we are the ones who originally contacted the NSA. Right now, he's cut off. He needs to know he has a powerful source of information he can contact."

Heather shook her head. "Even if we can come up with a way to convince him of all that, after we give away the cold-fusion device, we won't be able to snoop classified networks anymore."

"I'm sure you two little geniuses will come up with a solution to that." Mark turned and grabbed the wireless telephone, holding it out to Heather. "Do you want to make that call to Caldwell or not?"

After a moment's hesitation, Heather took the telephone from his hand and began to dial.

CHAPTER 37

It had been two nights since Freddy had dug up Billy Randall's empty coffin in Wickenburg. As soon as he'd pried the lid open with a crowbar and shone the flashlight inside, Freddy had hopped in the rental car and done his best impression of a NASCAR driver, hauling ass back to Barstow. His hunch that something was screwy had been right, and almost getting stuck on barbed wire, being chased by a stray dog, and eluding the cemetery's security guy had all been worth it. Despite being dead tired, he felt almost ecstatic. A brief pause at a truck stop to dump his dirty sweats, tennis shoes, and shovel into a dumpster had been the only delay in getting back to the Desert Inn. Since he'd never checked out of the Barstow motel, Freddy had stuck the "Do Not Disturb" sign on the outside door handle, stumbled into bed, and slept the day away.

Now Freddy found himself looking over the top of his hamburger, watching the setting sun shimmer in the heat that radiated up from the diner's asphalt parking lot. The waitress had stopped by to ask if he wanted coffee, and he'd laughed at her. What he wanted was water with enough ice to frost up the outside of the glass. Every time the diner door opened, it felt as if he were sitting beside a blast furnace.

Freddy wanted to talk to Dr. Bertrand Callow, the Barstow medical examiner who had signed off on the Randall report, but at home and after dark. Only a couple of things could make a man like that falsify an official report. Either he was one of the key conspirators in this whole mess or someone had scared the crap out of him. Freddy was pretty sure that it was the second, but if he was wrong about that, getting fired was going to be the least of his worries. Actually, now that he thought about it, he probably wouldn't live long enough to have many worries.

Dr. Callow's house wasn't difficult to find. You just got off Old California 58 and headed north on Camarillo Avenue until it stovepiped into Palermo Street. It was one of a handful of nice homes on the far north side of the street, backed up against desert open space. By the time Freddy walked up to the front of the house and rang the bell, the sky had taken on a dark shade of purple with a few wisps of burgundy still licking the horizon. At least the Western skies gave these poor desert rats something worth looking at. You damn sure couldn't watch the grass grow.

Freddy pushed the doorbell a second time. He could hear it buzzing inside. The light from the television flickered through the front windows although the plantation shutters prevented him from getting a good look inside. So the doctor was home, just not responding. Probably on the crapper.

After another minute, Freddy reached out and rapped the door hard with his knuckles, feeling the door move inward slightly under his hand. The thing wasn't locked. Hell, it hadn't even been closed hard enough to latch. A sudden uneasiness raised the hair along the backs of his arms, despite the heat of the evening. On impulse, Freddy pulled out his shirttail and wiped down the doorbell and doorknob before nudging the door open with his toe.

The television blared from a room just out of sight from the foyer, the sounds of battle amplified through a subwoofer so loudly that he could feel the concussion of cinematic artillery. Freddy stepped across the threshold, pushing the door closed with his foot.

Jesus H. Christ. If the bastard was taking a dump, he should at least light a match. The place reeked.

"Dr. Callow?"

Nothing.

Freddy felt himself move slowly forward, drawn toward the flickering light from the next room like some goddamn moth.

The living room opened up before him, the large flat-panel television occupying the wall on the left, its screen filled with combat as the war movie reached a crescendo of violence. Across the room a man sat in a recliner, his hand dangling over the padded leather arm, fingers open as if reaching for the gun that lay on the floor beside it. The television flared bright as another explosion shook the speakers, its light leaving little doubt about what Freddy was seeing. There, sitting in the splatter of blood and clumps of brain matter, was Dr. Callow.

CHAPTER 38

Heather glanced down at her watch: 10:43 a.m. Her mom had said she would be in the bank for only fifteen minutes, but it had already been twenty. Maybe she should have gone in with her mom, but banks were so darn boring. Add a little elevator music and they'd be as exciting as an elevator.

She'd always loved these shopping trips down to Santa Fe, but today she just felt wired. Perhaps someone had spiked her herbal tea with a healthy dose of caffeine. Whatever it was left Heather feeling irked.

It probably had nothing whatsoever to do with her mother or even with today. After all, it was Saturday, arguably the best day on the planet. More likely, her sense of hyperactivity was related to everything else that had happened this week.

Dr. Caldwell had arrived, they had all signed the papers, and he had gone off, redirecting the shipment of their cold-fusion science project to parts unknown. The judging committee had issued a statement that read:

"Upon further review, we the judges of the National High School Science Competition hereby conclude that, although the team from Los Alamos High School failed to properly document the derivations in one section of their report, the omission appears to have been unintentional. Nevertheless, the disqualification of the Los Alamos team remains in force. Although the error in documentation was an oversight, it was an egregious one..."

Wonderful. They had been upgraded from cheaters to incompetent losers. And although the paper had carried the story of the revised decision by the board of judges, that story was relegated to a page snuggled up against the classified advertisements.

At least the ravenous press feeding frenzy had died out and their houses were egged only every other day. At this rate, within a couple hundred years their popularity would be epic.

Just as Heather had about decided to go in and stand in line with her mom, Mrs. McFarland reappeared.

"Hi, sweetheart. Sorry it took so long, but I had to get something notarized and there was a line."

"No problem, Mom," Heather said, doing her best to sound nonchalant.

Heather swung her head in the direction of the intersection, her eyes scanning. For just an instant, she could have sworn she had seen the Rag Man. Her attention drifted to the traffic light. Odd. There it was again, that feeling of wrongness.

As she looked, a white Impala screamed around the corner, accelerating toward the yellow light, its engine climbing the RPM scale in a manner that indicated a floored gas pedal. As the light turned red, a blue van moved forward from the cross street, the faces of three young children visible through the van's side windows. The squeal of brakes was so loud that it hurt Heather's ears.

She wanted to close her eyes but couldn't, as the horrified faces of the three little girls in the van etched themselves into her brain an instant before the Impala impaled the side of the van.

Heather screamed.

How long it took her to realize her mother's arms were wrapped around her, she wasn't sure, but slowly her eyes refocused onto her mother's panicked face.

"Heather! What is it? Please, baby, tell me what's wrong."

Heather glanced at the intersection across from the bank parking lot. Nothing. No sign of the fatal car crash she had just witnessed, only normal traffic. She shook her head to clear the remnants of the vision. It had been so real.

As she started to answer her mother, she was interrupted by the squeal of brakes. Her head swung back toward the intersection as a large red pickup truck slammed into the side of a teal minivan, burying itself halfway into the passenger compartment, sending both vehicles spinning into a light pole and then into the plate-glass storefront beyond.

The other cars swerved to avoid the accident, miraculously coming to a stop with no further collisions.

"Oh my God!"

Heather's mother was already moving toward the accident scene, her running footsteps waking other bystanders from their shocked immobility. Heather followed, the sense of déjà vu so strong that she found herself struggling to wake up. But this time there would be no waking. It was all too horrifyingly real.

Mrs. McFarland was the first of the onlookers to reach the accident scene, the look on her face erasing any hope that lingered in Heather's mind that the accident was not as bad as it looked. Her mother was already speaking into her cell phone. She must have been dialing 911 even as she ran.

Several men reached the vehicles and began frantically tugging on the crumpled doors, trying unsuccessfully to get to the people inside the van. The driver of the truck had been thrown through the windshield and now lay with only his feet sticking out from beneath the overturned Dodge Ram.

Heather stopped about ten yards away from the scene, assaulted by a wave of nausea that brought her to her knees.

"Oh Lord."

As she doubled over, puking violently onto the sidewalk, the warble of sirens rose up behind her, but Heather never heard them. The thing that filled her head was the sound of the Rag Man's distant laughter.

CHAPTER 39

A wave of weakness assaulted Raul, something that he hadn't felt in a long time. If anything, he felt stronger with the passing of each day. His success in tapping into the external Internet had provided an exhilaration that drove him to speed up his work. But even with his augmentations, this work obsession was beginning to wear on him. On the plus side, it distracted him from his raw hatred for Stephenson, hatred so virulent it threatened his sanity.

Despite his growing familiarity with the shipboard neural net, Raul had to admit that understanding the alien technologies that made this ship possible remained well beyond his grasp. Perhaps he would never completely understand them, although he didn't really believe that. Every time he was able to fix another of the ship's circuits, more of the neural network came back online. And as that network improved, so did his mental capabilities. After all, he was thinking with it. At this point, it was merely an extension of his own brain.

What Raul had learned about the ship's technology fascinated him. Apparently, the alien race that had created it, which he had come to know as the Kasari Collective, had mastered a technology other alien races regarded as dangerous and unstable. The data records he had been able to piece together referred to those other races as the Altreians. And unlike the Altreians, who had adopted the use of subspace technologies, the Kasari had learned to manipulate gravity.

Actually, that wasn't quite right. They manipulated gravitational effects, completely in the absence of matter. The Kasari specialized in what earth scientists were just now beginning to investigate, the science of black holes and wormholes, where conventional mathematics breaks down.

Unlike a black hole, where anything that passes across its event horizon is crushed out of existence, wormholes created rips in the space-time fabric so that the distance between two places disappeared. It was the theory behind star gates—a way to travel from here to there by merely stepping through an opening.

It was the use of one minor aspect of the wormhole technology that had allowed Raul to tap into the Internet. He had managed to bring just enough of the ship's systems back online to produce the tiniest of these distortions, not so much a wormhole as a worm fiber.

In some ways, it helped him to think of these tiny wormholes like the optical fibers used in standard fiber optics. Except these fibers were not limited to light passing back and forth. They made it possible for any signal to pass through.

The process of directing the worm fibers was as natural to the shipboard control systems as tuning a radio. But it had still taken Raul a considerable amount of time and effort to learn to examine and tap into earthbound computer networks. He had no possibility of plugging in a network cable, but the worm-fiber link established a virtual splice into existing lines.

The downside of the gravitational technology was the massive amount of energy required to make the magic happen. From what Raul had learned, it was the reason the Altreians hated the Kasari so ravenously. The Kasari had created technologies that directly consumed matter, converting it to pure energy, and that energy provided fuel that had made the impossible practical, creating a thirst for resources that grew with the Kasari Collective's expanding capabilities.

Even the creation of the tiniest of worm fibers, such as Raul had accomplished, drained power from what remained of the ship's systems in a frightening manner, each attempt requiring a lengthy recovery period. Raul was filled with the worry that if he tried too much he might completely drain the reserves, something that might kill his ship permanently.

Still, he had managed to store up just enough power for this one experiment. Raul had tapped into the Santa Fe traffic management computer system just long enough to take control of the traffic cameras and signal lights at a busy intersection. At the key instant, he had extended the yellow light on one signal while allowing the other to go green, something that had produced the most amazing results.

Raul wished he could maintain the connection just a little longer so he could watch the response as emergency crews arrived, but he had already overtaxed the system. As he killed the worm-fiber link and switched all nonessential systems to standby, Raul grinned. Successful test.

Now, if he could just keep it all hidden from Dr. Stephenson for a little while longer…

CHAPTER 40

Dr. Donald Stephenson moved along the rows of cages, pausing to examine each rat in turn. Anyone else would have been completely outfitted in Level 4 Biohazard protective gear. But here, by himself in the infectious disease section of Rho Division, the time just past 2:00 a.m., Dr. Stephenson merely wore a set of hospital scrubs.

As he moved, he scanned the labels that identified the different cage groupings. Order Mononegavirales, family Filoviridae, genus *Ebolavirus*. Stopping before a cage labeled "species *Zaire ebolavirus*," he bent down to examine the occupant, a healthy brown rat with a white splotch on its head. Stephenson reached inside and grabbed the little fellow by the back of its neck. Ignoring the frightened animal's attempts to bite him, he held it up to the light.

Completely healthy. It was also perfectly predictable, but amazing nonetheless. Just two days ago the rat had been in the final stages of death from hemorrhagic fever, suffering from extensive bleeding from the nose, eyes, and anus. Dr. Stephenson placed the animal back in its cage, nodding with satisfaction. The latest strain of nanites worked every bit as well as the original, but these were much hardier outside the bloodstream, requiring no special suspension fluid to keep them functional until they were injected. The microscopic machines could survive in almost any environment short of a two-hundred-degree-Celsius oven. Even boiling water wouldn't harm them. With so many nations demanding them, this would solve their shipping problems.

To think that just across the huge open bay to the west, deep within the inner recesses of the Rho Ship, Raul had been his first human test subject for the new nanites. That had been a bit of a risk since Raul had already been infected with the original nanite strain. It had been entirely possible that the two strains would be incompatible, and if that had been the case, he might have lost a most valuable asset. Still, his reasons for subjecting Raul to the nanite upgrade were sufficient to make it a risk worth taking.

Other than some intense initial pain, Raul's system had accepted the new nanites very well. Judging by the pace at which Raul scurried about the equipment within the inner reaches of the ship, the young man had experienced no long-term adverse reaction.

And from what Dr. Stephenson had observed over the highly encrypted video link from the ship's interior, Raul had been very busy indeed. In a ship full of fascinating oddities, Raul now appeared the oddest, climbing up the equipment racks hand over hand or scurrying across the floor, dragging his umbilical bundle of cables behind him. Sometimes Raul would pause, the three-inch-long snakelike appendage that had replaced his right eyeball swiveling around in front of his face as it fed signals directly into his optic nerve.

While the deputy director had hoped that Raul would begin to understand something of the inner workings of the shipboard systems, the results of Raul's efforts had surpassed his best-case scenario. New activity in alien equipment that had been completely inoperative only a few weeks ago periodically sent power fluctuations through the ship's core, spiking the instruments Dr. Stephenson had positioned to detect such changes. Each time the ship had returned to a quiescent state once the transient effects died out. Nevertheless, the progress was nothing short of remarkable.

But it was also quite clear that Raul was being less than completely honest about what he was learning. That didn't matter to Stephenson. He needed Raul to continue his repairs of the damaged shipboard systems. So far, he had barely scratched the surface.

The thought of the extent of the damage that had been inflicted on the Rho Ship made Dr. Stephenson shake his head. He would dearly love to know what kind of weapons technology could have done that, especially since no Earth technology could put the slightest scratch in the ship's hull. It was the type of question he wasn't going to get an answer to unless Raul succeeded.

Of course, it was possible that Raul would try something really stupid. After all, Dr. Stephenson had known the boy was completely insane from the instant he first met him. The messianic complex that afflicted Raul had only been temporarily suppressed by his current imprisonment. His God complex was bound to reassert itself at some point, and when it did, Raul was likely to act out.

Turning his attention back to the healthy rat in the cage, Dr Stephenson pulled a small device like a penlight from his pocket.

Machines were funny things. You could have the finest and fastest car on the planet, but loosen a few lug nuts and watch out. It was something all machines had in common, even nanites.

Dr. Stephenson pressed a button on the device.

The rat let out a squeal that devolved into a damp gurgle. Within seconds, all that was left in the cage were bits of hide, hair, and bone, floating in a gooey mess. It was the second time he had attempted dynamically reprogramming the new nanites inside a living thing.

The first had been a most unfortunate necessity and had not involved the complete meltdown the rat had just endured. Dr. Nancy Anatole. So young. So brilliant. Such wasted promise. But recent events had clearly shown the existence of a mole within the Rho Project. The only ones with that kind of deep access to the data were Dr. Rodriguez and Dr. Anatole. Given his own research priorities, it could not have been Dr. Rodriguez, even if he wasn't dead. So that left Nancy.

The deputy director shook his head. Incredible to think that she could have resisted the special conditioning to which he had subjected her, that she could have continued to deceive him. She had been a strong woman. But not strong enough to survive the massive brain hemorrhage that had struck her down as she shopped among the Native American jewelry vendors in Santa Fe.

For several seconds Stephenson stared down at his latest handiwork before turning toward the chemical bath chambers that awaited him at the exit. No doubt about it, he knew how to loosen the lug nuts on the upgraded nanites.

As he stepped into the first of three decontamination chambers, stripped off his scrubs, and tossed them into the biohazard disposal unit, Dr. Stephenson grinned. When the time came, Raul would find out which of them was God.

CHAPTER 41

Heather's scream brought Anna McFarland out of bed and down the hall three steps ahead of her husband. Pushing open the door to Heather's room, Anna's hand flicked the wall switch to the on position, and she was momentarily blinded by the brilliance of the illumination.

"What's wrong?" Gil McFarland's breathless question echoed the one that had been about to roll from her own lips.

Across the room, as she sat upright in the middle of her bed, Heather's open eyes had rolled back in her head, the look of horror on her young face so intense that both parents whirled to look back down the hallway. It was as empty as it had been a second ago, surreally illuminated in sharp shadows by the light shining from Heather's open doorway.

"Baby?" Anna McFarland moved to the bed.

As she reached out to touch her daughter's face, something made her stop. Heather's eyes were moving as if she were seeing things move before her, things that only she could see. The way emotions played across Heather's face as those white eyes moved brought a chill to Anna's neck, a ripple that ran up over her scalp and down along both arms. Heather didn't even know she and Gil were there, her daughter's open-eyed dream state undisturbed even by the sudden bright light in her bedroom.

Anna reached out, gently cradling Heather's cheeks between her shaking hands, turning Heather's head so that she could see into those eyes. At first there was no reaction, and then, ever so slowly, Heather's eyes rolled forward, refocusing on Anna's.

"Mom?"

"I'm right here, baby."

Anna wrapped her daughter in her arms, letting Heather's body collapse against her own. Almost immediately, Anna felt Gil's strong arms wrap around them both. The assaulting rush of memories left her struggling for breath. The Saint Joseph's Hospital emergency room, Heather's feverish four-year-old body wrapped in her arms, Gil's big arms encircling them both.

Searching for anything to lift the dread that filled her, Anna glanced up. But instead of reassurance, what she saw in Gil's face was exactly what she'd seen there thirteen years ago, a fear as great as her own.

CHAPTER 42

Jennifer opened the door to let Heather in, concern rising up within her as she looked at her friend.

"You look tired."

Heather shrugged as she settled down on the couch across from Mark. "I'm exhausted. Mom and Dad found me sitting up in bed about two a.m. Apparently, I was having some sort of nightmare, dreaming with my eyes open. It really freaked them out."

Mark paused between bites into his cream-cheese bagel. "Christ. That would freak me out too."

Jennifer scowled at her brother, then refocused her attention on Heather.

"It's OK, Jen," Heather said, a sad look settling on her face. "That's exactly what I thought."

Mark looked as if he'd been kicked in the stomach. "I'm sorry. I was trying to make you feel better, not worse."

Heather's smile was weak. "It's not your fault. I've been feeling terrible since it happened."

Jennifer moved onto the couch beside her friend, wrapping an arm around Heather's shoulder. "So what happened next?"

"Nothing, at least not right away. But this morning, I heard Mom and Dad talking quietly about setting up an appointment with a doctor." Heather's face tensed. "I'm afraid he's going to order an electroencephalogram or a CT scan."

Jennifer felt the words tumble from her mouth before she could stop them. "But if they do that…"

"Exactly," said Heather. "They'll spot the difference in my brain activity. They'll discover our secret."

For several seconds complete silence reigned. Just then, Mrs. Smythe walked into the room. "What are you kids up to? I can't believe Heather is over and you didn't even tell me."

"Sorry, Mom," Mark's and Jennifer's voices merged into a single apology, something far from uncommon for the twins.

Linda Smythe laughed. "As if it were the first time. Can I get you kids something to eat?"

"No, thanks." This time the three voices merged as one.

For the barest instant, Linda Smythe looked hurt. Then a broad smile spread across her face. "Peanut butter sandwiches?"

Mark, Jen, and Heather exchanged glances.

"I guess we could go for that," Mark said.

"Good."

Mrs. Smythe disappeared into the kitchen. In what struck Jennifer as an incredibly short period of time she was back with a platter of peanut butter and jelly sandwiches.

"Thanks, Mom."

"Yeah, Mrs. Smythe," said Heather.

"My pleasure." Seeing them all staring back at her, Mrs. Smythe straightened and turned away. "OK, OK. I'll leave you to your private discussions."

Heather watched Mrs. Smythe depart before turning back to her two friends. "Sorry to bring you guys down with me. I just couldn't deal with this on my own."

Mark stood up. "Are you kidding me? Why wouldn't you come to us? Haven't we always been there for each other?"

"Of course we wanted to know," Jennifer said. "My God, Heather. We're all in this together."

Heather smiled. "Thanks, guys. You're the greatest. But I'm really scared. It's not just the doctor thing either. Last night's dream wasn't the first. I've been having them pretty often, usually when I'm awake."

"What do you mean, when you're awake?" Jennifer asked.

Heather sighed. "I don't know. I'll be doing something, and the next thing I know, it's like a déjà vu moment, like a rewind. Only part of it wasn't real, just a waking dream."

Jennifer's pulse quickened. "And before the rewind, what do you see?"

Heather stood up and began pacing back and forth in front of the couch. "I'm not really sure."

"You can't remember?" Mark asked.

Heather stopped. "That's not it. I remember just fine. It's like I'm seeing the future or something, not the distant future but something that is about to happen very soon."

"And does it come true?" Jennifer's chest felt as if it had been wrapped in chains.

"Yes. Not exactly the same as my vision, but close enough to scare the crap out of me."

Mark chewed his lower lip. "Maybe it's another side effect from the Second Ship. We've already experienced some amazing things."

"Seeing the future?" Heather shook her head.

"I don't think that's what's really happening," Jennifer said. "Think about it. Each of us has had our brains turned on to the max. You already had savant mathematical abilities. Maybe this is just an extension of the mathematics.

"Three-dimensional computer games are done with math. What if your brain is just working out the probabilities of stuff happening and painting a 3-D picture of the projected outcome for you?"

"If that's true, then how do I stop it?"

Jennifer wished she had a better answer. "I don't know, but right now, that's not our biggest problem. We can't let the doctors discover your abnormal brain activity."

Just then, Mark interrupted. "I have an idea. Do you remember when I tried the biofeedback meditation using the medical table on the ship?"

"You mean when you almost stopped your heart?" Heather asked.

"I didn't almost stop it. I just slowed it way down. With the biofeedback I was getting from the medical table, I was able to adjust my body response."

Heather sat down again. "What are you saying?"

"I'm saying that if I could do that, we might be able to learn to relax our brain activity so that it appears normal."

A light dawned in Jennifer's mind. With superior biofeedback, it might just be possible to learn how to do that. More than possible, it felt probable.

"Brilliant."

Heather stood up and headed for the door. "I'll tell Mom we're going for a bike ride. Meet you out front in ten minutes."

Jennifer shook her head. "Better make it twenty. I want to look up some information on the Internet about what normal CT scans and EEG readouts look like."

"Good idea."

As the screen door slammed shut behind Heather, Jennifer watched her friend disappear around the corner. As much as she regretted keeping secrets from Mark and Heather, maybe there really was hope after all.

CHAPTER 43

Heather had almost forgotten how good the alien headset felt on her temples. As soon as she entered the cave, climbed up into the ship, and slid the elastic metal band in place, a warm feeling engulfed her, almost as if she were coming home.

She was the first to enter the room they called the medical lab, followed closely by Jennifer and then Mark, each wearing a headset. Almost as if the ship knew what she was feeling, the colors in the room shifted to a softer shade, which highlighted the smoothly flowing elegance of each of the pedestals. Dear Lord, it was beautiful.

"I'll go first," Mark said.

Heather turned to face him. "Why you?"

"I already know how to manipulate the biofeedback. It's too bad we don't have more than one of these tentacle tables, or I could talk you through things as I'm doing it."

As if in response to his wish, the door in the far wall dematerialized, the one through which they had never been able to gain entry.

Heather gasped, then rushed forward, as if any hesitation might close off the newly opened doorway before she could peer inside. But Mark beat her to it, leaving only Jennifer hanging back. No shock there. Jennifer had always been the only one in the group with any sense.

The room was smaller than the medical lab, with a single large couch amid a forest of the clear tentacle tubes they had experienced on the table in the medical lab. These were bigger, though, filled with moving lights, almost like soap bubbles moving through a viscous fluid. If she hadn't been so excited by this new discovery, Heather could have just sat down and watched.

Mark stepped into the room, the clear tubes melting away from his path as he advanced toward the couch.

Heather reached for him. "Mark. Be careful."

"Why?" He turned to face her. "This ship could have killed us a hundred times by now."

"You make it sound like it is making a conscious choice not to. For all we know, if we press the wrong button or misuse a device, that could still be the ultimate outcome."

Mark shook his head. "Maybe, but I'm not getting that feeling about this place."

Heather concentrated, doing her best to send an intelligible query through the headset to the ship's computer system. Although her head flooded with imagery, she failed to make sense of it. Mark was right about one thing, though. This new room just felt right.

She glanced back at Jennifer. But if she was expecting her friend to inject a word of caution, she was disappointed. Jennifer had moved into the room with an air of expectation on her face.

If Heather hadn't known better, she would have thought that Jennifer had seen it all before.

Seeing no further objections, Mark slid onto the couch and leaned back. The room's response was startling. The tentacles swarmed over him, each one sprouting thousands of others, each with a supple, needle-sharp point moving to establish its own connection to his skin. If it had not been for the feelings of relaxation she was getting from the alien headband, Heather doubted she could have kept herself from screaming. And even though the look on Mark's face was one of complete relaxation, Heather had to concentrate to slow her own breathing.

Although Heather's attention was focused on Mark, she also noticed a slow, satisfied smile light up Jennifer's delicate features.

CHAPTER 44

Senator Connally stared over the microphones that lined the U-shaped table in the committee hearing room. Although the US Senate Select Committee on Intelligence held daily closed meetings here in room 219 of the Hart Senate Office Building, this one held an electric air, the kind he remembered feeling upon the approach of the worst Midwestern storms.

The other members of the intelligence committee stared at the head of the Department of Energy's Office of Intelligence and Counterintelligence, their faces displaying a wide range of emotions.

"So, Mr. Scott," Senator Connally began. "Let me get this straight. If I understand your opening statement correctly, it is your contention that the security around the Los Alamos Rho Project is adequate."

The blond man sitting across the meeting room pursed his lips, the effect narrowing the already thin line of his mouth, his blue-gray eyes flashing in the reflected light.

"That is correct, Senator."

"And would it also be your contention that the president's announced plan to release the details of the alien nanotechnology to the world constitutes no threat to national security?"

Adam Scott leaned closer to his microphone. "Senator, as you are aware, the president has only called for the release of the beneficial nanite technology, not the underlying details. That means we would be distributing the nanite serum but not the production details. Nothing is entirely without risk. However, in my judgment and in the judgment of the majority of the officials in my office, the benefits to national security outweigh the risks."

Senator Connally snorted derisively. "Really? And are you aware that the consensus within the military leadership disagrees with your assessment?"

Scott's face showed no sign of emotion. "Senator, that is hardly surprising considering the Defense Department's parochial view of the world. I would point out that there is a consensus within the intelligence community that agrees with the president on this. That includes the director of Central Intelligence, the FBI director, the director of the National Security Agency, and the director of National Intelligence."

"I notice you failed to mention that the initiative is vehemently opposed by the Defense Intelligence Agency. You also ignored the opposition of the previous secretary of defense and the previous director of the National Security Agency."

A slight smile creased the corners of Scott's mouth. "With all due respect, Senator, the DIA and the resigned secretary of defense are closely tied to the opinion of the Department of Defense, which I mentioned before. As for the recently deceased

NSA director, I hardly think a criminal's opinion deserves our consideration."

Connally felt the heat rise up through his neck and into his face. "Do you think this is funny, Mr. Scott? Because I can assure you that we, here on this committee, take national security matters deadly seriously. And while the fifteen members may disagree on many things, I believe you will find our tolerance for flippant answers in response to our questions to be nonexistent. Perhaps you would like to come back for a more extended session next week, along with a recall of your boss, the energy secretary."

This time it was Mr. Scott's turn to flush. He cleared his throat. "Senator, I apologize for any perceived slight. In the future I will ensure that my wording is more carefully considered."

"See that you do. Now, getting back to my original line of questions, are you aware of the subject of this week's special session at the United Nations?"

"Yes, Senator, I am."

"And you don't consider it alarming that more than ninety percent of the world's delegates joined in a resolution demanding that the United States immediately release all information on the alien nanotechnology into the public domain? There is also a call to turn the entire Rho Ship research program over to an international scientific committee in Europe."

"Senator, that response was exactly what we anticipated. However, that does not mean that we need to go along with their wishes. I believe that once the world community is able to evaluate, for itself, the beneficial results of the nanoserum, the response will turn to one of gratitude."

Senator Connally pursed his lips. "That seems to be the administration's theory. I'll come back to this line of questioning later. For now this committee recognizes the senator from Alabama."

By the time Senator Connally gaveled the hearing to a close and made his way to his car, darkness had fallen. By the time he pulled into his parking space at the Watergate, the first drops of rainfall had splattered his windshield, just enough to make the wipers squeal in protest as they smeared the dampness around.

Although every other senator was rushing to get out of town for the long holiday weekend, Connally was just glad to step inside his DC apartment and close the door behind him. Three years divorced, with two adult children who had moved to LA, he'd been left with the one thing he currently desired: a peaceful evening away from Washington's dogs of war.

Flipping on the light, Connally removed his coat and tie, hanging them neatly in the closet before making his way to the wine rack. He let his eyes linger on the labels as he lifted several bottles, replacing each in its spot until he found what he was looking for, a nice bottle of Alexander Valley Cyrus.

Swirling the red wine in the glass, he settled back in his reading chair and took a slow sip, letting the taste of the wine linger on his tongue. The way things were going, he wanted to savor every small pleasure.

The truth was that Connally was scared. His father had been a senator during the Cuban missile crisis. Connally remembered his old man telling about the terror that had gripped the capital in those days. Hell, the prospect of all-out nuclear war with the Soviet Union would scare the shit out of anybody. But it couldn't scare him any more than this.

The president of the United States had lost his mind. He had opened a box that even Pandora would have left untouched.

Connally took another sip and leaned farther back in the chair. Two weeks of hearings by numerous House and Senate committees had only slowed the pace at which events were progressing. And despite the fact that a number of groups had come out in frenzied opposition to the release of the alien nanotechnology, many of them from the base of the president's own party, most of the public remained enthralled with the prospect of a cure for all ills. Connally's own polls showed public support for the president's policy running at 67 percent.

Connally had to admit that it was damn hard to argue that letting sick people die was better than saving them. Hell, if he'd had a fatally ill child, he'd have been first in line for the stuff.

The military was against releasing it for obvious reasons. It wanted to inject American soldiers with the super juice and to hell with everyone else. The idea that he was on the same side of the argument as the military brass was enough to make Connally physically ill. And even though his reasons were entirely different, it made for a strange alliance, the antiwar liberal and the warrior elite.

Connally rose to his feet, moving to look out his window. Beneath him the Potomac wound its way toward the Atlantic Ocean, the lights of several boats glittering in the distance. Beautiful. Dear Lord, would it be this beautiful when nobody could die?

When he was a small boy, Connally's father had gotten him a Magic 8 Ball toy, the kind you held upside down and asked a question. Then when you turned it back upright, an answer would pop into the window. In his mind's eye, he could see his own answer pop into the window.

"Not bloody likely."

Connally knew that the nanites did not make a person immortal. They were just efficient little machines, scurrying around in your bloodstream, cleaning arteries, repairing damaged cells, killing infections, and fixing anything that didn't match the body's DNA encoding. They didn't make you immortal, just damn hard to kill.

What was going to happen to the world's population as those things were injected into the bloodstreams of the third world's prolific breeders? No more disease. But what about starvation? And how much longer would people live? A hundred and fifty? Two hundred? Shit. There wouldn't be room to walk.

War would take on a whole new violence. You couldn't just shoot people; they would just get back up and keep coming. You would need to dismember, behead, or vaporize your enemy.

His committee had been asking those questions of the president's team all week. And the answers that were forthcoming provided little solace. To a person they had sat in their seats and testified that all new advances presented challenges, but these new ones, like those before them, would be resolved. Besides, they had said, when you had a technology that would cure the world's diseases and save millions of lives, wouldn't denying that cure be worse than the crimes of Hitler and Stalin?

As much as Connally hated to admit it, he couldn't come up with a good counterargument. Certainly not one that carried that kind of weight.

Taking one last swallow of the red wine, Connally inhaled deeply, then turned and picked up his worn King James Bible from the table. Closing his eyes, he murmured a brief prayer for inspiration and let the Bible fall open to a random page. As he opened his eyes once again, a single verse jumped out at him.

"Father, forgive them, for they know not what they do."

CHAPTER 45

Heather opened her eyes, turning her head to glance at the glowing digital numerals on her bedside clock, even though it was entirely unnecessary. She knew precisely what time it was: 4:47 a.m.

Despite not sleeping at all the night before, she had never felt more rested in her life, which was great, considering all the stress she'd been operating under. She had only closed her eyes to enjoy the meditative state she experienced on the newly discovered tentacle couch on the starship. That experience had changed her in ways that she didn't understand but that felt right. As intense as her experiences with the ship had been up until now, they had been pale shadows of this.

Mark had gone first, remaining on the couch for a full hour, during which he had remained conscious, even asking to see the printed pictures of normal brain activity that Jennifer had brought along. Unlike with the medical couch, only the person on this couch could see the mental visions of the experience. Nevertheless, by the time Mark rose, letting the tentacles melt away from his body, he had seemed completely confident that he had mastered the desired technique.

Heather had gone next. Despite what she had observed with Mark, she had found herself completely unprepared for the sensations that stormed through her body and brain as the millions of needle points made their connections. It was beyond exhilarating, as if she had awakened from a dimly remembered dream.

Unlike with any other meditation she had ever tried, she had found herself simultaneously conscious of every nerve, every cell within her body. Slowing her breathing and heart rate, as she had observed Mark do when he first tried the couch in the medical lab, was trivial. Speeding up her metabolism was just as easy, requiring no significant level of concentration. She merely thought about what she wanted and it happened.

Heather had looked through Jennifer's pictures of brain activity, memorizing each with a glance before handing them back to Jennifer. With a slight shift of her thoughts, she had pulled up a mental image of her brain, shifting it to match the orientation in the photos. While this took more concentration than the earlier exercise, she had quickly gotten the hang of slowing the neural activity in each part of her brain, memorizing the feel of what she was doing as it happened. Even this had felt good, almost like letting a part of herself drift off to sleep.

By the time she rose from the couch, Heather had felt sure that she could duplicate the effects at will. The amazing part had come after she had relinquished the tentacle couch to Jennifer. The feelings of total connection to her body and brain had remained, unabated.

Last night's sleeplessness troubled her, but not in the way a sleepless night should have. It was as if she no longer needed sleep. The effect might not be permanent, but it was certainly odd. Combined with the oddities of yesterday's trip to the ship, it left her feeling distinctly uncomfortable.

Jennifer's reaction was what bothered her most. Heather had expected Jen to put up some resistance when Mark and then Heather slid onto the couch. Instead, she had seemed almost eager to watch them try it. And when Jennifer had climbed onto the couch, it struck Heather that she was already familiar with the thing.

Another thing that bothered her was just how good she now felt. Heather didn't know why that bothered her, but if this was how people on drugs felt, she could understand how you could get hooked. There it was. The thought of what she might feel like when she came back down off this mental high was what scared her.

A sequence of brilliant mental images flashed through her mind. It just didn't seem likely that this was a temporary effect. From the second she had climbed onto that couch, she had known that the ship was doing something to her, something that went well beyond what she had experienced on previous visits.

Heather slid out of bed and into her robe and slippers, wondering if her mom and dad were up yet. No, they weren't.

Heather froze. The answer had just come into her head. There was nothing particularly odd about that. Everyone had inner dialogue. But the feeling she got thinking about that answer sent shivers up her spine. This was no guess. Somehow, she just knew.

One thing was certain: standing here in her bedroom wasn't going to rid her of the strangeness. Perhaps a cup of tea wouldn't either, but it sure couldn't hurt.

By the time Heather seated herself in the lawn chair on her back deck, her knees drawn up almost to her chest, hands cradling the steaming mug, the first hint of dawn had softened the darkness in the east. Cool and crisp, with just a hint of pine scent on the smallest of breezes, the air that tickled her nostrils smelled different this morning. Even the chamomile tea seemed filled with subtle new flavors.

A rustling in the grass at the far edge of her yard attracted her attention. Sensing her gaze, a bunny lifted its ears momentarily before returning to its nibbling.

The sound of footsteps on the stairs interrupted her reverie.

"Good morning, Dad," Heather called toward the kitchen.

Gil McFarland stuck his smiling face out the door. "How did you know it was me and not your mother?"

"Dad, you're always the first one down."

"After you, that is. By the way, it's good to see you up early again. It's been a while since you played the early bird."

Heather laughed, something that sounded good, even to her own ears. "I guess I've finally caught up on my rest."

Her dad's eyes studied her for a moment, and then he smiled once again. "You're sounding better. Let me get some coffee going. Your mom and I will come out and join you in a little bit."

"Sounds nice."

A movement to her left snapped Heather's head around. There in the bushes just beyond the edge of the trees.

"Heather, what is it?"

The concern in her father's voice brought her back to reality. Somehow she had gotten to her feet, so that she now stood among the shattered pieces of her teacup. Barely audible in the distance, the Rag Man's maniacal laughter drifted up to her on the gentle breeze.

CHAPTER 46

Janet Price stared across the small central room of their hogan at Jack, his eyes locked on the laptop computer that sat on the wooden table, which alternately served as dining table, workbench, and desk. As she studied his lithe form, she could almost feel the tension that rippled the muscles beneath his skin. Like a coiled cobra, Jack was ready to strike.

A lump rose in her throat. She had always been independent, someone who lived on the ragged edge, a full rush of adrenaline her only addiction. Now she had acquired another. She had always thought of love as a myth, an illusion adopted by people who needed a crutch to help them through their boring little lives.

Janet knew the precise instant when she had tumbled over that mythical cliff. It had been that terrible moment when Jack had come for her, when she had stared up into those eyes as he told her to stay awake, the moment on that wooded ridgeline when he had turned back to hunt her pursuers. Perhaps she had allowed herself to fall because she had known she was going to die.

But Jack had not let her die. Even the unbearable pain he had inflicted on her with the injection of the nanite-tainted blood vials only made her love him more. Jack had come back for her, using every means at his disposal, demanding that she stay with him. With those actions, Jack had robbed her of her independence. She should hate him for that, but she couldn't.

Now Janet had another reason. She was pregnant. Leave it to those damn little nanomachines to fix everything. Even the relatively small dosage Jack had absorbed during his bloody fight with Priest Williams had apparently reversed his vasectomy. Since Janet now had her own nanite infection, she doubted that the pill would have worked either. Pretty soon the world would be left with condoms as the only viable means of birth control.

Jack didn't know, and Janet wasn't going to tell him until it became obvious. Her killer angel had enough on his to-do list without having that bombshell dropped on him.

Right now, the information on the laptop was at the top of that to-do list. That they had managed to charge the laptop batteries was a minor miracle of engineering. Despite the periodic assistance and supplies provided by Tall Bear, electric lines didn't run this far into the reservation's interior. And Jack hadn't wanted to attract the attention that the purchase of a generator might provide. So, using a variety of junk parts Tall Bear had scrounged up, and using the windmill to provide the rotary power, they had built one.

One thing about this high New Mexico country: wind was something available in abundance. A bank of a dozen car batteries provided enough storage to cover the brief periods of calm.

All of this had taken considerable time and effort, and only for the last two days had they been able to achieve a power signal clean enough to risk connection to the laptop's transformer. And even though they had power, an Internet connection was a bigger problem. There were no telephone lines, ditto for television cables or satellite equipment.

Still, Jack had been determined to get the computer operational. He wanted to review every bit of data on the system, on the off chance that there might be some clue as to who had betrayed Jonathan Riles and the rest of the team. Jack had always had a knack for disappearing from sight when he had to, sometimes for months at a time. But Janet could tell that this wasn't going to be one of those times.

Janet had been at the keyboard, having just started the computer up, when she saw it. There on her computer desktop sat a file that hadn't been there when she turned it off, a file with the ominous name "Jack You Need to Read This."

Since they had not been connected to the Internet, and since the computer hadn't even been powered on, there was only one reasonable possibility for the creation of that file. Some sort of virus had been inserted on her system that had been triggered when the system had restarted.

But that didn't check out. Janet had run a complete set of diagnostics, including state-of-the-art virus checks, all of which reported nothing unusual. More disconcerting was the creation date on the file. It had been created as the system was completing its initial boot-up sequence. That pointed back to a virus, something that she was convinced was not present on the system.

Jack finally shrugged. "Well, I guess we should find out what it says."

"That's what I was thinking," Janet replied, sliding back into the chair in front of the keyboard.

She opened the file. It was simple text, short and sweet.

"Jack. I am the NSA's original source about the Rho Project. I assure you that this communication is completely untraceable by any technology, Earth or alien. I have placed a chip on top of the CPU in this machine. It sends no signal and receives none. It works by means of what is called a quantum twin, a device for which there is only one counterpart. The quantum states of these two devices are always identical. If you apply a signal to one, it is applied to the other at the same instant. There is no intermediate signal to be detected. I tell you this so that you will know that this was originally an alien technology that I have mastered. No one besides myself is even aware that it exists, other than in theory.

"I tell you this so that you will not destroy this computer or remove the chip. I cannot trace you. I cannot tell where you are. All it offers is an instant means of secure communication.

"I also tell you this because I need you, and I believe you need the services that only I can provide. I am sure you are aware of my capabilities for penetrating secure networks, using other technologies at my disposal. You are, no doubt, cut off from your traditional lines of support and communication. Let me be that line. All you have to do to contact me is to replace the text in this file with your answer. I will be monitoring. Think it over."

"What do you make of that?" Jack asked, turning toward Janet.

"I think we need to open up the back of the computer and take a look at that chip. For all we know it might give away our location."

"Oh, we're going to do that, but I don't think we're in much danger of them finding us. If they could do that we would have already had some unwelcome visitors."

Janet closed the screen and flipped the laptop upside down. Extracting a small tool from the case, she removed the cover. Sure enough, there it was, a small chip glued directly atop the CPU.

"Well, that much of the message is true."

Jack nodded. "I have a feeling that most of it is true, although we can bet that this source has its own agenda."

Janet bent closer to the laptop. "I can't see any direct connections to the circuitry. The chip just looks like it was attached with superglue. The connection must be some sort of induction circuit."

"That doesn't seem possible using a chip of that size."

"If we buy the quantum twin thing, then maybe it is possible."

"You've got a point there." Jack grinned.

Janet turned her attention back to the exposed circuit board. "So what do you want to do? Do we deep-six the whole laptop? It may have been tampered with in ways that aren't this obvious."

Jack paused. "The laptop doesn't have any external connections, so the technology being used to communicate matches what the message said. Before we do anything else, I want to find out just how useful our new friend can be."

"How so?"

"Slap the cover back on that thing. We're going to ask our source for a good-faith deposit."

CHAPTER 47

Mark had been waiting at the door for half an hour, waiting for Heather, worried about her. He'd expected Jennifer to wait, too, but their mother had taken her shopping.

"How was the doctor visit?" Mark asked as Heather finally arrived.

Heather frowned. "Nothing happened."

"What do you mean nothing happened?"

"I mean the doctor didn't even examine me. He talked to Mom and Dad for a bit and then asked me a few questions. Then he referred me to another doctor."

"Another doctor?"

"Yeah, a shrink. Can you believe it? I have an appointment with her tomorrow."

Mark looked at Heather in alarm. As much as she tried to make herself sound casual, she looked angry and embarrassed.

Before he could ask her another question, she turned away. "Where's Jen?"

"She went to the mall with Mom. They'll be gone all day. Dad's at work; that just leaves the two of us."

"Any response on the message we sent Jack?"

"I don't know. I just left the system running the automatic resend program that Jennifer wrote. If he or Janet turns the computer on, they'll get our message."

"Let's check. And no, I don't want to talk about the doctor."

"I wasn't asking." But he was concerned. A shrink didn't seem right, especially since there was no way Heather could tell anyone what was really going on.

"Good," Heather said, heading for the stairs. "Let's go see if we got a response."

As Mark followed Heather into his sister's room, he paused at the doorway. That was another thing: Heather's problems aside, something else was wrong—right here, in Jennifer's room. He couldn't quite place it, but something didn't feel right. As different as they had always been, Mark knew his twin as no nontwin could. And something about her room was different. However, a quick glance didn't reveal what was off, and Heather was waiting. He'd figure it out later.

He followed Heather over to the small desk where Jennifer's laptop sat quietly running. Heather typed in the password, and the security screen was replaced by a view of the computer desktop.

Two programs were running, both minimized and out of view. Heather brought up the communication program that linked the QT on Jennifer's laptop to the one on Janet's laptop.

Heather almost jumped out of her seat. "Oh my God! They got our message and sent a response."

Immediately, all thoughts about Jennifer vanished from Mark's mind as he leaned over Heather's shoulder to read the message.

"All right. You know who I am, but I need more than your word that I can trust you. Prove it to me. Get me the name of the person who led the attack on my team. Nothing less will be acceptable. I'll give you a week to get back to me with the answer before I destroy this computer. Any attempt at contact without that answer and I will destroy the computer. You have my terms."

Mark was stunned. A glance at Heather's face confirmed that he wasn't alone.

"So Jack is alive," Mark breathed.

"Maybe so, but we can't give him what he wants."

Mark raised an eyebrow. "Why not?"

Heather glanced up at him. "Well, for one thing, we don't know the answer. Second, we can't hack our way into any network that might have the answer, because we don't have the cold-fusion tank anymore. Even though we kept the subspace transmitter, we don't have any way of generating the gamma flux it needs."

"Well, we're just going to have to come up with some other way of making the subspace transmitter work."

Heather shook her head. "Even if we could in that amount of time, where would we start looking? We have to have coordinates to tap into a network, and we don't have any idea who might have that information or what network the answer might be on. Besides, I don't think we should give Jack the answer even if we had it."

"Why not?"

"Even if he's working with us, Jack is a killer. We'd be murdering that person as surely as if we pulled the trigger ourselves."

Mark paced across the room. "Maybe that wouldn't be a bad thing. After all, these people killed Jonathan Riles and most of Jack's team. They're the ones working with Dr. Stephenson."

"We don't know that."

"What do your probabilities tell you?"

Heather pursed her lips. "I don't care. I'm not going to be part of killing someone."

Despite Mark's best efforts, she refused to consider it. Finally, he threw up his hands in frustration.

"OK. At least think about it until we get a chance to discuss this with Jen."

After a brief hesitation, Heather shrugged. "I'll wait until we talk to Jennifer."

Heather saved the message and minimized the program monitoring Janet's computer. As she did, she accidentally tapped the button that displayed the other running program. It was Jennifer's Internet browser, which showed that she had been looking at a news story about the search for Jack and Janet.

"Wait! Leave that up!" The urgency in Mark's voice caused Heather to look around.

Mark's gaze read the page at a glance and he reached across Heather to click the mouse, scrolling rapidly downward until he reached the end. For once, she didn't object.

"We're screwed," Mark said.

"What are you talking about?"

"That news story that Jennifer was reading. It says that the search for Jack has started focusing on the canyons farther west of town. I know the place they were describing. It's the canyon with our starship. With all those people, they're bound to stumble across our cave."

For once, Heather was too shocked to respond.

Mark's eyes settled on Jennifer's bed. Now he knew what had been bothering him. Something about the sheet was wrong. Jennifer had always been meticulous in the way she made her bed, but this morning she had left the sheet untucked, the end extending just below the end of the bedspread.

Drawn forward by his curiosity, Mark knelt down. Only the lower left corner of the sheet was untucked, as if the bed had been made and then the corner had been pulled out later.

Ignoring Heather's questioning gaze, Mark lifted the corner of the mattress.

"Oh, shit, Jen. What have you done?"

There, stuffed under the mattress, lay all four of the alien headsets.

CHAPTER 48

The canyon walls cascaded away before them. If not for the pounding dread in her heart, Heather would have marveled at the newfound stamina that had let her run along beside Mark with no need for a break during the entire trip out to the place they called the Mesa. On the steep slope far below, camouflaged amid the thorn thicket, lay the hidden opening to the starship cave.

Heather and Mark had left the alien headsets beneath Jennifer's mattress. With the search parties beginning to comb this area, the danger that they would be found with those in their possession was too great. Heather wasn't sure what Mark thought Jennifer had done, but the vision that had played out in her head upon seeing the headsets left her praying that she was wrong.

Mark studied the surrounding countryside carefully.

"I don't see anyone. How about you?"

Heather concentrated, noting every detail of her surroundings, a new vision forming before her mind's eye.

"I think the search parties are still an hour or so away from here."

Mark raised an eyebrow. "And how did you come up with that?"

"I don't know and I don't care. How did you read that article so fast? How did we just run all the way out here? You can believe me or not."

"OK. I wasn't trying to make you mad."

Heather took a deep breath. She had to get a handle on her stress. She wasn't mad at Mark; in fact, she was a little impressed and pleased he'd had the self-control not to bombard her with questions about the doctor.

"Let's just get down and check on the ship before they come," she said.

Mark led the way down the steep slope, going much more slowly now. With every step down that slope, the weight of impending disaster dragged more heavily at Heather.

"Oh no!"

Mark scrambled forward, leaving Heather's gaze unobstructed. On the slope below, where there had always been a holographic illusion masking the entrance, a huge cave opening yawned.

Following Mark as quickly as she dared, Heather stumbled into the cave's inky blackness. Not only was the holographic illusion that had masked the entrance gone, so was the soft magenta glow inside.

As her eyes adjusted to the reduced light level, she could see the curving outline of the ship, still resting where it always had. She moved forward reluctantly, her earlier vision coming back in full force, her worst fears confirmed. Either Jennifer had found some way to power down the whole thing, or it had just died.

Mark rushed forward, disappearing up inside the hole. Somehow, Heather could not muster the will to follow him. She knew what he would find, all the doors closed, the few rooms he could enter dark and lifeless.

After a couple of minutes, she stepped to the hole in the ship's belly.

"Mark," Heather called. "We have to get out of here. The lead search party is going to hit this canyon in a few minutes."

Almost immediately, he jumped to the cave floor, wiped at his face with the back of his hand, and turned toward the exit.

"Jennifer did this."

"Probably."

"I can't believe she didn't even tell us. She came out here and shut down the ship, knowing they would find it without the cloak."

"They would have found it anyway."

"She should have told us before she did it. She goddamn well should have told me."

Heather didn't know what to say. The way the tears streamed down her cheeks, she doubted she could say anything anyway.

Mark and Heather stopped at the cave entrance, took one last long look at their ship, then turned and began the long journey home.

CHAPTER 49

"Thanks, Billy."

Billy "Grinning Wolf" Enoso held out a disk fresh from the CD drive on his computer.

"You know you can count on me whenever you need something. Especially for something as interesting as this."

Tall Bear shook his friend's hand. "Yeah. Just make sure you keep it quiet. This is some bad medicine, *comprende*? Loose lips could get you and me both killed."

Grinning Wolf's mouth twitched, although the laughter stayed confined in his black eyes. "Never liked anybody enough to talk to them anyway."

"Good. Glad you got a chance to see me, then."

Tall Bear stepped into his Jeep Cherokee, slid the disk into the CD player, and pulled out onto the dirt road, which led back toward town.

For all their technological pride, sometimes the feds were so stupid you just had to laugh. In World War II, the US had come up with the brilliant idea of using native Navajos as code talkers, passing messages that the Japanese were unable to break. There had even been a recent movie about it. Yet here he was, communicating across the Internet with his source in DC via sound files recorded in Navajo.

True, he hadn't been bold enough to do it from his own computer. The government monitored people based on flags, those mystical keywords that attracted the attention of the computer gods. Having been the first on the scene of the Los Alamos truck ambush and subsequently on national TV in opposition to an FBI search had provided enough of those flags to ensure Tall Bear's communication would be monitored. Even the FBI could probably figure out what language he was using by now.

As the voice on the CD began speaking, Tall Bear found the tension rising in his shoulders and upper back. He didn't know what he had been expecting, but this wasn't it.

The Lakota Sioux had a term for greedy, scheming nonnative people: *wasi'chu*. Tall Bear had always liked the way that rolled off his tongue when he was angry. And right now the wasi'chu in Washington, DC, had him thoroughly pissed and pretty much scared shitless.

The man named Jack Gregory had given him a headful of information about what was going on at Los Alamos, information that had gotten the former director of the National Security Agency and most of Jack's team killed. Tall Bear had used his own sources to verify Jack's information, but this latest recording stunned him.

While the world was busy arguing about how and when the United States should release the alien nanite serum, a multibillion-dollar black market in the stuff had sprung up. Apparently, the going bid for an individual dose of the nanite serum was $250 million. Every old, sick billionaire and every cartel drug lord was desperate to get his hands on some of that juice.

Several of the families of the kids who had participated in the nanite clinical trials had already sold their blood for several million dollars per pint. Even though there was nothing illegal about that, the government had hushed it up and placed all of the families under Secret Service protection to prevent kidnappings.

But what worried Tall Bear was the whispers about Dr. Stephenson and his connections at the top levels of the US government, connections that were rumored to go much deeper than official. While you could pretty much discount most Washington rumors, these had come from a source who was rarely wrong. And what they whispered of was a third and far more dangerous alien technology.

How it could be more dangerous than this nanite crap, Tall Bear couldn't imagine. Didn't want to.

The CD recording ended, and Tall Bear brought the Jeep to a stop. He ejected the CD, got out, and laid it on the gravel, directly in front of his rear tire. Back in the driver's seat, Tall Bear spun his wheels, grinding the disk into a hundred pieces, sending them flying into the desert amid a plume of dust and rocks.

Despite all the help Tall Bear had provided thus far, he had reserved a final decision on Jack Gregory and his girlfriend. Now that decision was made. It was time to pay one more visit to the high hogan.

CHAPTER 50

"Where's my chopper?" Dr. Stephenson's voice crackled with annoyance.

"Sorry, sir. It was in the hangar for maintenance. A replacement is on its way now."

"I don't care if it's missing a blade. Get me a chopper here in the next thirty minutes or find yourself another job. Are you understanding me?"

"Yes, sir." The deputy director's secretary swept from his office, her face pinched and drawn.

Stephenson turned his attention back to the information streaming into his laptop. Unbelievable. After all these years, they had finally found the Second Ship. That damn Admiral Riles had ended up doing him the biggest favor he could imagine, and all because of the search for his rogue agents.

It was unfortunate that the search team that had stumbled across it had been a herd of local yokels with an AP reporter in tow. By now they had climbed all over the thing. Oh well, the military was en route to take control of that entire canyon, starting with the impact cavern. By this time tomorrow, that whole area would be under his direct control, a massive extension of Rho Division.

Stephenson picked up his cell phone and dialed.

"Major Adams." The voice on the other end was crisp with military efficiency.

"Major, this is Dr. Stephenson. What's your situation?"

"We have secured the cavern and escorted all the civilians back to the top of the canyon. I have a platoon of MPs establishing local security, but until we get a larger unit in here, we'll only be able to keep everyone back a few hundred meters."

"That'll be fine. I am going to be flying out there in the next half hour. Make sure you have someone up on the rim to clear a spot for my chopper to land."

"That won't be a problem, sir."

Stephenson flipped the phone closed and leaned back in his chair. Elizabeth might like to play the part of the abused secretary, but she was damn efficient. Whatever it took, she would have that chopper here on schedule. Then he'd get his first look at the starship that had shot down his Rho Ship.

But first he had a call to make. Even he couldn't keep the president waiting forever.

Halfway through his call with the president, Elizabeth signaled that his helicopter had arrived, something that annoyed him even further, since he couldn't get the damn politician to stop asking questions. Surely the president had some other schmuck on his staff who could brief him on this situation. As it was, Stephenson didn't have much information to give. Finally, the man shut up and said good-bye.

By the time the deputy director's helicopter settled down atop the finger of land above the starship crash site, Dr. Stephenson was having difficulty maintaining his traditional cool demeanor. He felt like a kid again, almost as he had on that day decades ago beneath Groom Lake, when he had been the one to open the Rho Ship.

As he stepped out of the aircraft into the gusts kicked up by the whirling rotor, Major Adams stepped forward to meet him.

"Follow me, sir."

Stephenson didn't like the major, but he admired the man's efficiency. No fawning small talk about how he had enjoyed his flight. Adams was strictly business. He knew what Stephenson wanted and wasn't going to waste any time accomplishing the mission.

The top of the mesa was quickly becoming a madhouse. Several of the search parties had now converged on the area, so that the number of locals now surpassed the number of FBI agents. And the FBI appeared none too pleased that the military had taken control of the site.

A reporter yelled after Stephenson, but he ignored the man. Overhead, two news choppers circled, one of them a traffic copter from Santa Fe. The military needed to get some more reinforcements in here fast or they were going to have a hard time keeping all the press away, much less the horde of curious people who must be heading this way as fast as they could rent horses, mountain bikes, or even private helicopters.

The canyon slope was steep and shale-covered, but within fifteen minutes Dr. Stephenson found himself at the entrance to the gaping hole in the side of the canyon. The military police had thrown up a generator, which belched smoke and echoed loudly out into the canyon as it pumped current through the cables that led into the cavern. Just inside the entrance, a bank of flood lamps illuminated the cave in garish brightness, the edges of the craft casting stark, motionless shadows against the back wall.

The starship drew him forward. Its sides were smooth and rounded, a circular ellipsoid, as opposed to the cigar shape of the craft that sat within his high bay back at Rho Division. The walls and ceiling of the cave showed clear evidence of the force of the impact with which this ship had come down, yet the starship's skin showed no sign of trauma.

Dr. Stephenson's gaze swept the dust-covered floor of the cave. Shit. The whole thing was covered with fresh footprints. He could just imagine the search team that found it jumping up and down, running here and there, whooping, hollering, and acting like the pack of idiots they were.

Ducking under a spot where the edge of the starship was wedged against the wall, Stephenson made his way to where an MP stood beside a stepladder. Accepting the flashlight offered by the MP, the deputy director paused, sweeping the beam upward.

A smooth hole had been cut through the craft's outer hull, extending upward through multiple decks and out the top side. As impressed as he had been with the damage done to the Rho Ship, it was now clear which had more power. This ship had been penetrated in a way that implied that this section of hull had been disintegrated, although Dr. Stephenson doubted that was the case. As he examined the smooth contours of the hole's lower edge, his confidence in his guess about the physics that had produced it grew.

Disintegration had nothing to do with what had happened here. A section of the ship had been transported elsewhere, as if a wormhole had torn the space-time fabric at that location. It had to have been an instantaneous, bounded singularity; otherwise the effects on the rest of the ship, and on Earth for that matter, would have been catastrophic.

Climbing upward, Dr. Stephenson moved through the craft with a precision born of refined purpose. Unlike the alien ship back at Rho Division, this one appeared to be completely powered down, not particularly surprising given the way it had been punctured. And although the military people had erected stepladders to allow access to each deck, large sections of the ship were closed off.

As he completed his tour, the deputy director shook his head in amazement. Each step of his inspection had increased the awe he felt, not for this ship, but for the technology of the Rho Ship. Although it had been brought down in the fight, it had survived with its power source at least partially intact, whereas this ship had died. It was no wonder. Everywhere he looked on this ship, smooth-flowing artistic lines gave ample evidence of wasteful inefficiency. While there was plenty of investigation to be done here, it was the type of work he could delegate to underlings.

As he turned to climb back down the ladders, a smile creased Dr. Stephenson's thin lips. Unless something far more interesting turned up here, he intended to keep his attention focused on the third alien technology.

Then the phone rang again. POTUS. What now? He cursed under his breath.

But it was actually the president's science advisor, calling from the oval office, asking him to come to Washington. As he hung up, he was cursing.

If there was anything stupider and more self-serving on this planet than politicians, Dr. Donald Stephenson couldn't imagine what it might be. To be pulled away from his work for an urgent meeting with the president of the United States was the height of folly.

Surely the president's national science advisor could have taken care of the chitchat without bothering him?

Dr. Stephenson's mood failed to improve on the walk back to his helicopter.

CHAPTER 51

Heather knew that time was running out, that they only had three days until Jack's deadline for information expired. And although she had worked out a theory that should allow them to modify the subspace transmitter so that it no longer required a gamma flux, they were having great difficulty getting the damn thing to work. Even if they managed to solve the technical problems, they still had no idea how they would find the information Jack wanted, and they couldn't even agree on whether or not they would give it to him if they could find it.

The only good thing was how the work took her mind off her other problems. Heather had hoped the last experience on the Second Ship would give her control over her visions, but it hadn't. If anything, they were worse than before, now that she no longer required sleep—even the meditation didn't always help. A random glance could trigger an experience so intense it seemed as if she had been transported to another time and place. The disconcerting glimpses were showing events farther out in the probable future.

Before, she had been seeing things only seconds before the event happened; now her visions placed her somewhere minutes or even hours in the future. And during the time Heather was lost in the visions, her body went into a glassy-eyed trance from which no one could wake her.

Heather's first visit to the psychiatrist, a tall brunette in her mid-forties, had consisted of nothing more than a seemingly innocuous set of background questions. For most of the appointment, she had been kept in the waiting area while Dr. Sigmund, "Call me Gertrude," had interviewed her parents.

Dr. Sigmund. What were the odds of getting a psychiatrist with that name? Although the answer to her own rhetorical question popped into her mind, Heather ignored it. At least she hadn't zombied out during the interview, thank the Lord. Still, her answers had been inadequate to prevent a follow-up series of appointments from being scheduled.

Heather turned her thoughts back to the work at hand. Jennifer was focused on constructing the computer simulation that would allow them to model Heather's latest equations, while Mark had gone off to research news stories on the FBI raid that had killed most of Jack's team.

The trouble with communicating through subspace was the quantum energy leakage across the normal space-to-subspace boundary. That leakage rate could be calculated easily enough with the assumption that the average redshift of observed stars at a given distance from Earth came primarily from energy leakage into subspace as opposed to Doppler shifting.

With a bit of oversimplification, each time a light wave took a step, it lost a tiny fraction of its energy to subspace. Since the most energetic light waves had the shortest wavelengths, they took more steps to go the same distance. And more steps meant more energy loss to subspace.

In the past, the three teens had needed the high energy of gamma rays to make the subspace transmitter work. It had only been after Heather had returned from the visit to Dr. Sigmund that a new idea had come to her.

If they could combine the right sets of normal wavelengths, it should be possible to form an interference pattern that would efficiently create high-energy wave packets. It was like the old science film of the Tacoma Narrows Bridge. A very ordinary forty-mile-per-hour wind had torn the bridge down, because gusts were timed so that each one made it oscillate higher, just like pushing a swing. Weak waves could add up if they were timed just right.

Jennifer had already written a program to control the hardware that would make this happen. The tricky part was to manipulate the standing wave packets to generate a usable subspace signal. The computer system clock had nothing close to the required accuracy. So Jennifer had built a circuit board to provide an oscillating crystal's feedback signal that her program used to correct the system clock.

The sound of the Smythe kitchen door opening into the garage brought Heather's head up in time to see Mark stride in, a broad grin spreading across his face.

"I've figured out how to give Jack the information he wants, but not in the way he expects."

Jennifer looked up from her computer on the workbench.

"OK. How is that?"

As Mark's gaze settled on his twin's face, a brief glint of anger darkened his features before he turned back toward Heather. She didn't know how long his bitterness toward his twin would hang on, but at least they were still working on the same team.

"I've read everything that is available in the public record, and I couldn't come up with anything that would point us to the classified computer network that might have the information. Then it hit me. Only someone with Jack's experience would know how to do that."

Heather nodded slowly, the light dawning in her mind. "So we just need to provide Jack with a link where he can find the information himself."

"Right. We need to let him feed in the coordinates of a building, and then we establish a link from here, feeding the information across the QT link to Jack's computer."

"I can do better than that if we can get the subspace transmitter working in time," said Jennifer. "I can drop a program on Jack's machine that will let him log in to our system here and do the search himself."

Heather's eyes narrowed. "I don't think it's a good idea to give him that kind of control over our subspace transmitter."

"We would still be in control," Jennifer continued. "We could limit him any way we wanted to. Maybe we would just give him a couple of hours of access on certain days. And we could monitor whatever he was doing."

Mark sat down on a stool on the other side of the workbench. "Jack would figure we were monitoring him."

"Sure. That's his problem."

Heather shook her head. "I don't like helping Jack search for people he is probably going to kill."

Before Mark could respond, Jennifer leaned toward Heather. "We can't control what Jack does. We can only hope that he's on our side."

As the three teens glanced from one to the other, Mark stood up.

"Then I guess you two better get this thing working before we run out of time."

"Where are you going?" Jennifer asked.

"For someone who does whatever she wants without telling us, you're awfully nosy."

"Fine. Forget it."

"I will."

The door slammed behind Mark before Heather could interject. Jennifer scowled after him, then turned her attention back to the computer. Deciding there was nothing she could say to break the icy quiet, Heather focused her thoughts back on the theoretical problem at hand.

Three days to produce a breakthrough of this magnitude wasn't much time. But if they were going to have any chance to pull it off, Jennifer was going to need Heather's help. Maybe if she focused hard enough, she could forget about the psychiatrist and the possibility that she might be going crazy.

CHAPTER 52

Mark's pace quickened, his anger rising as the front door slammed behind him. As he stepped out onto the street, he broke into a ground-burning jog, nothing fast enough to attract attention, just enough to burn off some of the energy building up within him.

He could feel his heart thundering in his chest, pumping blood through his body in massive pulses, which only fed his need to hit someone. Mark knew something was wrong with him. He had known it since their last experience in the alien ship. Ever since that day, his emotions had been jacked up, leaving him feeling stretched taut, a pinprick away from an explosion.

It wasn't just anger either. Every emotion had been amplified so heavily that he felt as if someone had shot him with an elephant-sized dose of adrenaline. Right now, the only way he knew to control it was to get away from everyone.

In addition to his becoming an adrenaline junkie, there were other changes going on with his body. For one thing, Mark wasn't sleeping. He just didn't feel the need. That was one change that didn't bother him. Although he had to stay in his room so that his parents wouldn't discover his sleepless nights, he had used the time to practice his speed-reading. The only problem he had run into with that practice was difficulty in turning the pages fast enough.

Another nighttime activity he had taken to was meditation. He had thought that if he could improve his already considerable meditation skills, then perhaps he could get control over the emotional thunderstorms that raged through his brain and body. However, when the adrenaline rushes hit, he had no time to begin a meditation, and once he was in thrall to the attack, it took several minutes of concentration to restore quiet to his mind.

His workouts helped, so he had thrown himself into a routine that even an Olympian would have found exhausting. Now, as Mark turned off the street, cutting out onto a bike trail into the woods, he could feel the muscles rippling beneath his skin. He had certainly put on some more muscle mass, but he wasn't bulked out. *Ripped* was the word that popped into his mind.

A stiff breeze had sprung up, carrying with it eddies of coolness that hinted at a coming storm. As the trail opened out onto the ridgeline, Mark could see the line of thunderheads in the distance, dark streaks of rain hanging like a curtain below them.

Good. Let the rain come. Maybe it would cool his overheated brain.

Mark increased his pace. It felt good to stretch out into a real run. His sister's angry face swam into his mind. Shit, after the way he had treated her, Jen had a right to be angry. Mark knew he should already be over his own anger at what she had done. Shutting down the ship had probably been what they would have done even if they had talked it over first. He should have already forgiven her, but he just couldn't.

The first drop of rain smacked him in the face, the big, fat globule splattering on his forehead as twin forks of lightning split the sky across the canyon. Mark's eyes focused on the scene ahead. Christ. He hadn't thought he had been running that long.

Half a mile ahead, the finger of land they called the Mesa came to a point, below which the Second Ship rested in its cave. But the spot no longer resembled the place they had come to know so well.

Military vehicles had been parked in precisely aligned rows just inside a newly erected chain-link fence topped with concertina razor wire. A guard bunker abutted the gate, and though he could imagine guards with machine guns pointed outward, Mark was unable to see them in the gathering darkness of the storm.

Another gust of wind brought a swarm of droplets splashing down, a swarm that was followed by a downpour as the sky opened up. There at the edge of the woods, as bolt after bolt of lightning ripped the black clouds, Mark stared in the direction of their lost ship, his tears washed from his cheeks by the rain.

CHAPTER 53

Freddy stared through the Nikon's viewfinder, the image magnified by the zoom lens until it seemed that he could reach out and touch it. The Gothic-style mansion looked as out of place in Podunk, California, as an igloo in Miami.

Built by a New Yorker named Winston Archibald, who had struck it rich selling dry goods to miners during the California gold rush, the place looked as if he hadn't been able to decide whether to build a cathedral or an English castle. Desirous of seclusion, Mr. Archibald had chosen a location near the rural community of Porterville for his monstrosity.

Once completed, the mansion occupied the center of 120 acres of lawns, hedges, and gardens, the entire compound surrounded by a ten-foot-tall wrought-iron fence. After his death, the estate had passed to the State of California, which had converted it to an asylum for the criminally insane.

Unfortunately for Porterville, an extremely violent inmate had escaped from the compound on Christmas Eve, 1949. His subsequent atrocities had caused an uproar in the horrified community, which had forced the state to close Archibald Mansion and transfer the inmates to more secure facilities elsewhere in the state.

In the years that followed, Archibald Mansion fell into disrepair. Then in 1986 the property had been purchased by the Henderson Foundation, the old buildings and grounds restored. Renamed Henderson House, the estate now provided round-the-clock care for patients suffering from severe mental and physical handicaps.

As a private foundation, Henderson House received its funding from a combination of private charities and the fees it charged for the care of its wards. From what Freddy had discovered in three weeks of snooping, many of the patients were the unwanted retarded spawn of the superrich. For others at the facility, there was no background information at all, but somebody was paying the bills.

The deeper Freddy dug, the more the Henderson House creeped him out. He hadn't been sleeping a lot, but the creepiness wasn't the cause. For one thing, he'd been following a convoluted money trail. He'd been able to call in a few favors from sources in the banking industry and at the Treasury Department, but the data they had provided was raw and unfiltered. And, as with all unfiltered data, someone had to do the filtering. While there was plenty here to keep an investigator busy for years, Freddy's interest was limited to recent arrivals at the facility.

He had been lucky to pick up the trail that had led him here. After he had uncovered the empty coffin of Billy Randall and the subsequent murder of Dr. Callow, the Barstow medical examiner, Freddy had tracked down Callow's secretary. Mary O'Reilly had been at work on the day the bodies of Billy Randall and his family had been picked up from the Barstow morgue. A night at the bingo hall had netted a description of the two men who had come to collect the bodies for transport to the LaGrone Funeral Home in Wickenburg, Arizona.

Mrs. O'Reilly, a talkative Irishwoman in her mid-forties, had remembered that the men had seemed out of place for funeral home employees. But when she had asked for identification, both men had supplied the proper credentials, which were promptly verified by Dr. Callow.

Except for the uncomfortable feeling that she had gotten from the two men, Mary could only remember one oddity. As one of the men had removed his identification card from his wallet, a second card had fallen onto the desk. Mary had reached out to hand it back to him, but the man had scooped the ID card up fast, as if he didn't want her to see it. Even though she hadn't been able to see much, she remembered a stylized logo, the letters *HH* connected in flowing golden script.

As the auto-winder on the Nikon buzzed, Freddy leaned forward, directing the camera at the massive gates that blocked the entrance to the old Archibald Mansion grounds. There, in flowing golden letters, the twin *H*'s of Henderson House filled his lens.

CHAPTER 54

Power. The pulse rippled through every fiber of Raul's extended being, from the nerve endings in his skin, along the neural pathways in the alien computers, crawling along the mechanical systems of the ship itself. Raul had never felt such exultation.

Even though it was what he had been hoping for, the resulting energy produced from this one tiny wave-packet disrupter surprised him. It was only one cell in a shipboard power-production grid that had once enjoyed billions working in tandem, but it was his first major repair. And it would allow him to do so much more without worrying about draining the limited shipboard energy reserves.

The technology behind the disrupter was relatively simple but made human nuclear technology seem laughable in comparison. Raul's ability to periodically tap into the Internet had allowed him to feed on information he hadn't learned in high school, information that the ship's neural network processed effortlessly. And whatever the ship knew, Raul knew. After all, his thinking was augmented by the ship's superior, although damaged, brain.

The human concept of quantum physics was really quite funny, beginning with the dual nature of light. Because scientists couldn't figure out how a photon could act like both a wave and a particle, they had just decided it was both, applying two completely inconsistent models to the same thing, a particle governed by waves of probability.

As if waves of probability could physically interfere with each other. Typical scientific nonsense.

The true comedy was in the way Earth technology attacked the problem of determining the structure of matter. In order to understand how particles were pieced together, they built giant accelerators to smash particles into one another at high speed so they could watch for what pieces flew out. It was like jamming a stick of dynamite up someone's ass and setting it off so you could examine his organs. What remained after the explosion was quite different from before.

Matter really had little to do with the notion of particles. The universe was actually made of *stuff*, a granular ether substance through which energy waves traveled. Those waves traveled through the substance at only one speed—the speed of light.

Certain combinations of waves could combine to form stable vibrational packets, something like musical chords. Only a limited number of frequency combinations formed stable packets, and these produced the elements in the periodic table.

But there were other wave packets that did not form harmonically stable chords. Unstable packets tried to get rid of the clashing frequencies, giving off radiation as they attempted to move to a more harmonious combination.

Most human nuclear reactors were fission reactors, which packed unstable elements tightly together so that the splitting packets combined with others, producing a chain reaction. Fusion reactors crammed together two relatively stable wave packets into one massively discordant jumble. The resultant mess radiated hard in its attempt to cast off the incompatible frequencies.

Both these processes were inefficient in the extreme. The way the disrupter technology worked was different. Since every particle is composed of a specific set of vibrational frequencies, the disrupter merely had to know what those frequencies were. Then it could send a complete set of canceling frequencies, an antipacket, which would result in an instantaneous and total release of all energy. Or it could cancel selected frequencies in the particle, resulting in controlled instability, which bled off energy at a controlled rate.

The disrupter cell could do either equally well. It could use any type of matter as fuel, although some elemental wave packets were easier to manipulate than others. Its other function was to collect the energy that had been released from the particle and pass that energy to the ship's systems. There was no need for energy storage. Matter was the stored energy.

Actually, that was not completely correct. The disrupters did require energy to start the entire process once they had been shut down. It was the one thing that had worried Raul about this test. The ship had a store of energy reserves, but these had been heavily depleted by Raul's worm-fiber experimentation. And even though a single disrupter cell was tiny, there was a risk that attempting to restart the repaired cell could drain the remainder of those shipboard reserves.

Fortunately, that had not happened. Now he had power. It wouldn't be enough to let him do everything he wanted, but it would increase the amount of time he could operate the systems.

There was something he needed, and this was going to help him get it.

Raul crawled higher along the wall, the set of umbilical cables that dangled from his amputated legs trailing along behind him. Extracting a specially designed tool from a hidden niche, Raul returned to the floor, propping himself against the near wall.

Taking a deep breath, he brought the instrument down to his leg stumps, slicing deeply into the skin around the umbilical. Dr. Stephenson's crude connections had served their purpose. It was now time to establish a more complete linkage with the ship. Besides, a tail was no fitting appendage for a child of God.

CHAPTER 55

Shift.

Heather struggled to make sense of the sudden change of surroundings, although she had no doubt what had happened. A fugue. It wasn't quite right, but it was the word she had come to use to refer to the eerie dream state into which her conscious mind was sometimes summoned.

The place where she now found herself was like nothing she had ever imagined. In the gray light, it was hard to focus her vision, almost as if she drifted in a fog. All around her, strange machines filled the room, odd conduits snaking among them in a jumble of chaotic connections.

She heard something, a skittering noise, but when she tried to turn toward it, she found herself unable to move, draped with some sort of invisible force that held her suspended above the floor.

Heather gasped. She hung in the air, face upward, completely naked.

Concentrating her efforts, Heather struggled, her renewed efforts having no more effect than her first. Something was with her here in the room, something that moved along the walls just outside her vision, something that was getting steadily closer.

A deep-seated dread consumed her, rising in intensity with each passing second. Heather increased her concentration, casting away the self-image-imposed limitations that usually blocked her from using all of her neurally enhanced strength. Straining until it seemed that she would tear every muscle in her body, Heather failed to produce the slightest change in position. She couldn't wiggle so much as a finger or a toe.

As a small child, she had once tried to crawl through a drainage pipe and had gotten stuck, her arms pinned to her sides. It had taken the fire department two hours to get her out. The sense of claustrophobic panic Heather had felt in that pipe washed her once again, hyperventilation further constricting her chest.

The other thing in the room was close now, so close she could feel the subtle current in the air from its excited breathing. In that air, Heather could feel a sick desire radiating toward her.

A hand caressed her cheek from behind, slowly making its way along her throat, the fingers quivering as they moved down along her chest. Heather braced herself against a growing revulsion, accompanied by a vague sense of familiarity, as a new purpose formed in her mind. She needed to see the face connected to that hand.

Shift.

Gasping for breath, Heather struggled to reorient herself. She was lying on a couch. As she looked up, she found herself staring directly into the intense blue eyes of Dr. Gertrude Sigmund.

CHAPTER 56

"Schizophrenia!" Gil McFarland was so shocked at Dr. Sigmund's diagnosis that his exclamation threatened to spray her with saliva.

"Not our Heather." Anna McFarland shook her head angrily.

"I'm sorry," Dr. Sigmund said. "But your daughter is suffering from an emerging psychosis, probably triggered by the recent traumatic events to which she has been subjected."

For once Gil McFarland was too stunned to respond.

"But you said schizophrenia," Anna continued. "Heather absolutely does not have a split personality."

Dr. Sigmund put a hand on her arm. "That is a common misconception. Schizophrenia does not imply a split personality. Your daughter is displaying some of the classic symptoms. She is suffering from delusions, hallucinations, and periodic loss of touch with reality. She is both seeing and hearing things that only exist in her head."

"So what does that mean? You said it was caused by her experiences, like post-traumatic stress, right?" Anna asked.

"No. I said that her psychosis was probably triggered by the traumatic events. I'm afraid that this condition is a disease of the mind, a disorder that can be treated but for which there are no cures."

Anna gasped, her hands flying to her mouth.

Anger clenched Gil in its anaconda coils. "I can't accept that. I want a second opinion."

Dr. Sigmund nodded. "I understand. But you should know that I have already consulted with two of the top psychiatrists in the country, Dr. Edwards and Dr. Mellon from the Henderson House Hospital in California. After reviewing the case file, they are both in agreement with my diagnosis. Nevertheless, I will fully support your desire to get another opinion from a doctor of your choice."

Anna McFarland's knees buckled, and she would have fallen if not for her husband's strong hands catching her and guiding her into a chair.

Sliding into a chair beside her, Dr. Sigmund leaned forward. "I know this is a shock, but I think it is very important that you hear it. Your daughter needs treatment before her condition worsens, which it certainly will. I have to warn you that right now is the time to act, before she becomes a threat to herself and to others. Her psychotic episodes are increasing in frequency and intensity."

"What kind of treatment do you think she needs?" Gil McFarland asked. "Counseling? Group therapy?"

Dr. Sigmund paused, a sympathetic look on her face. "I'm afraid that in a case such as Heather's, those methods will not suffice, although they may be helpful to you in learning to deal with her condition. She needs to begin a regimen of antipsychotic medication. Normally I would recommend olanzapine, but for Heather I would like to start with risperidone."

When neither Gil nor Anna McFarland spoke, Dr. Sigmund continued.

"It is very important that you listen to me carefully. Schizophrenia is a permanent condition, and it will take a commitment from you both to ensure that your daughter takes her medication and attends all clinical appointments. It is typical for patients to refuse to believe that they are ill. Heather will most likely be in denial.

"Your role is the hardest. It is your responsibility to force her to do what she will resist, even though she may rebel against you. But for her sake, you two must be strong. You should know that, based upon the severity of the symptoms I have observed, if Heather does not rigorously adhere to her treatment, long-term internment in a psychiatric facility is likely."

Once again, Anna McFarland gasped, this time breaking down into sobs as she buried her face in her husband's shoulder.

Gil McFarland held her tightly, then helped her to stand. "Dr. Sigmund. Thank you for your frank assessment. Anna and I will still want to obtain a second opinion. But be assured that if that assessment matches yours, we will do whatever is required to ensure Heather gets the best treatment available."

As they left the psychiatrist's office and passed through the waiting area beyond, Gil McFarland supported his sobbing wife. Glancing down at the love of his life, he wanted to scream. How had it come to this? He was supposed to protect his little wife and family. Now the most joyous creature he had ever known looked as if all the joy had been leached from her world. And as badly as he wanted to believe a second opinion would change things, Gil felt as if the spectral fingers of the banshee had just stroked the back of his neck.

Guiding Anna across the asphalt parking lot, Gil McFarland prayed as never before.

"Dear Lord, please save my little girl."

CHAPTER 57

The tension in the cabinet room had grown so thick that it threatened to acquire a gravity all its own, pulling the entire West Wing of the White House over the gathering event horizon. Vice President Gordon shifted his weight slightly so that his chin rested in the crook of his palm, his elbow supported by the polished mahogany table. His eyes drifted from President Harris to the sharp, expressionless visage of Dr. Donald Stephenson and then back to the president once more.

President Harris studied the image projected onto the view screen on the far wall, his frown deepening. "So, am I to understand that it is the consensus of the Joint Chiefs that the special commission's recommendation should be adopted?"

General Brad Valentine, the chairman of the Joint Chiefs, nodded slowly, his blue eyes locked unflinchingly with the president's. "Yes, sir."

Having just polled the members of his cabinet, the president was now faced with a dilemma. The special commission had been appointed directly by President Harris to fully assess all the national security and public safety issues associated with the impending worldwide release of the Rho Project's nanite solution. Although far from unanimous, the consensus recommendation was that the release should be delayed by at least two years, a time period that would allow independent scientific study of potential unknown side effects of the treatment, as well as time to formulate a comprehensive national policy.

So far, the lone dissenting voice in the cabinet had been Conrad Huntington, the secretary of state, who argued that pulling back on the US commitment at this point would incite outrage throughout the United Nations, the ramifications of which could be disastrous for US foreign policy.

President Harris looked down the table at Dr. Stephenson. "Don. The ball's in your court. I have to tell you that, based on the power of this report, I'm leaning toward delaying the release, despite the political capital that this is going to cost me."

Dr. Stephenson paused, leaning even farther back in his chair. "Mr. President, as anxious as I am to see an end to the horrible diseases that are the scourge of our planet, to see an end to the suffering of the poorest and most helpless populations of our world, I am forced to support the delay. Although all data points to tremendously positive results from the release, with an advance this radical, the potential risks are too great to be glossed over."

The look on President Harris's face matched the surprised intake of breath around the table. The president shook his head. "I must tell you, Dr. Stephenson, I'm stunned by what you've just said. Although my mind was pretty well made up already, this clinches the decision."

Turning to his chief of staff, President Harris stood. "Andy, see me in my office right after this. And bring Michelle with you when you come. If there's ever a time for her to earn that press secretary salary, this is it."

Rising from his seat, Vice President Gordon watched Dr. Stephenson walk from the room with the others, looking as if he'd just sat in on nothing more interesting than a high-school physics lecture.

Interesting. Very, very interesting.

CHAPTER 58

Mark glanced across the garage workshop at Heather, a lump rising in his throat. God, she was amazing. All week she had been forced to endure visits to three different psychiatrists, who each seemed to be intent upon drugging her out of her beautiful mind. Yet, despite the inner terror she must be feeling, she had managed to focus on the theoretical solution that would grant them new and improved subspace transmission capabilities.

And those efforts had been successful. Jennifer only had to finish the modifications to the controller, which would allow Jack limited remote access to the equipment, and they would be ready for a trial run.

"Bingo!" Jennifer's exclamation brought Mark's head around. "It's online."

Sure enough, the panel of multicolored LED lights twinkled in a manner that indicated the subspace transmitter was up and operational.

Jennifer looked at Mark. "Do you have the target coordinates?"

"Right here." He handed a piece of paper across the workbench.

Heather glanced at the text printed on the sheet. "The NSA again?"

"Why not? It's as good a test target as any." Mark grinned at her.

Before Heather had a chance to respond, Jennifer began typing the coordinates into the subspace transmitter control program. Watching his twin's fingers fly across the keyboard, Mark thought he detected just a hint of eagerness in her actions. Then again, why wouldn't she be eager? The controller was her design and represented a major advance from the crude controls for the original subspace transmitter.

As he watched the glittering LED lights on the display panel, Mark began to feel some of his sister's excitement. The thing was beautiful.

"I'm in," Jennifer breathed.

"Can you identify the network?" Heather asked, leaning in for a better view.

"Give me a sec."

The clicks of the keys reminded Mark of a snare drummer, so rapid that they sounded like the buzz of a drumroll.

"Looks like it's just an administrative subnet, but it is on the SIPRNet."

Mark nodded. "Good. Send the test message. Once we confirm that it's been inserted, we can break the link. Then we'll contact Jack."

Jennifer grinned. "It's done."

Mark leaned in to see what his sister had just transmitted. There on the computer screen, four short words clung to the white background.

"Hello, boys. I'm back."

CHAPTER 59

"What have you got?" Jack asked, leaning over Janet's shoulder as she worked on the laptop.

"It looks like our source has decided to answer your query."

"What did he say?"

"I'll read it. 'Jack. Even if I wanted to provide you the names of the people in charge of the raid on your team, I couldn't. As you probably suspect, I am not a spy and wouldn't even know how to search for that information. However, after careful consideration, I have decided to provide you with an interface to a very unique system.

"'I have transmitted a file to your laptop that contains instructions for remotely logging into my network controller. Through it, you will be able to access computer systems at any latitude and longitude you provide. And while that access will be detectable as an intrusion, your connection will be completely untraceable.

"'Although I will not be able to leave this connection up at all times, you will see a small green indicator on your screen when it is available to you. Should you decide to take advantage of this offer, I believe you will find it most useful.'"

Janet lifted her eyes from the screen. "That's the whole message."

Jack slid into the chair beside her. "Interesting."

"If this person isn't lying."

"That should be easy to test," Jack replied.

"You know he will probably be monitoring whatever we do across this link."

"So long as the guy doesn't get in the way of what I want to accomplish, that won't be a problem. Pull up that instruction file," Jack said, leaning over to kiss her cheek. "Looks like my deadly little computer hacker is about to get back in the business."

Janet's eyes followed Jack's lithe form as he arose and walked out the hogan's doorway. Despite her growing uneasiness, she trusted Jack's instincts.

Turning her attention back to the laptop, Janet opened the instruction file.

CHAPTER 60

Freddy Hagerman hunched forward, bathed in the dim red glow that struggled to keep the darkness at bay. A line of damp photographs dangled from clips along the clothesline, which stretched above the bathtub in the motel bathroom. As he studied a drying photograph in the makeshift darkroom, Freddy rubbed his chin.

His insistent need to cling to the old ways of doing things sometimes paid dividends. One thing you missed in digital photography was the way a photograph magically appeared from the foggy background as the development process continued. And for someone as good at that process as Freddy, there were moments as the picture emerged when otherwise hidden details stood out. One of those moments now stared him in the face.

Freddy had been photographing the exterior of the Henderson House compound for the last six days, from as many different vantage points as possible. He hadn't known exactly what he was looking for, but before he set foot on the property he would. One thing he did know: the more he watched the place, the more he felt that he was peering at one of those old horror movies, the ones shot in black and white.

That was stupid, of course, probably a side effect of the utterly bizarre architecture and the white-uniformed attendants who roamed the grounds. Still, Freddy was having a hard time shaking the irrational fear that had been growing in his mind.

But at the moment, his attention had been seized by a photograph of a helicopter landing on the back side of the estate. Freddy had been lucky to get it. The spot was mostly blocked from view by the buildings that surrounded it. Freddy had been in a spot on a hill opposite the gatehouse that yielded a very narrow line of sight to the helipad, when he had seen the helicopter approaching.

He had begun snapping pictures, following the chopper with his lens as it settled to the ground. All but one of those pictures had turned out to be useless. And Freddy might have missed the point of interest in this one if he had not been watching as the picture emerged on the photographic paper as it swam beneath the development solution. For a few seconds, a single face had clarified ahead of the background against which it might otherwise have been concealed.

Just visible in the image as it passed around the far side of the chopper, a familiar face angled toward him. Freddy leaned in for a closer look, shaking his head in astonishment.

Now what the hell was Dr. Donald Stephenson doing at Henderson House?

CHAPTER 61

A low hum throbbed through the interior of the Rho Ship, completely contained within the shielding mechanisms so that it, like the power surge that was producing it, remained well beyond the detection capabilities of the feeble human instruments that clung to the ship's outer skin. But Raul could feel it.

His connection with the ship had improved drastically since he had moved the umbilical cable from the base of his spine. The operation had taken a good deal of time, the complications having nothing to do with Dr. Stephenson's crude attachments. What had made things difficult was the need to maintain a connection to the ship's neural net while he performed the operation on the base of his own skull.

Raul couldn't just sever the old connections and move the cables up to be reconnected. That would have severed his link, leaving him without the knowledge to perform the brain operation that would reconnect him. So he had left the old connections in place while he began a separate operation at the base of his skull.

For several hours he had worked to implant a much more sophisticated device, one that extended a half inch from the back of his brainpan, just enough to provide an easy place to rehook the umbilical after he removed it. This outer hookup had to be simple. Once he disconnected the umbilical from his leg stumps, he would be on his own, cut off from the augmentation of the massive neural network that enhanced his mind. The task of reconnecting had to be accomplished while he remained in that reduced state.

Unfortunately, an unanticipated problem had almost brought a disastrous end to his efforts. After cutting away the umbilical connections to his lower spinal cord, Raul had experienced several minutes of self-doubt, accompanied by a feeling of great loss. Thoughts of Heather had bombarded his mind, leaving him nearly suicidal and almost robbing him of the will to reconnect. Only a sudden flash of hope had renewed his strength of will, a hope that had transformed into a new goal as the neural network connection had been restored.

It had been a close thing, but the danger had been worth the risk. The connections directly into his brain were so far superior to the previous ones that there was no comparison.

Dr. Stephenson's response upon seeing him the following day had been enlightening. The physicist had eyed him with interest, but there had been no hint of surprise in the man's mannerisms. If anything, he had seemed pleased.

Well, what Stephenson thought hardly mattered. Raul hadn't even seen the man in two days, and with his improved mental augmentation, that had been plenty of time to do what had to be done.

Raul let his thoughts drift to the machinery that powered the stasis field, the one that Dr. Stephenson had used to hold him immobile during the operations that had removed his eye and both legs. With a slight shift of his thoughts, Raul brought the machine online, manipulating the stasis field's lines of force as easily as he could wiggle his own finger.

A small scalpel rose from its resting place, steadied in midair, and then shot across the room, coming to a stop a half inch in front of Raul's face. It hung there, quivering as if it had just sunk its blade into a tree trunk. Once again Raul changed his visualization, the field compressing the metal scalpel with such force that it collapsed in upon itself, running like liquid mercury to form a shiny metal ball.

Raul let the ball fall to the floor as his torso floated into the air and began moving across the room, the umbilical cable attached to his skull trailing along behind him.

No. Stephenson wouldn't be bothering him—ever again.

CHAPTER 62

Most people found the inside of the Henderson House mansion more bizarre than the exterior, its freestanding spiral staircase occupying the center of the huge open foyer. The staircase went well beyond eccentric. It somehow managed to be simultaneously beautiful and hideous.

Built entirely of mahogany, it wound its way upward to a spot twenty feet above the marble floor, where it terminated in a platform supported by three archways. Narrow wooden walkways led outward along the tops of the arches to the inward-facing balconies that provided access to the hallways on the upper floor. Where the wood of the staircase connected to each metal arch, a face was carved. The wooden faces, one a man's and the other two women's, were contorted in expressions of agony, giving the clear impression that the touch of the metal arch was torture.

Even longtime staff often paused at the sight. Dr. Stephenson passed it by without a second glance, making his way directly toward the library.

A white-clad Henderson House staff member opened the heavy wooden door as he approached the room. As odd as most of the mansion was, the library felt comfortably normal, with a relatively small reading area, walls lined with bookshelves accessible via a sliding ladder. Seated at the circular table in the room's center, three men awaited him.

Dr. Anthony Frell, the chairman of the Henderson House Foundation, was on the right, rising from his chair and extending his hand in greeting. It was a gesture Stephenson ignored, turning his hawkish gaze on the man seated in the center.

He was Hispanic, his dark hair worn shoulder length, his mouth outlined with a Fu Manchu mustache and beard. The man's expression was one of thinly masked aggression, a look that was matched by the large man on his right. Jorge Esteban Espeñosa, the leader of the largest Colombian drug cartel, never went anywhere without his personal bodyguard.

Dr. Stephenson did not bother to sit down. "This meeting does not please me."

Espeñosa leaned back in his chair, bringing his booted feet up to rest on the table. "And I don't give a shit."

The drug lord extracted a cigar from his jacket pocket, snipping the end with a small cigar cutter. Striking a match on the side of his embroidered cowboy boot, Espeñosa drew in several puffs, blowing the smoke out in Dr. Stephenson's direction.

"It seems to me that you need a little lesson in who you are dealing with." Espeñosa smiled. "Don't get me wrong. The doses of the nanite formula you provided for me are most acceptable. But somehow, you seem to have gotten the notion that you can command me. Nobody commands Jorge Espeñosa. *Comprende*?"

Espeñosa exhaled another large puff of smoke, bringing his feet off the table and leaning forward. "And I don't like the inflated price you're charging for the formula. It cuts into my profits."

At a nod from the cartel boss, the bodyguard moved around the table, taking up a position just behind and to the left of Dr. Stephenson.

"It's bad for business. I'm sure you understand that." Espeñosa rolled the end of the cigar over his tongue, savoring the rich taste of the Cuban leaf. "So from now on, I'm going to set the price. All I have to do is let word of our arrangement leak out and your government would kill you for me. Don't forget whose *cojones* are in the vice."

Dr. Stephenson's face showed no sign of emotion.

Suddenly the bodyguard screamed, a sound that brought Espeñosa to his feet and sent Dr. Frell scrambling back into the far corner.

The bodyguard staggered forward, falling to his knees as his fingers clawed at his face, his fingernails ripping out large chunks of flesh. As the man looked up at his boss, his brown eyes exploded like grapes squeezed in a press, squirting out of their sockets in twin jets that splattered the front of the drug lord's shirt.

"*Madre de Dios!*" Espeñosa gasped as he staggered away from the dying man.

The bodyguard screamed again, a sound that degenerated into a gargle as his bones dissolved beneath his skin. Within seconds, the only thing that remained of what had once been a human being was a stinking, wet mess on the beautiful hardwood floor.

Both Dr. Frell and Jorge Esteban Espeñosa remained frozen in place, unable to speak, their backs pressed firmly against the bookcase.

Dr. Stephenson stepped forward, his eyes locking with Espeñosa's.

"I don't think I will be accepting your terms."

As he turned and began to walk from the room, Dr. Stephenson stopped to look back.

"By the way, if anything unfortunate happens to me or should I become displeased, then you have just seen a glimpse of your future. But your death will take considerably longer."

Moving out into the grand foyer, Dr. Stephenson paused momentarily, his eyes studying the spiral staircase, as if for the first time.

It really was a thing of beauty.

CHAPTER 63

Vice President Gordon's eyes opened at the soft knock at his bedroom door. Slipping silently from bed to avoid waking his wife, the vice president donned his bathrobe and opened the door. Sam Tally, the chief of his personal Secret Service detail, awaited, his square jaw clenched tighter than normal.

In a voice that carried only to the vice president's ears, the Secret Service agent spoke. "Mr. Vice President. The director of the FBI has been found murdered in his home."

"I understand," Vice President Gordon said, instantly assuming the commanding demeanor for which he was famous. Closing the bedroom door behind him, he nodded his head toward his personal office. "Let's take this conversation down the hall. Is there any connection to the hit on the FBI agent in North Dakota last week—Freeman?"

"We don't know for sure yet, Mr. Vice President, but the MO looks the same." Tally's voice held an unusual edge.

"Nasty business." He still couldn't get the photo from the crime scene out of his head— Freeman slumped on the kitchen floor, a knife in his gut, a name scrawled in Magic Marker across his forehead: Raymond Bronson. The name of one of the dead members of Jack Gregory's team.

"Tonight, when they found the FBI director's body, there was another name written on his forehead. Bobby Daniels."

"Another of Gregory's boys?"

"Yes, sir."

"I just can't believe Bill Hammond is dead."

"It gets worse. Both special agents assigned to ensure his protection were found dead outside the house. I'm afraid Mrs. Hammond is dead too."

"Marjorie? Jesus Christ."

"She must have stumbled on the killer as he exited the house. He cut her throat so violently her head almost came off. The house was a god-awful mess. The president wants you at the White House ASAP. He's gathering the whole cabinet for an emergency meeting."

"My driver?"

"He and the rest of your security team are already waiting outside."

"OK, Sam. Let the president's people know I'll be on my way as soon as I throw on some clothes."

The Secret Service man nodded, then turned and exited the room. Vice President Gordon waited until he was gone, then turned and picked up the encrypted Secure Telephone Unit, more commonly called a STU.

The STU-secured call was answered by an odd-sounding voice, the slight delay and echo indicative of the heavy encryption on the line.

"Yes?"

The vice president spoke softly. "Is the cigar ready?"

"The Colombian, just as you requested."

Vice President Gordon paused for just an instant, the code words that would change his life forever rising to his lips of their own accord.

"Smoke 'em if you got 'em."

CHAPTER 64

Surrounded by the machinery that filled this part of the ship, Raul hung in the air, suspended by the stasis field, which now responded to his mental commands as easily as his missing legs once had. His connection to the Rho Ship was better now, evolving in a way that changed with each of his repairs to the damaged shipboard systems. With each of the micropower cells he managed to bring online, his abilities increased. Not his mental abilities; those were tied solely to the neural network that formed the starship's computerized brain.

But each power increase allowed Raul to bring new systems online, giving him better control over the gravitational worm-fiber technology with which he had been experimenting. Initially, the worm fibers had provided a tiny point of access to a distant location, so small that he could only tap into existing communication networks. The power required for even those tiny space-time singularities was monstrous, each attempt bringing him close to draining his shipboard reserves. If he totally drained the power, then the neural network would fail, leaving him without the knowledge to repair the system.

That danger should have been enough to stop him from trying anything else until he had totally solved the power problem. But a stronger impulse consumed him: Heather.

In his darkest moment of despair, while he had briefly been disconnected from his starship, one thought had saved him, giving him a reason to reconnect. A new purpose seized his mind, a purpose that drove him to restore much more of the ship's former glory.

At this point, Raul didn't even have a good plan for accomplishing what he wanted. He wasn't worried, though. He would figure it out. Somehow, Raul would get Heather to come to him. Then he would introduce her to the power that came from a true connection. He would perform the operation himself so there would be no need to sacrifice those lovely legs.

Raul glanced down at his own legless torso. It wasn't so bad. He still had all the necessary equipment to slide between those legs. Then Heather would find out not only that he still lived, but just how well he could manipulate the spectral fingers of the stasis field. It was a shame he hadn't yet had any sexual experience to draw upon, but there would be plenty of time for practice when he had his soul mate. Once he hooked her into the ship, he would be able to monitor exactly what felt good and what didn't. Raul took a deep breath. He'd have Heather begging for more before she knew what was happening.

Noticing his rising heart rate, Raul turned his attention back to the task at hand. He could daydream later.

With the new matter-conversion cell operational, he'd been able to recharge the ship's energy storage units. With that reserve power added to what was produced by the two operational matter-conversion cells, there should be enough to create a larger worm fiber, one that could serve as an optical pinhole. Maintaining the worm-fiber viewer for several minutes should be possible.

The problem was that Raul didn't have enough power to do that and to completely mask the external effects such a worm fiber would produce. The best he could do was reduce the gravitational signature to a minimum.

Raul reached out with his mind, his neural network bringing the power cells up to maximum as he began the worm-fiber generation sequence. A tiny gravitational wave pulsed outward as the singularity came into existence, its extraordinary potential well contained by the alien technology that had brought it into being. It hung there in front of him, so tiny that no human eye could see it, no broader in diameter than a molecule, a place where *here* and *there* touched.

No longer aware of his own body, Raul's mind manipulated the massive computing power of his neural network, viewing and correcting for the changes in the singularity so that it stabilized despite nature's best efforts to destroy the microscopic abomination.

Raul shifted the controlling fields, drawing much more heavily on the power available to the system. Once again a gravitational pulse swept outward, this one larger than the last, possibly even detectable by Dr. Stephenson's instruments. The worm fiber bulged, quickly expanding to the size of a pinpoint visible to the human eye as Raul fought to reestablish control, something that required him to divert all available computational resources to the task. For several seconds the outcome of his efforts remained in doubt; then, as if it had just given up the fight, the new, larger worm fiber stabilized.

Without hesitation, Raul focused on the pinhole, changing the visible zoom level until he could see through it to the far side.

It was a perfect peephole, one side of which was here in the ship while the other side was wherever he chose. Raul recognized the outside of the building that housed Rho Division, but he did not have time to linger. Shifting the containment equations slightly, Raul experimented on moving the far end of the worm fiber. The first shift took him too far, the dense evergreen forest outside producing a momentary disorientation as he recalculated his position. British Columbia.

Three more jumps provided the necessary calibration of his equipment. Raul shifted the fiber back to central Los Alamos, moving it along rapidly now. The view froze on a familiar house, the windows now broken out by vandals, the flowers that had once graced the window boxes long since dead.

A momentary pang of remorse surged through Raul's mind at the thought of his dead father. Where was his mother? As Raul lingered, a sudden awareness of his rapidly dwindling power supply caused him to reassert self-control, once more moving the viewer along the highway at a speed no car could match. Reaching White Rock, Raul positioned the worm fiber outside another familiar house. It passed through the front door as if it had no more substance than a dream.

The living room was empty, as was the kitchen. A peek into the garage revealed that the family van was missing. So Heather must be out with her mom and dad. A wave of disappointment assaulted Raul, but he refused to allow it to slow him. Moving the viewer upstairs, he once again passed through a door, this time into Heather's bedroom.

Her bed was a double, the pillow covers and duvet done in beautiful hand-stitched floral patterns. As the power alarms sounded in his mind, Raul lingered just an instant longer, feeling his heart thumping in his chest as he stared at the place where Heather slept.

Allowing the worm fiber to collapse in upon itself as he powered the system down, Raul smiled. It would take several days to restore the energy reserves he had just used up. But when he did, he would be looking in on his old girlfriend once again. And next time he would make sure it happened around bedtime.

CHAPTER 65

With only the dim glow from the twin flat-panel computer monitors to combat it, the darkness crept through the room, a physical presence reminiscent of fog swallowing the Golden Gate Bridge. At the inner edge of the battleground where light and darkness struggled, the mahogany furniture was barely visible, the outlines blurry and indistinct. The smell of furniture polish hung in the air, adding a thickness that enhanced the room's claustrophobic contraction.

Dr. Stephenson leaned back in his chair, studying the recorded video stream from the starship's inner sanctum. Raul was performing as well as he had hoped, possibly even better.

Initially, Dr. Stephenson had been disappointed by the amount of time it had taken Raul to access and begin repairing sections of the starship's neural network. By the time he had gotten around to performing a self-modification to his own umbilical connection, Stephenson was beginning to wonder if he had made a mistake in selecting Raul as his subject. The lad was certainly bright enough to come to terms with his newly enhanced mental powers. The only question was the depth of the boy's psychosis, something that could either drive him to incredible achievement or leave him paralyzed with phobias from which there would be no recovery.

The operation that removed Raul's legs had been entirely unnecessary. That and the crude manner in which the umbilical connections had been established had been intended to provide motivation for change. Dr. Stephenson had been hoping to see Raul drive himself to redo the operation much sooner than he had. But now that the self-upgrade had been completed, the pace of Raul's advancement had quickened in a most gratifying manner.

The deputy director entered a command, and the computer screens shifted, the one on the right showing a new view of Raul hanging in the air, supported by the stasis field, which he now controlled. At the bottom of the screen, a timeline displayed exactly when each frame of the recording had been produced, the times calibrated through an atomic clock for accuracy before being encoded via closed-captioning into the video stream.

The other computer monitor was filled with instrument readings, each matched to its own timeline. The upper right corner of this monitor displayed a special set of readings. These had been received from the Ulysses spacecraft, now approaching the August 18 perihelion of its orbit around the sun.

The synchronization of all the data was tricky. It wasn't just a matter of matching the timelines. The times had to be adjusted based upon the locations and relative velocities of the instruments.

More of a problem was the sensitivity required of the instruments. He was looking for gravity waves, and those waves were weak. To measure a gravity wave required instruments to be calibrated to measure movements smaller than the nucleus of an atom. Getting rid of background noise generally required incredible efforts in vibrational shielding and damping. In addition, the devices had to be supercooled to close to absolute zero.

Only a few gravitational-wave experiments were being conducted around the world, and those were looking at relativistic objects such as supernovas or black holes. Fortunately, Dr. Stephenson's position allowed him to access all available data for the time period in question.

Raul had managed something truly remarkable. Two bursts of gravitational-wave activity had been measured during the day of this recording. The first of these had been quite small and might have passed unnoticed if not for the Doppler anomaly with the Ulysses spacecraft.

The second wave had been extraordinary, several orders of magnitude larger than any gravitational wave ever measured, a clear indication of a relativistic event in the near-Earth vicinity. Although scientists around the world were struggling to decide if the unexpected data was real or the result of faulty equipment, Dr. Stephenson knew precisely where it had occurred and the mechanism that had produced it. He had watched it happen.

Combined with the power surge his instruments had detected from the starship, Dr. Stephenson had been able to establish an exact timeline for the process. And that timeline confirmed his equations describing the third alien technology. If Raul could solve the power limitations under which he was currently operating, the starship would soon be supplying data that would provide the final answers Stephenson needed.

At that point, given the worldwide success of the first two alien technologies, the world governments would not hesitate to provide him the resources required for the next step. If they refused...well, he had another way to deal with that eventuality, although it would take every penny now flowing into his offshore bank accounts.

The image of the second alien starship popped into his thoughts. It was a lucky thing for the scientific team heading that investigation that Dr. Stephenson had been so busy with his work in Rho Laboratory. Otherwise, he would have had their collective asses in a sling long before now. He hadn't expected much, but those morons hadn't accomplished a damn thing.

Only the knowledge that the Second Ship's technology was far inferior to that of the starship here at Rho Laboratory kept him from taking direct control of that operation. That and the fact that the Second Ship was dead as a doornail while his was alive and under repair.

Dr. Stephenson stared at the image of Raul floating in the air, his gaze turned inward in concentration. It had been three weeks since the deputy director had set foot inside the inner section of the starship. Since Raul had gained control of the stasis field, it was prudent to wait.

So the deputy director would content himself with his observations and measurements while he let Raul keep working.

Dr. Stephenson smiled. As long as the kid remained useful, he would keep on living.

CHAPTER 66

After three weeks, Heather was amazed at the changes since she had started taking the antipsychotic drugs. As much as she had feared them and fought to keep from taking them, the daily dosage had turned out to be the best thing her parents could have done for her. She was sleeping again. She hadn't even known how much she had missed the ability to drift off to sleep and the wonderful feel of waking up to greet a new day.

Even more importantly, the disturbing mental fugues were gone. No more freaking everyone out while she made an unscheduled trip into zombie land. Her parents were so thrilled to have their daughter back to normal that their joy surpassed Heather's own.

There were a few downsides to the medication, but those were manageable. The biggest of these was the mild drowsiness she experienced after taking the pills. Heather had also acquired a very slight tremor in her left hand, something that Dr. Sigmund said was a fairly common side effect of the drug. While Dr. Sigmund was monitoring that, it was such a small effect that she had decided to stay with the drug, unwilling to change what was working unless it became absolutely necessary.

Heather had to agree with that logic. The only thing she hadn't shared with Dr. Sigmund was the troubling nature of her dreams. Usually Heather couldn't remember them. But these last few nights she had awakened with fragments of the same dream in her mind. A long black limousine lay on its roof against a tree, windows broken out, the gaping holes splattered with blood. As disturbing as this was, the viewpoint bothered her more. She appeared to be gazing at the limousine through some sort of telescope, the lens marked with a crosshair and tiny tick marks.

She concluded the dreams were probably just being caused by the bad news that had been all over the television. The FBI director had been assassinated, and that agent in North Dakota. All the news reports blamed the two killings on Jack Gregory, but despite a considerable body of evidence to back it up, Heather didn't believe it. For some reason the probability calculation in her head yielded only a 3.754 percent likelihood that Jack was the killer. After the way he had saved her life, the numbers would have to be a heck of a lot worse than that before she would believe it was Jack.

Sliding into her robe and slippers, Heather made her way down to the kitchen. Grabbing the can of Maxwell House from the cupboard, she spooned the coffee into the filter basket, poured in a container of water, and turned on the pot. Another oddity.

She had never liked coffee until three weeks ago, always making herself tea instead. The change had happened the morning after her first night's sleep, the day after she began taking the antipsychotic drug risperidone. She had slept until 6:30 a.m.

When she had walked down the stairs, the rich smell had been so enticing that she had asked her dad for a cup. That had been the first morning in a long while that she had sat at the breakfast table with her mom and dad, just enjoying their company. Something about that moment had etched a pleasurable association into her brain. Morning plus coffee equals comfort, or some nonsensical equation.

Without waiting for the pot to finish brewing, Heather poured herself a cup and returned the pot to its spot beneath the brewer. Sliding open the glass door that led to their back deck, Heather turned to look out to the east. The sun was just rising, the yellow brightness replacing the pink of sunrise. What a glorious day. She took it as a good omen for the first day of the new school year. After the summer she had endured, everything about school's return filled her with anticipation.

Her reverie was interrupted by her mom's arrival in the kitchen. By the time breakfast had come and gone, Heather found herself rushing to get through the shower and make her way over to the Smythe house. Mark and Jennifer were already downstairs waiting for her.

"You're looking perky this morning," Mark remarked, the worried look with which he had been watching her the last few days absent from his face.

"Thanks," Heather replied, sliding onto the couch.

"Let's just hope we're all feeling that way after the first day of school tomorrow," said Jennifer. "I'm not looking forward to the razzing we're likely to get over that science project."

"Look at it this way," Mark said with a smile. "We've already been thoroughly hosed. Might as well grin and bear it."

"Uh-huh," his twin snorted.

"Is that a new backpack?" Heather asked, pointing at the brightly colored bag beside the door.

"Yeah. Dad picked it out. This will be its first and last usage."

The look of disgust on Jennifer's face made Heather laugh despite her best efforts to contain it.

"I don't know," said Mark. "I think the school-colors thing you have going there shows good spirit. You just can't get too much green and gold."

Ignoring his sister's scowl, Mark tossed a pamphlet in Heather's lap.

"Have you taken a look at the student handbook?"

"Since when have you started reading the student handbook? How'd you even get one?"

"Mom picked it up at the PTA meeting. I thought it might be good for a few laughs."

"So was it?"

"I think a couple of rules got added just because of our junior year."

"Such as?"

"Well, for one thing, the school dances section expressly states that sophomores and freshmen are not permitted to attend junior-senior prom."

Heather chuckled. "They had that rule last year. It was waived because our junior class didn't raise enough money."

"Yes, but this year they highlighted it in boldfaced letters. And get this part: no peeing in the hallway."

Heather made a grab for the book, scanning rapidly down through its pages before she noticed the snicker.

"Mark!" Her foot just missed him as he dodged sideways. Fortunately, Jennifer landed a punch on his shoulder.

"Ouch."

"What does it say about displaying your butt in public?" Jennifer asked.

"OK, OK," Mark said, holding up his hands in protest. "I was just trying to add a little levity. No use getting personal."

Seeing his wink, Heather smiled. God, it was good to have things back to normal.

CHAPTER 67

The blackness in Mark's room softened as it moved away from the corners. Faint hints of red illuminated the objects that occupied the space, the luminosity changing as the red numerals on the digital clock switched to a new time: 4:16 a.m.

This time of night was the quietest. Even the latest of night owls had already found a way home from whatever sport had kept them out and about. Before long, folks on the early shift would be making their way to relieve sleepy compatriots at the local mini-marts, but not yet.

Sitting up in his bed, his back propped up by a pile of pillows, Mark let his eyes roam freely. His night vision was improving with use, but then again, what wasn't?

No longer requiring sleep left plenty of extra time for thinking. It was something Mark was thankful for. The days were filled so full of activities that there was little time for learning about the ongoing changes to his mind and body.

The list scrolled through his mind: strength and reflexes that were off the charts, perfect memory, enhanced hearing, enhanced vision, speed-reading. Although his thought processes were up across the board, he had acquired a special affinity for languages that was every bit as amazing as Heather's savant mathematical abilities and Jennifer's computer wizardry. It had gotten to the point that his mind could master a language as he listened to it or read it.

Mark had discovered another odd ability by accident, during one of his language practice sessions. He had been listening to an online language course, copying the native speakers' pronunciations and intonations, when Jennifer had walked into his room.

"You sound just like the people on the tape."

"Thanks," Mark had replied.

"No. I mean exactly like them," Jennifer had said. "The men and the women."

"Right."

"Play it back in your head if you don't want to believe me," Jennifer had called over her shoulder as she ducked back out into the hallway.

As he thought back on it now, his twin sister had been right. Replaying the scene in his mind, he compared the sounds that had come from his mouth to those from the speakers. He had been so intent upon matching the tones of the native speakers that he had somehow managed to mimic their voices so effectively he could barely hear any difference from the original.

He would have been thrilled with his progress if not for the difficulties he had been having controlling his emotions. Yesterday he had even snapped at his mother, an action that brought tears to her eyes. And although he had apologized, guilt had plagued him the rest of the day.

Mark's raging adrenaline rushes presented such a danger that he had been focusing his attention on finding a way to control them. So far he had enjoyed only limited success. Meditation worked but wasn't practical. Most situations that produced an emotional response found him in the middle of an activity, which provided no opportunity to sit down, cross his legs, and achieve a meditative state.

While meditation had its limitations, it provided complete relief, something that had led Mark to practice it every chance he got. He had read every book and article he could get his hands on about the various meditation techniques.

A Rosicrucian technique had become his favorite, allowing him to achieve the feeling that his mind was truly disconnected from his body, free to float around as he willed it. Starting with a sequence of deep, slow breaths, Mark focused on feeling just his toes, one at a time. Once his mind was completely focused on a single toe, he would allow his consciousness to move to the next one, gradually working his way up the body until it got to his scalp. Although the technique took a considerable amount of time, the euphoria he felt upon completing the exercise made him reluctant to come back down. Mark was sure that the key to self-control lay buried in a deeper understanding and skill with meditation, but so far that key had eluded him.

As he sat there in the darkness, a sudden sense of being watched nudged him, the intensity of the feeling making his scalp tingle.

Night's blackness draped the outside of his window, its face unbroken by any hint of a presence there. His door was closed, and there was no sign that someone stood waiting just beyond that. Mark's senses heightened to such a level that he could taste the air moving in and out of his mouth. He allowed them to sweep the room free from his conscious will, relying on the thought that whatever hidden clue had alerted him would guide him to the source.

Down the hall, he could hear Jennifer's rhythmic breathing. No doubt she was as awake as he was, lost in her own thoughts and meditations.

Whatever it was that had disturbed him felt closer than Jennifer. Not far at all. The conviction that something was there in the room with him grew stronger with each passing second, although he couldn't see anything that appeared to be out of place.

The glowing red numerals on the clock beside his bed shifted to 4:24. The subtle change in room lighting would have been nearly invisible to him only a few months earlier, but now the slight shift in intensity pulled his gaze to a spot an arm's length past the foot of his bed, just below eye level. There was nothing there, just a general sense of wrongness about that point in space.

As Mark focused his vision at that spot, the clock numerals changed once again. It happened so quickly that he could almost believe he had imagined it, but he hadn't. Mark played the scene back in his mind. In that instant when the light had changed, the smallest of glints had reflected back at him, as if from a tiny bubble of dew at the tip of a blade of grass.

Swinging his legs out from under the covers, Mark rose from the bed, keeping his eyes locked on the tiny pinpoint of wrongness as he moved slowly toward it. Whatever it was, it was damn hard to see, even with his enhanced neural pathways processing the data. Reaching a spot only a couple of feet away from whatever it was, Mark stopped.

Despite the dim light, he could now see the distortion more clearly. There was nothing there except for a pinpoint that blurred his vision of what lay beyond. There was no sign of whatever might be causing the distortion.

Mark circled the spot slowly, positioning himself so he could look back through it toward the glowing clock on his nightstand. There it was, suspended in the air. A tiny pinpoint of nothingness, ever so slightly twisting the light that passed through it.

Something about the oddity hanging there in the air raised the hair along the back of Mark's neck, sending a little shiver down his arms. Whatever it was, it wasn't a natural phenomenon. Of that Mark was certain.

Leaning in so close that his eye was less than an inch away from the disturbance, Mark focused his consciousness, letting every one of his neurally enhanced senses dance across it. No sound issued forth, but the air in its vicinity seemed different, as if it had acquired texture from the thing's proximity.

Although it was so small that it would have been invisible to most people, the center of the pinpoint looked different, almost like a hole into another place. As Mark moved in closer, trying to understand what he was seeing, a vision of another room resolved itself in his mind. From his limited perspective, he could see only a fraction of the place, just enough to see that it was cluttered with strange cables and equipment, the scene lit with a dim gray, shadowless light.

Ever so slowly, Mark moved around the pinhole, his view of the strange room changing as he did. Something moved at the corner of his field of view, but when he shifted to get a better angle, it was gone. Suddenly, something blocked the other side of the pinhole, completely obscuring his view of the room beyond. Mark inhaled deeply, struggling to slow his racing heart.

There, staring back at him from the far side of the distortion, was a dark-brown human eye.

CHAPTER 68

Darkness draped this small section of the quiet White Rock residential neighborhood. It pushed up against the houses, the streetlamp that normally pushed back at it having burned out two nights ago. It flowed in close, snuggling, tasting the shadowed corners like a lover nibbling at an enticing earlobe.

Raul watched the two houses, his gaze lingering on the house on the right before turning toward the other. For the last several weeks, he had worked around the clock to bring two more of the microscopic power conversion cells online. He had intended to make use of that power much earlier last night, hoping to catch a view of Heather in her bath.

But Dr. Stephenson had picked that time to pay Raul a visit, one that had lasted through the evening and well into the early morning hours. As annoyed as Raul had been at the interruption of his plans, Stephenson's conversation had been intensely interesting, so interesting that it had altered Raul's thoughts about his future.

After Dr. Stephenson had left, Raul considered waiting for another night to look in on Heather. Given the power consumption caused by the creation and use of the worm fiber, it would take him several days to recharge, even with his new power cells. To proceed was completely illogical, but he had waited so long to see her that he couldn't bring himself to wait, not even one more night.

Now here he was, his worm-fiber pinhole positioned just past the end of her driveway, about to change his mind. Even if he did look in on Heather, it would only make things worse, seeing her lying in her bed bundled up in covers, a nightmare of frustration. Raul directed his gaze to the left.

Mark Smythe, the jock who imagined himself as Heather's protector. That was his house.

Anger surged through Raul's brain, the feeling transmitted around the neural network within the Rho Ship and then returned to him, its edge honed to razor sharpness. An old enemy was near, one who enjoyed a physical proximity to Heather that Raul was currently denied.

His perspective shifted as he willed the worm fiber forward, passing through the wall of the Smythe house, then upward into the hallway upstairs. On one side of the stairway, a single closed door awaited, while in the other direction three doors led into rooms, two on the left side of the hall and one at the far end.

Certainly the master bedroom would be the one off by itself, that direction offering nothing of interest to Raul. His attention focused on the door at the far end of the hallway. That would be the one. Raul was sure of it. The athlete would have been the dominant of the two children, naturally acquiring the better bedroom at an early age.

The worm fiber moved in that direction, slowly now. It passed through the door and into the room beyond, Raul's awareness taking in every detail of the dimly lit room.

Bringing the fiber to a stop just beyond the foot of the bed, Raul shifted the light amplification of the scene, letting his altered perceptions change the image until it appeared as light as if the midday sun were directly overhead. Unlike squinting through a tiny pinhole, the unique capabilities of the alien computing system allowed him to view the scene from any angle, a clear projection into his mind.

Instead of being asleep, Mark Smythe sat at the head of his bed, his legs crossed in a deep meditative posture. The jerk thought he was Bruce Lee or something.

A gradual change moved over Smythe's features. The muscles around his eyes tightened, his gaze sweeping the room as if he was looking for something. Hard as it was to imagine, Smythe seemed to have somehow sensed the presence of the worm fiber and was actively searching for it.

But that was impossible. The distortion itself was no larger than the point of a pin. Nobody's eyesight was good enough to see that from ten feet away, even in broad daylight. Especially not in a dark bedroom. But despite all logic to the contrary, Smythe's eyes locked directly on the pinhole.

Swinging his legs off the bed, Smythe arose, moving straight toward the fiber. At a distance of a couple of feet, he paused, circling slowly around Raul's viewport, his gaze never wavering from the lock it had on the target.

Raul adjusted his own viewpoint, increasing the zoom on the face that leaned closer. Amazingly, Smythe seemed to be trying to see through the worm fiber from the other side. If he could see the pinhole, then perhaps he could get a glimpse of what lay beyond.

Raul moved, letting the stasis field sweep him toward the spot where his end of the worm fiber hung amid the machinery. So the bastard was trying to see him. Fine.

Raul leaned in, moving his one remaining eyeball within an inch of the worm fiber, his anger boiling through the neural net.

View this, bitch.

Raul held the pose for a full ten seconds before initiating the command that dissipated the localized gravitational distortion. He continued to stare at the spot long after it had gone.

Smythe. What was it with that guy? Applying every bit of the neural network that now augmented his brain, Raul forced himself to calm down, focusing his thoughts on his enemy.

For the longest time Raul had known there was something unusual about Mark Smythe. It was amazing he hadn't analyzed it before now. Smythe had shown oddities that went beyond being just an amazing high-school athlete.

Coordination was one thing, but Raul had seen the guy slam the captain of the football team up against a locker and hold him there with one hand. At the time, Raul thought that Doug Brindall had let Mark get away with it to avoid a suspension for fighting. But now, thinking back on it, a different conclusion presented itself. Smythe had been the one holding back. The power in that grip was enough to snap the quarterback's neck, and Doug had known it.

What had the tabloids said about Smythe? Something about his being an alien. That was ridiculous. But he was a freak, and his dad worked on the Rho Project, something that Raul knew a bit about.

But how much did he really know? While he was now a part of the alien ship and had access to the functional portion of its neural network, that didn't mean he knew much about the rest of the Rho Project. Despite last night's enlightening conversation, there was no doubt that Dr. Stephenson was keeping many things from him.

The nanite research was one piece of the puzzle. Certainly, other people had been subjects for that testing. It only stood to reason that Smythe had undergone some additional type of modification.

A new wave of anger swept through Raul's neural network. So Dr. Stephenson thought his other pet pupil was good enough to let out in public, made into some freakish superstar athlete, while Raul was having his legs amputated and being locked away in the ship.

Well screw him. Screw them both.

The stasis field lifted Raul up toward the ceiling, to a spot where he could survey the entire room, a thin smile splitting his lips.

If it meant he had to bring more of the ship back online to be able to reach out and touch them, then that was exactly what he was going to do.

CHAPTER 69

It was a subtle change, barely noticeable, even to Mark's enhanced synapses. One second the tiny disturbance was there, hanging in the air three feet from his bed; then it was gone. Without having to look around, he knew it had departed. As strange as his room had felt only a moment earlier, the space now radiated normality.

If he hadn't been able to replay the events in his mind, Mark might have thought that he had just experienced a waking dream. But the aberration had been all too real, a tiny window to another place. Mark had peered through it, although his glimpse had been severely limited by his narrow field of view. With such a small, short look, he didn't have any idea what the purpose was of the equipment he had seen, nor of the strange cables that snaked around it.

Mark did know one thing. Someone had been watching him from the far side, and he had to assume that that person's view had been superior to his.

Walking to the window, Mark looked out across the fifty feet of lawn that separated the side of his house from Heather's. The sky had lightened to the point that the predawn contrast made the ground look darker than before.

Outside, the darkness seemed to thicken as he watched, moving between the two homes like a living thing, coiling around Heather's house, seeking entrance. The burned-out bulb of the nearest streetlamp provided no opposition to the encroaching blackness.

Mark shook his head to clear the illusion. Unable to shake the morbid sense of dread that assailed him, Mark grabbed his sweats from the back of the chair, dressing quickly. He left the room and made his way silently downstairs, then out the front door into his driveway.

The eastern sky was much lighter now, laced with streaks of pale lavender where it touched the mountains. A car moved along the street headed toward the main highway, its headlights sweeping past his house in twin beams that pushed at the shadows. Then it was by, its twin red taillights flashing brighter at the stop sign before disappearing around the corner.

As the car's headlights receded, the sense that the darkness was a living thing flowing back between the houses returned stronger than before. Mark turned toward the McFarland house, making his way toward the gap he had observed from his window. Unlike in some of the newer residential areas, no wall separated the houses here.

An unofficial lawn-mower boundary was barely visible, its location changing from week to week depending on whether Mark's dad or Heather's had been the last to operate his riding mower. Mark paused at the grass boundary.

To his eyes, the darkness hid nothing, merely providing a different spectrum from daylight, a detailed grayscale image lacking the warmth of the daylight colors. Standing here in the grass, looking out across the lawn at Heather's house, the dark feeling acquired a name: fear. Not for himself, but for her.

He moved around behind the McFarland house, letting his feet take him where they would. With every passing second, the sky lightened, fading the predawn shadows into the background. Heather's back lawn, like his own, ran back about fifty feet from the house before descending steeply into the rocky canyon below. There was a point just before the edge where the lawn refused to venture, the abundance of pine needles making the soil too acidic for growth.

When this neighborhood had first been built, the trees had been cut back away from the houses, so that now only one huge pine remained, rising up outside Heather's window, just around the far corner of the house. Mark moved toward it, his thoughts involuntarily turning to the Rag Man. Odd. Maybe it was because this was the tree he had climbed to kidnap her from her room.

It didn't really matter. That bastard wasn't going to threaten anyone, ever again. Jack Gregory had seen to that.

As he moved behind the McFarlands' back deck and rounded the corner, Mark glanced up at Heather's window. Her bedroom light was on. Not surprising. Heather had always been an early riser, and even though she was sleeping again, the antipsychotic drugs had not changed that.

Searching for anything that might have elevated his concern to its current level, Mark spun in a slow circle. Nothing. Not a goddamn thing out of the ordinary.

Yeah, right—nothing but a tiny hole in the fabric of the universe materializing in his bedroom. That was damn sure enough to freak anybody out.

Now that he thought about it, it was a miracle he wasn't running around waving his arms and screaming, "Oh my God! We're all gonna die!"

Not that most people would believe him. Heather would. But he wasn't going to tell her, at least not yet. She'd been through so much lately that he wasn't about to lay more stress on her. Besides, whatever it was had been looking at him.

Something like that had to have its origins in the Rho Project. But why would it look in on a high-school kid? Maybe Jennifer had been right about his attracting too much attention to himself. Whatever it was, Mark wanted to have a theory before he discussed this with the two girls.

With one more glance up at Heather's window, Mark turned back toward his house. At least for now, this was his problem and he would figure it out on his own.

CHAPTER 70

Indian summer. Janet had grown up in the Northeast, where that term meant a late fall return to warmer weather. Here in the high desert of New Mexico, it had taken on a whole new meaning. Late summer storms had become a daily occurrence, their arrival presaged by towering thunderheads trailing curtains of rain, stabbing at the ground with their jagged spears of lightning and shaking the canyons with the heavy rumble of thunder. The wall of thunderheads building in the distance showed every indication of delivering another of the violent performances that made her wonder if the small hogan could remain standing.

Janet loved the storms for the diversion they provided from the strands of loneliness with which her isolation bound her. Jack had been gone for three weeks. Like some great crocodile sliding into the Nile, he had departed, leaving her alone. And although she had not heard from him directly, she knew he was out there, somewhere back East. He had given her specific instructions to stay put and stay focused, correlating the pieces of the puzzle as she hacked her way through secure networks around the globe.

So Janet had stayed, making use of the quantum twin link to their source's magical Internet gateway. She still had no idea what technology enabled her to enter precise coordinates and then connect to any network at that location. The systems that attracted her interest were all highly classified networks, physically isolated from any type of external access and protected by the best shielding that could be constructed.

But despite their layers of protection, the classified networks she targeted might as well have been broadcasting an open Wi-Fi signal. It was as if she had just plugged a Cat 6 cable into the remote hub. Once she was in, the data access was easy. Hardly anyone bothered to encrypt data on the network, relying on the protection provided by the network itself. Unfortunately, that was where the easy part ended. There was so much data to search, so many subnets to access, that finding the clues she needed was daunting.

If Janet hadn't been quite as good as Jack knew she was, the task might well have been impossible. It was one of the reasons he had left her here, in the most secure location available to them, a place that provided no distractions from her task.

Janet pushed back from the laptop and glanced down at her stomach. She was starting to show. Somehow, Jack had seen it weeks ago. He had actually seemed pleasantly surprised that she was pregnant, a response that had shocked her to her core.

Not that she had expected him to fly into a rage or anything like that. Jack never lost control. Janet wasn't really sure what she had expected, just not happiness. But then again, maybe she had misread him.

Standing up, she moved outside the small hogan that had become her home, at least for the indeterminate future. The wooden windmill spun in the gusty afternoon breeze, the rise and fall of the pump shaft producing a rhythmic thumping sound as it performed its dual duty of filling the tank with water and driving the small electric generator, which provided the trickle charge to the batteries.

"*Ya'at'eeh.*"

The Navajo greeting turned Janet toward Tall Bear as he stepped out of the juniper thicket some thirty feet east of the hut. Over his shoulder he carried a large burlap bag.

"Tall Bear. It's good to see you." Janet smiled as she moved toward him. She doubted that anyone else besides Jack could slip up on her unnoticed the way Tall Bear could.

"I figured you would be getting low on groceries," he said, pausing just long enough to return her hug before ducking into the hogan to set down the heavy bag. Straightening once again, Tall Bear nodded. "I like what you've done with the place."

Janet's laugh brought the hint of a smile to his lips.

It had become a standard joke on these delivery visits. The hogan was a typical eight-sided female hogan with log walls, dirt-covered roof, dirt floor, and no windows. Its single door opened to the east in order to welcome the dawning of the new day. At one time it had been the principal type of Navajo family abode; although still common, hogans were rarely used for housing anymore. This far back on the reservation, the old building, the accompanying small mud sweat lodge, windmill, outdoor mud oven, and water trough might as well have been invisible, so well did they blend with the rugged canyon country that surrounded them.

The only furniture was the small square table, four wooden chairs, and a wood-post double bed. Janet had taken a couple of the tanned deer hides from the walls and spread them out as rugs. She had also fashioned a lampshade of sorts for the bare bulb, which dangled on a cord from the ceiling. A large pottery water basin and pitcher sat atop a crate against the north wall, the closest thing this place had ever seen to running water.

A refrigerator was out of the question. Even a small one would drain too much of the precious electrical supply that the windmill generator could produce. That was dedicated to her laptop, the single lightbulb, and her one luxury, a small oscillating fan.

"So what goodies have you brought me today?"

"Well, let's see." Tall Bear dumped the contents of the sack onto the floor.

"Hmmm. Meals ready to eat. Beans. Freeze-dried entrées. The works."

"Don't forget the toiletries. You know the elders didn't have the luxury of those things."

Janet raised an eyebrow. "Much as I love roughing it, TP is high on my priority list. But where are my manners? Thanks again for hauling all these supplies up here. Have a seat while I get you some water."

Tall Bear slid onto one of the chairs as Janet grabbed the pitcher, filling a tin cup and setting it on the table in front of her friend. It was odd to think of him that way, but that was exactly what he had become. The tall Navajo cop, with his long raven hair hanging below his shoulders, had proven his reliability time and again. Not only had he guided them to this remote hideaway, but he had been their only means of getting critical supplies from town. While she and Jack were capable of sustaining themselves off the land indefinitely, Tall Bear's help had given them a base of operation.

Besides that, Jack trusted the man, and Jack's intuition about such things was never wrong.

"So what's the news from civilization?" Janet asked, sliding into a chair across from him.

"Internet down?"

"You know what I mean. What's the local gossip?"

Although she had access to all the news sites, Janet had found the Navajo a font of information. For one thing, he was a cop and a damn good one. More importantly, he was privy to a network of sources that stretched across the country and beyond, a web of communication links among native communities dotting North, Central, and South America. Despite all her years working with the CIA, DIA, and NSA, Janet was stunned by the true reach and capabilities of that network. As tightly secretive as was the cell structure within Al Qaeda and its affiliates, the cellular nature of these native communities put that to shame. And invariably, within each grouping of native people there was a subgroup in which the old longing for independence ran deep.

Tall Bear leaned back in his chair, rocking it back until it balanced precariously on two legs, his hand interlaced in his long black hair.

"It's not good. This nanite goo is the new meth, only the world is addicted to this stuff even before they've taken a hit. Shit. Everybody wants it."

Janet nodded. "From what I see on the Net, the UN is pushing pretty damn hard to speed the public release. Luckily, the president seems to have had a change of heart on how fast he wants to push it out the door."

"Only because some of his right-wing base is in rebellion. But he won't be able to hold back too long. There are whispers about a new black-market source for the stuff, distribution through the drug cartels, that sort of thing."

"It's gonna get ugly."

"Already is. Beheading has become the preferred gangland method of execution. They don't know who's on the juice, and they just aren't taking chances."

"So is the new source real?"

"Hard to say for sure. At first, the stuff was only available from the blood of someone who had undergone the treatment. But it seems like there is just too much available on the market. Of course, a lot of the stuff is probably fake."

"It's pretty easy to check whether someone got the real stuff or not. Just stick a knife in them."

"And that's the trouble. There are way too many reports of freak healers to think they are all false. For there to be a second source, someone might have reverse-engineered the formula."

"Or there is a leak in the Los Alamos security."

"Wouldn't be the first time." Tall Bear frowned. "But I think something else is going on. I just can't quite put my finger on it. This has the feel of powerful sponsorship within our own government."

"Why do you say that?"

"Call it a hunch. The way this is being investigated by the FBI and Treasury feels wrong. The whole thing feels more like a cover-up than a real investigation."

The rumble of thunder echoed through the canyons outside the hogan. Tall Bear rose from his seat.

"Well, I better be getting back to the Jeep. It's a two-mile hike, and it sounds like I might get wet if I don't hurry."

"You could wait out the storm here," Janet offered.

"Can't. I go on duty at six o'clock, and there are a couple of other errands I need to run before then."

Janet followed him outside and hugged him again. "Well, thanks for the supplies and the company."

As Tall Bear stepped back, he glanced down at her stomach. "How're you feeling?"

Janet patted her stomach and smiled. "Everything seems to be progressing normally."

"Morning sickness?"

"Not yet."

For just a moment, it seemed that a shadow passed across Tall Bear's features. Then he smiled. "Not all women get it. Maybe you're one of the lucky ones."

"One can only hope."

"Have you heard from Jack?"

"Not in over a week. When I need to get information to him, I encrypt it and post it on one of the public Internet sites we both monitor. Jack does the same."

"Does he know you're pregnant?"

"Yes."

"Sorry. You can tell me it's none of my business."

"Don't worry. I'm not shy."

Tall Bear laughed as he turned away. "That thought never occurred to me."

CHAPTER 71

Jennifer sat on Heather's right, looking out the school bus window intently enough to make Heather wonder whether the scenery along the route to Los Alamos High had changed. Mark sat by himself two rows up. That was probably a good thing. She didn't want to talk to him right now. It had been a long time since she had been this mad at anyone, and for it to be Mark that she was angry with was a new experience, one that she could have done without.

Heather had awakened on the first day of school with that special thrill of anticipation that this day always gave her. What in the world had possessed him to bring her down like this?

Heather had known for a while that Mark was less than thrilled with the idea that her parents had her on antipsychotic meds. Until this morning, he had never directly challenged her on the subject. But whatever good sense he had shown heretofore had evaporated as they waited for the bus. He'd actually had the nerve to say that her mom and dad were drugging her out of her mind and that she was crazy for knuckling under to their wishes.

If she hadn't been quite so mad, Heather was sure she would have been reduced to tears by the verbal assault from someone she loved so dearly. She wasn't going to let that happen, though. Mark wasn't the one suffering from the horrifying mental fugues that had been ripping apart her reality, leaving her trembling with fear that she might completely lose her mind. He had no right to judge her or her parents. No right.

A sudden jolt as the rear tires of the bus climbed up over the curb as it turned in to the high school brought Heather's thoughts back to the present. New bus driver. Heather hoped the bumpy entrance to the school grounds wasn't a sign of things to come. In response to her mental question, the image of her old Magic 8 Ball toy came to mind, the answer swimming into view through the blue liquid beneath its lens.

"Don't count on it."

Without bothering to dwell on the unpleasant thought, Heather allowed herself to be swept from her seat, carried along by the excited throng toward the entrance to the high school, and then into the hallway beyond. When she glanced around, Mark was gone, as was Jennifer. So much the better. All she wanted right now was some sense of return to normality, something that the bustling high-school hallway promised to deliver.

First-day activities consumed her: class schedules, new teachers, book issue, locker assignment, assembly. Most of her classmates seemed genuinely happy to see her.

Only Paulette Carlton and her troupe of snobettes got in her face.

"Look what we have here," Paulette exclaimed with an expert flip of her long blond hair. "A certified national science contest award winner. Nation's biggest cheat."

The other three girls, all members of the cheerleading squad, laughed loudly as they passed by in Paulette's wake, Heather's scowl lost on their backsides. Watching them from this angle, Heather could understand their popularity with the boys: lots of waggle and vocabularies that didn't include the word *no*.

Grabbing her chemistry notebook from the locker, Heather pushed the pride of Los Alamos High School's cheerleading squad from her mind and headed toward her next class.

A small group had gathered just outside the classroom, and to Heather's dismay, she saw that Paulette and the kitty cats were among them. Just as she was about to put her head down and duck by the cluster into the classroom, Heather caught a glimpse of the person at the center of everyone's attention.

Jennifer Smythe stood smiling and chatting amiably, the group around her as enthralled by her presence as if Elvis had just walked into the building. Heather stopped to stare. Even the cheerleaders appeared to be trying to crowd nearer, as if they couldn't bear to be excluded from Jen's inner circle of admirers.

Unable to believe the evidence presented by her own eyes, Heather edged closer, ignoring the sound of the bell calling her to class. Suddenly, Jennifer's laughing eyes caught her own and a feeling of gentle longing filled her mind. As Heather watched Jennifer turn that sparkling gaze from person to person, a chill spread through her body.

With the probability equations forming a torrent in her head, Heather understood. Her shy little friend was in the midst of becoming. The only question was...becoming what?

CHAPTER 72

"Coach, I'd love to go out for the football team, but I can't."

Mark knew that the words sounded false as they passed through his lips. Coach Crawford's eyes locked him in place.

"I want you to listen to me, son. I would never talk to you like this if I hadn't already had a discussion with your parents. Your father told me he had encouraged you to try out for the football team. I'm sure you know that he was an all-state defensive end when he went to high school in Albuquerque."

Mark nodded. *Oh crap, here it comes*, he thought.

"Now I know that you see a future for yourself in college basketball, and I understand why Coach Dickey doesn't want you to risk injury playing football, but the truth of the matter is that high school is what makes a young man. If you look at the great athletes, the greatest among them excelled in multiple sports. They never let fear make their decisions for them. Not fear of failure. Not fear of injury. Hell, not even fear of a tough coach.

"They believed in themselves. It's that kind of belief that makes a winner. Do you understand what I'm saying, Mark?"

Mark swallowed hard. "Yes, Coach. I believe so."

Coach Crawford slapped his shoulder firmly enough for it to be heard across the hallway. "Good. I'm not going to ask you to make a decision right now. You made your initial choice when you didn't come out for summer tryouts and two-a-day practices. Your muscle definition says you have a great work ethic and self-motivation. If you give it a chance, football will give you the confidence and belief in yourself it takes to be a real winner."

He patted Mark on the shoulder once again. "Think about what I said."

Before Mark could respond, the coach turned and walked down the hall toward the gymnasium. Mark stood by his locker, watching the coach disappear into the crowd of students hurrying on to their next classes.

Great. He was being spied on by some Rho Project anomaly. He had made Heather so angry that she wasn't even looking at him, much less speaking to him. Now the high-school football coach had implied he was a coward for not trying out for the football team. Could the first day back at school get any better?

The real pisser was that Mark wanted to play football, wanted it more than he wanted to play basketball. He wasn't the least bit worried about getting hurt. What worried him was that he couldn't control his adrenaline. In the rush of excitement, he might hurt someone horribly.

A year ago he would have gone for it, figuring that his enhanced reflexes would allow him to keep from hitting anyone too hard. That was even truer now. What scared the crap out of him was that, in the heat of the moment, he might *want* to hurt someone. Shit. All it took to send him into an adrenaline-stoked rage was for Heather to smile at some boy down the hall. And it didn't seem too likely that the referees would let him call time-out after every play so he could meditate.

"Mark Smythe!"

The authoritative tone spun his head in the direction of the sound.

Principal Zumwalt stood three feet away, his gaze locked on Mark's face. "Come with me, young man."

Without waiting for a response, the principal strode away down the hall toward his office with Mark in his wake, the students parting around them like the Red Sea for Moses. As they stepped into his office, Principal Zumwalt motioned for Mark to take a seat and then closed the door behind him.

The principal moved around his desk, seating himself so that he stared at Mark across steepled fingers. As the silence dragged on, Mark began to wonder if he was expected to be the first to start talking. However, since he had no idea why he was even sitting here, he resisted the impulse to speak.

"Mark, I know that Coach Crawford spoke to you about trying out for the football team. I want you to know that his approach was out of line and I will be speaking to him about it."

"Sir, I appreciate it, but that's not really necessary."

"In my mind it is. And I wish that were the reason that I called you to my office."

Principal Zumwalt paused again, and with each passing second, the oppressive atmosphere of the closed office deepened.

"There are times when being a high-school principal is unpleasant in the extreme. Although what I am about to tell you affects your sister and Heather McFarland as well, I called you in first since you are the most deeply impacted.

"The Los Alamos School Board met last night to discuss proposed sanctions for the alleged plagiarism that led to your team's disqualification from the national science competition."

Mark inhaled deeply. Oh Jesus, not that again.

"Even though no formal finding was issued by the judges, the school board felt obliged to reexamine the facts of the incident to see if you violated school standards in a way that brought dishonor to this institution and to the community as a whole.

"I'm sorry to have to tell you this, but the board has decided that all three of the members of your science team will be banned from all extracurricular activities for the entire school year."

Mark was too stunned to speak.

"That means you are banned from participation in high-school clubs, band, and high-school athletic teams. For you that means no basketball."

Mark swallowed hard to clear his throat. "But, sir, surely there is something we can do, some appeal we can make."

"I'm afraid not. The school board is the final authority in this matter, and they have spoken. I'm sorry."

Unable to remain sitting, Mark rose to his feet. For several seconds he stood there staring at Principal Zumwalt, feeling as sick as if he had just been kicked in the groin. Unable to find anything else to say, he merely nodded, then turned and walked out of the office into a suddenly alien hallway.

Rage at the injustice of it all rose up within him until he found himself shaking. Desperate to get outside before he did something he would regret, Mark stumbled through the front doorway and began running along the highway toward home.

If they didn't want him playing basketball, fine. He didn't want to play for that goddamn intellectual-snob high school anyway. As the ground swept past beneath his feet, a single thought hammered the inside of his skull.

Screw them. Screw them all.

CHAPTER 73

El Chupacabra. The blood beast of the shadows, a creature of the South American night, seldom glimpsed and never caught.

Eduardo removed the lens cover from the scope and settled into his hide position. He had not picked the nickname that now provoked such fear throughout the Colombian cartels, but it suited him. He was death incarnate. He didn't just enjoy killing. It sustained him.

There were only two other professional killers who could be compared with him. One was Carlos the Jackal, hardly a worthy comparison. The other was still out there among the sheep, very much like himself. Hunting. But the one known as the Ripper would come for him. Eduardo would see to that. And then El Chupacabra would be the only name whispered in dark places.

But right now, business called. Below him, the George Washington Parkway rounded a gradual bend along the west bank of the Potomac, the heavy foliage ensuring he could not be seen from the ground, especially not from the highway. Two narrow windows through the trees provided twin sight lines to the road. The crosshairs steadied on the nearest section of highway.

Killing a president wasn't supposed to be easy. The biggest problem was a general dearth of information critical to making the hit. The US Secret Service was very, very good at what it did, and one of the things it did was protect the specific information that made killing easy. Travel by motorcade was one of the times when the president was most vulnerable, since the entire route could not be as thoroughly secured as the departure and destination points. Therefore, a combination of armor, deception, and misdirection were the primary tools used to ensure the president's safety.

Which car the president was riding in, his seating position in the car, the exact route of the motorcade, the time of departure—all of these were zealously guarded secrets. But not today. Eduardo's inside source had provided incredible detail, the last update coming in via encrypted text message just five minutes ago. Everything was go.

As the police escort entered his peripheral vision and then moved through the crosshairs, Eduardo felt the familiar tingle where his cheek welded itself to the stock of the AS50 sniper rifle, down along his arm and into his hand, terminating where his finger rested against the trigger. In rapid succession, the vehicles flashed across his sight line as he counted. Now!

Although it was secured to the thick tree branch in a vise and despite the weapon's incredible recoil-damping mechanism, the recoil of the three incendiary, armor-piercing fifty-caliber rounds rocked the weapon back into his shoulder. It didn't matter. The killing pattern had been perfect, the first round entering through the forward edge of the armored limousine roof, each subsequent round four inches behind it.

Without waiting for any reaction from the convoy, Eduardo grabbed the handle that dangled below his branch and let himself fall outward. His momentum snapped the string that had secured the pulley in place and swept him down the steeply angled cable into a thicket on the water's edge.

Filling his lungs with air, he slipped beneath the river's murky surface, feeling his way along the rope that guided him down to the submerged scuba gear. Opening the valve on the tank, he cleared his mask, then grabbed the underwater sled that would pull him to safety.

As the propeller spun up, El Chupacabra smiled inside the scuba mask. Killing a president shouldn't be this easy.

CHAPTER 74

The cacophony in the White House briefing room made it difficult for the television audience to discern what was being said. In the midst of the melee, CNN's star White House reporter, Rolf Larson, held sway.

"As we have been reporting for the last hour and a half, the president of the United States was assassinated this morning as the presidential motorcade made its way toward a political rally in Rockville, Maryland. Despite the best efforts of the staff at Walter Reed National Military Medical Center, President Harris was pronounced dead at ten twenty-five a.m., leaving this city and the rest of the country in shock.

"Although details of the assassination remain unclear, sources within the FBI and the Department of the Treasury indicate that it is only a matter of time before the killer is caught and brought to justice. Even now a broad net has been cast around the

Washington, DC, area, with all highways and airports shut down, ports and waterways sealed, so the assassin cannot escape."

The reporter paused as the CNN anchor interrupted. "Rolf, this is Karen Whitcomb. Can you tell us if you are hearing anything from your extensive contacts within the administration and the Justice Department about who the killer might be?"

Rolf nodded into the camera. "Karen, although no one is willing to go on record at this early stage of the investigation, my sources are telling me that this is almost certainly the work of the same man believed to have conducted a string of recent assassinations. I am, of course, speaking of the man at the top of the most-wanted list of every law enforcement agency in this country. Jack Gregory, better known by his street name, the Ripper."

"Rolf, this is truly shocking information. Thank you so much for the type of inside reporting that only you can deliver. I'm sorry, but I am getting word that the new president, formerly Vice President Gordon, is about to speak to the nation from the Oval Office. We go now to the president of the United States of America."

The image on camera shifted to the presidential desk in the Oval Office. The newly elevated president stared into the camera, framed by windows, his eyes shining with moisture as his jaw tightened with determined resolve.

"My fellow Americans. It is with deepest sadness that I assume the mantle of the presidency. We have all just endured a most terrible shock, one that has left the nation stunned with its loss."

President Gordon's eyes narrowed. "But before I speak of that loss, let me assure you, the American people, that this vicious murderer, who has attacked our nation, has failed in his principal aim. This cowardly act has accomplished nothing except to rob a generation of a fine leader, a man I was proud to call a friend. I assure you that the wise constitutional measures that the

Founding Fathers put in place are functioning. This government goes on without interruption.

"I also want to say something to the man who murdered our president. Know this. No matter where you run, no matter how deep you burrow—no power on earth can stop us from finding you. As president, I vow this on the Constitution of the United States of America."

President Gordon paused to clear his throat. "Now, let me speak of my friend. President Harris was a man of vision. He was a man who knew who he was, a man elected by the people of this country because they looked into his eyes and recognized a man who would always do what he believed was right.

"This fine man, a man I was proud to serve under, put his very life at risk by doing exactly what he pledged. He cracked open the dark shroud of secrecy that has hidden wondrous technologies away from mankind. By opening the Rho Project to worldwide view, he took a tremendous risk, one that has now cost him his life.

"Once again, I am here to say to this assassin and to those who sponsor him…you have failed! The people of the United States of America will never be cowed or intimidated. In the face of tribulation, we will persevere. If you think that, by this atrocity, you have slowed the release of Rho Project technologies, then you are sadly mistaken. You have only redoubled our national resolve."

The president dabbed at his damp eyes with a clenched knuckle.

"I pledge to you now that, as your president, I will follow through on the noble work started by this great man. I ask for your prayers and support in the difficult days to come. May God be with Mary Beth and the rest of the Harris family. May God be with us all."

CHAPTER 75

Garfield Kromly blinked into the glare of the headlights as he turned onto Jefferson Davis Highway. Shit, he was tired. Two a.m. and just getting home. Barely enough time to catch a cat-nap before heading back to Langley. A left on Fifteenth Street and then straight across Crystal Drive and he was back at the apartment he had called home for the last eleven years. Water Park Tower South.

The high-rise apartment tower, or condo if it tripped your trigger to call it that, ran north-south, bowing gently away from the river. It was exactly the opposite of its twin tower a little farther north. A pair of parentheses, offset from each other in an oddly artistic way, each having a side that looked out over the Potomac River, just north of Ronald Reagan Washington National Airport.

Kromly pulled into his parking spot, rolling down the window to nod at a pair of CIA agents prominently posted near the building entrance. And those were just his visible guardians. Amazing, really. Since President Harris's assassination the day before, all high-level CIA staff had their special bodyguards, the CIA's best of the best, assigned to babysitting duty. And that was in addition to the security that had locked this city down as tight as a snail's ass, turning what was normally a half-hour drive at this time of the night into an hour-and-a-half crawl down the GW Parkway.

Clicking the lock button on his keychain, Kromly left the red Mustang convertible wedged in close to a black Caddy that had pulled in crooked and made his way inside the large foyer. The ride to the eleventh floor was notable only for the seventh-floor light that failed to illuminate. Nothing surprising about that. Lucky number seven just wasn't coming up lately.

At the door to his apartment, Kromly fumbled with his key ring. Damn. Gonna have to get rid of some of these things. He couldn't even remember what two of the small ones unlocked.

The door swung open to a dark apartment, the only light coming in through the large window that looked out across the Potomac to the Washington Monument and the rest of DC. Without bothering to switch on the light, Kromly moved to the window. God, he loved this city. Since Pam had died, his work, one bedroom, a small kitchen, a living room, and this view were all he had to keep himself sane.

Looking down at the Potomac, Kromly shook his head sadly. Another president shot down in a motorcade, this time only a few miles from this very spot. The assassin had made the shots that had almost cut the president's body in half and slid down a zip line into those muddy waters to make his escape. Except for the fifty-caliber rifle secured to the tree and some ancillary equipment, the killer had vanished without a trace.

Kromly stiffened. Had he heard something? His hand moved toward his shoulder holster.

"I wouldn't."

The familiar voice raised the fine hairs along the back of his neck. Kromly let his hands fall back to his sides, turning slowly toward the speaker. There in the darkness across the room, a shadow leaned back in his reading chair.

"Jack."

A low chuckle. "Now, Garfield. Is that any way to greet an old friend?"

Kromly struggled to control his elevated heart rate, applying the same techniques he had drilled into field operatives for the last thirty years, including the man who now sat shrouded in darkness. His ultimate student.

"Sorry. I didn't expect to see you."

"Not surprising. Have a seat."

Kromly moved to the couch, keeping his hands well away from his body at all times. No use giving Jack an excuse to pull the trigger. Not that he needed much of an excuse, not after what had happened to his team.

"Why, Jack?"

"Why what?"

"Why the president?"

Jack paused several seconds, the silence in the room growing thicker with each passing moment. Kromly considered triggering the panic button on his key ring but discarded the idea. Jack would kill him before his hand reached his pocket.

"How many years have we known each other?"

Kromly cleared his throat. "Seven."

"How long has it been since you considered yourself my friend?"

The question stunned him. Christ. Jack had been the best student he had ever had at the CIA. He was the whole package: dynamic personality, quick wits, lightning-swift reactions. But it had been his instincts that set him apart. Jack had always seemed to sense what was about to happen before it did.

Kromly had been drawn to the young man early on, pulling strings to get Jack the assignments he desired. And Pam had loved him like the son they had never had. She had succumbed to breast cancer shortly after Jack was reported killed in Calcutta. It just seemed that she had lost her will to keep fighting. If a young god like Jack could fall, then maybe she could let go, too.

"I guess it was when I thought you were dead." Kromly felt the anger edging into his voice. "You damn sure didn't go out of your way to let me know that wasn't true. You must have been busy those two years. You'll have to forgive my not being thrilled to see you now."

"I know you were advising the FBI unit that took down my team."

Shit. This was it. Nothing to do now but bend over and kiss his ass good-bye.

"You know me well enough to know that you'd already be dead if I wanted that," said Jack.

"Yes." A faint glimmer of hope that he might yet see another sunrise sharpened Kromly's focus. "I'm listening."

"You think I killed the president."

"There aren't many who could have made that hit. You're at the top of the list."

"But here I am, sitting in your living room."

Kromly shrugged. "You might have stopped by to scratch another name off your list."

"You're still alive."

"True."

"When were you first aware that Admiral Riles had a special NSA team looking into the Rho Project?"

"I only found out shortly before his suicide. The FBI was keeping the investigation very close-hold."

"What do you know about what Admiral Riles was up to at NSA?"

"Not much more than was in the press. He was trying to discredit the Rho Project in order to prevent the president from publicly releasing the technologies coming out of it."

"Let me paint a different picture. Admiral Riles called me in on a meeting at the NSA in early January of this year. The subject of that meeting was what was being called the New Year's Day virus. I led the team that secured a computer from the house in Glen Burnie."

"Then Riles exceeded his authority by sending your team in on that one."

"Maybe. He had a presidential finding. That was good enough for me."

"OK."

"The NSA was able to extract information from that computer which could only have come from within the Rho Project. The Rho source indicated that something was dangerously wrong inside the project."

"Pretty weak justification to send you to Los Alamos. Why didn't Riles notify the FBI? That's their area."

Jack shifted positions ever so slightly, the movement producing a barely visible reflection of the DC lights from the barrel of a weapon.

"I don't know how he justified it. I do know he had a damn good reason to think the Rho source was legitimate enough to send me to check it out. That investigation left no doubt in my mind that the project is corrupt, with support from the highest levels of the government. I sent back an interim report along with the decapitated body of Carlton 'Priest' Williams."

Kromly shook his head. "You're losing me. Other than your personal vendetta, what did Priest have to do with any of this?"

"Other than being the sick psycho bastard he always was, his blood carried proof of secret, illicit testing of alien nanotechnology outside the confines of the national laboratory."

"Yeah, I read about it in the papers. But that story is old news. Dr. Stephenson explained it a couple of weeks later."

"About the time the FBI came after my team."

"Coincidence."

"Let's talk about coincidences. First, I send my report to Riles. Two days later he is dead. Second, I steal Priest's body and provide evidence to the reporter who broke the nanite story. Immediately my team is taken down. Third, the president starts to back off on his commitment to release the Rho Project nanotechnology, and he is assassinated."

Kromly shook his head. "You left out a couple of other killings in the sequence. The FBI man in South Dakota and the FBI director, both people you had good reason to kill. That also applies to the president."

"That's true. You still have the scenario you have been operating under, the one that assumes Riles went nuts and that I'm a revenge killer working my way back up the chain of command. Everyone is so busy barking down that trail, they can't see any other possibility."

Jack stood. "I came here to tell you something's very wrong with the work being done within the Rho Project, wrong enough to make someone kill the director of the NSA, the director of the FBI, and the president of the United States."

"Jack, that's one crazy story."

"I'll make you a deal."

"I'm still listening."

"You tell me you'll do some digging into what I told you, and you'll live to see tomorrow. Lie to me and you're dead."

Kromly stared at the shadow standing above him. It hadn't been the barrel of a gun that had glinted in the dim light, it had been Jack's knife. There was no doubt in Kromly's mind that judgment was now being passed.

"I, ah"—Kromly swallowed hard to wet his throat—"I'll look into it."

"Right answer. Sleep well, my old ex-friend."

The cold spray of knockout gas hit Kromly in the face as he was inhaling, wrapping his brain in a fog in which the carpeted floor rose up to kiss him. He hadn't felt the Berber against his cheek since he had made love to Pam on this floor. As everything faded to black, one last thought graced his mind.

I miss you, baby.

CHAPTER 76

Heather had the pillow wadded so tightly in her hand that the seam had split, sending the goose down puffing out through the rip, but that wasn't what held her vision. She was so close to recalling the dream from which her violent shaking had awakened her. Deep inside her head, something hammered to get out, the pressure building to the point that her skull threatened to explode.

"God, just let me see it," Heather breathed.

But it wasn't happening. The more she tried to focus on the strands that remained of the dream, the faster they unraveled. A gasp of frustration slipped from her lips as she pushed herself upright in bed, the sudden movement sending fifty-four feathers floating away like a line of tiny paratroopers leaping from the back of a combat aircraft.

The sound of a door closing at the far end of the hall brought her back to the moment. Was it morning? The light coming into her room said it was, but what day? Was it Saturday already?

Heather stood up, then immediately sank back as a wave of dizziness narrowed her vision. The feeling passed as quickly as it had come. Must have stood up too fast. Moving more slowly this time, she made her way across her bedroom and slid into her summer bathrobe. It took her two tries to tie the bow that held it closed, so badly was her hand shaking.

Heather held her hands out before her, palms down. There was no doubt that the unremembered dream held a terror and a need that called to her, but it wasn't causing this. The tremor was only in her left hand and had been getting worse for the last two weeks, a side effect of her new antipsychotic drug, Thorazine.

She regretted mentioning the rising intensity of her unremembered dreams to Dr. Sigmund. The doctor had increased her dosage and then switched drugs altogether in an attempt to bring peace to Heather's sleep, expressing a fear that if the dreams got stronger, they might reassert themselves in her waking life. As for the drug's side effects, Dr. Sigmund had assured Heather and her parents that they would most likely stabilize when the drugs and dosages were finalized.

A shower. That's what she needed. Worry damn sure wasn't going to fix anything.

As she stepped into the hallway, she almost bumped into her mom.

"Oops. Sorry, Mom. Didn't mean to run you over."

"I was just coming to wake you for breakfast." Mrs. McFarland smiled, the early morning light accentuating the lines in her face. It seemed to Heather that her mother had aged ten years over the course of these last few months.

"Do I have time for a shower first?"

"Sure, but not a long one. The Smythes will be over in half an hour."

"OK. I'll hurry," Heather said as she stepped into the bathroom and closed the door behind her.

By the time she had washed her hair, letting the pulsing showerhead massage the back of her neck, Heather finally felt ready to mix with other people. Throwing on some faded jeans and a summer blouse, she made her way down to the kitchen.

Although the pancakes and bacon were fabulous, the jovial atmosphere of their weekend get-togethers failed to make an appearance. Their parents' conversation turned to the assassination of the president, leaving little room for pleasantries.

Heather caught Mark staring at her left hand, although he quickly averted his gaze. It was stupid to let something that trivial upset her, but it did. Their attempts at conversation evaporated, leaving the adult discussion unchallenged. By the time breakfast ended, Heather could hardly wait to leave the table.

As she made her way to put her dishes in the dishwasher, Mark moved up beside her.

"Can you come over for a while? We need to talk."

Heather looked into his eyes, but failed to see any hint of the disapproval or worry she had been expecting.

"I guess I can stop by for a few minutes."

"Good. Jen and I'll be waiting."

Heather found the twins in their garage, standing in the corner they had come to call their workshop. Jennifer leaned back against the tool bench, her arms folded across her chest. From her smug expression and the thunderclouds gathered behind Mark's face, Heather could tell that she had interrupted an argument.

Mark's face lightened as he saw her.

"I didn't come over here to get involved in another fight," Heather said as she walked toward him.

Mark swallowed. "I don't want to fight with you."

"Just with me," said Jennifer.

"That's not fair, and you know it."

"Do I?"

Heather held up her hands. "I don't care. Lately it seems like all we do is argue. I'm sick of it."

Mark took a deep breath, and Heather noticed the muscles in his face relax.

"Point taken."

"So what did you want to discuss?"

Jennifer leaned forward. "He wants us to hack into the Rho Project."

"What?"

"That's not what I said." Mark glared at his sister. "But we do need to talk about what is happening over there and what we should be doing about it."

He pointed at the laptop computer that sat on the workbench. "Ever since that damn science contest, we've only done one thing. Leave that computer up and running so Jack and Janet could access it using the quantum twin link to their laptop. We've been so involved in our own problems that we've had our heads stuck in the sand, hoping that Jack and Janet would work a miracle and stop the Rho Project."

Heather felt her heart rate tick up a couple of notches. "I don't know what else we can do."

"Besides nothing? We can get back in the game."

Jennifer laughed. "You seem to have forgotten that we already played that game. That went really well. Head of the NSA dead. FBI director dead. President Harris dead. Jack's team destroyed. Jack and Janet on the run. Dr. Stephenson more powerful than ever. Face it, Mark. We lost."

"Not to mention," said Heather, "we don't have the Second Ship anymore. Stephenson has it."

"I'm not saying things don't suck. But I know this: every second that goes by, Stephenson is making progress on that Rho Ship. And that scares the crap out of me."

Heather stared at him. Never, in all the years she had known him, had she heard Mark admit that he was scared of anything. She could feel the probabilities swirling in the back of her mind. Something had happened to him that he wasn't sharing.

"So what are you suggesting?"

Mark's eyes locked with hers. "I don't know why, but we were the ones who found the Second Ship. We were the ones it chose to change."

"Yeah," said Jennifer. "Us and the Rag Man."

"Mark," Heather interrupted, "the ship probably would have changed anyone who tried on the headsets."

"OK. Doesn't matter. Right now, we are it. And I think that if we don't fight this thing, the whole planet is going to get flushed right down the toilet, just like all those worlds we watched being destroyed in the imagery on the Second Ship."

The air of smugness left Jennifer's face. Heather could see that, for all the bluster from her friend, Mark had struck a nerve in her too.

He moved in closer to Heather, invading her personal space in a way that focused all her attention back on his face.

"So what do your probabilities tell you?"

Heather felt a blockage rip loose in her head. It wasn't a vision, but the equations in her mind cascaded through a set of multidimensional matrix calculations. For several seconds she just stood there, so involved in the complexity that she almost forgot that Mark and Jennifer stood next to her.

As a new wave of dizziness came and went, she slumped down into the chair beside the workbench.

"Heather?" Mark asked. "You all right?"

When she looked up again, she felt her jaw tighten.

"We'd better get busy. We have a lot of work to do."

CHAPTER 77

Mark had been meditating for more than three hours, periodically pausing to mentally tag everything about what he was feeling. The idea had come to him shortly after he had finished savoring the last piece of Mrs. McFarland's legendary apple pie at dinner. When the final morsel had been swallowed and the wonderful sensations in his mouth were only memories, it had come to him.

Memories. Thanks to the augmentation he had received on the Second Ship, his memories were perfect in every respect. Sitting on the couch he had played back the memory of eating the slice of pie, the flaky texture of the crust, the sweet tang of the fresh apples, the cold smoothness of the vanilla ice cream as it mixed with the still-hot filling on his tongue. He could feel it, taste it, smell it every bit as realistically as the original experience. Amazing.

If he could do that with an experience like eating, maybe he could get control of his emotions using the same technique. The problem with meditation was that it took time. But remembering how he felt took almost no time at all. If he could play back the feeling in his mind, every detail the same as it was during meditation, he should be able to achieve exactly the same brain state.

Retiring to his bedroom, Mark sat down on his bed, vividly recalling how he had felt during one of his meditation sessions. Almost instantaneously he was there, calm yet completely alert, aware of every hair on his skin. There was no doubt in his mind that if he had been hooked to a device that displayed his brain waves, they would have been exactly the same as during that past meditation.

Thrilled with this new discovery, Mark moved his memory around through different parts of previous meditations, adjusting his brain state accordingly. One thing he determined was that he needed a better system of recalling exact levels of meditation, depending on the state he desired to achieve. Borrowing Jennifer's idea of tagging memories in a scheme that let her easily find the memory she desired, Mark set to work. Rather than playing back and tagging parts of old meditations, he started fresh, taking himself through a wide variety of meditative techniques, progressively going deeper and deeper. As he did, he began setting the mental tags at points he thought he might want to recall quickly.

Finishing with a close approximation of the deathlike trance in which he had frightened Heather and Jen on the starship, Mark brought himself back to full alertness with a shift of thought.

Rising from the bed, he pumped his fist in the air. "Yes!"

Despite the Second Ship enhancements to their brains, most of that potential was completely untrained and yet to be explored. Mark had no idea what might lie along those unexplored neural pathways, but tonight's success left him more eager than ever to find out. In one fell stroke he had accomplished something that had eluded him for weeks—he had regained his sense of self-control.

CHAPTER 78

So close. As Heather watched Jennifer's fingers stroke the keyboard, she could feel the equations in her head converging. The software approximations Jen had implemented on the computer were almost within the variance allowed by Heather's mathematical derivations.

For two weeks, the three friends had immersed themselves in the new project, to make a miniaturized version of the subspace receiver-transmitter. To make it truly portable, this one had to be no bigger than a laptop computer and include its own internal power supply and wave-packet generator. The only truly challenging piece of the effort was this last item.

To generate the wave packets that produced the proper range of frequencies to create the tiny gamma pulses required laptop modifications. That meant the addition of four central processor chips and four floating-point processors. Even these additions proved inadequate until Heather worked out a mathematical approximation, which provided much faster computational solutions.

News reports from around the world only added to their sense of urgency. The new president had requested, and been granted, a special assembly of the United Nations, one in which he brought down the house. Never had a United States president been given a larger or longer standing ovation from the traditionally hostile assemblage. Not only had he acknowledged the legitimacy of the UN's requests for access to the Rho Ship's nanotechnology, he had promised to begin worldwide shipment of the serum by Monday, November 5, a date that provided time to ramp up production and to get the necessary congressional approval.

This last had proven to be the sticking point, with a small but vocal congressional minority joined in adamant opposition to the plan. House approval was a certainty, but the Senate appeared to be just short of the support required for cloture, the three-fifths majority required to cut off filibusters. At least that had been true until yesterday, when the leader of the opposition, Senator Pete Hornsby of Maine, had been killed in a fiery automobile accident on the Acadia Byway as he returned from a Bar Harbor weekend getaway.

Heather looked down at the modified laptop and then across at Mark, who was also watching intently as Jennifer ran through what they hoped were her final software modifications. Without Mark's incredibly steady hand doing the microsoldering, there was no way they could have completed the circuit-board changes that had been required. Feeling her own quivering left hand, Heather was certain that she could not have done it. Even Jennifer lacked the complete control of her neuromuscular system manifest in each of Mark's movements. As they watched him work through the lens of the microscope, his hand was as steady as a rock. If his hand had wavered at all she would have seen it, but it hadn't.

"Got it." Jennifer's voice snapped Heather's gaze back to the computer screen.

A glance told her all she needed to know. Jennifer's program was working even better than they had hoped.

"Beautiful," Heather said, putting her arm around Jennifer's shoulder.

Mark grinned broadly. "Gotta hand it to you, Jen. You play a mean keyboard."

Jennifer smiled at her brother for the first time in weeks, an act that gave Heather a glimmer of hope. Since the government discovery of the Second Ship, the twins had barely spoken to each other. That, combined with Jennifer's strange new aura of self-confidence, had made Heather wonder if the estrangement might not become permanent, something that would be nothing less than a tragedy.

Heather's eyes took in the data scrolling across the display, her savant brain comparing the readouts against the equations the program was intended to model. Good. Better than good.

She nodded. "Looks like it's ready for a trial run."

"About time," Mark said.

He had been champing at the bit for weeks, desperate to find out more about what Stephenson was up to. Initially, Mark had argued they should use the computer and subspace transmitter that was already set up and working, but Heather had talked him out of it. The heavy pattern of access on that system meant that Jack and Janet were on the trail of something important. To use it would have meant disconnecting them, a thought that filled Heather with a deep sense of dread.

"You have coordinates for me?" Jennifer asked.

Mark recited the coordinates for the L-shaped Rho Division building. "Location is 35.83333 degrees north latitude, 106.30303 degrees west longitude."

Jennifer initiated a new feature of the program she had just finished, a scan that adjusted the coordinates in tiny steps, searching for any computer networks within a short distance of the given location. For over a minute, she remained focused on the readouts as the scan progressed.

Finally, she looked up. "Looks like we have a hundred and thirteen separate subnets in the building."

Mark shrugged. "Pick one."

"Might as well. We're going to want to check them all," Heather agreed.

"OK, but it's going to take quite a while to make sense of the data going across each subnet."

"See if you can isolate any that Dr. Stephenson is using," Mark suggested.

"That might be tough."

"We should be able to pick up Stephenson's activity by the way others respond to him," said Heather. "Dad says he has scared the crap out of everyone on his inner team."

Jennifer paused. "OK. It's worth a shot. If I can latch onto a response chain, I can sniff the IP packets for the IP address of the computer Stephenson is using."

"He may be using more than one," said Heather.

"Most likely. All we can do is try to follow the bread-crumb trail."

Suddenly, Jennifer leaned forward, staring closely at the computer readouts from the scan. "Now that's weird."

"What?" Mark and Heather asked simultaneously.

"I have no idea. It looks like another computer network in the building, but it's not using any form of Internet protocol, at least none I've heard of. From the look of the data signature, it must be one of those new massive parallel systems the lab is working on."

"Why do you say that?" Mark asked.

"The data is just zipping around in one localized area, appearing and disappearing on separate nodes." Jennifer paused, a stunned look spreading across her delicate features. "Christ. I can't make any sense out of it."

"Maybe the data is encrypted," Heather said, leaning forward to look over Jennifer's shoulder.

"Maybe. But I don't even understand the dataflow. Must be some new type of neural net."

Mark stiffened. "Or an old one. What if you've accessed the computers on the Rho Ship?"

Heather's gaze locked with Jennifer's wide eyes.

"Oh shit."

CHAPTER 79

Raul felt the anomaly as a tingle in his skin. Turning away from his repair work, he let his consciousness roam the ship's neural network. The data disruption was tiny, a semirandom power variance jumping here and there among the neural nodes, briefly sampling node strength before moving on.

A probe!

The shock of realization stunned him. The Rho Ship's systems were being probed from an external source, something that none of the scientists who had worked all these years on the Rho Project had even come close to accomplishing. Until moments ago, Raul had believed this impossible.

Raul increased his focus, bringing every working part of the Rho Ship's massive neural net to bear on his analysis. If only he had made more repairs to the ship's data storage banks. Perhaps they held some data that would give him a better idea of how this could be happening. Instead, he had been so busy repairing the matter-disrupter power cells that he had delayed further work on the ship's computing systems. Now that decision had come back to bite him on the ass. Well, there was no help for it. Raul would just have to make do with the tools he had.

As he began analyzing the nature and pattern of the probe, it disappeared as suddenly as it had begun. Odd. Had it noticed his sudden attention? Raul replayed the incident, noting every detail of the intrusion.

The signal strength had been very low and had just appeared, moving around inside his neural network in jumps. That in itself was quite fascinating. There was no sign in any portion of the neural network that something had passed through it. The signal had just appeared at various points as if out of nowhere.

Out of nowhere! Almost like what he had been able to accomplish through his worm fibers.

Raul rechecked the data, cross-correlating with gravitation readings from the other instruments. Except for the low-level gravitational flux from the Rho Ship itself, there was nothing out of the ordinary, certainly nothing of the magnitude a gravitational singularity such as that would produce.

So this wasn't a gravitational technology. That left subspace manipulation as the most likely source of the anomaly. Subspace! The technological realm of the Altreians.

Raul felt his heart rate jump. Had the Altreians somehow managed to track the Rho Ship to Earth? Shit! In its current damaged state, this ship was in no condition to survive an Altreian attack. If that was the case, he was trapped in a bottle that was about to be shot off the fence.

But that scenario didn't feel right. Raul reexamined every measurement associated with the probe. The signal strength was far too weak to have been an Altreian scan. It had also been too random, almost as if the source of the probe had not known what it was looking at. With the Rho Ship's shielding inoperative, an Altreian scan would have been very powerful and would have simultaneously engulfed the entire neural net and all other shipboard systems.

Raul looked around the room in which he hung suspended in the stasis field. The artificial lens that had replaced his right eye swiveled in the socket, the hinged mechanism extending from his head to zoom in on the panel where his umbilical cable connected to the ship. No doubt about it. If he wanted to have enough computational power to figure this out, he was going to have to get back to work on the computing systems. For too long he had delayed the next round of self-surgery, the drastic step that would grant him the level of access he now needed.

Raul had imagined himself beyond fear, but now that he faced the reality of what had to be done, a deep dread made him weak in the knees. Glancing down at the empty space where his legs had once connected to his hips, he managed a smile. Perhaps not.

Then, taking a deep breath, Raul turned back toward the umbilical connection panel, letting the stasis field gather the surgical devices that would be required. His artificial eye telescoped into a thin flexible tube, extending to a point where it could focus on the spot where the umbilical entered the base of his skull. Having acquired sufficient skill with his field manipulation, Raul could control the instruments without using his hands. Unfortunately, he would have to remain completely conscious throughout the operation. The necessity of allowing the ship's neural net to monitor the surgical progress meant that he didn't even have the freedom to damp down the pain.

At least, bound by necessity, here in the dim gray light at the heart of the Rho Ship, he retained one essential freedom. He had the freedom to scream.

CHAPTER 80

"Oh shit!"

"Back out of there!" Heather gasped.

Jennifer's fingers were already flying across the keyboard, activating the commands that would jump the subspace transmitter to other coordinates, still within the Rho Building but onto a conventional computer subnet.

Jennifer leaned back. "Done."

"Thank God." Heather suddenly remembered to breathe.

Mark had begun to pace beside the workbench. "You know what this means? That damn Stephenson has somehow managed to activate the alien computer system on the Rho Ship. God only knows how long he has had access to it."

Jennifer shook her head. "Just because it's turned on doesn't mean he's able to understand the data. It's like nothing I've ever seen."

"I wouldn't make that bet. What about you, Heather?"

"Me either. I'd say there's roughly an 84.61538 percent probability that he's gotten at least some control over the system."

"Roughly?" A grin softened the worry lines in Mark's face.

Heather shrugged. "That still leaves two chances out of thirteen that I'm wrong."

"Well, let's hope you're wrong," said Jennifer. "From the way the alien data pattern was changing, I'd say something noticed our intrusion. I'd rather think it wasn't Dr. Stephenson."

"I'm not sure I like thinking about what else might have noticed us either," said Mark.

"Well, they can't have figured out much," Heather replied. "We were only in there a few seconds, randomly hopping around the neural net. There's no way to trace the subspace signal back to us."

"No way we know of," corrected Mark.

Heather closed her eyes. "Even an alien trace is highly unlikely."

"Please don't recite the odds. We'll take your word for it."

An angry response had just started to form on her lips when she noticed Mark's quick wink. He'd been pulling her chain, and she'd almost rewarded him.

As Heather stared, Mark's face blurred ever so slightly. For a moment, it seemed that his eyes hollowed and long, greasy blond hair hung over his shoulders. Then the vision was gone as quickly as it had come.

How long had it been since her last dose of medication? Five hours and thirteen minutes. More than an hour overdue.

"Sorry, guys. I've got to go home and take my meds. Mom's probably about to come looking for me."

Jennifer raised an eyebrow. "What about this?"

"I don't know. I think it's safe to keep searching for Stephenson's computer, so long as you don't access that ship. Wish I could stay and help, but I can't. At least not until tomorrow. See you then."

As she made her way out of the workshop, Heather felt another vision building in her mind. Without pausing to wave good-bye, she broke into a run, letting the door slam behind her.

CHAPTER 81

After midnight, the silence that crept into the strange rooms and corridors that honeycombed Henderson House thickened until it could almost be felt on the skin. It emerged as the day's second of three shifts checked out, replaced by the late-night crew. This much smaller assemblage consisted primarily of security staff who retreated to their stations, surrounded by monitors displaying the moving images from the building's black, bulbous glass eyes, lost in the magical pages of the twin Ks, King and Koontz. The glass camera housings were almost everywhere, their output tied to motion sensors and computer analysis software that used sophisticated algorithms designed to alert the guards should something out of the ordinary occur.

One of these monitors showed a janitor working next to a trolley filled with an assortment of mops, brooms, buckets, and chemicals strong enough to kill germs by smell alone. The janitor had started the shift clad in snow-white coveralls that had now turned dingy, his rolled-up left sleeve dripping brown water from the retrieval of a scrub brush lost to the depths of the mop bucket. His graying crew-cut head bobbed in a hypnotic rhythm as he swung the industrial mop slowly back and forth across the tile floor, each swing revealing the Grateful Dead tattoo that covered his right forearm.

The janitor returned the mop to its bucket and pushed the trolley around the corner into a narrow hallway that led only to the public restrooms and a large janitor's closet. Fumbling with a heavy key ring, he unlocked the closet door, reaching inside to flip on the light. Then, pulling the cart inside, he closed the door behind him.

The dimness of the lone 40-watt bulb caused him to pause momentarily to let his eyes adjust. For several seconds the sharp shadows from the double utility sink hid the pipes beneath it. The janitor removed the thick Coke-bottle glasses and placed them on a shelf, rubbing his eyes with his fingers. Then, without bothering to empty the mop bucket, he reached his damp left arm deep inside the murky water, extracting a plastic bag from the bottom.

Drying the packet with a towel, he unzipped the ziplock bag and removed a small recorder and a tiny microphone at the end of a long, thin cord. The janitor worked quickly, inserting the plug into the microphone jack on the recorder and then kneeling to lower the mike through the slits in the floor drain beneath the sinks. When it reached the bottom of the thirty-foot cord, he placed the recorder behind one of the sink pipes. Then he slid a particularly foul-smelling bucket of bleach over the drain, hiding both the microphone cord and the recorder.

Straightening once again, he rubbed the base of his back, returned the glasses to their position on his nose, and pushed the cart back into the hallway. He paused to turn off the light and lock the door behind him before once again picking up the hypnotic mopping motion that made him all but invisible to the guards and their monitors.

It had taken him six weeks of calling in every underworld IOU he had amassed over his career, as well as the bulk of his life savings, to obtain the fake identity that had passed the security checks and allowed him to get this job. But the janitor had no doubt that the investment would prove well worth the cost.

Several times, in the deep, post-midnight silence of Henderson House, he had heard the noises percolating up from the depths of the facility, from the lower levels to which he was denied access. Sometimes they were like distant screams. At other times the sounds hinted at something far more horrible. They were so strange and distant that he could have almost believed he had imagined them.

But if there was one thing his ex-wives agreed upon, it was that imagination was a trait he completely lacked. As he worked the mop steadily back and forth, the thinnest of smiles tweaked the corners of Freddy Hagerman's mouth. Imagination indeed.

CHAPTER 82

Mark came over to the house by himself.

"Where's Jennifer?" Heather asked as she opened the front door.

"Grounded for life."

"Jennifer?" She couldn't believe it.

"The one and only."

Before Heather could quiz him further, her mom entered the living room, still in her Sunday best. "Well, hello, Mark. Where's Jennifer?"

"Hi, Mrs. McFarland. Jennifer had something she had to do, so it's just me."

Mrs. McFarland smiled as she continued toward the door to the garage. "It's not that we're not glad to see you too. I've got some errands to run in town myself. There are some leftovers in the fridge if you kids get hungry."

As the door closed behind her, Heather plopped down on the couch across from Mark. Finally they'd have a chance to talk. Mark had wanted to for a while, she knew. "OK. Spill it. What happened with Jen?"

Mark shook his head. "Well, you know how odd she's been acting these last few weeks. Last night she snuck out and went to a party with some of the cheerleaders."

Heather's mouth dropped open. "Snuck out?"

"After Mom specifically told her she couldn't go."

"You're kidding!"

"I didn't believe it myself. Dad blew a fuse."

"I can imagine. Have you talked to her? Jen must be pretty shaken up."

"Not so you'd notice. I stuck my head into her room this morning, and she was just sitting at her laptop like nothing had happened. She just laughed in my face when I asked about it."

A frown spread across Heather's face. "Mark, I'm really worried about her."

"You and me both."

"There's something she's not telling us. Ever since the science contest, her abilities have been changing in ways I don't understand." Not that she hadn't had enough on her own plate to make it hard to find time to figure out Jen's issues.

"It started before that. I should have noticed it when she started jogging at night."

"That doesn't sound like her. When did she do that?"

"Shortly after school let out for the summer. I noticed it, but I was so wrapped up in what I was working on that I didn't really press her about it."

"How often was she doing it?"

"Every night, I think."

Heather felt a knot form in the pit of her stomach. "She was going out to the ship!"

Mark slapped his palm to his forehead. "Damn it. Of course. That's what she's been hiding from us." Mark didn't seem surprised Jen would hide something from him, but they were siblings. To Heather it was something new.

"It explains how we got into that room we could never open before," she said. "Jen must have figured out how to access more of the ship's computers. And somehow that closer link has changed her."

"She's taken the next step. But what are we supposed to do about it?"

Heather closed her eyes. She had the feeling that she should be able to see something important, something that she couldn't quite pull to the forefront of her mind. "I don't know."

Mark leaned forward, his deep-brown eyes locking with hers. "There's something else I want to discuss with you. Please don't get mad at me."

Heather felt herself tense. Oh great. Here it comes.

"It's not just Jennifer that is changing," Mark continued. "It's all of us. She's just changed faster than us, most likely because of her visits to the ship. But I've struggled all summer to get control of myself. Then there are your visions."

"Don't go there."

Mark swallowed hard, but continued. "I'm not going to preach at you. But I want to ask you to do one favor for me."

"You can ask, but I'm not promising anything."

"I won't pretend to know how hard this has been for you. But I've been hiding stuff too. All summer I've been having a harder and harder time controlling my emotions. It's like I get a heavy-duty hit of adrenaline over the least little thing."

"Sounds like PMS," Heather said, immediately regretting the snippy remark.

Mark nodded. "I probably deserved that. But if it's PMS, then it's the type that makes me want to break things, including people. The problem is, I could do it. Last week I almost hit Jennifer, and I don't mean any friendly little love tap. I could have killed her."

Seeing the dread in Mark's face, Heather believed him. Dear Lord. What were they all becoming?

"But then I discovered something. You know how hard I've been practicing my meditation routines. The trouble is that meditation takes time. At least it used to."

"What do you mean?" Mark now had Heather's complete attention.

"I discovered that I can just recall how I felt during a certain meditation, and it puts me there. Think about it. We all have these perfect memories. For us, remembering something is exactly like reliving it. Anyway, once I had the idea, I began mentally cataloguing a variety of meditation levels. I can drop into any one of them almost instantaneously."

Before she could respond, Mark's eyes lost their focus, his chest stilling to the point that she thought he had stopped breathing. But it was moving, just in a very slow rhythm.

Fascinated, Heather moved over to his chair and reached out to feel the pulse in his right wrist. She waited, counting, then relaxed. A steady twenty-four beats per minute. Within seconds it shifted to fifty-three beats per minute and his eyes resumed their normal alert expression.

"Wow!" was all she managed to say.

"And that brings me to my favor," Mark said, his face as serious as Heather could remember seeing it. "I don't think the ship is changing us into something inhuman. I think we were right from the beginning, that it's just released all of our human potential. The problem is that we don't have any idea what that means. Maybe a thousand years from now, or a million, every human will be using every part of the brain. But we're just stumbling around trying to figure out what new thing is going to happen to us next.

"As scared as we are of what is happening, I think we've got to accept these gifts and learn to use them. I want you to let me teach you the meditation trick. Then I want you to stop taking the drugs they have you on."

Heather had known what was coming the instant Mark had started talking, but his demonstration had at least made such a thing seem possible.

"I don't know if I can."

"I know. You've always been as aggressive and confident as I am. Do you remember that day when you talked me into climbing Ship Rock on the hard side? That's still your personality."

"Maybe."

"No maybe about it. You're not going crazy. You have a gift for seeing visions of the most likely outcomes. You just have to learn to turn it on or off at will. Maybe that's as simple as remembering what it feels like when a vision is coming on or when one isn't. I don't know, but we need to find out. I think we're going to have to learn to use every bit of our augmented brains and bodies to have any hope of stopping the Rho Ship and Dr. Stephenson. Besides, after what that bastard has done to us, I want to nail his ass to the wall."

For several seconds Heather remained still, remembering the feel of that climb up the sheer face of Ship Rock, the thrill of fear as she dangled from the wall, and the exhilaration of reaching the summit. Ever so slowly, she nodded.

"How do you want me to start?"

CHAPTER 83

Having spent the day working with Heather, coaching her on several of his favorite meditation techniques, Mark was as optimistic as he'd been in the last six months. Heather was always great at whatever she put her mind to, and once she had decided to master the techniques he had shown her, she was nothing less than amazing. Sometime around three o'clock, as the Thorazine dissipated from her system, she had wavered under the impact of an impending vision. But Mark interceded, physically shaking her until she regained her focus on his face. Then, ever so gently, he made her recall one of the meditation levels she had achieved.

The memory of how she had felt during the meditation worked its magic, completely banishing the vision and its associated sense of loss of control. Heather was so thrilled that she hugged and kissed him, something that almost caused Mark to lose his own self-control. He was quite certain that, if the kiss hadn't been quite as best-friendish, he would have devolved into a lovesick idiot instead of her self-control coach. As it was, he barely managed a congratulatory smile and some generic words of encouragement.

Fortunately, the moment passed before he succeeded in making a complete fool of himself. The next part of their practice session was the most dangerous anyway, and he'd need his full concentration. To practice turning off the visions, Heather needed to learn to turn them on at will. That meant having her focus on how it had felt just before she succumbed to her past hallucinatory experiences.

Their only goal for now was to have her practice stopping the visions as they began. Mark had Heather seat herself on the couch where he could watch her closely, promising to wake her from her trance if she didn't bring herself back within one minute. She nodded that she was ready, then inhaled deeply, letting her breath out slowly. As Mark watched, Heather's eyes acquired a faraway look, as if she were no longer in her living room but was looking out over a distant landscape.

Mark glanced at the second hand on his watch. When he glanced back up, deep lines of anxiety had etched themselves across Heather's beautiful face. Another quick glance at his watch showed that less than fifteen seconds had passed. There was no way he was going to let her go through a full minute of whatever was scaring her so badly.

Mark had just reached out to gently shake her shoulder when he saw the change. A look of peaceful bliss replaced the worry lines as her breathing slowed and steadied. With a gentle smile, Heather touched his hand, her eyes once again fully alert to his presence.

"I'm OK. It worked."

Mark suddenly realized that he was the one who hadn't been breathing, something he remedied with a gasp of relief. "Wow.

The look on your face scared the crap out of me. It was so intense I was afraid you weren't going to be able to snap out of it."

Heather sat up. "It was so hard to remember that what I was seeing wasn't real. Once I was able to think of that, remembering the meditation was easy."

"Can you remember what you were seeing without slipping back into the vision?"

Heather nodded. "Jennifer was there."

"Where?"

"I'm not sure. She was doing something with her mind. Then she looked at me and grinned. Something in that look spooked the hell out of me. That's when I remembered to try to bring myself back."

"Well, at least that worked."

Heather's smile returned. "I think it's going to take quite a bit of practice to get good at going in and out."

As she tried to stand, her legs wobbled and she would have fallen had Mark not been there to steady her.

"You OK?"

Heather straightened. "I think so. Just got a little light-headed for a second. That must have taken more out of me than I thought."

He must have looked concerned, because she laughed out loud. "Mark. I'm really OK now. You can let go."

Mark released his grip on her arm. "OK. I think that's enough practice for today."

"Don't worry, I'll take it easy until I get the hang of this."

The sound of the garage door rising caused her to put a finger to her lips. "Not a word to Mom and Dad. They'd never go for this."

"What're you going to do about your meds?"

"Dr. Sigmund has them watching to ensure I take the pills. I'll have to fake swallowing them."

The conversation was interrupted by Gil McFarland's entry into the house, grocery bags in each hand.

"Hello, Mark. How'd the study session go?"

"Hi, Mr. McFarland. I think we've got it down pretty well."

"That's good," Mrs. McFarland said as she followed her husband into the kitchen. "Biology tests can be tough."

Mark helped carry in the rest of the groceries and then excused himself, giving Heather a quick hug. For once, Mrs. McFarland did not invite him to stay for dinner.

He found his mom and dad watching television in the living room, an old *Bonanza* rerun. Mark had seen this one, the episode where Hoss and Little Joe thought they had found leprechauns on the Ponderosa. It was one of his favorites. Seeing that his parents were chuckling at a particularly hilarious sequence, Mark resisted the urge to ask about dinner and made his way upstairs.

Pausing just outside Jennifer's closed door, Mark considered knocking but decided to wait until after dinner to talk with her. Except for the last couple of months, he had been as close to his sister as any twin could be to another. She had always seemed so frail, a delicate but brilliant source of light in his life. He had always imagined himself her protector, and although it now seemed that Jennifer no longer wanted or needed his protection, he was determined to restore their mutual affection. Perhaps if he did a little less talking and a lot more listening, that could happen.

After dinner would be better. Besides, he hadn't gotten in his workout yet today. If he hit the weights for a half hour, he should have time to shower before *Bonanza* ended. Closing his door and locking it, Mark glanced at his unmade bed and the pile of dirty clothes in the closet. He had intended to carry those down to the laundry room. Oh well, no use picking up the room now. It wasn't that many hours until he'd be getting back into bed anyway.

Mark added weight to the Olympic bar until there was no more to add. He had been wanting more, but that would have meant trying to explain to his dad why four hundred and fifty pounds wasn't enough. He didn't actually know what his max lift might be. He'd never had the privacy required to find out. Not that it really mattered. The neural augmentation he had received on the Second Ship had made his muscular system so efficient that it seemed he could do pretty much whatever was required, at least for any physical activity he had attempted to date.

Mark changed into his sweat suit, lay down onto the workout bench, and lifted the barbell from its support, the weight causing the bar to bow slightly in the center. Inhaling deeply, he lowered the bar to his chest, exhaling as he raised it to the original position, repeating the action in a smooth, steady rhythm. As he worked the bar, Mark employed one of his newest mental tricks, playing back one of his favorite Evanescence albums in his head, letting Amy Lee's haunting voice power his arms, every note exactly as he had heard it through his headphones.

When Mark had completed what he thought of as a mini-circuit and showered, he could hear his mother calling from the kitchen. God, he hoped Dad had grilled burgers. His nose told him the good news as he reached the bottom of the stairs: it was a cheeseburgers-and-hot-dogs night.

"Thought you were going to let me eat your share." His dad grinned as Mark grabbed a plate.

"Hah. I was just cleaning up after my workout."

Mark piled his plate high with pairs of burgers and dogs, then set about adding a healthy stack of condiments.

"Don't forget the potato salad," his mom added. Seeing him eye the bowl with suspicion, she laughed. "Don't worry. I didn't make it. I bought it at the store."

"Oh good," Mark said without thinking. "Oops. Sorry, Mom. I didn't mean that the way it sounded."

Once again, Linda Smythe's laughter trilled out. "Yes, you did, but it's OK. I may be a lousy cook, but I'm an incredible shopper."

As he reached the table, Mark looked around. "Where's Jen?"

"Oh, she's out with some of her school friends."

Mark almost dropped his plate. "What? I thought she was grounded."

Mrs. McFarland shot a quick glance at her husband. "She is. But we had a very nice discussion with her this afternoon, and your father and I decided that it would be OK to let her have a break for this evening."

Mark fought to regain his composure. A break? This was her first day of being grounded. As he sat down, he felt his appetite fading.

"So who're the friends that she's visiting?"

"Jillian Brown and Kristy Jacobs."

Mark almost choked on the first bite of his sandwich.

"The cheerleaders? Wasn't that who she got grounded for seeing in the first place?"

His dad nodded. "I know it sounds odd, and I guess it is when you look at it that way. But like your mom said, we had a very nice chat with Jen today. Sometimes you have to be able to recognize that the right thing to do isn't necessarily the logical thing. We both felt this was the right thing to do."

"Can I get you another soda?" Mrs. Smythe asked as she headed for the refrigerator.

Mark shook his head. "No, thanks, Mom. I still have more than half of mine left."

And just like that, the conversation turned to his school schedule, the interesting new piece of electronics his dad was working on at the lab, his mom's male hairdresser's new boyfriend, anything but Jennifer. That doorway had closed, the subject locked away like a crazy relative in the cellar.

Mark forced himself to finish everything he had put on his plate, despite his sudden loss of appetite. Then, after helping clean up the kitchen, he excused himself, proclaiming his need for a couple more hours of study before tomorrow's biology test.

He'd been intending to study for the test but couldn't get his mind off his parents' inexplicable decision to temporarily waive Jennifer's grounding. The theory that formed in his mind on that subject put him into a slow-boiling rage. Only through using his meditation technique was he able to cool down and wait for Jen to get home. Anyway, he wouldn't know for sure until he got a chance to ask her about it.

The wait proved to be a long one. By the time a car pulled up outside to drop her off, Mark's clock showed 1:03 a.m. Oddly enough, his parents seemed as unconcerned about her lateness as they had about allowing her out in the first place. This was confirmed when Jennifer ducked into their bedroom to kiss them good night.

As Jennifer retreated to her bedroom, Mark moved out of his, his hand catching her door before she could close it. He stepped inside.

Jennifer stared at him, a look of amusement on her face. "It's a little late for a brotherly chat, don't you think?"

"What did you do to Mom and Dad?"

Jennifer pushed the door closed, then turned back toward him. "I have no idea what you're talking about."

"I think you do."

"OK. Since you know it all, you tell me."

"I know about your extra little trips out to our ship. I've seen the way you've been affecting people around you. You've learned a new trick."

"Relax, Mark. I'm the same twin sister you've always known."

Suddenly, a sense of well-being enveloped him, a wonderful calmness reminiscent of the deep alpha-wave patterns from some of his meditations. Shit, she was doing it to him. Using the reverse of his meditation technique, Mark pulled forward the perfect memory of his previous anger.

He leaned in close. "Sorry, Jen. Your little mind games won't work on me. I don't care what you do to your vapid little cheerleader friends, but you stay the hell out of my head. Stay the hell out of Mom's and Dad's heads too."

Jennifer grinned, the look sending a chill down his spine and ramping his anger to the next level.

"I can't believe you'd do that to Mom and Dad. But since you don't give a shit what you're doing to them, why don't you drug their food while you're at it?"

The look of fury that swept Jennifer's face peeled away her calm facade. "Don't you ever talk to me that way again. In fact, don't even talk to me. Get out of my room. Now!"

Mark wheeled, pulled open the door, and strode rapidly down the dark hallway toward his room. Behind him, he heard Jennifer's door close and lock. Fine. If she wanted to be that way, then screw her.

As his anger faded, a wave of deep depression settled into the hollow it left behind. Mark knew he should recall his meditations and get control of his emotions. But somehow, standing at his window, staring out at the darkness that separated his house from Heather's, he just couldn't bring himself to do it.

CHAPTER 84

Blackmail was such an ugly word. Freddy preferred to think of what he was doing as justified persuasion, at least in this instance.

Sometimes underworld contacts could give you things on people that background checks couldn't uncover. It was why corporate and even government background investigations failed to ensure secrets were safe. And Benny Marucci had connections most underworld kingpins would have envied.

Everybody had something to hide, something personally embarrassing or worse. When it came to security guards, the need to hide those things rose to a whole new level. And when it came to a shakedown, the combination of children and porn dealt the blackmailer the equivalent of poker's royal flush.

Freddy hadn't needed something on all the Henderson House security people, he'd just needed a weak link, and Benny Marucci had found it in the person of Damien Ridick. The fifty-eight-year-old Ridick was happily married with five children and eight grandkids. A retired US Army MP, he'd worked security at Henderson House for the last thirteen years. He was a man with a lot to lose.

It gave Freddy all the leverage he needed. It also made Ridick a reluctant and dangerous ally, one he didn't relish accompanying through the warrens beneath Henderson House at 1:30 a.m. Freddy would have stayed a million miles away from all of this if it hadn't been for what he'd heard upon playing back the contents of his hidden recorder. Sounds alone, even the most horrifying sounds, weren't enough. They'd left him no choice but to see for himself what was happening in Henderson House's lower levels.

Reaching another locked door, the fourth so far, Ridick turned toward Freddy.

"We've got to be out of here in twenty-five minutes," Ridick said, tapping his watch. "I've got the video circuits on loopback, but if we take any longer, we risk Kane coming back early from his lunch break."

Freddy just nodded. It was hard to talk to night-shift people. They ate breakfast at dinnertime, lunch when most folks were deep in REM sleep, and dinner for breakfast. It was an upside-down world, but the sounds worming their way out through the sealed steel door didn't reassure Freddy that things were about to become more normal.

Ridick swiped his badge, then placed his right palm on the scanner, holding it still as a red laser beam swept across it. The door slid open and Freddy stepped through, stride for stride with Ridick, straight into the howling depths of hell.

It wasn't a long hallway, just long enough for twelve padded cells, six on each side, Plexiglas instead of bars keeping the occupants inside. If it wasn't for his first sight of those occupants, Freddy wouldn't have believed the volume of screams could have come from so few people. And he was pretty sure that these were, or had been, people.

Looking at Freddy's face, Ridick sneered. "Better not barf unless you want your DNA spread around."

Freddy didn't bother to respond; he was still trying to adjust, trying to ignore the sudden chill, the way the hairs had risen on his arms. He pressed the RECORD button on his digital recorder before taking out his camera. Removing the lens cover, he began walking along the cells on the right side, his camera clicking like a silenced machine gun as it captured frame after frame. And as he watched in fascination and horror, the beings within the cells changed...mouths, eyes, and other appendages sprouting from their bodies as others dissolved away. Freddy had the eerie impression that these things were experimenting, seeking perfect form through an endless sequence of trial and error. Apparently, the process was far from painless.

One of the things caught his eye, and the sorrowful longing that flowed through that glance almost froze Freddy's soul. He just hoped the lens captured it.

"What do you think of the next-generation nanite formula?" Ridick's voice carried a strange mixture of humor and revulsion. "The docs haven't quite worked out all the kinks yet."

No shit, Freddy thought.

He reached the far end and began working his way back down the other side, his concentration so perfect that he failed to notice Ridick step up to one of the Plexiglas cells behind him, but the unexpected sound of the door sliding open spun him around.

Freddy wasn't as young as he'd once been, but he wasn't slow either. Especially when he was scared shitless. And the three-legged horror that launched itself out of that cell at him lent him a special kind of speed, enough to pass Ridick on his way to the yawning exit. The guard tried to grab him, but Freddy's elbow across his nose sent Ridick stumbling backward.

Sensing the thing behind him, Ridick pulled his pistol, placed the muzzle against the thing's forehead, and pulled the trigger. And though that slowed the monstrosity, it didn't stop it from tearing into the security guard's flesh, mixing its blood with Ridick's.

Ridick's screams joined those of the others in that hall.

Freddy found himself at the door, his camera still clicking in his hand, watching the thing atop Ridick healing, watching the process spread to the unfortunate man as he continued to shriek.

Then, as the three-legged, once-human creature turned its attention to Freddy, he slammed his hand on the red CLOSE button, sending the door snicking into place, shutting away the madness that lay just beyond. Sorry, Ridick. He knew he should have felt more for the man, but Ridick had tried to set that thing on him.

As he turned and made his way back to the elevator, in his head he could still hear the screaming.

CHAPTER 85

Heather didn't need to glance at the clock on her nightstand to know that it had just ticked past 2:00 a.m. As the Thorazine had continued to dissipate from her system, she had lost her need for sleep. And as it departed, the visions hammered at her consciousness. The one good thing about that was that she was getting plenty of practice shutting them off. Over the last several hours, her confidence had grown to the point that she let herself wade more deeply into some of the waking dreams, just to test her ability to exit them whenever she desired.

But going deeper left her exhausted. Luckily, one of the meditation techniques proved extraordinarily restorative, thirty minutes leaving her as refreshed as a full night's sleep.

Heather had run through the probabilities from each test, and there could be little doubt that Mark was right. What she was experiencing had nothing to do with losing her mind. It was a side effect of exploring a new region of her brain. While their link to the Second Ship had unlocked the full potential of their brains, it had left them stumbling blindly through that vast, unexplored landscape.

But that was OK with her. Exploration of her potential might be dangerous, but Heather had always enjoyed risk. The knowledge that she wasn't going insane empowered her.

Thrilling as that realization had been, a new discovery currently held Heather's full attention. She had stumbled upon it by accident. As she prepared to immerse herself in another vision, she was momentarily distracted by a moth that brushed her hair.

Heather felt her perspective shift, her view of the moth zooming in until it seemed she was trailing along behind it. The flutter of its wings was preternaturally loud as it bobbed left and right in some dark space. The sight of clothes lined up on hangers triggered her recognition. This was her closet.

Suddenly the moth's forward momentum ceased. It spun about, flapping harder than ever, but going nowhere. Long sticky strands clung to its wings, legs, and thorax, each movement only increasing its ensnarement.

Heather focused her thoughts, drawing herself into meditation, which returned her to the present. Looking around the room, she found the moth perched atop her lampshade. Without hesitation she arose from her bed and walked directly to her closet. She opened the closet door, switching on the light as she reached inside.

There it was, high up in the far left corner, the same web she had seen in her vision, a fat black spider moving along an upper strand. Interesting.

Heather grabbed one of her tennis shoes, reached up, and smashed the spider, sweeping the web away. Wiping the shoe on the carpet, she paused as she set it back where it belonged.

What had just happened? Had she changed the moth's and spider's futures? That was certainly true, but she'd done it to prevent one of her visions from coming true. No doubt about it. Her mind was doing a version of its math thing, allowing her to visualize the most probable outcome of a scenario. Just because she experienced the vision didn't mean it couldn't be changed.

The other interesting aspect of this vision was that it had focused on what she had been thinking about. Maybe she could learn to control that too.

But it didn't explain the visions that came at her from nowhere. Maybe her subconscious was picking up signals that her conscious mind failed to notice. It was going to take a lot more experimentation to come to grips with how this really worked.

Returning to her bed, Heather paused to look at the moth. "You owe me, big-time."

A smile spread across her face at the thought that she had just become the first superhero for hapless insects.

Heather rearranged her pillows so that she could sit back against the headboard and settled in for another round of deep meditation. It wouldn't do to start the next exercise even slightly tired from the last, at least not until she had gained more confidence.

Morning came quickly, the first light of dawn bringing her out of her practice session. She was so eager to tell Mark about her progress that Heather considered sliding into some clothes without showering. A quick glance in the mirror changed her mind. Even a good friend deserved better than that.

By the time she had showered, dressed, and made her way downstairs, she could hear the Smythes talking to her parents by the front door.

"Hi, everyone..." The words froze on Heather's lips as she saw the grim faces. Mrs. Smythe's eyes showed clear evidence that she had been crying.

Heather's mom reached out to put an arm around her. "Jennifer's gone."

"Gone?" The panic that clutched at Heather's chest robbed her of her breath.

Linda Smythe began to sob softly, burying her face in Mr. Smythe's shoulder. It was Mark who answered her question, his voice cracking with emotion.

"She ran away sometime in the night. She left this note."

Heather took the paper from his hand. There, written in Jennifer's beautifully precise handwriting, were the words that removed all doubt.

"Dear Mom and Dad. I'm so sorry to hurt you this way, but I have to find my own place in this world. I love you both. Say good-bye to Heather for me. Jen."

No mention of Mark. The realization struck her like a slap in the face. As her eyes locked with his, all doubt faded away. The omission had not been accidental. Jennifer had known exactly how to hurt her brother, and from the look in those eyes, she had been successful beyond her wildest dreams.

CHAPTER 86

"And what does that mean?" The confusion in Heather's voice matched the darkness that had crept into Mark's soul.

Staring at the empty place on the bench in their garage workshop, Mark felt as if he had been repeatedly kicked in the stomach. It was gone. Jennifer had taken the newly modified laptop, the one containing the miniaturized subspace receiver-transmitter.

"Jesus!"

Heather's exclamation caused him to look toward her as she scrambled to move the folding stepladder across the garage.

Suddenly, a deeper understanding widened Mark's eyes. Racing to Heather's side, Mark helped her position it. After spreading the metal legs and sliding the locking hinge into place, he scrambled up.

With one hand, he raised the ceiling panel and slid it aside. The attic space was dark, but to his eyes it appeared dimly lit, the slatted two-by-fours separated by faded yellow foam insulation. A quick shove of his powerful arms lifted him up and into the attic, where he crawled along the support slats until he reached the lowest point of the overhang.

Mark reached out, sliding his hand under the insulation until it came to rest on the long, flat box they had placed there weeks before. Pulling it free, he backed up until he could sit erect. Heather moved into the attic beside him, staring down at the closed box, which now lay across his lap.

For an instant Mark hesitated, his eyes fixing on Heather's as he worked up the nerve to look inside. Heather beat him to it, reaching across to tilt up the lid. At first he thought it was OK, that they were still right there, safely hidden away. Then the lid came fully open.

Heather rocked backward, a soft moan of dismay escaping her lips.

Unable to believe what he was seeing, Mark could only stare into the box. Of the original four alien headsets, only two remained.

"Goddamn it," Mark breathed. "Jen! What the hell have you done?"

Hearing no response from Heather, Mark glanced sideways. Staring straight through him, she leaned back against one of the roof-support frames, lost in a vision that clouded her eyes. If it hadn't been for the intensity of the look on her face, Mark would have shaken her, would have tried to bring her back to the present. But somehow, pulled forward by a fascination that he couldn't fight, Mark leaned in close.

As he watched Heather's jaw clench in determination, Mark knew this was no random fugue that had come to claim control over his beautiful friend. As strange as it seemed, deep in her savant mind, Heather was hunting. And although it raised the hair along the back of his neck, this was one hunt Mark was unwilling to interrupt.

CHAPTER 87

Dr. Hanz Jorgen, chief scientist in charge of research on the recently discovered Bandelier Ship, had set up a makeshift office inside the cave that housed the dead starship. The name had come from the press, Bandelier being the national monument adjacent to where the second starship had been discovered. Now, as the setting sun cast deep shadows through the steep canyon outside, a darker shadow crept across Jorgen's plump face.

Dr. Stephenson sat on a folding metal chair, directly across from Dr. Jorgen's desk, watching Dr. Jorgen struggle to control his emotions.

"I don't at all agree with that characterization of our status."

Dr. Stephenson's eyes narrowed. "Well, Hanz, how would you characterize a total lack of progress?"

Jorgen ran a plump hand across the top of his shiny bald dome, as if seeking some hair to pull out. The dampness at the armpits of his rumpled white shirt seemed to grow darker by the second.

"Just because we haven't managed to open the doors into the inner compartments or power up any of the ship's systems doesn't mean we haven't made progress. My report documents the results of our tests on the composition of every part of the ship we can reach, both interior and exterior. By the way, I seem to recall there is a large section of the ship you have at Rho Division that your team has been unable to access, despite decades of work."

"Ah, yes, your report." Dr. Stephenson smiled as he extracted the thick document from his attaché case, leafing through pages he had covered with red markings. He flipped to one of the dog-eared pages. "'Exterior chemical composition…unknown. Material defies all efforts to extract a sample.'"

Stephenson turned to another page. "'Although the texture of the materials comprising the interior surfaces, couches, and panels indicates a much different molecular composition than that comprising the ship's outer hull, we have, as yet, been unsuccessful in extracting samples for chemical analysis…All efforts to power up shipboard systems have proven ineffective.'"

Glancing up at the ruddy face of Jorgen, Dr. Stephenson sneered. "*Unknown…unsuccessful…ineffective*…everywhere I look in this piece of garbage you call an interim progress report, that's all I see. Those aren't my words, they are yours. Let me tell you something, Dr. Jorgen. I don't call lack of success progress. You give me one example of something tangible that your team has come up with, and I'll get off your ass."

Jorgen's plump face had gone well past red, acquiring a deep shade of purple, his blue eyes bulging as if they were ready to shoot forth like potato pellets from a spud gun.

"Did you even read our conclusion?" he sputtered.

"That's why I came to pay you this visit." Dr. Stephenson flipped to the last page. "Let's see...Based upon the failure of all of our tests to identify any of the materials from which this ship is constructed, we have concluded that they are of extraterrestrial origin, the result of a superior alien technology.'"

Dr. Stephenson rose from his chair and tossed the document onto Dr. Jorgen's desk. "Extraterrestrial. No shit. Consider this your six weeks' notice. Get me something useful or start shopping around for someplace else to work."

Without giving the hyperventilating scientist a chance to respond, the deputy director turned and exited the cavern.

While the steps that had been cut into the hillside leading to the top of the canyon had greatly improved ease of access, it still left most people huffing and puffing, but the hike didn't even stir Dr. Stephenson's heart rate from its steady forty-six beats per minute. Passing the military guards without bothering to acknowledge them, he made his way back to his helicopter and was soon airborne for the short flight back to Rho Division.

It occurred to him that his pressure tactics might backfire with Jorgen. The man was a heavyweight in more than physical appearance, having won a pair of Nobel Prizes for his work in basic materials science. There was no questioning the man's intellect, possibly a close second at the laboratory to Dr. Stephenson's own. In addition, Dr. Jorgen exercised a tight network of political connections from his days as scientific advisor to the president. And although President Harris was dead, those connections had not died with him.

Still, in Dr. Stephenson's experience, anger was sometimes a more effective motivator than fear. That Jorgen was one of the few people on the deputy director's team who didn't fear him only spurred Stephenson's aggressive nature. In most cases, he would have wanted to discuss several interesting aspects of Jorgen's report, but today Dr. Stephenson found himself distracted by the amazing changes in Raul.

Again, the lad had subjected himself to an intensive round of self-modification, intended to integrate himself more closely into the alien ship's neural network. This latest operation had been drastic and involved such dangerous surgery that Dr. Stephenson had considered making Raul stop. Unfortunately, by the time he had checked in on the cameras monitoring Raul's activities, the operation had progressed beyond the point where it could be halted safely.

Besides, Raul would certainly resist any effort to stop him. The boy had acquired an amazing level of control over the alien stasis field and was using it to perform the self-operation with finer control than his own hands could have achieved. There was little doubt that Raul could use that same field to atomize anyone who entered his compartment, if he chose to do so, although that didn't necessarily apply to Stephenson.

Working on the theory that the ship itself was driving Raul to perform the dangerous surgery, Dr. Stephenson had decided against trying to interrupt its progress. Instead, he had spent the entire night closeted in his private office, watching the monitors in fascination as Raul worked.

By 3:00 a.m. Raul had completely removed his skull above his eyebrows along a line that passed just above his ears and then all the way down to where his neck connected to his head. From the way he screamed, it was clear that he needed to feel every nerve in order to feed that data back through the Rho Ship's neural network. Apparently, the pain formed the data that told him exactly how deeply to cut, and the accuracy of those cuts had to be perfect. Almost as fast as each section of the skull was cut away, the nanites in his blood stopped the bleeding, although they could not regenerate the major tissue losses.

Once Raul had exposed the entire top and side portions of the brain, he paused to remove a large number of small crystalline chips from the Rho Ship's circuitry. Actually, the stasis field opened the panels and removed the chips, large numbers of them seeming to disconnect themselves and float randomly around Raul. Satisfied with his preparations, Raul rotated himself in the air until he floated facedown. Then, as if they were an attacking swarm of small insects, the chips descended on his exposed brain, inserting themselves into exactly positioned microcuts created by Raul's manipulation of the stasis field, its razor lines of force acting like a thousand tiny scalpels.

And in his pain, Raul's screams were replaced by a high-pitched mewling sound, a sound that Dr. Stephenson would have thought human vocal cords incapable of producing for more than a few seconds without inflicting permanent damage. The vibration of Raul's vocal cords intensified until Stephenson could almost hear them tear and reknit themselves as the nanomachines worked to repair the damage.

The operation ended midmorning, the final steps of the procedure the most fascinating of all. Having completed the insertion of the thousands of microcrystals into his brain, Raul removed the umbilical cable that connected him to the ship. His new freedom left him floating freely in the air, legless, his one artificial eye swiveling about on its hinged arm, his brain sitting naked in the open dish of his lower skull.

Raul moved across the room, pausing in front of a machine, the purpose of which Dr. Stephenson had never determined. The mechanism pulsed, producing a transparent gel which Raul extracted into a clear blob, barely larger than one fist. The gel floated up until it hovered just above Raul's head, then began to flow out and across the surface of Raul's brain, spreading so smoothly that it completely covered every exposed section of gray matter.

Suddenly, Dr. Stephenson knew why the gel looked so familiar. It was the same transparent stuff that wrapped the conduits that ran throughout this section of the ship: flexible, but so hard that a diamond drill bit was unable to scratch it. Although he couldn't be certain, the deputy director thought he understood how it worked. It was a nanomaterial, something that could harden instantly once given the proper command or become as flexible as Silly Putty given another.

The jolt as the helicopter touched down disrupted Dr. Stephenson's recollection of the scene. As he stepped down, feeling the rotor wash swirl around him, the deputy director of Los Alamos National Laboratory smiled. Whatever had suddenly driven Raul to connect himself so extensively with the Rho Ship had just accelerated Stephenson's timetable. He'd let Raul explore his limits just a bit longer before he reminded the young man who was really running the show.

CHAPTER 88

Power! The sensation storm in Raul's brain crawled through his body like an overdose of crystal meth.

If he had thought himself connected to the Rho Ship's neural network before, what was he now? Yesterday he had felt as if the massive alien neural network was a part of him. Now it felt as if the brain and body of Raul Rodriguez were only tiny pieces of what he had now become.

As he scanned the data storage, fragments of memories floated before him…the Rho Ship hurtling through the wormhole that had brought it to this solar system…the attack by the Altreians…the direct hit of his gravitational vortex weapon on the Altreian vessel…the shock of impact from the Altreian subspace distortion beam.

Raul tried recalling more of the confusing imagery, but the damage to the data storage elements was too great, yielding only unintelligible fragments for his examination. Without much more significant repair, the rest of the historical data would remain inaccessible.

A detailed systems check revealed the true extent of damage from the Altreian subspace weaponry: power production at 0.000352 percent capacity, the neural network operating at 9.317 percent of normal, 0.1231 percent of data access capability online, weapons systems inoperable, navigation systems inoperable, propulsion systems inoperable, communications systems barely functional.

One piece of the data excited him. A subsection of the communications apparatus appeared to have survived with only minimal damage, a testament to the extreme gravitational shielding that had protected it. Housed within the most heavily protected area, the Rho Ship's intelligence-gathering capabilities pulsed with a healthy heartbeat, only awaiting sufficient power to perform the information-gathering and scanning capabilities for which the system had been created.

One other interesting piece of information introduced itself to Raul. The Rho Ship hadn't had a crew for its last mission, its operation controlled by the onboard artificial intelligence. Unfortunately, the purpose of that mission was lost in the damaged data banks, hidden away as effectively as a single grain of sand at White Sands National Monument. But it was still there, and Raul knew that, given time, he would uncover it.

With a slight shift of his thoughts, Raul brought up a three-dimensional diagram of the ship's systems, coloring the various pieces with a color scheme displaying relative status. Spinning in his mind, it looked like a bloody mess, the display showing only occasional specks of healthier yellow and green colors. Although the overall status was disheartening, he now knew where to focus his efforts for the fastest payback.

Raul glanced up at one of the cameras Dr. Stephenson had installed to monitor his progress, a slow grin spreading across his face. It wouldn't be long now until he showed the deputy director who was going to be using whom.

CHAPTER 89

The lights of Las Vegas lit the low clouds in a neon-color storm that was like nothing Jennifer had ever seen. Across the street, Céline Dion's wonderful voice activated the fountains of the Bellagio, pulling Jennifer toward it, along with a horde of tourists. As she listened, she found herself unable to suppress a smile. "A New Day Has Come." How appropriate.

Strolling past the mass of spectators crowding forward to get a better view of the dancing fountains, Jennifer made her way into the luxurious lobby. Ignoring the long line at check-in, she made her way directly to one of the young women currently assisting another group of customers.

Spotting Jennifer standing behind the couple and their two small children, the woman glanced up.

"I'm sorry, but if you're not with Mr. and Mrs. Alfonse, you'll have to wait in line like everyone else."

Jennifer ignored her.

"Excuse me, but my mom and dad are in the casino somewhere and I left my key in our room. You'll find the reservation under Wilkinson. Mr. and Mrs. Gerald Wilkinson. I'm their daughter Gale."

As the woman's eyes locked with Jennifer's, they softened, a sympathetic look spreading across her face.

Turning back to the couple in front of her, the hotel clerk held up one finger. "I'm sorry. Give me just a second to help this young lady get back into her room."

In less than a minute Jennifer found herself in the elevator, key in hand, making her way up to the twenty-ninth floor, then to her mythical parents' room, one of the penthouse suites occupying the top seven floors. As she opened the door, Jennifer paused, gasping in delight. A powder room was located just off the marble entry. Overlooking the living area, the wet bar fronted the credenza on the back wall.

Throwing her arms wide, Jennifer turned into the bedroom, then stopped to gaze at the spectacular view offered by the floor-to-ceiling windows. Continuing her tour, she moved to the "Hers" bathroom, her eyes taking in the large whirlpool tub, vanity, illuminated makeup mirror, and separate water closet with toilet and bidet. After that, the "His" bathroom, with shower, bench, and steam jets, was a bit of a letdown.

Jennifer giggled to herself. "He" would just have to suck it up while she enjoyed all the luxury the suite had to offer.

The fake identities and reservations for her make-believe family had been trivial, even the credit cards, social security numbers, and Cayman Islands bank accounts. It was truly amazing what someone who knew how to manipulate the world's computing systems could do when she put her mind to it.

Laying her backpack on the desk, she pulled out the laptop, the power cord dragging the two alien headsets out with it. For some reason the sight of the translucent headbands sent a chill flowing up her spine, accompanied by a momentary pang of guilt. Perhaps she had been hasty to take them both; surely hers would have been enough.

As she fingered them, Jennifer noticed something. Although they appeared identical in every respect, she somehow knew which one was hers, almost as if it recognized her in a way the other one did not. As she thought back upon each time she, Heather, and Mark had gone out to the Second Ship, she realized each of them had always picked up the headset he or she had initially tried on. It was odd that she hadn't noticed it before.

Jennifer considered putting on her headset but discarded the temptation. Although she knew somehow that the ship would activate if she tried on the headset and commanded the computer link to activate, the thought of attracting Dr. Stephenson's focus stopped her. Besides, she had more pressing business to attend to.

She pushed the two headsets back into her pack and slid into the chair, leaning forward as she logged in. Having been seriously disappointed in the Windows hard-drive encryption software, she had written her own, and it was this algorithm that made it impossible for anyone else to log in and access the system. Even if the hard drive were stolen, there was only one other person on the planet who could decrypt it: Heather.

Jennifer pushed the thought of her friend from her mind. That was a weakness she could not afford to succumb to, at least not right now. She glanced up at the mirror, the sight of her new self startling her momentarily. Her long brown hair was gone, cut boyishly short, dyed black, and spiked up in a mildly Goth look. A lacy black dress, lace-up, knee-high black boots. Even without any piercings, something she had no intention of inflicting on her body, she couldn't recognize herself.

Still, it wouldn't fool the dedicated professionals who might be looking for her, especially if they were studying video. Since her parents had no doubt now made her a milk-carton girl, that was a concern. And although Las Vegas, with its millions of visitors, was a great place to lose yourself, closed-circuit video was everywhere.

A high-speed wireless Internet connection was available from the hotel, but Jennifer didn't connect to it, at least not directly. Instead, she brought the subspace transmitter chip online, scanning for computer networks close to her location. It took her three hops to find what she was looking for: a network with links to the hotel security system.

Security system network administrators were notoriously paranoid, and from what Jennifer observed as she hacked her way through the layers, the Bellagio staff took that paranoia to a new level. Every time she thought she had cracked the final level of security, she found another router, firewall, subnet mask, or encryption scheme.

When she finally managed to gain access to the cameras and video playback systems, she pumped her fist in the air. "Gotcha!"

Filling her screen with small windows for video display, Jennifer located the sequence of monitors that covered her path through the hotel, from entrance to lobby desk, all the way up to her room. Scanning back in time until she found her own image, she set to work editing the saved video data, carefully replacing all Jennifer pixels with background data from other frames.

As fast as she was, the task took almost an hour. Not good. She was going to have to write some custom video-editing routines if she didn't want to spend a quarter of every day doing this sort of thing.

Jennifer pressed the combination of keys that locked out her computer screen and stood up, stretching her arms and rolling her neck until she felt a series of small pops. Then, making her way across to the king-size bed, she sat down in the middle of it to take in the full reality of the room.

Jennifer let her eyes roam freely. The place practically dripped elegance, from the bathroom tile to the plush carpeting in the bedroom. A penthouse suite all to herself. If only Heather and Mark could see her now.

As she sat upright in the exact center of the bed, Jennifer realized that she was rocking slowly back and forth, hugging herself as if her mother's arms wrapped her from behind. Feeling a tremor work its way into her breathing, Jennifer clenched her teeth. This was stupid. She wasn't Tom Hanks, curled up on a flophouse cot in the movie *Big*. Nobody was yelling and shooting in the next room. This was a penthouse in the Bellagio, for Christ's sake. And she was damn sure the one in charge of what was happening.

For Jennifer Smythe, the days of being a little girl were gone… forever.

CHAPTER 90

"What you got, Fielding?" Annoyance painted McKinney's voice almost as red as his hair.

Bobby McKinney had been running cyber-security operations for the MGM Mirage and its owned hotels for so long he could sniff potential trouble just from the reactions of the system administrators. He was known as a man who was completely incapable of sitting still, constantly making the rounds of every one of the Las Vegas hotels that operated under the MGM umbrella, poking his nose into all aspects of the most sophisticated security system outside of the NSA. Today it was the Bellagio's turn to endure his presence, the tired, nervous movements of the systems administrator showing the stress his twenty-hour workday and probing intellect produced.

The young computer technician glanced up from his workstation and shrugged. "Don't know yet. Could be nothing."

"What could be nothing?"

The technician ran a hand through his long blond hair, sweeping it back from his face in a movement that reminded McKinney of a schoolgirl. But, while Larry Fielding might straddle several sexually ambiguous boundaries, he was one of the best young computer geniuses in the entire company.

"Let me show you." Fielding turned back to the keyboards stacked in front of him, an arrangement reminiscent of a pipe organ inside the Mormon Tabernacle. His long, slender fingers touched the keys so rapidly and softly that he seemed to be stroking them.

The flat-panel monitors surrounding him changed to show the blackjack tables. As he stepped the video forward frame by frame, he oriented the view on a single table and the young Asian man sliding into a just-vacated seat. The dealer had just finished filling the shoe with the cards she had extracted from the Shuffle Master. With a small smile, the man pushed a stack of black chips onto the betting mark. Fielding froze the display.

"I spotted this guy when I was reviewing the table data. He played at five different tables, always making his big bet just after he sat down, winning all five of those first bets. After that, he reduced his bet and continued to play at that table for twenty or so minutes."

McKinney's eyes watched the video jump from table to table as the man played his first hands.

"Here, take a look at his expression as he places that first bet," Fielding continued.

McKinney leaned in closer. "Intense, isn't he? I'd bet his heart is doing one-twenty or better."

"Now, watch his face as he continues to play. You'd swear it was two different people. There!" Fielding slowed the video to a crawl.

McKinney nodded. "Bored stiff. Looks like a guy who can't wait to walk away from the game."

"Exactly what I thought."

"What I want to know is why my computer security team spotted that instead of the pit bosses?"

Fielding smiled. "You'll have to ask them."

"I intend to." McKinney looked down at the computer technician. "But someone who figured out how to tamper with the shuffle machines isn't what's bothering you, is it?"

The technician pointed at one of the frozen video frames on the display. "It was so subtle I almost missed it. You see anything funny in the background?"

McKinney grabbed a chair and slid up beside Fielding, his blue eyes scanning the video frame. "Nothing out of the ordinary."

Fielding left the display as it was, pulling up footage from additional cameras on the other monitors. These new views were not of the blackjack table, but of the hotel staff checking in guests. Each image showed the same exact time as the frozen frame at the blackjack table.

At first, McKinney failed to notice the connection. These new angles showed the check-in counter, which could be seen from a distance in the blackjack table shot. As he glanced back and forth between them, it hit him.

Seeing the light dawn in his eyes, Fielding pointed at a spot just over the Asian man's shoulder. Just visible through the crowded background, a darkly dressed girl leaned across the check-in counter in discussion with a clerk. It was the only shot that showed her.

"I've played all the video forward and backward. There's not another shot of this girl from any camera in the building."

"None?"

"I've checked backward and forward from the time of this shot. Nothing."

McKinney rubbed his chin, then raised his voice enough for everyone in the data center to hear him. "OK, everyone listen up. We have a situation. I want a priority search of all our systems focused on the girl in this shot. I want to know everything about this young lady, especially her parents and how they managed to hack into our systems. Fielding will brief you. Take your direction from him."

"What about the Asian?" Fielding asked.

"I'll take care of that situation with the bosses. You stay focused on the data intrusion. Check all the camera data files to see when they were last modified." McKinney pointed at the clerk across the desk from the girl. "And get me the name of that hotel clerk. I want to have a chat with her."

McKinney paused at the door and looked around at the technical team staring at him, raising his voice once again. "One more thing. You will not discuss this with anyone except me. Is that clear?"

The response from everyone present almost brought a smile to McKinney's lips. It sounded like a basic training unit's response to its drill sergeant. That was good. Even the new people had been taught whom to fear.

CHAPTER 91

Union Station sat at the nexus of DC, the restored Beaux-Arts architectural majesty of the metro and rail transportation hub giving bold testament to the thesis that not all government money is wasted. Since the completion of the remodeling in 1988, it stood as Washington's most visited symbol of rebirth, a phoenix risen from the ashes of decay. Even the busy shops and restaurants fitted flawlessly into the elegant architecture. It reminded Kromly of a beating heart, pumping humanity through the veins and arteries of the nation's capital.

Garfield chewed slowly as he leaned against the wall, letting the freshly baked, buttery warmth of the soft pretzel dissolve on his tongue. The line at Auntie Anne's Pretzels was even longer than usual, especially for a Friday midafternoon, with people trying to get an early start to their weekends.

A woman in a navy-blue pantsuit stumbled as she stepped away from the counter, spilling her soda and dropping her handbag on the ground.

Garfield stepped forward, bending down to help her gather her things.

"That was so clumsy of me," she mumbled as he handed her purse back to her. "Thank you."

"Don't mention it."

Then she was gone, disappearing into the throng of humanity headed toward the train platforms.

Garfield finished the pretzel, licking the salt from his fingers as he paused to throw the wrapper into the waste receptacle. Then he turned and headed toward the multilevel parking garage, the computer disk he had retrieved from the open handbag tucked safely in the inside pocket of his sports jacket.

CHAPTER 92

"I can't believe you didn't tell me!" Heather's anger leaped from her lips.

"I'm sorry. I..." Mark paused, his tongue searching for the words. "I was just so excited to know something you and Jennifer didn't. It was stupid."

"Damn right." Heather knew she was hurting him, but she couldn't stop herself. "As hard as I've been working to figure things out, I can't believe that all this time you knew how speed-reading could help, and you kept it from me."

"I'm sorry."

"You know what? I can't talk to you right now. Just give me some space."

Mark stepped back, her words slapping him in the face as effectively as if she had used her open hand. For a second he stood there, his deep-brown eyes shining with moisture. Then he turned and strode from her room, leaving Heather alone.

The void that settled into the room with his departure put a lump in her throat. Heather was angry with Mark, but now that she thought about it, the speed-reading revelation had only been one more brick on the pile of frustration that weighed her down. Since she had come to terms with her latest savant gift, she had been working her ass off trying to master it, but that goal kept drifting beyond her reach, as elusive as the end of the rainbow. Not that she hadn't made huge strides in understanding how it worked.

Chess. Heather could play entire games in her mind. She could beat any computer chess opponent with ease, and she suspected the legendary Deep Blue computer opponent would present no more of a challenge than any of the others. How could it when her mind could run through an endless number of game variations with a thought? But compared to the complexity the real world presented, chess might as well have been tic-tac-toe.

Her brain gathered every bit of data available to it, including some subtle details well below the level of her conscious thought, constructing most-likely scenarios and doling them out as visions so vivid that she often found it difficult to remember she needed to come back to reality. Thank God Mark had taught her the meditation trick that kept her in the present until she made a conscious choice to let the hallucinations take her.

Heather had made a number of important discoveries. First, she could control the subject of the visions, at least partially, by concentrating on a particular thing as she let herself go. And the answers she got from her waking dreams were incredibly accurate in the short term.

But the longer-term probabilities got weaker and weaker, their likelihood depending on the quality and quantity of her present information. Just as in chess, the possible outcomes shifted based on what the other players might do, their possible actions opening up whole new universes of nonlinear fractal mathematics. But in chess, humans and computers played the game completely differently. A human master could sense the correct move without consciously having to play out all possibilities the way a computer would. Heather had acquired an enhanced combination of both methods, her mind picking only the most worthy choices to be played out in each step.

Every attempt to go further into the future left Heather so exhausted she could barely summon the energy to bring herself back. Despite the terror of the thought that she might lose herself in a land of permanent hallucination, Heather drove herself deeper. And with each attempt, each venture further out onto that ledge, she could feel herself grow stronger.

Heather glanced down at the digital photograph Mark had taken of her during one of her visions. There she stood in her own kitchen, silhouetted against the stainless steel backdrop of the GE refrigerator. Something about her expression made it appear that she was staring straight ahead, despite her wide-open eyes having rolled so far up in her head that only the whites were visible. Not a particularly good look on her. No wonder she'd scared her mom and dad to death. Christ. Staring into those white eyes was enough to make you want to crawl under the bed.

But that fear was nothing compared to the force that drove her to the limits of her enhanced endurance. No matter how many scenarios she examined, the waking dreams had left her convinced of one thing. If they didn't find Jennifer, horrors beyond anything she had ever imagined would sweep them all away.

Heather had seen her mom and dad die horribly so many times that she couldn't bear to think about it. Mark died. Jennifer died. But each time Heather was left behind, wanting to die but unable to do so. Depending on what she and Mark did in her visions, the hallucinations changed, but in every one where they failed to go after Jennifer she lived out the stuff of nightmare. Although Heather couldn't see the face of her enemy, she knew with a cold certainty that something was coming for them, and if she and Mark didn't leave soon, it would kill everyone she loved before turning its attention toward her.

Heather glanced down at the speed-reading course materials Mark had left on her bed. As angry as she had been at him for keeping the information from her, she could have kissed him for finally bringing it to her. There was so much she needed to know, but this had to come first.

Piling pillows high against her headboard and sliding back against them, Heather grabbed the books and began scanning them into her memory. Whatever it took, she wasn't going to leave this room until she had mastered the contents. As she leafed through the materials, a chill of anticipation worked its magic on her attitude. No matter how badly life seemed to have stacked the odds against her, she was not without talents, and this new skill would only make her stronger.

And with Mark, she was not alone. For the first time, she felt that new strength bubbling up within her, pushing back the darkness that lurked at the edges of her soul.

Hang in there, Jen. We love you. Wherever you are, we're coming.

CHAPTER 93

Three forty-two p.m. Jennifer glanced at the digital display at the lower right corner of her laptop monitor. What she had expected to take a couple of hours had turned into an all-day project, although the outcome was far better than she had originally envisioned.

Shortly after starting development work on her video editing program, the idea had hit her. Why should she be spending all this time every day manually hacking into the hotel security systems to find and edit video frames that contained her image? Surely she could come up with an automated way to do that.

The first part of the problem involved facial-recognition software, something that would have been difficult for someone of lesser talent, which basically meant everyone else on the planet. The algorithm she selected used a combination of relative facial measurements based upon a matrix comparison. Since she had already produced an OpenGL three-dimensional representation of her face, all she needed was the routine that would identify key facial features in each image frame, grab the measurements from that image, and compare against the stored data matrix.

Ironically, the hardest part had nothing to do with the complexities of facial recognition. The camera imagery involved more than just faces. It did no good to just erase her head; she had to find the face and then resolve the outline of her body by forcing a comparison against earlier and later frames from the same camera. While not overly difficult, the first several algorithms took way too much computer time to process, and although she refined the program several times to optimize the calculations, the results were still way too slow.

The real problem was the laptop. It just didn't have the kind of speed bigger systems had. Then a new idea presented itself. Of course. The hotel was loaded with networked high-end computing systems. Why not use their system to do the work for her? After all, she already had a virus she could insert the new code into, the same New Year's Day virus they had originally used to contact the NSA. With a few modifications, it could be programmed to limit itself to the hotel subnets, processing all imagery products, looking for a match to her face and replacing her image with background data copied in from other frames or with background approximations if other frames were unavailable.

Jennifer took a deep breath, then reached forward and initiated the virus launch sequence. A button press on her screen and it was done. Just like that. No bells. No whistles. But the virus had been released and was already replicating itself throughout the designated Bellagio subnets.

Pushing away from the desk, Jennifer stood up. Such brilliant work and nobody here to see it, nobody to tell her just what an amazing thing she had just accomplished. Heather and Mark would have been oohing and aahing, telling her how they couldn't have done it without her. But that was OK. She was beyond them now.

Down on the street below, just loud enough to penetrate the insulated glass, a lone siren's wail drifted into the room.

CHAPTER 94

Mark swallowed hard, steadying his hand under the microscope for the last circuit-board connection. This one had to be perfect. The last time he had done this there had been no pressure, just the joy of being able to impress Heather and Jennifer with his complete mastery of every nerve ending and muscle in his body. And they had been duly impressed with the results of his modifications to the miniaturized subspace transmitter.

But that had been before Jennifer had taken that laptop and run away. This time, he and Heather had been forced to apply the same modifications to the other laptop, the one that had been connected to the larger power supply, the one reserved for Jack and Janet's access. Even though it meant taking that system offline, there was no help for it. He and Heather needed it worse than Jack and Janet did; at least Heather was convinced of it.

Mark completed the connection and glanced up, his eyes locking with Heather's. God, he hoped she was right. What the hell? Heather was always right. So why was the doubt shining so brightly in her beautiful eyes? Thankfully, she was no longer angry at him; that had blown over like a sudden summer storm. It had become harder and harder for him to take her disapproval or anger.

"Ready," Mark said as he tightened the screws that secured the board to the laptop casing, a few quick motions restoring the outer cover to its normal state.

"Power it up." Heather took a deep breath. "The program worked for the other laptop, so if the circuit holds up, this should work too."

"It'll hold up," said Mark. He sure as hell hoped he was right. This was the last thing they had to have working before they could go after Jen. As crazy as his twin had been acting, he was still desperate to find her. The other pissant stuff didn't mean anything. Getting Jen back safe was what mattered.

As the laptop finished booting, Heather slid it over in front of herself. She might not be as fast as Jennifer on the keyboard, but she was no slouch. Activating the subspace transmitter, she set the signal location, watching the readouts as she adjusted the wave-packet synchronization.

"The Rho Project?" Mark asked, glancing at the coordinates she had entered.

"I won't be in long enough to be noticed."

Mark nodded. "OK. Just so it's a quick in and out."

"Almost done." Heather pressed the TRANSMIT button. "That's it. We have confirmation of packet insertion."

She shut down the transmission and brought up a second software control panel, this one of her own design.

"Now to find out if my math's as good as advertised." Heather's lips moved in a nervous tic that might have been intended as a smile.

As much as he wanted to, Mark found that he was having difficulty watching. So much depended on this next test. Heather had come up with the idea that the alien headsets remained in contact with the Second Ship even when it was powered down, so that they could send commands that would bring its systems back online. And if they did, that meant those subspace signals could be detected.

Of course, it wasn't that easy. First, you had to have a subspace receiver capable of detecting them. Second, you had to know the precise location to which the signals were directed. Third, you had to know the wave-packet characteristics of the headsets in order to separate the signals from the background noise. They had the first two answers. Now they would find out if Heather's theory about the headbands transmitting a periodic ping to mother held any water.

Heather reached down into her backpack and pulled out her alien headband, setting it on the workbench beside her. She held out a hand and Mark gave her his own headband, which she placed beside the other. Although she could have performed the test with just one band, Heather wanted both so she could analyze the Fourier transforms of the subspace signals. Even if everything else worked, if those signals were too different, she might not be able to get a trace on the two headbands in Jennifer's possession.

Mark leaned in close, his head almost even with Heather's right shoulder. The data scrolled along the left side of the display, a jumble of digits forming a cascade of numbers. Shit. For the first time in his life, he wished he'd paid a little more attention in math class. He was stuck, helplessly waiting for Heather to say something.

Instead she leaped up, catching him around the neck in a hug that threatened to leave bruises.

Her breath stirred the hairs in his ear as she spoke. "Look's like tonight's the night. Let's get packed."

~ ~ ~

Raul raised his head until he seemed to be staring directly at the circuit panels that covered the room's ceiling. The anomaly had been so brief that he had almost missed it. He certainly wouldn't have noticed it without his new linkage, but now, as he analyzed the data on his neural net, there could be no doubt.

Another subspace probe had penetrated the Rho Ship.

CHAPTER 95

Pauly Farentino moved through the mass of humanity toward the Union Station exit to the parking garage, his right hand hidden inside his jacket pocket as he screwed the linear inertial decoupler (LID) and silencer onto the nose of the Glock 9mm. Unlike the Beretta, the Glock used a Browning action, which tilted the barrel down after about a quarter inch of recoil, letting the slide move freely backward to eject the spent round. Without the recoil assistance provided by the LID, the inertia of the suppressor prevented this tilt. It was an added complication that just didn't matter. Pauly had done this so often it came as naturally as shaving.

He increased his pace slightly, making sure to keep his target in sight. The transfer had been so smooth that Pauly would have missed it if he hadn't recognized the man helping Natalie Simpson recover her bag. Garfield Kromly. That meant that Kromly had the disk. It also meant Pauly had a new target.

Even though this raised the operation profile way above the hit he was being paid for, there was no time to call in the Colombian. Kromly had to be taken down before he could get to a computer and access that data. Pauly could report this new development when the job was done.

A homeless man blocked his path through the crowd, thrusting out a greasy palm in supplication.

"Out of my way," Pauly said, stepping in just close enough to send an elbow into the fellow's gut.

To his surprise, the blow failed to land. In a movement Pauly only saw from a corner of his eye, a knife glittered, then plunged forward in three quick strokes.

Trying to bring the Glock around toward this new threat, Pauly stumbled, a scarlet fountain spraying from his throat onto the people crowded around him. As the screaming bystanders scrambled to get away, Pauly felt the wet slipperiness of the floor rise up to kiss him.

The red eyes of the vagabond followed him down.

CHAPTER 96

Her face, arms, and legs tanned to a dark brown, Janet stared at her reflection in the mirror, another of the small but regular gifts from Tall Bear. She had dyed her already dark hair black and clothed herself in the manner of modern Navajo women, which she thought of as avant-Arabic. Plumped out with her advancing pregnancy, she doubted that even Jack would recognize her at first glance.

Now, as she surveyed the hogan that had been her home and office for the last several weeks, Janet double-checked her pack. She had the laptop, her nine-millimeter subcompact, and an assortment of false documents.

Shit. She had been so close to sending her next communiqué to Jack, information he desperately needed to know, that the loss of the link to her mysterious source of Internet access had come as a complete shock. It had been so reliable, she had begun to take the amazing capabilities of the system for granted, hacking her way along progressively more complex links in her search for the people who had betrayed Jonathan Riles and his team. If not for the urgency of her need to contact Jack, she would have waited a few days, just to see if the link restored itself. But that was out of the question.

Although Janet didn't yet know the name of the person behind their betrayal, she had been able to trace a string of encrypted communications originating from within the White House, possibly from someone within the new president's inner circle. Just as importantly, the messages had been directed to Jorge Esteban Espeñosa, the head of the largest and most violent of the Colombian drug cartels.

Piecing together what she could obtain directly from CIA and FBI files had brought her to a dead end, but early this morning Janet had gotten a break. As she checked one of the Interpol subnets she had been monitoring, she discovered an obscure report from a Caracas field operative assigned to track the movements of the Espeñosa cartel's top hit man. Eduardo Montenegro, aka El Chupacabra, aka the Colombian. Apparently, the Colombian had dropped out of sight completely just before the string of US killings attributed to Jack, including the assassinations of the FBI director and the president.

Janet had run a complete background check on El Chupacabra. The man had weighty dossiers at the CIA, the FBI, and the ATF, but the French government files had the best information. The hit man had come to the attention of French Interpol because of his interest in all data related to Carlos the Jackal. Following this line of inquiry, the French security services had discovered that the Colombian had a much stronger obsession, the American killer code-named the Ripper.

Janet stepped out into the gathering twilight, pausing just long enough to fill her twin canteens from the water tank. After looking up at the stars starting to populate the darkening sky, Janet glanced down at her stomach. No use crying over something she couldn't change. She sure wouldn't get to the end of her long trail by standing here.

Hitching her pack higher onto her shoulder, Janet began climbing the arroyo that led up to the ridgeline south of the hogan. Whether she was fat and pregnant or not, Jack needed her, and Janet was about to reenter the game.

CHAPTER 97

A knock on the door brought Jennifer bolt upright in bed, sunlight streaming from the floor-to-ceiling windows hot on her face. What time was it? She had fallen asleep without bothering to undress. She had dreamed of her mom and dad holding each other in grief as Mark and Heather laughed joyfully in the adjacent room, as if her brother and best friend were glad that she was gone.

The door in the other room opened before she could protest.

"Hello? Maid service?"

Jennifer cleared her throat. "No, thank you. Could you come back later?"

"*Sí, señorita.*" The click of the door closing once again brought Jennifer's heart back out of her throat.

Jesus. It was only the cleaning lady. You'd think she'd never stayed in a hotel before.

Jennifer rose from the bed, stretched, and ran her fingers through her hair, surprised by how little of it there was. She had heard of people having lost limbs and still feeling them, but phantom hair? Please.

The window beckoned to her, and she answered the call, moving right up against the pane, looking out and down across the cityscape below. Something about the bright sunlight on the streets of Las Vegas seemed wrong. Like Dracula's castle in daylight, it was somehow diminished, robbed of the glory that only darkness could bring. She had really been looking forward to the luxury of this penthouse suite, but the opulence of the Bellagio made her feel so small and out of place that she might as well have picked the vampire's castle as her lair. That would have better fitted her mood.

A shower would help. Maybe the hot steam of the "His" shower would do more to lift her spirits than a jetted bath.

As Jennifer finished toweling her hair, she realized just how hungry she was. She'd seen a Waffle House down a side street on her cab ride over, but if she ate in one of the Bellagio's restaurants, she could charge it to her room. Since she was short on cash at the moment, that option seemed to make more sense, even if it did mean she would have a lot more of the camera video to clean up later. That thought didn't bother her. She needed to write her video-editing tool anyway, and that would give her a chance to do both at once.

By the time she had made her way down to the buffet line, Jennifer was so hungry she suspected the other guests could hear her stomach rumbling. She considered dining at the Café Bellagio or at the Pool Café, but she just couldn't resist experiencing all the buffet had to offer. The wait proved worthwhile, although she felt a bit embarrassed at the number of foods she selected to sample. As if anyone here cared.

A glance at the table to her left revealed a family with six kids attacking plates piled high with pastries. From the way they were inhaling the food, this clearly wasn't going to be their last course, either.

Jennifer rose from the table and began walking through the crowd, back toward the elevators that would carry her up to her room. As she walked, she glanced up at the black glass domes housing the hotel's video surveillance cameras. No doubt about it, these Vegas casino owners were one paranoid bunch. They made it hard for an honest young woman like herself to maintain her privacy.

As soon as she opened the door into her suite, she saw that the room had been cleaned while she was gone. A moment of panic sent her rushing into the bedroom. Seeing her laptop on the desk where she had left it, she quickly checked her backpack, a wave of relief passing through her body as she saw the two alien headsets tucked in right where she had left them, atop the extra clothes that comprised the remainder of her wardrobe.

Jennifer knew she would have to remedy the clothing situation shortly, probably with a trip to some shops right inside the hotel. Right now, though, it was time to start doing what she had run away to do. Ever since her last trip to the Second Ship, she had known what was required. It had just taken her a while to come to terms with the fact that she could never take those steps while under her parents' supervision, and although it would have been nice to have Mark and Heather's help, they just weren't ready. Maybe they never would be.

The Rho Ship was out there, and its technologies were about to be spread around the planet. Once that genie was completely out of the bottle, there might be no way to put it back in. From what she had seen in the Second Ship data banks, no civilization that had succumbed to that addiction had ever been saved.

Heather and Mark believed that they could stay safely on the edge of the fight, dropping little hints to government agencies in the hope they would recognize the evil and put a stop to it. Jennifer no longer held such illusions. Even the deadly Jack Johnson or Gregory, whatever his real name, had failed to stop the Rho Project. In the process of their meddling, the president of the United States had paid the ultimate price for trying to slow the Rho Project's forward march.

Jennifer slid onto the chair and typed in the password, which bypassed her laptop's encryption program. Anyway, she was through playing second fiddle to Mark and Heather. She'd been the one to discover how to access the Second Ship's internal data banks, and it had accepted her. It had chosen its champion, and no matter what anyone else thought, Jennifer was it.

The time for half measures was over, but her next actions were going to require money and lots of it—more fake identities, more offshore bank accounts. Jennifer grinned. In an odd way, she was about to become the Robin Hood of her day. She had already identified over a dozen drug-cartel bank accounts that were begging to have some of their ill-gotten gains put to better use.

Having spent the last few weeks analyzing how the cartels laundered their money, Jennifer found their methods almost laughable. They had certainly never seen anything like the convoluted money trail she was about to inflict upon them. And if it caused the various cartels to suspect one another, so much the better.

To Jennifer, this was the fun stuff—and she was good at it. Too good.

CHAPTER 98

Bobby McKinney pushed his way into the room, followed closely by Danny Norman, the Bellagio security chief, the coolness of the room causing him to rub his hands together for warmth. Computer centers were still commonly cooled to temperatures that would make an Eskimo reach for his parka, a relic of the days when real computing meant massive Cray supercomputers or perhaps even before that, when vacuum tubes attempted to do a fraction of the work an acid-etched piece of silicon wafer now performed.

Larry Fielding rose to meet him. "You're not going to believe this."

"Show me."

Fielding slid back into his spot in front of the bank of keyboards and monitors. "You remember the shot from the blackjack table?"

"The one with the girl in it?"

"Right."

"What about it?"

"Take a look for yourself."

McKinney studied the image on the high-resolution display. "Not this one. Where's the one with the girl in it?"

"This is the same shot. Only now she's gone."

"What about backups?"

"The story's the same on every one of our copies."

"What about the tape?"

"That's just it. I pulled the tape and same story there. But get this. The last modified time on the tape was just a few seconds after I finished loading it. It looks like someone edited the data on the tape as I was bringing it up."

"Bullshit!"

"That's what I thought too. But look here." Fielding zoomed in on a section that showed the hotel counter. "See the color artifact here, and then along here. The background's been edited to replace this section of the image."

"How?"

"I would say someone was using a program like Photoshop except that it happened too fast."

"Edited, but not perfectly."

"Right. Looks like it was done by some sort of computational algorithm running in the background."

"On our system?"

Fielding shrugged. "Pretty much has to be. And that's not the worst of it. I ran a check of all of the video data since then, looking for any odd color artifacts, such as edge blurring or pixel copies."

The computer technician's fingers danced across the keyboard. "Watch this little video segment."

A video clip showed a crowd of people just outside the Bellagio Buffet. It lasted just over thirty seconds and, on the first pass, McKinney failed to notice anything out of the ordinary.

"OK?"

"Now watch it at one-quarter speed," said Fielding.

Once again the video showed the line moving toward the cash register. Then there was a glitch, a faint ghosting that moved through the display like an echo.

"Freeze that," McKinney said. "Now back it up frame by frame."

For the next several minutes, he studied the imagery as Fielding took him frame by frame through the clip.

Larry Fielding spun his chair to face McKinney. "This evening I've picked up some similar anomalies in video from around the hotel. It looks like the data is being edited almost as fast as it is recorded. Just like the tape."

"Shit." McKinney straightened. "Tell me someone made a hard copy of the original picture of that girl."

"Afraid not."

Fielding was just geek enough to fail to recognize the jeopardy that answer put him in. Fortunately for him, he was also too valuable to throw away, at least for now.

Turning toward Norman, McKinney clenched his teeth. "Danny. I don't care what kind of trouble you have to go through, but I want pictures of every guest entering or leaving their hotel rooms for the next two days. And I mean pictures from cameras that use film."

Danny Norman's mouth dropped open. "How the hell am I supposed to do that?"

"I don't give a damn. It'll give you and that overpaid staff of yours something to figure out." McKinney shoved his index finger into Danny Norman's chest. "Don't disappoint me."

Danny froze, as if considering a response, then turned on his heel and stormed out the door.

McKinney pulled a stick of gum from his pocket, removed the paper and foil wrappers, and folded it into his mouth, letting the rush of saliva soften it as he chewed. Looking around at the startled faces in the room, he raised his voice.

"Show's over. Back to work."

Then he walked out through the door Danny had just slammed.

CHAPTER 99

The lights on this section of Maury Avenue had seen better days. Now, well past midnight, more gangbangers than pedestrians prowled the streets of Oxon Hill, Maryland. The area had a reputation, sometimes deserved, sometimes not. Here tonight, a block southeast of DC's Southern Avenue, danger filled the air. It was this atmosphere that called El Chupacabra. Tomorrow he would be on a private jet back to Bogotá, but tonight was his.

He strolled down the dark street, occasionally detouring into alleyways, drinking in the fear that seeped from the windows of the houses, from the occasional passing car on the streets. He had grown up in the barrios of Lima, Peru, and this felt a little like home—a bit more upscale, but death was out there, waiting to claim the unwary.

Since Eduardo was old enough to remember, the fear demon had been a constant companion. His mother had been the first to introduce it. Now, in ways so profound that they recalled the spirits of the Incas, it had become his one true lover.

Several times he was tempted to walk right up to one of the groups of young black men in his three-thousand-dollar Armani suit and use a line from one of his favorite Jackie Chan movies, "Wassup, my niggas!" just to see them go wild, to bathe in their blood as they flailed their guns at him. But their hate would not satisfy his hunger. What he wanted was fear.

A car turned into a driveway on the north side of the street, three houses down from the alley in which Eduardo stood watching, the engine coughing and sputtering in protest as it switched off. The door opened, silhouetting a tall black woman against the cab lights, her clingy dress and spike-heeled shoes making a statement about her profession. Not a hooker, whose work for the night would be far from over. More likely she was an exotic dancer at one of the clubs that nuzzled up against the nearby military bases.

The woman leaned back into the car, bending down to reach across the seat for her purse, a posture that heated Eduardo's blood. She would serve his purpose nicely.

The woman slammed the car door and pressed the lock and alarm button on her key ring twice, the second time producing a short squawk from the car horn. Then she strode rapidly to the door, glancing around quickly before sliding her key into the lock, opening the door, and stepping inside. As the lights inside the entryway went on, Eduardo remained in place, watching the shadow of her movements in front of the windows.

The next light to come on was on the second floor, the position of the room marking it as a child's bedroom across from the master. Just a quick on and off, Mama checking in on the kiddies. Was there a Mr. Stripper? Not likely. Neighborhoods like this were the reason for the sky-high American statistics on single mothers. No sign of a second car. Eduardo very much doubted he'd meet the man of the house. But if he did, so much the better.

Moving across the street, Eduardo slid into the shadows, moving right up against the houses as he made his way toward his target. The building was a two-story brick structure divided into two-bedroom units, each with its own driveway and yard, many separated by chain-link fences. Pausing only briefly to survey the front, he moved around the side of the building and into the treelined space, which gave the houses some separation from the busy Southern Avenue.

Looking at the large trees that spread their branches right up against the building, Eduardo smiled. How inviting. Climbing was one of his specialties, and a climb like this wouldn't even wrinkle his suit.

The light in the kitchen sputtered and then blossomed in all its fluorescent brilliance, allowing him to glimpse the face of his target as she moved in front of the window to reach up into a cupboard to grab a plate. With a face like that and a body to go with it, the stripper had to be pulling down some good money.

The woman moved to the refrigerator, and Eduardo turned back to the tree, effortlessly moving up along its branches until he reached the master bedroom window. He pulled two small oddly shaped tools from his pocket, cut away the screen, and then slipped one through the crack where the first of twin latches held the window in place, wiggling it back and forth until he could feel the latch lift.

Repeating the process with the second tool, he popped the other latch free and slid the window fully open, pausing just long enough to secure his equipment before slipping into the dark bedroom.

Eduardo, more at home in the partial darkness than he was in full daylight, surveyed the room. It wasn't much. A queen-size bed, a single nightstand, a four-drawer dresser, a closet, an open door into a small bathroom, and another leading out into the hall.

No hesitation. Eduardo moved silently out the door, ears attuned to the movements in the kitchen below, his footsteps taking him to the other doorway, the one leading into the second bedroom. He turned the knob, pushing the door open just a crack. Then, hearing no squeak of hinges, he opened it a full twelve inches, just far enough to allow him to slide through. A night-light plugged into the near wall revealed a twin bed, its headboard decorated with Power Rangers cutouts, a pattern that was repeated on the blue-and-orange comforter that was tucked in tight around the sleeping little boy's neck.

Good mama.

Reaching inside his jacket pocket, Eduardo removed a flat plastic pouch, pulling out a sheet of precut strips of duct tape, each pressed up against a special 3M film. It was a kit of his own design; the plastic film had a coating that let the duct tape stick only slightly, allowing it to be soundlessly peeled free, adhesive preserved. In addition to the duct-tape packets, the kit contained a number of the plastic cuff strips that had become a favorite among both the law enforcement and drug trafficking communities.

In movements so quick and efficient that he was done before the child had struggled back to wakefulness, Eduardo stuffed a roll of gauze into the boy's mouth and slapped a strip of duct tape across it, cuffing hands and feet together behind the child's back. Hoisting the squirming form over one shoulder, Eduardo stepped back out into the hallway, closed the door, and walked back to the mother's room.

Without a pause, he set the boy on the bed, his back pressed against the headboard. A quick twist with another of the plastic cuffs secured the child's throat to the bedpost tightly enough to produce tiny gagging sounds whenever the boy moved but not tightly enough to choke him unconscious. The boy whimpered, tried to scream, but the sound was so muffled that Eduardo barely heard it himself, a small snuffling, like a rat in a garbage can.

Removing his jacket, Eduardo moved to the closet, selected an empty hanger, and hung the jacket beside a knee-length black skirt. He placed his shoulder holster and stiletto atop the dresser, continuing to disrobe until he stood entirely naked, the remainder of his suit hanging neatly beside the jacket. Then, picking up the knife, he stepped into the darkened corner behind the open doorway, the handle of the Beretta clearly visible in the holster atop the dresser, six feet away from the wide-eyed boy bound to the headboard.

Filled with anticipation, Eduardo grinned. After tonight, the Americans would finally have proof of El Chupacabra's existence.

CHAPTER 100

Mark held Heather's arm as he walked her down the line of cars in the dark parking lot, her eyes as white and unseeing as the full moon in the night sky overhead. Suddenly her eyes rolled back to normal.

"This one," she said, pointing at the car to his right.

"You sure?" Mark asked.

"I'm sure. Just do it."

Mark ran the coat hanger down between the driver's-side window seal and the glass, jerking back up with a quick stroke that popped the latch on the old Ford Pinto. Reaching under the steering column, he ripped away the plastic covering and pulled out the wires, found the pair he was looking for, and stripped the insulation to short them together and ignite the engine.

By the time Heather had moved to the passenger door, Mark had unlocked it and settled into the driver's seat. Heather sat down beside him, slamming her door.

"She may be ugly, but at least she's old," Mark said with a grin that showed more bravado than he felt.

Heather managed a smile. "Let's just go."

Mark knew she didn't like stealing a car any more than he did, but she had worked out the odds in her visions. No other method of travel except hopping a freight train provided them much of a chance of escaping capture. The problem with the freight-train idea was that they still had to get to Santa Fe before they could hop on one going in the right direction.

Mark headed out of town, taking Highway 502 toward Santa Fe. From there they'd get up on I-25 until they got to Albuquerque, where they could catch I-40 west.

"How long do you think we have until they sic the cops on us?"

Heather shook her head. "Our folks won't miss us until morning."

Mark wasn't sure about that. It seemed all they did anymore was hurt their parents. But no matter how hard he tried, he couldn't come up with a better solution.

"And the guy whose car we just stole."

"He's in the bar, and I don't think he planned on leaving before closing time. By then he probably won't be sure if he drove or caught a ride with a buddy."

Mark had to agree. "I doubt if he'll be in any big rush to report his DUI ride home was stolen."

"Borrowed."

"Whatever. How far west are we going?" Mark asked.

Heather shrugged. "Several hundred miles at least. I could only get a direction from the headband signal. We'll need another direction reading from a new spot before I can pinpoint Jen."

"Right. Triangulation."

"Same general concept. But subspace geometry is non-Euclidean, so it's not quite as simple as laying down a map and drawing a couple of intersecting lines."

Mark grinned. "That's why it's a good thing I have you along, eh? To handle all that jazz."

"And all that jazz." Heather reached over and touched Mark's arm. "I'm so glad I have you with me. I don't think I could do it by myself."

Mark squeezed her hand, a lump rising in his throat. "I'll always be here for you. I swear it on my dead mother's eyes."

Heather laughed out loud at the old B-movie line. "Thank you. I think I'll sleep now."

True to her word, Heather leaned over until her head rested on Mark's shoulder, and closed her eyes. Long before they reached Santa Fe, she was sound asleep. For the next several hours, the pressure of her head slowly put Mark's shoulder and right arm to sleep as well, but he ignored it. God's archangel Michael could come down and smite him for all he cared, but he'd be damned if he'd make a move to wake her.

Her head rested on his shoulder. If Mark could have made the moment last for eternity, he would have. And, just so, they passed through Santa Fe, then Albuquerque, then Gallup, as the stars rose higher in the sky and the moon sank toward the west.

Jennifer was out there somewhere to the west-northwest. What she was trying to do, he had no idea. Mark just knew that he wanted his sister back, wanted the three of them back to what they used to be. But that wasn't likely. Jennifer was a runaway, and he and Heather were now car thieves, all of them pulled forward by forces well beyond their control.

Mark's thoughts went back to the day when he had found the Second Ship, when they had first tried on the alien headsets. If he had known then what he knew now, how they would be augmented, how it would change their lives so drastically, would he have even tried the damn thing on? Would he have even ventured near the alien starship?

The answer struck at his heart. Yes. God help him. Given everything he had learned, everything they had suffered to this point, he would still have done exactly the same thing.

As the white lines that divided the lanes of I-40 swept by beneath him, Mark looked up at the sinking full moon. If he could have bayed like a werewolf, he would have.

CHAPTER 101

It was very late and Raul was tired, a feeling that he hadn't experienced for a long, long time. The harder he worked, the more the Rho Ship responded to his efforts. Even Stephenson seemed impressed. Not that he gave a shit what Stephenson liked. Raul found himself thinking of Heather again. In the end all his work to repair the ship centered on the same thing. He was lost without her, constantly trying to picture her face in his mind, to recall the sound of her voice.

Every new power cell he brought online brought him closer to his dream, closer to the reunion that was destined to be. And just as he was becoming a god, she would become his goddess.

Raul glanced down at his legless body. As much as he loved the look of Heather's long legs, as much as he loved to picture them wrapped around him, they would have to be removed. It was only right that the two of them should float here in this room, legless, but with a power that would shake this world. Once he had cut her lovely legs from her body, there would be no running away from him, ever. Not that she'd want to. How could she?

The latest of the subspace probes worried him. The Altreians were still out there, and somehow they had found his ship. At first, Raul had thought that the subspace probe must have come from the dead ship in the Bandelier cave, but a scan of all Rho Project data on that ship indicated that it showed no signs of activity, no energy fields whatsoever. Dr. Stephenson checked on it periodically but showed no active interest in the ship or its technology. As much as Raul hated the man, he had to admit that the deputy director was a brilliant scientist. If there had been anything that warranted concern, Stephenson would have been all over it.

But tonight was not about Stephenson, or the probe, or even the ship. Tonight was the first night in a long time that he would indulge his fondest desires. It had been so long since he had taken any time for self-pleasure that he could barely contain his excitement. And that excitement swept away the fatigue his round-the-clock work had inflicted upon him.

Pooling the ship's new power, Raul felt himself floating upward in the stasis field until he stilled at the exact center of the chamber, drawing upon the nexus that would form the strongest and most stable worm fiber he had yet constructed, one that would let him follow Heather through the hours of the evening, from undressing in her bedroom to her bath and back again. Perhaps he might even be able to pass a breath through the fiber to ripple the fabric of her nightgown, a soft lover's touch that would tickle her with excitement.

He smiled. *It's all right, my lover. It's OK to want without yet knowing who it is you want.*

The worm fiber formed in the air before him, the gravitational improbability swirling as he brought the incredible power of the Rho Ship to bear on it, stabilizing the instability, directing it according to his will.

The parlor inside the McFarland house swam into his vision, empty and dark except for a small light from the kitchen. Moving his viewpoint into the kitchen, he found it empty, the light coming from the illuminated time display on the microwave oven: 3:00 a.m.

Raul moved the fiber upward until it passed through the ceiling into Heather's room. Empty. The bed perfectly made. No sign of after-school activities, no tossed-aside backpack, no books scattered on the desk. No clothes scattered about. What the hell?

Raul moved down the hallway to the bathroom. Nothing. No naked girl in the shower. Nothing.

In growing desperation, he swept into the master bedroom. On the bed, fully clothed, Mr. McFarland held his wife, who sobbed inconsolably on his shoulder, his face a mask of despair as he spoke with great animation on the phone. The combination of Heather's empty bedroom and the looks of loss on her parents' faces could only mean one thing.

The stunning realization hit Raul in the chest like a sledgehammer. Heather was gone.

The worm fiber collapsed. Hanging in the air of the Rho Ship's inner chamber, Raul screamed. And as he screamed, the electrical energy built in the air around him until it arced outward, connecting the walls to his fingertips in one undying web of lightning that failed to defuse the shock of loss that drained his soul.

CHAPTER 102

Heather yawned and stretched, wiping the sleep from her eyes. It was morning. At least the sun was thinking about rising above the eastern horizon, a peachy glow having lit the skyline outside the car window.

"Good morning." Mark's voice brought her head around. He leaned in the open driver's-side car door.

But he had aged at least ten years. What the hell? Had she slipped into one of her visions while she slept?

Seeing the shock in her expression, Mark straightened, the age lines melting from his face as he did, leaving the boy she knew.

"Sorry I startled you. Just wanted to try out my new look."

Heather opened her car door and stepped out into the brisk morning air. "What just happened?"

Mark shrugged. "I had been driving all night, just thinking about things as the car rolled along, stopping for gas here and there while you slept. I got to wondering how we would get by without being discovered. I mean two kids our age. We'd stick out like a sore thumb. Then, just about an hour ago, it hit me. Our age."

"Our age? What do you mean?"

"Think about it. What does it mean to look older? Mostly it has to do with the age lines in people's faces."

Something clicked in Heather's head. Of course.

Mark nodded. "So I stopped the car and started working on it in the mirror. If you scrunch your face, you get a ton of wrinkles. Then I just started relaxing a single muscle here and there, changing the look gradually until it matched a picture of some thirty-something people in the magazines. Once I had a look I liked, I memorized its feel. With our kind of neuromuscular control, we just have to recall the feeling to get that look back."

"Show me."

Mark's face moved, the slight age lines in his forehead and at the corners of his eyes and mouth producing a remarkable transformation. It was like looking at a different person.

"Wow!"

Heather's heart hammered in her chest. Moving to the car mirror, she tilted it outward. Then, repeating the technique Mark had described, she scrunched her cheeks and forehead, feeling all the muscles tense, forming lines across her face. Then, one by one, she let them relax, retightening some to match the facial lines on a woman she had seen in *People* magazine.

Within thirty minutes Heather had mastered the lines of that look. She was sure she could pass for a woman in her early thirties.

As she demonstrated the finished product for Mark, he clapped his hands. "Hello, Mrs. Robinson. I don't know if a young man like me should be seen with you. People will talk."

"You know what this means?" Heather asked.

"What?"

"We're going to need new fake IDs."

Mark slid back into the driver's seat, reaching across to open the door for Heather. "Somehow, I don't think that's going to be a problem."

Starting the car, Mark took the access road toward the freeway on-ramp. On the radio, Rod Stewart began crooning "Maggie May." When he reached the verse about the morning sun really showing her age, Heather glanced at Mark, and together, they began to laugh. As the sun peeked over the distant mountains, they kept laughing, while the tears rolled down their cheeks.

CHAPTER 103

Without taking a break for lunch, Jennifer sat at the keyboard, working her magic. Five million dollars. That was the amount she had transferred from three Swiss bank accounts controlled by the Espeñosa drug cartel into a handful of separate Cayman Islands bank accounts. If it had simply been direct transfers, Jennifer would have been finished long ago, but that would have been stupid. Instead, she had moved the money through a web of transactions around the world, all recorded over the last week, deals that included arms purchases in the Middle East and commodities options on the Chicago Board of Trade.

She was a time walker. At least, Jennifer could make her data trail walk back through time, searching out all records of transactions and inserting new ones, careful to trace the entire audit trail. When in doubt that she had tracked down all the related computer records, she inserted a virus, corrupting records in a way that would make a trace of her activities almost impossible.

The Espeñosa cartel was just the first of many such thieves' dens she planned on inflicting financial pain upon in her quest to establish a financial empire. A growing dread forced her to hurry. The new president had pledged to release the nanite formula for distribution to Africa on Friday, announcing that millions of doses were already on Navy ships headed in that direction. He had chosen Africa because it, of all continents, was the most desperately afflicted by the scourge of disease, especially AIDS. It had also been the most ignored by past US administrations. Now it was to become the model for American humanitarian efforts.

Jennifer shuddered. Those poor people. So desperately willing to take any risk in order to survive. But what choice did they have? In their situation, she would probably have done exactly the same thing.

Not all addictions were chemically based. How many people could get by without their cars or air-conditioning or refrigeration or electricity? The truth was that mankind was addicted to technology. What Dr. Stephenson and the president offered was only the next logical step in that addiction. But it was a step that horrified Jennifer beyond words.

Hearing a knock, Jennifer pressed the key sequence that locked out her computer, then walked to the door.

"What is it?" she called out.

"Complimentary turndown service," came the woman's voice from the other side of the closed door.

"No, thank you."

"Hello?"

"No, thank you," Jennifer said again.

The key turned in the door. As it opened, Jennifer stopped it with her foot.

"I said, no, thank you!"

"*Perdón, señorita,*" the maid said, bowing her head. But when she raised it again, a spray of mist squirted into Jennifer's face.

Before she could grasp what was happening, Jennifer felt her legs buckle. As everything faded around her, a redheaded man stepped forward to catch her.

"Hello, young lady. You have a lot of explaining to do. But first you are going on a little trip."

Jennifer felt herself stuffed into the bottom of the maid's cart. Then, as it rolled back out into the hallway, everything went black.

CHAPTER 104

Janet slipped the end of the key device into the car ignition switch, pressing a button on the side that engaged the tumblers. With a twist of her wrist, the lock turned, sending the engine of the Ford Explorer rumbling to life. God, she loved civilization, if you could call Santa Fe, New Mexico, civilization. The place felt as if she had been swept back in time five hundred years, the narrow streets of old town Santa Fe certainly never designed for the modern automobile, much less two lanes of traffic.

She was tired, more tired than she had been in weeks. But Jack needed her, and so sleep would have to wait. Her first priority was to get herself to a safe spot where she could establish an Internet connection. Then she could uplink the information that would give Jack what he needed to know. After that, well, she would think about that when she got to it.

The baby kicked in her belly. Her baby. Jack's baby. Janet rubbed her abdomen and smiled. Life had certainly gotten more interesting. What sort of mama would she be? What sort of baby would she have?

There were certainly plenty of people out there trying to make certain that she failed to live to answer those questions. Her hand moved to her hairpin, the narrow spike spinning in her fingers, coming to a stop in her clenched fist, its razor tip glittering in the early evening sunlight.

Fine. She would be ready for them.

CHAPTER 105

Jennifer coughed, opened her eyes, then closed them again as pain pounded her skull. The headache made it difficult to think. She just wanted to roll over, pull her covers up around her, and go back to sleep. Then she remembered.

Once again her eyes popped open, and this time she kept them open. For several seconds her disorientation made the sights and sounds confronting her unintelligible. She was on some kind of couch, an uncomfortably narrow couch, and there was a loud thrumming in her ears, along with a babble of nearby voices, mostly speaking Spanish. As the fog in her brain cleared, she understood.

She was on an airplane—some sort of small jet. From the spacious layout, it seemed to be some sort of corporate aircraft, certainly different from the personal space afforded by a B-group ticket on Southwest Airlines. Jesus. What had happened to her?

Gently moving her wrists, Jennifer was surprised to find that she was not tied up. A quick personal inventory revealed that, aside from her throbbing head, she had suffered no apparent bodily injury. Indeed, someone had taken the trouble to cover her with a thin blanket.

Jennifer struggled to a sitting position. Seeing her looking around, the redheaded man she had seen as she passed out rose from his seat and moved to sit across from her. He appraised her with his intelligent blue eyes, simultaneously cold and curious.

"Can I have a drink?" Jennifer asked, her voice coming out as a hoarse croak she barely recognized.

"Certainly," the man replied, signaling to a young woman, who immediately brought a bottle of ice-cold water.

Jennifer drank deeply, finishing the small bottle in several long swallows. When she looked up again, she had managed to establish at least a small degree of calm.

"Who are you? Where are you taking me?"

The redheaded man's eyes narrowed. "My name is not important. Your next stop is Medellín, but we won't be landing at the José María Córdova International Airport."

Jennifer's eyes widened. "Colombia?"

The redheaded man smiled. "Good girl. So unusual for a girl your age to know her geography. But then you're a very unusual girl, aren't you?"

Jennifer worked to get her bearings, but her thoughts were foggy, her senses dulled.

"I don't understand."

"Maybe not now, but you will. Señor Espeñosa is very anxious to meet you." The man smiled, but his lips held no mirth.

Jennifer felt her throat constrict as a growing terror gripped her. Dear God. What had she gotten herself into?

CHAPTER 106

Heather and Mark stepped out of the FedEx Office twenty-four-hour copy center in Las Vegas with their new IDs in hand. With the right person creating the digital images, the right materials, and a good enough laser printer, it was amazing what you could create. And Heather was the right person. Add an empty copy center and a clerk weighed down with 3:00 a.m. sleepiness, and she could work miracles.

Once outside, Mark looked at the driver's licenses in the light of the bright neon signage. He had to admit that they were good enough to fool anyone who didn't actually work at the Arizona Motor Vehicle Division. Robert Foley, age twenty-nine, and his wife, Rebecca Foley, age twenty-eight, from Tempe, Arizona.

"Not bad, Mrs. Foley." Mark grinned, handing the Rebecca Foley ID to Heather. When he looked in her face, it was like looking at an older woman, something that he found strangely erotic. Well, come to think of it, it wasn't all that strange or unusual.

"Thanks, Robby." Heather smiled back at him, opening the passenger-side door and sliding into the seat.

Mark climbed in and started the car. They had agreed that he would do the driving, since they needed Heather to do her white-eyed savant thing from time to time, an activity that tired her so that she needed sleep. It struck Mark as a little odd, since he no longer needed or desired to waste time in an unconscious state.

"How about that?" Mark asked, pointing to the Super 8 motel down the block.

Heather nodded. "Looks good to me."

Mark pulled to a stop under the overhang. "I'll check us in."

Although it took several rings on the bell to wake the sleeping desk clerk, he completed the check-in process with no difficulty. Once they had parked and carried their bags to the room, Heather flipped on the light, then paused in the doorway.

"A king-size bed?"

Mark felt his face redden. "Sorry, he didn't ask, and I thought he might be suspicious if I asked for two beds. After all, we're supposed to be married."

"Uh-huh."

"I'll lie on the floor if you want."

When Heather paused to consider it, Mark continued. "Even though it looks pretty darn uncomfortable."

"Hey, wait a minute. You don't even sleep."

"No, but I rest and I meditate."

Finally she shrugged. "Oh, all right. Just make sure you stay on your side."

"I can't believe you even think I wouldn't."

"Right."

Mark let Heather shower first before taking his turn. By the time he'd put on a fresh set of clothes and returned to the bedroom, Heather was fast asleep beneath the covers. Mark lay down atop the covers on the other side of the bed, rolling onto his side. As much as he knew he should be thinking about the next steps in their search for Jennifer, he just lay there watching Heather sleep beside him, her gentle breathing the most wonderful sound he could imagine. It was another of those moments he intended to record in his memory, down to the last perfect detail.

He could've watched forever. Then Heather sat bolt upright in bed, knocking him over the side.

"Mark!"

Almost before the word was out of her mouth, he had recovered and was on his feet beside her, his hands clenched into twin fists.

"What's the matter?"

Heather scrambled out of bed, grabbed her backpack, and pulled the laptop out onto the table.

"We've got to leave. Jennifer's in trouble."

CHAPTER 107

Garfield Kromly stared at the report on his desk. The brown double wrapping still lay on the floor where it had fallen as he removed the outer covering of the classified package. This was just one more piece in the puzzle, a jigsaw that had begun to resolve itself from the information on the disk he had gotten at Union Station. And as badly as he wanted to believe something else, anything else, it was looking more and more as if Jack Gregory was right.

At this point, Kromly was sure that someone at the top level in the White House had assisted in the assassination of President Harris; he just didn't yet know who that someone was. As for the connections to the Rho Project and the upcoming release of the alien nanotechnology, he had come up with little more than a string of very odd coincidences. He was going to need something much stronger than that to break this thing open.

Kromly glanced down at the computer disk that lay beside the package he had just received. Along with a host of circumstantial evidence, it contained the digital recording of a phone call from the White House, made just minutes before the president had been killed. It might just be the break he had been looking for. Unfortunately, the recording was encrypted using some of the most sophisticated hardware and software available to the United States government. Without the STU encryption key, his chances of deciphering it were practically nonexistent.

His hopes of at least getting a voiceprint from the scrambled data had proven fruitless. Perhaps the folks at the NSA could have done it, but all who had gone that route had found themselves very, very dead. And although Kromly didn't fear death, he had no intention of rushing to embrace it either. There was too much at stake for the country for him to get himself killed just yet.

Already he'd been lucky. The man who had been killed at Union Station, not far from where Kromly had entered the parking garage, had turned out to be a mob hit man named Pauly Farentino. A more thorough check into Farentino had revealed that he had been seen following Natalie Simpson before she reached Union Station. It didn't take much imagination to guess that he had seen the exchange outside Auntie Anne's and had switched targets on the fly.

The public story that Farentino was killed by an angry vagrant was laughable. While Farentino wasn't the smartest guy on the block, the man had earned a reputation as a vicious and dangerous killer. Unfortunately for him, in the middle of the crowd at Union Station, he had crossed paths with a much more dangerous predator. The knife work was too precise. Two quick cuts severing each side of the throat in a manner designed to produce the maximum spray of blood, something to shock the surrounding crowd, drawing their focus away from his face.

But it was the third and final wound that left no doubt in Kromly's mind as to the identity of the killer. The long knife had punched straight up, entering Farentino's head just beneath the chin, punching its way up through his mouth and into his cranial cavity with enough force to drive the blade and several splinters of bone deep into the hit man's brain. The person who had killed Farentino had wanted to make sure that he could not survive his injuries, even if he had been treated with the nanite serum.

Kromly shook his head. So now he owed Jack his life, twice if you counted the fact that Jack hadn't killed him when he could have. Apparently, Jack wanted to make sure he lived long enough to complete the task he had agreed to.

Maybe he'd have to put Jack back on his Christmas card list after all.

CHAPTER 108

From her barred window, Jennifer watched the backslapping, laughing men below, several carrying rifles slung loosely across the crooks of their arms. From the look of the activity, preparations for some sort of celebration were well under way. Heavily laden workers moved back and forth, dropping off supplies and setting up tables and chairs beneath a large awning that had been erected between the wings of the hacienda-style mansion. A glance at the sky revealed the reason for their hurry. Rain was coming, and from the look of the thick clouds creeping down from the peaks of the surrounding mountains, it was going to be a gully washer.

She pulled back from the bars, the tears that had dripped from her cheeks leaving damp spots on the stone windowsill, precursors of the coming storm. She lingered for several moments, then stepped down from her perch atop the single bed, her eyes making a circuit of the room. It was tiny, barely large enough to hold the bed. A foul-smelling bucket occupied the farthest corner at the foot of the bed, across from a heavy wooden door. Moving across the space separating the bed from the door, she twisted and pulled on the handle, but it was useless.

Backing into the corner farthest from the stinking chamber pot, Jennifer slid to the floor, her hands rising to cover her face as sobs shook her body.

CHAPTER 109

The wireless Internet connection at the Days Inn on Macon Cove was the best Janet had been able to get since she had left New Mexico headed east on I-40. Not being an Elvis fan, she'd never actually stopped in Memphis before tonight, but she was dead tired and damn glad to see the hotel room.

Janet stared down at the news story front and center on her laptop screen, stunned by the realization that hammered her. She had been checking news out of Los Alamos when she saw the article on the disappearance of three Los Alamos High School students, Mark Smythe, Jennifer Smythe, and Heather McFarland. Apparently, Jennifer had run away several days before, followed shortly by Mark and Heather, the conjecture being that those two had gone in search of her. Both sets of parents were horribly distraught, begging the public to come forward with any information on their missing children.

As disconcerting as was the news, it was the date of Mark and Heather's disappearance that slapped Janet in the face. November thirteenth. The exact day her connection to her secret Los Alamos source had gone off-line.

Everything snapped together in her head. All this time she had been looking for a person she had assumed to be a scientist working on the Rho Project. Instead, it was one or more of those kids, operating right under her nose all along. Hard as it was to believe that those three wonderful young people were capable of hacking into the world's most secure computer networks, that they had somehow managed to gain access to highly classified Rho Project information, suddenly it all made sense.

All those times Heather McFarland had been in the middle of deadly situations had always struck Janet as odd. What had Jack said about the psycho who called himself the Rag Man? Something about the way his speed and strength seemed supernatural. Then there was Heather's involvement with the family of Raul Rodriguez, whose father had been a top scientist on the Rho Project. Dr. Rodriguez was dead, Raul Rodriguez missing, Raul's mother insane.

Then there was Mark Smythe, an abnormally gifted young athlete. Mark had been at Janet's house the day Priest attacked her. Somehow he had survived his encounter with that killer. As far as she knew, Priest had kidnapped only women for his sick pleasures. Why hadn't he killed the boy? Something about his encounter with Mark must have raised Priest's curiosity to a level that he couldn't ignore.

Another thing Janet had never understood was why Heather, Mark, and Jennifer would plagiarize from a top scientific team for their entry in the national science contest. Everyone had just assumed that three kids couldn't do work that advanced on their own. Apparently, that was another in a long chain of bad assumptions, the type of assumptions Janet would never have made if she had been observing adults.

No. There was something very, very special about those kids, something that Jack had to know about. Janet had already posted the encrypted information Jack needed about the Colombian assassin known as El Chupacabra onto the Internet. But the identity of their secret Rho Project source was too sensitive and important to be posted on the net, no matter how good her encryption and data hiding. This was something that had to be delivered to her partner in person.

Janet looked over at the bed, thinking back to a dingy youth hostel outside of Paris, another time she and Jack had been on the run. When she had asked Jack why they didn't keep moving, he had laughed and thrown himself down on the bed, eliciting a puff of dust and an angry squeak from the worn box springs.

"Even sleep is a weapon."

As she made her way to bed with the image of Jack burning brightly in her mind, Janet smiled. It was a weapon she intended to put to good use.

DC could wait for one more day.

CHAPTER 110

Jorge Esteban Espeñosa's arrival at his compound three days later brought about a change as radical as Jennifer's sudden departure from the Bellagio. Suddenly she was moved from her tiny cell to a huge bedroom on the upper level of the hacienda, and although the door was still locked and guarded, the bedroom and the attached bathroom were even more elegantly furnished than her Bellagio suite.

A maid brought her an entire wardrobe of beautiful dresses, some of which hinted at a long-lost Spanish court, others soft and elegant peasant dresses. The maid spread an assortment of matching shoes and accoutrements alongside them on the bed, then looked Jennifer up and down with eyes that showed no hint of sympathy. It appeared that the Goth look would no longer be an option.

In heavily accented but clearly distinguishable English, the dark, matronly woman spoke.

"*Señorita*, my name is Gloria. I am here to make you presentable for your dinner with Don Espeñosa. Please, follow me."

Unable to get her bearings quickly enough to form a question, Jennifer followed the maid into the bathroom, where steam wafted gently upward from the huge freestanding bathtub.

"Undress, throw your dirty things in the wastebin, and then bathe yourself, thoroughly. Call me when you are done and I will assist you with your clothes and hair." A frown spread across Gloria's face as she studied Jennifer's short black hair. "I will be in the next room."

For several seconds after Gloria's departure, Jennifer stared after her. Then a glance at the tub set her into motion. There was no telling how long she would be given, but if this was her last night of comfort in her short life, Jennifer was determined to indulge in the bath for as long as possible. It was remarkable how little emotion remained within her as she tossed her filthy clothes into the trash bin. She felt as if she had been wrung out and hung over a line to dry in the wind.

That changed the moment her small right foot slid into the water. A wave of ecstasy sent a shudder through her body as her naked torso slipped slowly into water hot enough to pink her skin. Jennifer continued to slide down into the tub until her entire head sank beneath the surface, the ripples distorting her view of the beamed ceiling twelve feet overhead.

She didn't know what the sick old drug lord might have in mind for her, but at least for the moment, she could block out those thoughts and the discomfort and fear that had gripped her so tightly these last few days. In her present world, there was only room enough for her and this wonderful tub of liquid bliss.

Perhaps a half hour passed before a knock on the door and Gloria's voice brought her back to reality.

"*Señorita*? Are you ready, or do you need me to help with that too?"

"Just a minute."

The implied threat that the maid would come help her finish her bath brought forth an annoyance that bubbled into her voice. Something about her sudden anger felt really good. How long had it been since she had shown the least bit of spirit? Christ. One second she had been at the Bellagio, so full of herself and her mental superiority, and in the next she had turned into a sniveling, helpless child.

If she was going to survive, she had to get her shit together and use some of the gifts she had been granted. Most of all she had to use her head.

Jennifer stepped out of the tub and toweled herself dry. Without bothering to wrap herself in the towel, she took a deep breath and stepped out into the bedroom.

"Well, it took you long enough!"

The maid's eyes swept Jennifer's body before locking with her eyes. As they did, Jennifer centered, letting her mind attune to what she saw behind those dark orbs.

Despite the number of times she had experienced the sensation, the experience of feeling another person's mind gave her a rush. It wasn't that she could hear the other person's thoughts. It was more like a jazzed-up version of what some twins reportedly experienced, a sharing of feelings, an exchange of desires, longings, fears. Only this exchange was entirely under Jennifer's control.

As with everyone Jennifer had tried this on, the feelings in Gloria's head were a complicated mixture at the conscious and subconscious level. The woman was certainly nobody Jennifer would ever want to establish a friendship with, a burned-out shell filled with frustrations, fears, and petty jealousies that crowded out any of the finer emotions that might have once been there.

Fine. If she couldn't accentuate the positive, there was always the other side of the coin. Jennifer focused, selecting the maid's fear of authority, twisting and amplifying it as she held the woman's gaze.

The change in Gloria's expression was instantaneous.

"*Perdón, señorita.*"

The woman lowered her head, almost as if she expected to be struck across the face, but having just glimpsed the woman's soul, Jennifer felt no sympathy.

Turning toward the vanity, Jennifer glanced back over her shoulder. "Help me with my hair. Then we will try on some clothes."

Exactly fifty-eight minutes later, the maid knocked on the door to Don Espeñosa's private terrace.

"Yes?"

Opening the door, the maid curtsied, a sight that almost brought a smile to Jennifer's lips as she waited just behind and to the left of the massive hand-carved teak door.

"Well, bring her in."

Jennifer stepped forward, pausing when she was just across the threshold, her breath catching in her throat. The terrace opened out onto a spectacular view over the city of Medellín. It and the surrounding mountains formed the most beautiful sight Jennifer had ever seen, its grandeur dwarfing the Spanish opulence of this private dining area and the elegantly dressed man who had just arisen from his chair.

When, after several seconds, her eyes focused on her host, she was surprised to see a warm smile on his face. Don Espeñosa's eyes swept her body, lingering on the delicate, flowing lines of the white peasant dress and the colorful silk sash tied about her waist. Jennifer's short coal-black hair had been softened ever so slightly with an orchid just above her right ear. The man's gaze left a tingle of self-awareness that made her notice the tropical evening breeze across her bare arms and shoulders, the feel of the sandal straps between her small toes.

Don Espeñosa stepped forward, taking her hand and raising it gently to his lips, the surreality of the moment making her head spin.

"Welcome to my humble home, Señorita Smythe."

CHAPTER 111

"Welcome to my humble home, Señorita Smythe."

The petite young girl standing before him opened her mouth as if to say something, but the shock of hearing her real name robbed her of her voice.

Don Espeñosa smiled, lowering her hand from his lips. He had been looking forward to this meeting more than anything he had done in a long, long time. It was quite funny, really. In almost any other scenario, he would have personally supervised the videotaped torture and killing of someone who had dared to touch his personal bank accounts, then posted the video on the Internet as a warning. But his standard response didn't fit this situation.

Somehow, this teenage girl had hacked a network of banks and casino security systems in a way that all his high-paid computer experts hadn't begun to figure out. Combine that surprising fact with the discovery that she was a runaway whose father worked on Dr. Donald Stephenson's top secret Rho Project in Los Alamos, and she had Jorge's full attention. That didn't mean he wouldn't rape and kill her, but he would take his time deciding.

The drug lord bowed his head ever so slightly. "I must apologize for the conditions in which you have been kept. Had I not been away when my people brought you in, I would have ensured that you received proper treatment. Unfortunately, some of those I employ can be a bit overzealous in their efforts to protect my interests."

Leading her to the small table, Don Espeñosa pulled out her chair. "But let us defer such talk until after dinner."

The speed with which the girl regained her composure amazed him. A soft smile spread across her lips as she slid into the chair he held for her.

"Thank you, Don Espeñosa."

The don moved to his own seat, a snap of his fingers bringing two members of his waitstaff to the table.

"May I offer you something to drink? Some wine, perhaps?"

The young lady laughed, her easy, comfortable manner surprising him once again.

"I'd rather have a Diet Coke if you have one. Otherwise water's fine."

"I think we can manage that."

Jorge spoke a few words in Spanish, and one of the servants scurried away as the other poured a small amount of red wine into the don's glass. Jorge swirled the red liquid several times, smelling it before taking a sip. Seeing his nod of approval, the servant filled his glass, set the bottle on the table, and began serving the appetizers.

As the first servant returned with the Diet Coke, Don Espeñosa leaned forward so that his elbows rested on the table.

"So, Jennifer…it is OK if I call you Jennifer?"

"My friends call me Jen."

There it was again, that unnatural maturity and self-confidence.

"Very well then, Jen. What do you think of my city?"

Jennifer paused, her gaze taking in the city nestled in the valley below his hacienda. The purple sunset crawled across the sky above the western mountains, its rich palette forming a backdrop to the lights that were just beginning to wink on across the valley.

"Glorious." The tone of her voice confirmed the sincerity of Jennifer's comment.

Throughout the appetizers and the leisurely meal, Don Espeñosa continued to study the girl. To observe the way she enjoyed their casual dinner conversation, one would never suspect that she had been held prisoner in a filthy cell for more than two weeks, probably wondering just how she was going to die. Jorge had been around many self-confident people who would have crumbled under similar circumstances.

But there was something else about this girl from Los Alamos, something he couldn't quite put his finger on, something that raised the small hairs along the back of his neck whenever he really focused his attention upon her. *Madre de Dios.* What was there about this child that could do that to him?

As the servants cleared the dessert plates, leaving them alone to sip their after-dinner coffee, Don Espeñosa hardened his voice.

"Now that you've had a chance to enjoy your dinner, perhaps you wouldn't mind telling me why I shouldn't kill you here and now."

For the first time all evening, Jennifer Smythe allowed her eyes to lock with his. Never in all his life had Jorge seen anything like them. The way they reflected the candlelight made him dizzy, as if he were standing on the edge of a great precipice, looking down into depths no living soul had ever seen.

And as Don Espeñosa stared into those eyes, he answered his own question.

CHAPTER 112

From the place where Raul floated in the stasis field, high up on the far northeastern wall of his wounded home, he stared down at the one who had just entered the room. No matter how much he hated the man, he had to admit Dr. Stephenson had balls. Not the standard brass ones either. Knowing the kind of mastery Raul had achieved over the alien systems, the man must have had *huevos* of tempered steel.

Raul let his mind roam the neural net, manipulating the lighting until it formed a virtual star field, a simulation of the starship hurtling through space as it exited a wormhole. The effect made it appear that Raul was a god, hurtling through the heavens as he levitated high above the strange platform of alien equipment.

"Having fun?" Stephenson's voice was as flat and unimpressed as if he were watching a child playing hopscotch on a chalk-marked sidewalk.

"As a matter of fact, I am," Raul responded, amplifying his voice so that it boomed through the room, the reverb level shaking some of the instruments hard enough to produce a rattle.

"Then I suggest you get serious and come over here, where we can discuss something of importance."

The anger that bubbled up inside Raul could not be contained. He knew he needed Stephenson, but that didn't mean he couldn't hurt the man, just a little. Just to let him know who he was talking to. Just to teach him to show a little respect.

As if it were a part of his own body, Raul grabbed control of the stasis field, amplifying the lines of force so that they solidified into an invisible net, dropping it from above so that it draped Dr. Stephenson's body. Then he began to squeeze.

The corners of Dr. Stephenson's mouth twitched in what Raul at first thought was a grimace, but which spread ever wider until he recognized the expression for what it truly was: a grin. With no more effort than it took him to step from the shower, the deputy director stepped forward, passing through the force field as if it weren't there.

What the hell? Raul lashed out, smashing an empty metal case beside Dr. Stephenson and then throwing his full will into a wall he erected directly in front of the man. Once again, Stephenson stepped through the stasis field, his eyes locked on Raul as he moved along the narrow walkways between the machines that filled most of the floor space.

Raul scanned the neural network, running a full set of diagnostics on the equipment that powered the stasis-field generator, on the generator itself, and on the computing systems that he used to control it. All were operating normally. Then how in God's name was Stephenson moving through something that would have contained a full-blown fusion reaction?

The physicist stopped almost directly below Raul and then began slowly rising up through the air until they stared directly into each other's eyes. Raul's disbelief at what he was seeing almost made him miss the cause. But there it was in the data stream that swam through his neural net.

It wasn't that Stephenson was unaffected by the stasis field. Somehow, he was overriding Raul's control. That particular shipboard system was responding to both of them, and where their wills were in conflict, Dr. Stephenson was winning. It was responding to a higher master.

"Are you ready to hear what I have to say?"

Dr. Stephenson's grin departed, leaving his face as cold as the machinery behind and below him. As Raul's anger and frustration gave way to amazement, he felt himself nodding in affirmation.

"Good. As much as I appreciate what you've been able to accomplish so far, I have a new project for you." Dr. Stephenson paused, his eyes studying Raul like a rat in his lab. "I think you'll get a thrill from what I want you to do."

Raul recovered his equilibrium enough to speak. "Like what?"

"Let's just say that if you can do this, you'll be able to reach out and touch someone."

A sudden light dawned in Raul's mind. "God in heaven!"

Stephenson repeated his earlier question. "You ready to listen?"

Raul was.

CHAPTER 113

Mark glanced across the car at Heather, the age lines of a twenty-eight-year-old lightly etched in her perfect face, her hair cut fashionably short, her beautiful brown eyes hidden behind the dark sunglasses that she now wore whenever they were in public. The precaution against being observed in one of her white-eyed fugues had become so habitual that she now often forgot to take them off. Mark knew that if he reached over and removed them right now, he would see those eyes gone white.

The last few days had taken a toll on both of them. Thanks to Heather's power and her relentless speed-reading of every piece of news and rumor on the Internet, they now knew Jennifer was in Medellín, Colombia. They had confirmed it by performing a complicated subspace triangulation to the signals from the missing alien headsets.

Putting together the money for the trip had been the easy part. Heather could win at any gambling game, from poker to roulette. The craps tables were her favorites, since she could throw the dice with such amazing accuracy that she only lost to avoid standing out. Even the slot machines proved no challenge to her savant mind. Within a few minutes of watching, she could determine the way any machine's random number generation algorithms worked. Game over.

They changed from casino to casino, from game to game, intentionally losing to throw off suspicion, but steadily building the cash they would soon be needing. Heather always seemed to know exactly when to back off on her current winning streak.

The real problem had been getting the passports and visas needed to get into Colombia. These weren't the type of documents you could just whip up at your local FedEx Office. But Las Vegas abounded with people who, for the right price, could produce whatever fake documentation you needed.

Only a couple of blocks to go now before the car reached their destination. If everything went well, they'd walk in, plop down the envelope with the seventy-five thousand dollars, pick up their documents, and go. If everything didn't go as planned, well, that's what Heather was working out the odds on as he drove. She wouldn't have the last pieces of data she needed until they walked into the building and met the person who awaited them.

In the meantime, they had rehearsed the most likely scenarios a dozen times. Mark felt stretched taut, like a cable holding some great span of bridge. Except the bridge that he supported was this girl he loved more deeply than he would have believed possible. It must have happened ages ago, but it was their mutual quest for Jennifer that had brought him to the full realization of his feelings.

And he hadn't even told her. How could he? With all the pressure she was under, how could he lay that on her?

Mark turned right off of Oakleigh onto Evening Dew Drive. The neighborhood was upper-middle-class residential, just east of the ridgelines rising up to Frenchman Mountain. Certainly not the kind of place you'd expect to find an illicit printshop for hire. Mark pulled into the driveway just as the late-afternoon sun disappeared behind the high peaks to the west.

As he reached across to gently squeeze Heather's shoulder, his voice nudged her. "Heather. You with me?"

She turned toward him and nodded. "Good to go."

"OK then, let's get it over with."

Mark reached across the seat for the envelope of cash, but Heather stopped him. "Let me take the lead. Just stay by me and watch for my signal."

Although Mark felt prepared for anything, this wasn't good. Her last vision must have taken her down one of the more unpleasant paths.

Opening the door and stepping into the driveway, Mark shrugged. "Whatever you say, boss."

As he followed Heather to the front door, he willed his face into a mask like the ones he had observed on some of the high-roller bodyguards at casinos downtown. Ignoring the doorbell, Mark rapped three times on the door, then twice more.

Listening carefully, he made out the footsteps of three men, two moving away as the other approached. Three heartbeats matched the movements. A door closed softly just before the front door opened.

The man who smiled out at them looked like any male head-of-household a census taker would expect to meet in this neighborhood, a neatly dressed, blond-haired, blue-eyed man in tan cotton Dockers and a Michael Jordan golf shirt. Even the sandal straps matched the tan lines barely visible on his feet.

"Mr. Billings?" Heather asked.

"Yes?"

"I'm Amanda Fowler, and this is my associate, Jason. I believe you were expecting us."

"So I was. Please, come in."

Mark stepped in first, his eyes scanning the interior in a way Mr. Billings noticed. As soon as the door closed behind Heather, the warm smile faded from the man's face.

"You have my money?"

Heather patted the fat envelope. "I would like to see our documents first."

Billings smiled, this time allowing a slight sneer to warp his lips. "Follow me."

Heather stumbled slightly, and Mark reached a hand out to support her arm, thankful that the sunglasses hid her eyes.

Billings paused momentarily, looking at Mark. "She on drugs or something?"

"Cut the small talk and show us the documents. Then you'll get your money."

"Fine. No need to get pushy."

Billings led them into a small study just off the dining room. A large executive desk occupied the center of the room, and Billings slid into the chair behind it, reaching down into a drawer as he did.

"Easy," Mark said, stepping up beside him so he could see into the drawer.

"What? You think I'd pull a gun on you? In this neighborhood?" Billings pulled a large manila envelope from a file and emptied its contents onto the desktop.

Heather flipped rapidly through the passports and visas, then slid the cash-filled envelope toward Billings, watching as he counted. "Satisfied?"

The smile returned to Billings's face. "Actually, I've run into some unexpected costs associated with the urgency of processing your order. I'll need another twenty-five grand."

"No. We'll pay the agreed price and not a penny more."

Billings cleared his throat, and as he did, Heather nodded toward the closed door behind him.

Mark exploded into action, his thunderous side kick catching the door as it started to open, the violence of the blow ripping the hinges from the frame and catapulting it back into the garage, sending two large men rolling backward against a jet-black Suburban.

Continuing his forward momentum, Mark's fist crashed into the jaw of the nearest as he attempted to bring a gun around. Without bothering to watch him hit the ground, Mark grabbed the right arm of the second man, feeling the muscles in the three-hundred-pound frame tense with effort as he struggled to wrap his massive arms around Mark's body.

With a yell of satisfaction, the big man dragged Mark toward him. What happened next changed the yell into a scream. Mark's grip tightened, snapping the bone of the right forearm, sending the sharp end jutting out through the skin, accompanied by a spray of blood that robbed the big man's face of color. Without releasing his grip, Mark pivoted, sending his elbow crashing into the side of his opponent's head. The sound of the heavy body hitting the floor was like that of a dropped watermelon. The screaming stopped.

Mr. Billings froze, too shocked by the explosion of violence to move.

Heather leaned in close, her voice barely rising above a whisper as she gathered the documents into her handbag. "As I said. Not a penny more than the agreed price."

"F—fine." Billings's eyes remained locked on Mark as he moved back into the office.

As they turned to leave, Heather turned toward him one last time. "Make sure this closes our business dealings. I'd hate to send my associate back for a more vigorous discussion."

Billings swallowed. "We're all done here."

"Good."

Mark walked Heather back to the car and backed out of the driveway. As they rounded the third corner onto East Washington Avenue, Heather leaned forward and vomited onto the floor mat.

"Oh, Christ," she muttered as the gagging subsided. "That's so gross. Sorry."

"Don't worry about it. I felt the same way after I broke Priest's neck. At least until the asshole shot me in the butt with that tranquilizer dart."

Heather laughed. "But you don't have to sit here smelling it."

"Oh, I smell it."

Her elbow caught him in the shoulder, interrupting the grin just as it got started.

In a matter of minutes they were on Highway 147 headed west out of Las Vegas. Vomit cleanup would have to wait for a truck stop on I-15, somewhere along the road between there and Salt Lake City.

CHAPTER 114

Freddy Hagerman leaned back against the tree in the darkness, feeling the rough bark through his wet shirt. His breath panted out hard enough to scrape the skin from his throat. As a child, his mother had always given him a shot of Jack Daniels and honey to cure a sore throat. If he survived the night, he vowed to revisit that treatment. Hold the honey.

Now that he had stopped, the warmth that had come from his desperate scramble to get away from Henderson House leached away in the icy water that dripped from his clothes. The tremors that had started in his extremities now moved into his core, growing in power until his teeth chattered audibly.

His janitor's pants were ripped from crotch to knee, thanks to an old piece of razor wire just beneath the surface of the stream. Just how badly he had cut himself, he could only guess. Considering the fact that he hadn't yet passed out, the wound couldn't be that bad. Then again, the shaking might not be solely due to hypothermia.

Freddy sank to the ground, hugging the small pack with his camera and recorder tucked damply inside, trying to clear his head enough to come up with a plan. A quick review of his situation wasn't comforting.

His damned car was half a mile away, inside the Henderson House compound. No chance of getting that. In his desperate flight he hadn't even had a chance to grab his jacket. At least the dogs had lost his trail in the stream. If he could just make his way down to the lake, he could steal a boat. Not that a boat would take him far on that little lake, but it would give him more separation from his hunters. Plus, if he could get down to the flood-control dam, it was only a short hike to a warehouse where he had seen some interstate trucks and trailers.

After that…well, one step at a time.

Lake Success had a marina just a short distance from where Success Valley Drive crossed Highway 190. To Freddy it sounded as if it had been named at a multilevel marketing convention. Hell, if he got that far, he might just sign up for their business opportunity himself. After all, a little extra soap never hurt anybody. Those poor bastards in the depths below Henderson House could have used some.

Freddy shook his head to clear it. He must be frickin' delirious. One thing for sure, if he stayed here much longer, he'd find himself down in that hellhole. So much for his second Pulitzer. So much for putting a stop to that madness.

Patting the camera bag one last time, Freddy forced himself back into the cold water. He might have lost all the photos left hanging in his hotel darkroom, but what he carried in that bag was enough. Enough to bring down Dr. Stephenson. Enough to bring down a president.

CHAPTER 115

Pieces of the alien machine floated in the air around him as Raul worked, each one tracked and catalogued by the ship's improving neural network, each compared against specifications stored deep in the Rho Ship's database.

If he had worked hard before, it was nothing compared to the way Raul now drove himself. As shocked and angry as he had been to discover Dr. Stephenson's ability to override his commands to some of the Rho Ship's systems, the task the deputy director had offered him had captured his imagination so vividly that Raul put everything else aside. Dr. Stephenson's interest was focused on a particular machine, one that had been heavily damaged by the weapon that had sent the Rho Ship crashing to Earth.

For more than twelve hours, Dr. Stephenson had taken Raul through a series of equations and diagrams illustrating what he wanted done and making an offer so attractive that Raul had leaped at the opportunity. As he had listened, applying the full computational powers of his networked brain, he found himself more and more impressed with the span of Stephenson's intelligence.

Somehow, without Raul's level of access to the Rho Ship's alien computing powers, the physicist had figured out the purpose of the machine in question. Not only that, he had worked out, with amazing accuracy, the underlying theory of its operation. Looking at the equations was like opening a vault in Raul's mind, unlocking parts of his database that, although damaged, filled in pieces of the jigsaw puzzle he would need to get the thing working again.

Another shocking development was the way his data search revealed blocks of historical data on the alien technology that had enabled the Rho Ship to travel the stars. Unlike the Altreians, who had employed subspace technology, the Kasari had mastered the manipulation of gravity. Their ability to warp the space-time continuum extended well beyond the little worm fibers Raul had been able to re-create, allowing for the production of much larger discontinuities, holes in space large enough to transport objects the size of the starship.

The larger the hole, the greater the spanned distance, the more time it needed to remain open, the greater the energy needed to produce the space-time fold. The machine he was working on was what made the large folds possible. And even though there was no way the Rho Ship's damaged power systems could produce anything close to an interstellar fold, it should be possible to produce one sufficient for earthbound transport. That was the breakthrough Stephenson wanted.

And in return, he had offered to let Raul pass through and return with a companion of his choosing. Raul's heart rate and breathing increased as his mind played with that thought. He would create a doorway through which he could pull Heather back to him, a completely untraceable action that would deliver his soul mate. And once Raul had her where he was a god, he would introduce her to pleasures beyond her wildest imaginings.

Raul refocused his attention on his work. At the current rate, repairs to the machine would be complete in another 184 hours and 13 minutes. After that he needed to shift his efforts back to the repair of additional power cells. What he needed to do would certainly take far more energy than he currently had available, especially since he needed to maintain plenty of shipboard reserves. It wouldn't do to transport Heather but kill his Rho Ship in the process. Once it was completely drained, there would be no way to restart it.

Raul flexed his mind, feeling the energy crackle through his neural network, drawing on the working power supplies to fuse two damaged conduits.

One hundred eighty-four hours, 12 minutes, 23 seconds... and counting.

CHAPTER 116

The rural house just off Mattaponi Reservation Circle backed up against heavily wooded Virginia countryside. Although the tribe claimed over four hundred members, the number of residents living on the 150 acres of reservation land that snuggled up against the Mattaponi River had shrunk to around seventy-five. Seventy-six if you counted Janet. Clad as she was in the manner of the locals, with her dark hair, dark skin, and pregnant belly, few outsiders would have given her a second glance.

Tall Bear's connections never ceased to amaze her. She had been accepted into the tiny community with a warmth and protectiveness beyond what she could have expected. And although she received more than a few questioning looks from the young ones, the stoic elders of the river people quickly squelched any open inquiries. Janet didn't know what Tall Bear had told them, but they seemed to regard her with a respect reserved for heroes from the Indian nation's proud past.

The location was exactly what she needed, an isolated community just on the northwestern side of West Point, Virginia, less than three hours' drive from DC. She'd been given access to a high-speed Internet connection and provided with food, fresh clothing, and a secure place to stay. The nine members of the tribal council had been unwilling to accept her thanks. Whatever they thought she was doing had been deemed worthy of their support. As far as they were concerned, that ended all discussion of the matter.

So while the tribe went about their daily business, Janet returned to hers. Jack was out there somewhere within half a day's drive from where she sat with her laptop. The first thing she needed was to let him know what she'd learned about the Colombian known as El Chupacabra. Next she needed to ask Jack for a meeting time and location to share her theory about the McFarland and Smythe kids.

Janet smiled to herself as she rubbed her abdomen. Jack's child. What would he think when he saw her dark-brown, round little body? It'd be worth the trip just to see the expression on his face. At least she hoped it would.

Pulling the Heckler & Koch 9mm Compact from the small holster strapped beneath her left arm, Janet set it on the table beside her laptop. Even after she finished posting her coded message to the Internet, it might be a long wait before Jack got back to her.

Might as well get comfortable.

CHAPTER 117

President Gordon leaned back in his chair, feeling the even bulges in the burgundy leather press against his back. Pushing away from his desk, he glanced at the narrow grandfather clock that occupied the wall between the window and the large painting that hung immediately behind his desk: 10:36 p.m.

The White House Treaty Room had always been his favorite. He had to admit that his late predecessor's interior decorator had hit a home run with the room's simple elegance. The off-white walls and ceiling perfectly framed the dark furniture, and even the wildly colorful rug somehow added to the room's comfortable feel. Its location next to the Yellow Oval Room on the second floor of the White House made it the perfect private office.

Hearing the distant rumble of thunder, President Gordon walked to the window that looked out across the Truman Balcony over the South Lawn. As a flash of lightning ripped the sky, he began to count off the seconds. Six, seven, eight. The rumble was louder this time, only a mile and a half away. Fat raindrops spattered the room's eastern window, although none carried beneath the overhang to strike the panes where he stood.

Sliding the latch, the president lifted the window, letting the damp, musty-smelling air fill his lungs. The Secret Service hated for him to stand by a window, much less an open one. Didn't matter. He was the boss and he'd do as he'd always done, exactly as he pleased.

Washington, DC, rarely got thunderstorms this late in the year, November lending itself more to cold, foggy rain. Tomorrow some damn fool congressman would probably be on television claiming this was proof of global warming.

Gordon glanced up at President Grant's portrait staring down at him, as if he were expecting something. Shit. The whole damned world was expecting something.

The news out of Africa couldn't have been better. Although there'd been some trouble with rioting at distribution centers that ran out of serum, the Marines had quelled the mobs with no loss of American life. And in every region where the nanite formula had been delivered, the effectiveness of the treatment had stunned the world monitoring organizations.

Doctors Without Borders reported the complete eradication of HIV and AIDS in the injected populations. Not just AIDS. Every single known disease was being wiped out across Africa. There were even reports of late-stage Ebola virus infections being cured.

But such success had a price. Riots had broken out in countries that were not on the early-distribution list. Despite the extensive US production program, the United Nations was up in arms over the limited quantities of serum currently available. They wanted nanites and they wanted them now. When the

United States refused to publish the procedure for manufacturing the nanite serum, several countries established scientific programs to reverse-engineer the formula by extracting blood from people who had received the injections or by stealing shipments of formula from the distribution centers.

The Russians and Chinese had gone so far as to threaten a military response if the United States failed to assist them in setting up their own production facilities, only backing down after President Gordon threatened to stop all serum shipments.

Not that everyone was thrilled with the worldwide distribution of nanites. Several Muslim leaders had issued a fatwa proclaiming that the serum was a product of Satan and that anyone using it was condemned, both in this life and the next.

Gordon shook his head. No virgins for them.

Numerous American Christian groups hadn't been happy about the nanite serum either. Between the religious nuts and the right-wing conspiracy theorists, the Secret Service was so busy following up on presidential death threats that he couldn't sneeze without five agents throwing their bodies on top of him.

The sound of the secure phone ringing brought the president out of his reverie. Returning to his chair, he lifted it to his ear.

"Yes?"

"Mr. President, this is Bob Adams."

"OK, Bob, what's wrong?" A call from his national security advisor this late at night was never good news.

"We've got a problem at Henderson House."

"Go on."

"Last night, a janitor without the appropriate clearance gained access to the underground levels and then escaped from the building. So far he's managed to evade the special security teams sent out to collect him."

"Why am I just now finding out about this?"

"Apparently, Dr. Frell felt the situation could be contained before he reported it."

"That stupid bastard!"

"Unfortunately, it gets worse. The janitor was using a false identity."

"How'd it pass security checks?"

"That's just it. This was a very professional job, fake background investigation, the works. We still don't know how he managed it. From items our team found in the hotel where he's been living, we know who it was."

"And?"

"And it was Freddy Hagerman. DNA samples from blood found on razor wire at Henderson House confirm it."

George Gordon clenched his right fist so tightly that his fingernails dug into the skin of his palm, the small cuts healing before he could notice. The name left him cold. Freddy Hagerman. The *New York Times* reporter who had broken the Priest Williams story.

"Listen to me, Bob. You know as well as I do what a public release of information on that program would do to us, to the country." President Gordon paused. "I want this moved to absolute top priority. I don't care what it takes; I want you to nail that son of a bitch before he can go public. You follow me?"

Bob Adams cleared his throat. "Yes, Mr. President."

"And get me Dr. Frell. I want his ass on the next plane to DC." President Gordon slammed the telephone into its cradle without waiting for a response.

The rumble of thunder rattled the window frame, pulling the president's gaze outward once again. No doubt about it. The coming storm would be a bad one.

CHAPTER 118

Jennifer rolled over in bed, stretching her arms until they were fully extended above her head. The clean smell of freshly laundered linens reminded her just how much her circumstances had improved this last week.

The light of the early-morning sun slanted into her room through the French doors, opened wide to the balcony. A loud squawk brought her gaze around to the bird perched atop her open laptop. It was about the size of her hand, its body a brilliant orange from its underbelly to the tip of the long, pointed crest that extended outward from its forehead. Jorge had told her it was a vermilion cardinal, a species native to Colombia and Venezuela. Beautiful.

But it was sitting on her laptop. Probably getting ready to poop all over it.

“Hey. Scat!” Jennifer tossed a pillow in its general direction, sending the bird flying back out through the balcony doors toward the gardens below.

A low chuckle caused her to sit up abruptly, pulling her sheet up to her chest.

“I see you had an unwanted helper.” Jorge Espeñosa leaned back in the wicker chair across the room, his warm smile spreading the narrow lines of his Fu Manchu mustache.

Jennifer relaxed. A little. “Don Espeñosa. You startled me.”

It was the truth. Not needing sleep, Jennifer had been deep in meditation, but not so deep that she shouldn’t have heard him enter her room and sit down. What she really wanted to do was tell him to get out, but she still wasn’t sure exactly how much control she had over him.

“My apologies. I thought you’d be up by now. It’s a beautiful morning. I came up to invite you to breakfast. There is someone I would very much like for you to meet.”

Jennifer let her gaze wander out the window to the gardens that dominated the north side of the drug lord’s estate. “Will we be eating down on the patio?”

“Precisely.”

Jennifer smiled. “Sounds lovely. Give me twenty minutes.”

Don Espeñosa rose from the chair. “Twenty minutes then.”

As the don closed the door behind him, Jennifer made her way to the shower, discarding pajamas as she went. Standing under the pounding water, she thought about who she would be meeting. Clearly it was someone the don thought important. His voice had held a hint of uncharacteristic eagerness.

This thought gave her pause. By reputation and from her limited dealings with the man, she knew that Jorge Espeñosa had few attachments. He had no wife or children. His only brother had been killed in a battle with Colombian government troops thirteen years ago. His paranoia and distrust of others had led him to create a security structure composed of independent cells, each constantly checking on the others, each cell leader reporting directly to the don.

But within that paranoid mind, Jennifer had found a deep loneliness. Ironically, it was by manipulating both the loneliness and the paranoia that she had gained such rapid acceptance into his inner circle, something that had produced a great outcry of distrust from his other advisors. And although Jorge Espeñosa listened to their concerns, he disregarded them.

For her part, Jennifer had moved rapidly to prove herself worthy of his trust. Don Espeñosa had set her up with the finest high-speed network money could buy, through which she had immediately begun a scan of all of the cartel accounts. Within hours, she had identified twenty-seven different transaction traces, some initiated by the US government, some by the Colombian government, some by other cartels.

By the end of the first day, she had not only cleansed the suspect transactions, she had hacked her way back through the computer networks conducting the trace, eliminating each record trail at the source.

And as Jennifer worked, the Espeñosa cartel's top computer experts watched her, stunned by what they were seeing. Her delicate fingers worked the keyboards that surrounded her workstation so rapidly, they found themselves unable to follow what she was doing. But they knew she was breaching the toughest computer firewalls as easily as a husband brushed aside a wedding veil.

By her third day in her new job, cartel operatives began receiving reports that the US Internal Revenue Service and the Drug Enforcement Administration were in a panic about the worst cybernetic attack in history. Although the full extent of damage to their computer archives was being kept secret, rumor had it that data critical to several ongoing investigations had been completely destroyed. Even worse, their effort to restore the data from off-site archives was being circumvented by an aggressive new type of computer virus.

Jorge Espeñosa was so thrilled that he had asked her to implement a new computer tracking and security program for all cartel accounts.

Jennifer finished dressing, selecting a pink cotton blouse to go with her white cargo pants and sandals. Then, with one more glance in the mirror, she made her way down to breakfast.

The north patio dining area was the most beautiful spot on the entire estate. In the midst of flower gardens rivaling those she had seen on a family trip to Lake Chiemsee in Bavaria, several outdoor tables protected by colorful umbrellas provided an atmosphere so inviting that Jennifer often found herself lingering over her meal, reluctant to finish.

This morning several of the tables had been set with trays of fresh fruit, hot pastries, and a large assortment of cold cuts, breads, and cheeses. Don Espeñosa sat alone at a table set for three. Seeing Jennifer, he arose from his seat.

"Come. Let's fill our plates. I'm afraid my other guest will be a bit late."

Jennifer had grown accustomed to the buffet layout so favored by Don Espeñosa. Although he could order whatever he wanted, the drug lord most enjoyed making up his mind by looking at an assortment of food spread out before him.

Jennifer filled her plate, but Don Espeñosa seemed distracted, taking just half a grapefruit. He sprinkled it with salt before digging out a slice with his spoon.

"So who am I going to meet?" Jennifer asked.

"Someone whose judgment I trust completely." Jennifer searched Don Espeñosa's face for a smile, but found none.

"Mysterious."

Jorge leaned back in his chair, lifting a cup of frothy cappuccino to his lips before responding. "I don't mean to be. As a matter of fact, I'm a bit nervous." Recognizing what he had just said, the drug lord smiled. "I don't believe I've ever said that before. You see? You confuse me. I'm not a trusting man, yet I find myself trusting you. My key people all tell me to go slow, that I'm behaving irrationally."

Jennifer felt a flash of anger. "The same people who provided such great security for your accounts? I think they're angry about me making them look bad."

Jorge laughed. "That's exactly what I told them. Of course, I said it with a gun in my hand."

Jennifer's mouth dropped open. "You didn't kill them?"

"No, of course not. It just lets them know I'm not in the mood for an argument."

"I make you nervous?"

"A poor choice of words. You make me feel different. Unusual. It's why I wanted you to meet my associate, so he could form his own impression. I think you'll find him interesting."

Suddenly, Don Espeñosa glanced up. "Ah, here he comes."

As the don rose from his chair, Jennifer turned to see a very handsome young man walk out onto the patio. With dark hair and light skin, dressed in a mocha suit, he moved with easy grace and self-confidence.

"Jennifer Smythe, I would like to present my good friend, Eduardo Montenegro."

Jennifer stood, extending her hand, which was grasped and gently raised to Eduardo's lips. The touch, cool and soft on the back of her hand, matched the look in those beautiful dark eyes.

So this was the one whose judgment Don Espeñosa trusted more than his own. So be it.

Jennifer took a deep breath and centered. Then, with a small smile on her lips, she stepped across the threshold of those dark orbs and into the soul beyond.

CHAPTER 119

From the moment El Chupacabra stepped onto Don Espeñosa's lush patio with its colorful native tile, bright umbrellas, and the elaborate buffet spread across tables in a manner that would have made the Mirage Hotel managers hot with jealousy, he knew what elevated his heartbeat. It wasn't the lavish spread. Not the smell of orchids. Eduardo had been on this patio so many times that these failed to arouse his interest.

It was the girl.

Don Espeñosa rose from the table, his hand extended in greeting.

"Jennifer Smythe, I would like to present my good friend, Eduardo Montenegro."

Although he met the grip with his own firm clasp, Eduardo's gaze was drawn past the drug lord to the young woman rising from her chair, the one Don Espeñosa had been so anxious for him to meet. Petite, not more than seventeen, her coal-black hair cut short and sexy, accentuating the line of her slender neck. Even in a casual blouse and pants, her body called to him, young and supple with a hint of unusual strength and grace.

Eduardo had always had a special hunger for such young women. They hadn't yet learned if they liked to scream. With Eduardo, they all did.

But there was something different about this one, something that drew him more than could be explained by the proud, upward-tilting chin, the narrow waist, and the firm little tits and ass.

As Jennifer stood, Eduardo moved past the don, gently grasping her extended hand and raising it to his mouth. The trick with a woman's hand was to let your warm breath stroke the tiny hairs on its back, barely allowing your lips to graze it. When done correctly, the quick contrast of warm breath and cool lips raised goose bumps across her body.

Eduardo lifted his gaze slowly, rewarded by the sight of the gooseflesh tightening on those slender arms. Gotcha. Then his eyes locked with hers.

For a moment he was held by them, a gaze so intense that he felt as if he had been strapped into a chair and jolted with fifty thousand watts of juice. A force moved in his head, and it wasn't him.

As a boy in Lima, in the madness and desperation that had taken his mother, she had turned to the old ways, searching among the lost souls of the poor for someone who could teach her the dark magic of the Incas. And as she pulled her young son from one rat-infested barrio to the next, she had found a native woman who taught her the Inca rituals.

Some scholars thought the Inca Empire had been built by their attainment of enlightenment, a knowledge of science akin to that of the Egyptians. But the Inca had built their empire on fear. They worshipped it. Their elaborately designed rituals produced fear beyond that ever achieved by any society before or since.

Eduardo knew. After all, Inca rituals required a subject. And his mother had kept her own small subject close at hand.

It is often said that when a man is first exposed to wickedness, he is appalled. But if he remains associated with that wickedness for long enough, he comes to accept it, then finally to embrace it. Eduardo had found the same to be true of fear.

In those years of ritualistic torture at the hands of his mother, Eduardo had come to accept his own fear and to worship it in others. She had taught him well. He almost regretted killing the witch. Almost.

Eduardo felt a sudden cold sweat dampen his skin. As hard as it was to believe, this girl had the talent his mother had tried so hard to attain, the ability to join minds with another. In his head he could feel her, her touch strong but soft, seeking to know him, but for what purpose?

Rather than resist the intrusion, El Chupacabra opened himself wide. The girl's powers were so strong he felt that he might not have been able to resist them anyway. Why not let her see the whole package?

A sudden change in the intrusion pounded his head. She was scrambling now, no longer seeking to burrow more deeply, her efforts reduced to a desperate scramble to break the connection.

Fear. Its glorious purity flowed from her mind into his, each wave so intense that it threatened to bring him to climax where he stood, amid the orchids and roses on Don Espeñosa's private patio. When he was a teen, he had first experienced that rush of sexual release as he plunged the knife again and again into his mother's dying breast. It was as if he had been sprinting, his heart hammering in his chest, filling his arteries and vessels with a thunder that demanded release. He hadn't felt anything this intense since that first kill, but here it was again.

As close as he had come to all his special victims, seeking to immerse himself in the ritual of fear, those experiences now seemed empty. Here was pure, fresh terror, dripping directly into his mind in a way he'd never dreamed possible.

Then it was gone. The girl, whose hand he still held, slumped toward the ground.

Eduardo caught her as she fell, guiding her unconscious body back into its seat.

"What the hell?" Don Espeñosa's gasp of surprise brought Eduardo back to the present.

"She fainted."

"I can see that. Why?"

Eduardo turned his face toward the drug lord and grinned. "What can I say? I have that effect on women."

Don Jorge Esteban Espeñosa's brow darkened momentarily, then his expression broke into a grin even broader than Eduardo's. "Uh-huh. Well, you just keep your dick in your pants. This one's mine. Besides, I brought you here to get your opinion of the girl, not to offer her up as Chupy bait."

Eduardo glanced at the girl slumped in the chair and shrugged. "What's to say? I like her."

"I don't give a shit if you want her. I want to know if I can trust her."

Eduardo studied Don Espeñosa's angular face. "Trust her? Why?"

Don Espeñosa signaled with his hand, and a servant appeared out of the doorway. "*Manuel, Señorita Jennifer está enferma. Llévela a su cuarto.*"

"*Sí, señor.*"

As the servant lifted Jennifer in his arms to carry her back to her room, the drug lord nodded at Eduardo.

"Walk with me."

For forty-five minutes, Eduardo walked with Don Espeñosa, listening intently to his description of how this girl had come into his possession, how this teenager had hacked her way past the best security the cartel's computer experts could provide to access his accounts, how she had hacked Bellagio security, and how, given the opportunity, she had turned her talents to frustrating the US DEA and IRS.

It was clear that Jorge Espeñosa had developed strong feelings for this child prodigy. But he was, above all else, a paranoid schizophrenic who could never fully trust anyone. So he had called in El Chupacabra, a man known for his ability to see through the veneer with which people draped themselves, all so that the drug baron could feel safe in his decision to keep the girl, to put her to work for him, to eventually make her the first Señora Espeñosa.

They had long since made their way out of the gardens, winding their way up one of the mountainous paths that led into the secluded north end of the estate. A black-and-yellow bird darted through the branches high above, its high-pitched keen giving testimony to its annoyance at the disturbance on the trail below.

Eduardo stopped and turned to look directly into Jorge Espeñosa's dark-brown eyes.

"So you want to know what I think of her?"

"I do."

Eduardo paused. "You know me and my first impressions."

"Never wrong."

El Chupacabra smiled. "I hold my own."

"And your impression of the girl?" The tension in Jorge Espeñosa's voice was palpable.

"As I said, I like her. And yes, I'd like to screw her. But we can't always get what we want."

Don Espeñosa laughed, a little too hard, as if any other assessment from Eduardo would have been too horrible to bear.

"I would, however, like to do some double-checking. Do you mind if I do some of my own digging into her background?"

"Fine."

"I'll want to search her things."

"My people have already done that."

"That's them, not me."

Stepping back slightly, Don Espeñosa studied Eduardo's face. After a couple of seconds, he shrugged. "Do whatever you want, so long as it doesn't involve laying a finger, or any other body part, on the girl. Like I said, she's mine."

Eduardo smiled his most disarming smile. "Agreed."

The don turned and began leading him back down the trail toward the main part of the estate. High in the trees, El Chupacabra spotted, for the third time, two riflemen with sniper scopes.

Would the don have been so foolish as to try to give a signal to his snipers if Eduardo had pronounced the girl unworthy? What kind of hold had this strange girl established over the drug lord?

One thing was certain. He very much looked forward to finding out.

CHAPTER 120

The gentle breeze kissed Jennifer's cheek softly enough to nudge her toward wakefulness without startling her. She had almost forgotten how good it felt to wake up slowly.

Carried up on the breeze, the thick fragrance of Don Espeñosa's gardens brought her back to the present. With a start, Jennifer sat bolt upright in the bed. What had happened? How had she gotten here?

She'd been at breakfast. Don Espeñosa had been there, introducing her to…to…

A shudder started at the base of her neck and amplified until she had to clench her fists to stop the shaking in her hands. Eduardo Montenegro.

She'd barely touched his mind, not nearly as deeply as she'd linked with the many others on which she'd used her special ability, but what she'd felt there had been horrible. Something had rubbed against her, sending her mind recoiling, struggling to find its way back to the light of her own body. But she was so deep in shock that she had lost the thread that could guide her back. She only knew that she had to get away from the horror she had mentally embraced.

Every time the thing had touched her thoughts again, she had retreated, scrambling ever deeper into the darkness, erecting barriers in her mind, wall after wall of them, each higher and thicker than the last. But instead of blocking out the thing that pursued her, her panic had seemed to feed it, drawing it onward like a beacon in the night.

Then a kind of mental count had begun to tick down, starting at ten, and she'd known that if she didn't find her way back to her own head by the time that count hit zero, whatever was coming would pull her into a madness from which there would be no escape.

The memory was so intense she felt the bile rise up in her throat and had to force it down. Clearly she'd escaped, but it had been close.

Jennifer had delved into many minds, not the least of which was Don Espeñosa, the boss of the most violent and largest of the South American cartels. Although she had found it filled with cruelty, greed, and paranoia, there were parts of his mind that loved beauty, that longed for basic human affection, and in those parts Jennifer had comfortably roamed. Even playing on his greed and paranoia had presented little challenge to her abilities.

But touching Eduardo's mind would always terrify her beyond words. It was a blackness in which unthinkable thoughts and feelings squirmed and wriggled, each tendril seeking to pull her deeper into the abyss. In that mind she had felt no hint of light.

Once again the memory overwhelmed her. This time she failed to shift her thoughts in time, the heaves emptying her partially digested breakfast onto the sheets spread across her legs.

"Perfect!" Jennifer muttered as she tossed the sheets into a pile, then headed for the bathroom to wash the acrid taste from her mouth and the filth from her body.

Under the splash of water hot enough to send waves of steam rising from her skin, Jennifer tried to calm herself. But this time her concentration failed her. She'd heard of people so deep in shock that they couldn't stop shivering, but until now she'd only imagined what that was like. Now, standing in Turkish sauna–style steam, she found herself shaking like the last leaf on a maple tree, the cold autumn wind tugging and twisting at the tiny stem that connected her to reality.

In Arizona, on the rim of the Grand Canyon, the Hualapai Indians had built a stunning new attraction called the Skywalk. Tourists could cross the massive glass walkway balanced a mile above the Colorado River and extending a full seventy feet beyond the canyon rim. Jennifer had never had the chance to visit it, to walk away from the edge with only a transparent layer between her small body and the canyon bottom a mile below. Now she felt as if she stood at its very center, not wanting to look, but with eyes drawn irresistibly toward the abyss.

Jennifer turned off the water, walked out of the small shower, and wrapped herself in a thick white towel. If anything, she felt colder now than when she had stepped in to warm up, the tremors in her hands having migrated into her core. She considered climbing back into bed, piling the covers atop herself as she curled into a fetal ball. But the thought of the mess in the sheets killed that idea.

What she needed was something only the Second Ship could provide, that sweet sense of well-being she had experienced on the alien couch. Only now she'd gotten herself into a state where any memory threatened to pull the wrong one. She couldn't bear that again. Not now. Not ever.

Frustrated, Jennifer made her way past the open French doors leading onto the balcony, the warm breeze chilling her like tendrils of marine-layer fog. She thought about closing the doors, then discarded the notion. The chill wasn't real, only a figment of her extensive imagination. She knew what she needed, and it wasn't beyond the doors to the balcony. It was in the closet.

Pulling open the slatted doors, she stepped inside to pull her suitcase from the highest shelf. Jennifer dropped it on the floor, her fingers fumbling at the zipper like those of a junkie struggling to get to her fix.

There, in the inner zippered pocket, she found them, the two translucent alien headbands, exactly where she had left them. To Don Espeñosa's men, they'd been of no more interest than any young girl's hair decorations. So much for judgment.

The second Jennifer touched the one that was uniquely hers, she felt better. It was one of the oddities of the alien halos that only the one to which you had originally become attuned worked for you. And once they had attuned to you, they didn't work for anyone else, at least not while you lived. After that, Jennifer didn't know and didn't want to find out.

With both headbands clutched in her hand, she walked across the room to the wicker chair in which Don Espeñosa had sat that morning. Tossing the other halo on the coffee table, Jennifer slid into the chair and pulled her knees up to her chest.

Then, taking a deep breath, she positioned her own halo on her head, letting the small beads slide into place over her temples.

CHAPTER 121

Three thousand miles away, in a temporary shelter he had come to think of as home, Dr. Hanz Jorgen scanned the papers spread across every square inch of his desk.

The article that currently held his attention had received scant notice from the scientific community, much less from the general public, but he found it fascinating. In it, Dr. Paul Silas of Northwestern University focused on the asteroid named 2004 XY130. Although the asteroid had far less than one chance in a million of striking Earth, its potential impact would produce an explosive force in excess of two thousand megatons, more than a hundred thousand times the force of Little Boy, the bomb that had been dropped on Hiroshima in World War II.

A buzzing in his pocket alerted him to the presence of his cell phone. Having tried unsuccessfully to find a ring tone that was only mildly obnoxious, Jorgen had long since adopted the vibrate-only cell phone policy for himself and his staff.

He flipped his open, lifting it to his mouth. "Jorgen here."

"This is Bill Franks."

Dr. Franks's distinctive voice crackled with excitement.

"I can tell that, Bill. What is it?"

"You better get down here, Hanz. Something incredible is happening."

Without bothering to utter a word of response, Dr. Jorgen hoisted his large frame from the chair and headed out the door, flipping the cell phone closed as he ran. Although no one would think it to look at him, Dr. Jorgen could move with the agility of a man half his age and weight when he needed to. And right now, making his way rapidly down the steep stairs cut into the side of the canyon, he needed to.

Dr. Franks waited at the bottom of the steps, his face even paler than usual in the bright midmorning sun.

"What is it?" Dr. Jorgen asked between panting breaths.

Bill Franks pointed at the spot where the high desert mesquite had been cleared to open a path into the starship cave. The entrance was gone.

Dr. Jorgen rushed forward to touch the hillside where he had walked out of the cave just two hours before, bringing himself up short when his hand passed into what appeared to be solid ground.

"What the hell?" He pulled his hand back, somewhat surprised to see it reappear intact.

"It's come alive."

Dr. Jorgen was renowned for his quick wit and ability to rapidly analyze changing scientific data, but now he felt as if his thoughts were stuck in mud.

"The alien ship." Dr. Franks grinned like a boy who'd just found his older sister's diary. "A few minutes ago. It just came on."

"And this?" Dr. Jorgen pointed to the illusory wall in front of him.

"Some sort of advanced hologram. It appeared at the same time."

"Out of my way." Dr. Jorgen had to get inside the cave. As excited as he'd been when he first laid eyes on the alien starship, this went beyond that.

The darkness beyond the hologram was not complete, but it surprised him. The banks of lights his team used to study the exterior of the starship had all been turned off, leaving a magenta glow, which seemed to emanate from the air itself.

Bill Franks stepped up beside him. "We turned them off to better see this."

At the far end of the cavern, Dr. Jorgen could see the smoothly curved bulk of the starship, completely draped with the metal scaffolding that supported the researchers and their equipment.

Dr. Jorgen took two steps forward, then stopped one more time to stare at the unearthly illumination.

"Beautiful. Just beautiful."

CHAPTER 122

Losing one's fascination with life was like dying, and El Chupacabra had no intention of doing either. He knew how to watch, and he knew how to wait. This was how it worked. Watch and wait.

Eduardo could have just searched Jennifer's room, going through her personal things with the same unmatched thoroughness that had made him the world's best assassin. Instead, he strolled out past the north end of Don Espeñosa's gardens, found a tall tree, and climbed.

As he lifted himself onto a concealed branch that provided a nice armrest, Eduardo pulled the Swarovski EL 10x32 binoculars from a cargo pocket on his trouser leg. They were easily the best compact binoculars in the world, perfectly waterproof and nitrogen-filled so that they never fogged, even in the Amazon. Eduardo loved them, especially now that Swarovski had removed the slight golden bias present in the lenses of earlier models.

Aiming the binoculars at Jennifer's balcony, Eduardo adjusted the focus. The white French doors were open wide, embracing the spectacular view of the gardens and mountains on the north side of the estate. An outside sitting area with a small round table and two deck chairs sat immediately above and to the right of the patio where Eduardo had met the startling young lady. From this angle Eduardo had a clear view of almost the entire bedroom beyond.

Jennifer Smythe still lay asleep beneath a sheet on her bed, the heavier covers having been turned back by the servant who had carried her up to her room. The bedroom was as Eduardo remembered it, having stayed there in one of his previous visits to the estate. A wicker reading chair and coffee table sat across the room from the bed, near the door that opened in from the second-floor hallway. One thing that was new was the oak desk on which a laptop computer sat open, the screen saver's multicolored fractal lines cutting a swath across the blackness.

Eduardo shifted his eyes to the sleeping girl. Almost as if she felt his gaze, the girl's sleeping form shifted. As she stretched her arms high above her head, a smile crept onto her lips. Then, with a start, Jennifer Smythe sat straight up. She continued to sit there, her stillness interrupted only when she leaned forward and puked in her own lap. He continued to watch as Jennifer jumped out of bed, wadded the sheets, dumped them into a pile and disappeared into the bathroom.

Eduardo smiled, remembering the feel of her fear as their minds had touched. She gave *good head* a whole new meaning.

Spending much less time in the shower than he would have expected, Jennifer reappeared, wrapped in a white robe. She moved quickly across the room and opened the closet, and although the closet door partially obscured his view, it seemed that she pulled something from a high shelf, possibly a suitcase or large bag.

Whatever she was after did not take her long to find, and the change in her face as she reemerged from the closet was clear. She had entered in a panic of intensity, but now the girl radiated hope.

Jennifer paused, tossed something onto the coffee table and plopped into the wicker chair. Again, Eduardo adjusted the binoculars' zoom and focus.

A narrow, three-quarter loop of metal or shiny plastic lay on the coffee table. What was that? A headband? Shifting his gaze back to Jennifer, Eduardo saw that she held a similar band, gazing raptly down at it. Then, inhaling deeply, she slid the band onto her head, positioning it more like a military headset than a young girl's decorative headband. The analogy wasn't exactly right. The ends of the band were positioned over her temples, not her ears, but the intent looked the same.

Once again Jennifer's expression underwent a remarkable change, the worry lines in her face disappearing as he watched. Her brown eyes remained open, but the look became distant. It wasn't that they lost focus. Instead, they focused on something that only she could see.

For the next forty-seven minutes, Jennifer Smythe remained in the chair without moving, the relaxed intensity of her expression unchanging. Then, as one would get up from a movie when the theater lights came on, Jennifer arose from the chair, removed the headband, and deposited it and its twin back in the hidden container in the closet.

Dressing with a purpose and alacrity that Eduardo would not have believed possible only a few minutes before, the young lady walked confidently out of her room, closing the door behind her.

Without hesitation, Eduardo pocketed the binoculars and dropped from the tree, sprinting toward the house along a path that avoided the garden. He emerged from the woods between a freestanding six-car garage and the servants' entrance. Two white-coated cooks raised their eyebrows questioningly as he moved through the kitchen, but upon seeing who it was, returned quickly to their business.

He passed through a pair of swinging doors into the narrow service hallway and opened the first door on his right. Taking the stairs two at a time, Eduardo paused only momentarily before stepping into the second-floor hallway.

Finding it empty, he walked to Jennifer's door, twisted the knob, and stepped inside. After closing the door behind him, he moved to the closet. Eduardo pulled the twin slatted doors open, flipped the light switch, and stepped inside. The closet was a large walk-in, a small assortment of clothes hanging from only one of the four available clothes racks, the emptiness adding to the closet's apparent size.

Glancing up, he could see a single charcoal-colored suitcase on the top rack. Eduardo lifted it down, setting it gently on the closet floor. The suitcase was divided into two compartments with three zip-up pouches for holding shoes and accessories. Both main compartments were empty, but in the second of the accessory pouches he found what he was looking for: the mysterious headbands.

Sitting cross-legged beside the suitcase, Eduardo selected one of the bands, running his fingers over the entire surface. It appeared to be metal, but not of a type he recognized, its surface refracting light in a way that gave it the illusion of translucence. The material flexed, but gave an impression of great strength and durability.

Could it be an artifact? His mother had spent her adult life looking for magical Incan artifacts, studying photographs and drawings of ceremonial pieces. But those had all been complex designs. These bands were elegant in their simplicity. Could one of these have produced the apparent trance he had watched Jennifer slip into?

Only one way to find out.

Eduardo slid the band he held over his temples in the manner he had seen Jennifer do, counting slowly backward from ten as he did.

Nothing.

Disappointed, he returned it to the zippered pocket before turning to examine the remaining band. It appeared identical to the first in every respect. So much for that theory. Eduardo started to place it back in the zip-up pocket alongside the first, then paused.

No use breaking old habits. In his book, thoroughness was next to godliness.

Spreading the band slightly with his hands, Eduardo slipped it into place on his head. For a moment it seemed that the small beads at both ends adjusted themselves for comfort. Indeed, a low-frequency vibration began producing a relaxing massage.

Once again he felt disappointment. So this was just a relaxation gadget, probably something she had gotten in a Sharper Image store.

A lifetime of close familiarity with pain did little to prepare him for the explosion in his head. It felt as if a million holes had been drilled into his skull, each with a tiny micro-Taser inserted, all simultaneously firing their fifty-thousand-volt pulses directly into his brain. He tried to pull the headband off but found he could no longer control his body.

Thoughts flashed through Eduardo's mind. Was this it? Had he finally succumbed to an elaborate trap?

Shift.

The closet was gone. He floated in a transparent bubble in the vast darkness of empty space. A ringed planet darted by, its many moons careening away as his ship banked so hard that it seemed the gravitational strain would destroy it.

Then he saw it, flitting across his field of vision, far ahead. It expanded in a magnified view, surrounded by circles and cross-hairs as his ship tried to get a lock on the target.

The long cigar-shaped craft he chased suddenly emitted a swirling vortex that rippled through the space between them, a narrow tube that bent and twisted his view of the stars on its far side.

His ship torqued hard right and dropped, the space-time ripple passing within a hundred meters of him. In response, a beam of solid red pulsed outward from his own ship, missing the cigar ship but pulverizing a small asteroid as he passed through a field thick with the spinning rocks.

Ahead, a blue planet with a single moon loomed large, and the other ship raced toward it. Almost simultaneously, both ships' weapons fired again.

His red beam played across the cigar ship's surface, bubbling and warping its hull, as the vortex beam punched through his own ship. All maneuvering control lost, his ship plunged onward, and the surface of the blue planet rose up to meet him.

The scene winked out. The closet returned.

Eduardo found himself leaning back against one of the shoe shelves, his legs still crossed, his arms hanging limply at his side.

His mind struggled to reorient itself. What the hell had just happened? An answer came to him. At least he thought it was an answer, although he couldn't identify the symbols that floated in his brain.

Of course. The headset.

Eduardo reached up and removed the headband from its perch atop his head. Immediately the unfamiliar imagery stopped. But a strangeness lingered. All those years of torture and suffering at his mother's hands had given him a special awareness of each and every nerve ending in his body. It was one of the things that made him strong and fast. He was aware of things long before others sensed them. Now that awareness had been ramped up to an altogether new level. It was as if he had been blind but could now see, deaf but could now hear. He squeezed his hand into a fist, and that too felt different.

Staring down at the seemingly insignificant metal circlet in his hand, Eduardo understood. He'd been right the first time. It was an artifact, although its origin and powers were far stranger than he had imagined.

Rising to his feet, Eduardo retrieved the other alien artifact from the zippered pocket and returned the now-empty suitcase to its place on the shelf.

Then, with the artifacts clutched firmly in his left hand, Eduardo Montenegro made his way out of the building by the same route by which he had entered.

Yes, today his mother would have been proud of her son.

CHAPTER 123

Gone!

Shock smashed into Jennifer's head like a wrecking ball. She played back the memory of placing the suitcase on the top shelf, comparing it against the position from which she had just retrieved it. Not the same. As if she needed confirmation that the precious alien halos had been stolen.

Weak with dread, she stumbled out of the closet, her eyes stabbing toward the desk where she'd left her laptop. There it sat, untouched.

It didn't make sense. Why would a thief leave the laptop and take the apparently worthless headbands? If it had been Don Espeñosa, she would have sensed it in his mind. The answer that flashed through her brain left her shaking with anger and dread.

Eduardo. He must have been spying on her as she awoke, must have seen her make the connection to the Second Ship.

God, she was stupid! Jennifer felt like grabbing her short hair in both hands and ripping out chunks of hair and scalp. But self-flagellation wasn't going to solve her problem. She had to act and act quickly.

That sick son of a bitch had taken them, and she was going to get them back. Eduardo might be a monster, but he had no idea whom he was dealing with.

Jennifer burst out the doorway with such force that she almost knocked down a maid.

"*Perdón, señora.*" Jennifer's voice carried a deep sense of urgency. "*Donde está Don Espeñosa?*"

The woman recovered her equilibrium and pointed down the hallway. "*El señor está en la biblioteca.*"

Jennifer's Spanish was nowhere near as good as Mark's, but she could get by. The don was in his private library. Although Don Espeñosa loved it, Jennifer had only been in the room one time. The high-ceilinged, windowless space, with its twin leather chairs, dark hardwood floor, and tall bookshelves made her feel that she was trapped at the bottom of a well. The thick odor of cigar smoke only added to the oppressive atmosphere that permeated the room. For a lover of books to abhor a room filled with them seemed terribly wrong, but that was how she felt.

Two sharp raps on the door preceded Jennifer's entrance into the drug lord's inner sanctum. Don Espeñosa sat in the right-most reading chair, a fat Cuban cigar wedged between the index and middle fingers of his left hand, a hard copy of Dean Koontz's *Watchers* open in the other. His angry look faded as he saw who dared to interrupt his private time.

"Ah, Jennifer." The don set his book aside. "So you decided to take advantage of my library after all."

"That's not why I came." Jennifer's tone caused Don Espeñosa's left eyebrow to rise. "Something has been taken from my room. Two pieces of personal jewelry."

The drug baron motioned to the other chair. "Sit down and tell me about it. None of my staff would dare take anything in this household."

Reluctantly, Jennifer forced herself to sit, although the tension in her body kept her at the forward edge of the chair.

"It wasn't your staff."

"You saw the thief?"

"Not exactly." Jennifer hesitated. Don Espeñosa had said Eduardo was a personal friend, but there was no substitute for directness. "I believe Eduardo took them."

Don Espeñosa's eyes narrowed. "You are sure of this?"

"I am. There were two decorative headbands, gifts from my mother. I want them back."

The drug lord smiled. "Such spirit in so small a package." He puffed deeply on the cigar, breathing out a large plume of smoke before continuing. "Eduardo is a friend, but he is also a man of strange passions. I told him not to touch you, but it would not be beyond him to take a memento from someone such as you."

Jennifer's anger bubbled over. "Then make him give them back."

"Unfortunately, he left the estate thirty minutes ago." Noting her distress, Don Espeñosa put a hand on her arm. "Do not worry. I will send word that I want them returned as soon as he gets back from his business trip."

Jennifer made no attempt to hide the bitterness in her voice. "Knowing what he was like, why did you introduce that man to me?"

After another long draw on the cigar, Don Espeñosa leaned back in his chair. "You know I have developed a fondness for you. In my business, such sentiment can get a man killed. I have known Eduardo for several years, and he possesses a number of unusual talents. He was here because I asked him if I could trust you. Before he left, he stopped in to tell me."

Jennifer felt her chest constrict. "And his answer?"

The glowing ash at the end of the Cuban had grown so long it threatened to tumble to the hardwood floor at any moment. "He said I had stumbled upon a great treasure, a true prodigy. And he said I could trust you not to leave me."

"Did he say how he knows this?"

The don's eyes locked with hers. "Because you love your parents. Because you don't want Eduardo paying them a special visit."

Her psychic ability left no doubt. Don Espeñosa was telling her the truth. But manipulating Don Espeñosa wouldn't stop Eduardo from following through on the threat, even if the don ordered him not to. The beast had peered into her mind, and he would know.

There would be no leaving for Jennifer Smythe.

CHAPTER 124

Loading docks are never located in the best parts of town, and Manhattan Island's were no exception. It was a rough place, where men got hurt on the job and some men got hurt as part of much darker business. It wasn't exactly where Freddy had wanted to end up, but burrowed deep in the ass end of a long-haul truck, hidden among the cargo, he hadn't been in a position to ask the trucker to drop him someplace more convenient. For that matter, the way he'd been passing in and out of consciousness, he was lucky to have awakened at all.

He'd picked this particular truck out of the others at the Kansas City loading docks for two reasons. First, it had a shipment headed to New York. Second, it was pulling one of the new canvas-sided trailers, the kind that were so common in Europe. Perhaps that hadn't been such a great move. While it made it easier for him to slip inside, it did the same for the wind, and

November wasn't the greatest of times for a ride from Kansas to New York in a windy trailer. Especially with an infected leg.

Freddy leaned back against the warehouse wall, struggling to catch his breath in the dark alley. Funny about that. He'd sliced himself badly on rusty barbed wire, but that was healing up nicely. Overconfidence was what was busy killing him.

Should've known the feds would be all over his cell phone. Hell, he had known it. Just hadn't expected them to be on his ass the instant he used it. Who would've thought the people trying to shut him up were that good? And his editor hadn't even answered. Gutless bitch.

Only incredibly good luck and a passing train had saved his ass. If you call catching a bullet in the left calf lucky. Now he looked the part of a drunken vagabond, having swapped his old clothes and a C-note for his current wardrobe, courtesy of a Kansas City wino named Phil. The filthy garb was probably what had infected his wound.

Maybe he should've grabbed some of that new juice they were injecting into those poor bastards below Henderson House. Freddy shuddered. No, thanks. He'd take his chances with gangrene.

Freddy felt his left wrist for his watch. Gone. Shit, he'd given that to the wino, too. Really hadn't been in a good bargaining frame of mind when he'd made that deal. He looked around. Judging from the level of activity on the docks, it was somewhere between midnight and four in the morning. Good. That gave him a little time to do what he needed before it got light.

As a kid, he and some of his pals from the neighborhood had often come down to check out the docks after dark. Between that and a couple of news stories that had brought him down here later in life, he had more than a passing familiarity with the area. Although cell phones had killed off the old-style pay phones, there were still a few around the docks that the phone company had never bothered to take out. At least that had been true a couple of years ago. If they were still there, if he could get to one, and if it still worked...if, if, if...

For three and a half city blocks, Freddy staggered and swayed through the dark buildings, his near-perfect imitation of a drunkard more the result of his bad leg and raging fever than any brilliant acting on his part. Just as despair began to consume what little hope remained, he spotted it. While the chain that had once held a phone book had long since snapped off, the metal-wrapped cord and handset remained intact.

Raising it from its cradle, Freddy cursed. No dial tone. He jiggled the toggle within its cradle. When the familiar tone warbled in his ear, Freddy gasped with relief. He didn't know how far it was to the next phone, but he didn't think he could have made it.

He dialed zero and the operator's voice responded, bright and clear.

"Operator. How may I help you?"

"I want to make a collect call to Benny Marucci." Freddy recited Benny's number from memory.

"Who may I say is calling?"

Freddy hesitated. Based upon his experience with the cell phone call, the NSA, CIA, FBI, and every other three-letter agency in the government probably had banks of computers listening to the country's phone lines for any mention of his name.

Then it came to him. With the popularity of several recent mob-family television series, Italian-American slang had gained wide popularity. Old-school Benny Marucci hated that crap with a passion. Of course, that had only made Freddy go out of his way to use the words and phrases in his greetings. It was their game.

"Tell him it's from his goombah."

After several seconds, he could hear Benny's sleep-filled voice answer.

"Hello?"

"This is the operator. I have a collect call from a Mr. Goombah."

Another pause. "I'll accept the charges."

The operator spoke again. "Go ahead, sir."

"Benny, it's me."

"You don't sound too good."

"Been better. Hate to call, but you're the only one I could think of."

"You sure know how to stir the pot. Where you at?"

"Remember where your cousin Vito got whacked?"

Vito Calini had been a low-level mob enforcer who had gotten the cement-shoes treatment back in '88, on these loading docks.

"Uh-huh. Do you see any cranes from where you are?"

"One right in front of me, two more off to the left."

"OK. When you hang up, I want you to crawl back into the shadows and wait right where you are. Someone will come for you."

"How will I know them?"

"You'll know. Don't go anywhere, *cugine*." Benny hung up without giving Freddy a chance to respond to being called a young tough-guy wannabe.

"Couldn't if I wanted to," Freddy said into the dead handset before setting it back in its cradle. Then he staggered back to the side of the building.

By the time the black Lincoln Town Car pulled up beside the telephone, the gray light of dawn was fast approaching. Freddy had already started hobbling forward when two big, mean-looking hunks of mob muscle stepped out and, none too gently, thrust him into the backseat, sliding in on either side of him.

The car was rolling before the doors slammed shut.

Freddy automatically glanced back as the car made its way along the docks, but saw no sign of anyone following them. The driver swung the car around a truck and into a side alley. Immediately the truck backed across the alley entrance, blocking any access from that direction.

The black sedan turned again, this time down a much tighter alley, before swinging into an open bay door. The driver pressed the switch on a garage-door remote, sending the large metal door rumbling closed on its track.

"Hey, watch it!" Freddy exclaimed as one of the tough guys dragged him from the car, sending pain shooting through his leg.

Instead of taking it easier, the other tough guy grabbed his right arm, and together they dragged him down a set of cement steps. Freddy had never been big on ethnic slurs, but these two guidos were starting to piss him off. They opened a thick door and pulled him into a concrete cellar, closing and bolting the door behind them.

Freddy didn't like the look of the place, not one little bit. He'd done stories on places like this, places where the mob manufactured fish food. A pair of fluorescent lightbulbs burned in a fixture on the ceiling, minus the softening filter of a plastic cover.

He expected to be strapped onto a metal chair in the center of the room. Instead, the bigger of the two enforcers half-carried him to a chair beside a shop bench on the far wall. Dropping to a knee, the big man ripped open Freddy's bloody pants leg.

"Shit!" Freddy gasped as the pain forced beads of sweat out of his forehead like water from a squeezed sponge.

"Shit's right," the big man said. "Franky, get a look at this leg."

Franky ambled over, glanced down, then grinned at Freddy, revealing a mouth badly in need of an orthodontist. "You like that leg?"

"Used to," Freddy managed between clenched teeth.

"Well, it won't bother you much longer, will it, Jimmy?"

Freddy knew he must be missing something. Probably the fever making him delirious, but this conversation wasn't sounding good at all.

"Listen, guys. Maybe I should just be on my way. Don't want to trouble you."

"No trouble at all," Franky said, moving so that he was behind the chair.

As the one called Jimmy picked up a power tool from the workbench, Franky pinned Freddy to his seat in a grip that threatened to crack ribs.

"What're you doing? Goddamn it! I'm a friend of Benny Marucci's!"

As Jimmy retrieved a bucket and walked toward the chair, his grin returned. "Oh, we know. Benny said to help you disappear, and that's what we're going to do."

Jimmy pulled a handheld recorder from his pocket, pressed the small red RECORD button, and set it on the workbench. In a swift motion that belied his size, Jimmy looped a plastic tie around Freddy's good ankle, binding it tightly to the steel chair leg. Then, lifting the damaged leg so that it rested on the bucket, he switched on the jigsaw.

As the saw bit into the skin and bone just above Freddy's left knee, he began to scream, the sound echoing in the concrete room until it drowned out the high-pitched squeal of the saw. And despite the blood that splattered the case, the small gears on the old cassette tape recorder continued to spin.

CHAPTER 125

President Gordon sat at his desk in the Treaty Room of the White House; the voice on the secure phone was the one he'd been expecting.

"So, Bill, what have you got for me?"

"Good news, Mr. President. Freddy Hagerman is dead."

"You have confirmation."

"DNA, and lots of it. It seems that our boys weren't the only ones after Mr. Hagerman."

"How so?"

"A few years back he did a series of stories on New York crime families. Apparently, one of them held a grudge. Some of their boys ran him through a crane pulley down on the docks. Most of the body went in the river, but police found a mangled leg and lots of blood on the big cable spool."

The president hesitated. "All they found was a leg?"

"No. If that was it, we wouldn't be certain he's dead. The mob left a bloody cassette tape at the scene. Must've wanted to send a message."

"They recorded the kill."

"Just the audio. Pretty nasty stuff. You can hear them working on Hagerman with a power tool. Must've run him through the crane after that. Reminds me of what the mob did to one of the FBI boys a few years back."

"You're sure it's Hagerman on the tape?"

"Voiceprints match. One more thing, Mr. President."

"Yes?"

"When someone screams hard enough, the vocal cords start ripping. Permanent damage. The boys in the lab ran an analysis on Hagerman's screams. At the end, his throat must have been a bloody mess."

"Thanks, Bill."

The president hung up the phone and leaned back in his high-backed leather chair, feeling the weight lift from his shoulders for the first time in over a week. He hadn't admitted to himself just how much the pressure had gotten to him. If Hagerman had been able to leak the information on what was happening in the tunnels beneath Henderson House, the government would have had a serious shit-storm on its hands.

One major threat put to bed. And with the information his source in the CIA was providing, he felt confident that the remaining threat would be dealt with soon. Even though they still didn't know Jack Gregory's location, it was only a matter of time.

The CIA had some talented contractors, but Gregory made him nervous. After what had happened in Los Alamos, the president was in no mood to take any chances this time. That's why he'd recalled the Colombian.

The president looked out his window and smiled. Freddy Hagerman dead!

Tonight he'd break out a glass of that Chivas he'd been saving for just this occasion. When the Colombian nailed Gregory, he'd finish the rest of the bottle.

CHAPTER 126

Sitting in the beautiful terrace dining area of the Hotel Poblado Plaza in the heart of Medellín's business district, Mark couldn't begin to allow himself to relax. So intense had been his concentration on the drive from Bogotá to Medellín that he had heard the movement of the soldiers' hands on their weapons at each checkpoint, had monitored their heart rates and breathing for any sign of increased stress.

But the trip had gone remarkably smoothly. They had flown into Bogotá to avoid taking a direct path to their target, staying just long enough to purchase an old car, the transaction made in cash. Thanks to Heather's gambling talent, there was no shortage of that. Their papers had aroused no suspicion, and after listening briefly to the intonations of local people, Mark had adjusted his Spanish so that he now sounded like a native.

In years past, traveling the road between Bogotá and Medellín would have been tantamount to carrying a "Please kidnap me!" sign. With the left-wing guerrillas, the right-wing paramilitary groups, the bandits, and corrupt soldiers, any attempt to travel the Colombian countryside carried with it the near-certainty of disaster. But that had changed in recent years, and while dangers still existed, the risk was acceptable.

Besides, Heather had given the travel plan her savant blessing.

Mark glanced across the table, watching her sip cappuccino, her eyes hidden behind her dark sunglasses. Heather's powers were getting stronger—much stronger. All this practice peering into the future had been exercising her brain in ways he couldn't even begin to imagine. And although at times she still needed to go into a deep trance, she was now able to pick up changes that might affect their plan while carrying on normal conversation. She called them eddies, small events that produced large impacts later on. If anything was out of place, he could count on Heather to spot it. His job was to be ready when she did.

They knew where Jennifer was being held: the estate of Jorge Espeñosa, the most feared drug lord in South America. Triangulation of the missing headbands had confirmed it. Bad news. Jen couldn't have gotten herself into a worse spot if she'd been thrown into a Colombian prison.

Now they were sitting on the terrace of one of the nicer hotels in Medellín, having spent the last two days dreaming up a plan that gave them a chance to get Jen out alive. Today was to have been the day of reckoning. But this morning, everything had gone to hell.

Overnight, the headbands had been moved, this time to Washington, DC.

Although Mark had been stunned by the discovery, at first he had believed it was a piece of good luck. After all, it would be far easier to rescue Jennifer in the United States than from the drug lord's compound. Heather had just quashed that idea.

Mark looked at his plate. The half-eaten scrambled eggs and bacon had grown as cold as his formerly hot coffee, his appetite having dissipated along with their heat.

"So you don't think Jennifer's in DC?"

"No," Heather said. "I can feel her in my head. She's close."

"Then how the hell did the headbands get to Washington?"

Seeing Heather's eyebrow rise, Mark backpedaled. "Sorry. I'm just not liking what I'm thinking right now."

"I know. It's not good."

"So what're we going to do about it?"

"Nothing. Stay focused on getting to Jen."

"And our plan?"

"Unchanged."

Mark smiled, attempting to show a confidence he didn't feel. After all, what good was perfect muscle control if you couldn't use it to lie to your best friend? He reached across the table and touched Heather's face, gently removing her sunglasses. Just because she said this was their best chance didn't mean their odds of surviving the day were good. And before he got up and led her out of this hotel to whatever destiny awaited, he wanted to look into her beautiful brown eyes one more time.

Heather seemed to sense his thoughts. Shit, for all he knew, she was hearing them. Her own brave smile parted her lips. He wanted to lean across and kiss them so bad he actually started to lean forward. Instead, Mark swallowed hard and returned her sunglasses to their accustomed spot on her nose.

"Ready?" Heather asked, standing up.

"Ready."

Mark flexed his muscles as he rose to his full height. One thing he swore to himself as he turned toward the door: he wasn't going to die before he got to deliver that kiss.

CHAPTER 127

Having left their cash in the hotel safe before ditching the car in the nearby barrio, Mark and Heather walked the last mile along the narrow winding road that led to the Espeñosa hacienda's front gate. Aside from the curious stares of a few onlookers, no one attempted to stop them.

Mark had almost forgotten what it felt like to look seventeen, although he felt older than Methuselah. He glanced over at Heather. Young or old, she still looked wonderful.

To say this plan bordered on madness would have been to give it the benefit of the doubt. When they had first begun to discuss how to rescue Jen, Mark had envisioned some sort of Rambo assault, bad guys pinned down by his withering gunfire as Heather led Jennifer to safety. There had certainly been nothing in his plan about two seventeen-year-old kids strolling up to the front gate and asking Don Espeñosa to see his prisoner.

When Heather had first described it to him, he had laughed out loud, thinking she was pulling his leg. It reminded him of the time his basketball coach had drawn up a last-second play for Jacob Mahoney to shoot the ball, on the theory that the other team would never expect it. No kidding. Jacob had been wide open. Right before he missed everything but the kid playing the tuba behind the hoop.

The only good thing Mark saw in the plan was that they wouldn't have to fight their way in. That and his faith in the little savant who had thought it up. But there was also the fact that they had been through so much, had seen so much, since they'd discovered the second spaceship. Every time he thought something was impossible, reality upped the ante.

As they reached the top of the low hill occupied by the Espeñosa estate, Mark inhaled deeply, glancing at Heather once again. No sunglasses and her eyes were normal. Good. Nothing in her savant mind had identified a serious problem with the way things were unfolding, at least nothing wrong enough to force her to go deep. As he refocused his attention on the armed guards beside the massive wrought iron gate ahead, the words of the X-wing pilot in *Star Wars* played in his head. "Stay on target. Stay on target."

The guards certainly didn't appear concerned about the two high-school kids walking toward them, not reacting until Mark touched the gate.

"Hey, what are you kids doing there?" the guard on the left yelled in Spanish, not bothering to raise the submachine gun cradled in his arm. "Get away from the gate!"

Mark responded with flawless Spanish of his own. "We're here to see Don Espeñosa."

This brought a round of loud laughter. "And what makes you think he wants to see you?"

Mark took another deep breath. Here it was. "Because he has my sister."

The change in the guards was immediate, their machine gun muzzles rising in unison. Mark had never before looked directly down the barrel of a loaded weapon, certainly not one gripped with a twitchy trigger finger. Now, with two of those round black holes pointed directly into his face, he decided he didn't like it.

The gate opened, and one of the guards grabbed Mark's arm, shoving him face-first against the railing as the other motioned for Heather to face the fence beside him. Covered by his partner's weapon, the swarthy fellow with the Che Guevara hairdo frisked him, cuffed his hands behind his back with a plastic tie, then repeated the procedure with Heather.

A quick glance at Heather showed tension in her face, but no white eyes. Everything was still on plan. Wonderful. That made him feel so much better.

Mark and Heather were pulled inside the compound, and while one guard placed a call on his cell phone, the other pushed them along the driveway leading up to a sprawling two-story house with arches that opened into a central patio area. At the base of the steps leading up to a pair of twelve-foot-tall wooden doors, the guard brought them to a stop.

"Where are you taking us?" Mark asked, drawing a sharp jab in the back from the muzzle of the machine gun.

As if in response to the question, the huge doors opened outward, revealing an elegantly dressed man sporting a Fu Manchu mustache and a thick cigar clamped in his teeth. Five khaki-clad bodyguards as big as pro wrestlers moved down to take charge of the prisoners.

"Thank you, Umberto," the man said, taking a puff on the cigar as he stepped closer to Mark. "You may return to your post."

The guard gave a stiff salute, pivoted, and walked rapidly back toward the now-closed gate.

Don Espeñosa smiled. "So, you are Mark Smythe. Your sister has told me so much about you. And this must be Heather McFarland."

Heather was the first to react. "Where is Jennifer? Can we see her? It's safe. No one knows we're here."

If anything, the drug lord's smile grew broader. "Oh, I know. You two have been all over the American news channels. The mentally unstable friend and the distraught brother searching for his runaway sister. Quite a tabloid story."

The smile faded from the don's face. "Take them to the gym and wait until I get there."

The bodyguards grabbed Mark by each arm as he and Heather were dragged forward, not into the house, but through the arches that led into the beautiful central patio. Mark's mind spun, and he realized he was breathing hard. Despite the unpleasant tone he had heard in the don's last command, it was still possible that he was having them taken to the room where Jen was being held. Or maybe he had gone to get Jennifer.

The gym turned out to be a large room on the west side of the patio. Unlike the tile that had covered the entranceway and the walkway under the overhanging porch, black rubber mats covered the floor. Two mirrored walls reflected the racks of dumbbells and Nautilus equipment that filled the right side of the workout room. A chrome bar ran along the left wall, the kind ballet dancers used for stretching their legs, and that part of the floor was clear of equipment. A closed door in the far wall apparently gave access from within the main house.

Mark felt a metal handcuff slapped onto his right wrist just above the plastic tie. Then his back was shoved up against the weight rack and the second cuff applied, securing him to the equipment. Another drug thug cuffed Heather's wrists to the dancer's bar.

Anticipation hung in the air like campfire smoke, an anticipation that didn't feel right. The bodyguards looked like kids waiting to open their Christmas presents. Before Mark had time to think about that, Don Espeñosa entered the room, closing the door behind him.

No Jennifer.

He walked directly up to Heather. "So, you two thought you could just walk up to my estate and demand to see Jennifer Smythe. I guess word of my fabled good nature has reached your ears."

Two of the bodyguards snickered.

The don lifted Heather's chin with his hand. "What's wrong with her? Some kind of fit or something?"

Mark caught sight of the milky white of Heather's eyes. Shit. She'd gone deep.

"No matter," the don said, nodding toward Mark. "Kill the boy, then we'll have some fun with this one."

Before the bodyguards could turn to comply, Heather's brown eyes rolled back into place. With a noisy hawking sound, she spat directly in the don's face, the wad of spittle splashing his nose and left eye.

Don Espeñosa's lip curled into an ugly grimace as he wiped at his face.

"Wait!" His command brought the bodyguard who had begun to advance toward Mark to a halt.

The drug lord turned his attention back to Heather. "So you care about this boy, huh? OK. Then we'll let him watch before we kill him."

With a grin that became a sneer, the don signaled four of the thugs forward. "Uncuff her hands and stretch her out here on the floor."

To Mark's horror, the men released Heather's handcuffs, and although she struggled mightily, they pulled her down onto her back, one pinning each of her arms while two more spread her legs. Don Espeñosa knelt down between them, reaching forward to slowly unbutton Heather's blouse, one button at a time.

"Ah, Smythe. I bet you've never had a chance to do this. Don't worry. I'll let you watch."

To Mark, the panting breath of the men, the sound of the racing hearts pumping blood into the bulges in their pants, the smell of their sweat, felt like the rupture of hell's gate, and from that gate poured a firestorm of rage that scorched his brain.

Mark's heart pulsed in his chest, sending a massive surge of blood and adrenaline coursing through his arteries.

With a snap loud enough to spin Don Espeñosa's head in his direction, the metal and plastic of his double handcuffs split apart.

CHAPTER 128

Jorge Espeñosa heard a mighty crack behind him as he opened another button on Heather's blouse.

What the hell was that? Jorge spun toward the sound, but failed to comprehend what he was seeing. The Smythe boy was loose and moving, a look of rage distorting his face into a werewolf mask of hatred. Then the face blurred as the boy spun toward Carlos, the lone standing bodyguard, his fist moving so fast that the drug lord couldn't follow it.

Carlos's head exploded like a melon hit with a sledgehammer, the force of the blow spattering globs of blood, bone, and brain across the five men crouched over Heather McFarland. Then Smythe was on them.

As he reached for his Beretta, Don Espeñosa felt the kick break his arm and cave in his chest, the amazing force of the blow sending his body spinning across the room, where the impact with the wall broke his neck. As he slid to the floor, unable to twitch a finger, his face settled into an angle that provided a view of the carnage raging fifteen feet away.

Even as he hurtled forward, he could hear the wet screams behind him, could smell the coppery odor of blood. Smythe wasn't just killing the bodyguards, he was ripping them apart, pummeling their heads into a mush that even their nanite-infested bloodstreams had no chance to repair. Impossible. Nobody could move that fast or hit that hard. Nobody.

Don Espeñosa felt his own unnatural healing process restore the broken parts of his body, weaving his torn spinal cord back together, rewarding him with a river of pain. One thing he knew for certain: if the nanites didn't hurry, the boy demon was going to finish ravaging what remained of the bodyguards and turn his attention to a more entertaining victim, one he had saved for last.

His hand moved, a jerky motion that didn't accomplish anything, but which gave Jorge hope. And with that hope came panic. Just a few more seconds. That was all he needed to get enough control to reach his shoulder holster and put every bullet in his gun into the Smythe thing. He just hoped bullets would kill it.

As he struggled to move, Jorge's hand spasmed, but a quick glance toward the center of the room wiped away all hope. Smythe was coming, looking as if he'd just finished bobbing for apples in a barrel of blood.

And in those eyes…no pity.

CHAPTER 129

It was raining, the same bloody rain Heather had seen in her nightmare. Although the vision had ended a minute earlier, it seemed that the nightmare world had merged with the present, leaving her struggling to understand whether this was real or just another part of her hallucination. A warm wet blob splattered her face and hair as bodies that had just crouched atop her came apart, sending up great fountains of arterial spray.

Screams bubbled wetly, dying out as the mouths that uttered them lost all shape. And in the very eye of this hurricane of death, Heather stared up at the avenging archangel that Mark had become.

"I know what you are becoming." The laughing voice of the Rag Man echoed in Heather's delirious mind.

What Mark had become was what she had made him. She had seen this future, and yet she had knowingly set it in motion by spitting into Don Espeñosa's face. It was that or let Mark die.

Heather struggled to sit up in the slick red pool that covered the floor around her, not caring that her blouse had been half-torn away, exposing her bra. She felt sick, not just in her stomach, but in her soul. The image of Stephen King's *Carrie* stared back at her from the mirrored wall. Except it wasn't a bucket of pig blood that soaked Heather. And Carrie hadn't been covered with all these wiggling globs filled with nanites struggling to repair the irreparable.

Heather retched a single dry heave before she managed to shift her memory to the couch on the Second Ship. But she couldn't linger in that memory. The rain had stopped, and Mark was moving across the room toward the crumpled body of Don Espeñosa.

"Mark, stop!"

Her voice tugged at him like a jockey trying to stop a runaway horse. He slowed but didn't come to a complete halt.

"Mark! Look at me."

Mark grabbed the drug lord at the collar, lifting his broken body in one hand, as if it had no more weight than that of a baby. Heather could see Don Espeñosa was healing rapidly, although his arms and legs still only managed short spasmodic jerks.

"Mark! Look at me," she repeated, struggling to her feet.

Ever so slowly, Mark's head turned back toward her, the rage melting from his face as he stared at her.

Heather stepped forward. "We need him alive."

Espeñosa's hand twitched upward.

"I wouldn't," Mark said, his grip tightening until the drug lord's eyes bulged. Don Espeñosa's hand dropped back to his side.

Mark's gaze returned to Espeñosa. Reaching the shoulder holster, Mark removed the Beretta and slipped it into his own belt.

"And why do we need this piece of trash?" he asked.

"To take us to Jennifer, for one."

Heather noted his eyes moving across her half-naked torso, though she was spattered with blood, his stare bringing a flush to her cheeks. Spotting a rack of clean towels, Heather grabbed two, draping one over her shoulders while she scrubbed at her face and hair with the other.

Mark set the drug lord against the wall, standing over him in a posture that indicated his good luck might not continue to hold.

Heather grabbed more towels, handing some to Mark, who began scrubbing at his own sticky body. They certainly weren't going to come clean, and their clothes were ruined, but it helped.

"Someone will have heard the screams. They'll come," said Mark.

Heather bent down to stare into Espeñosa's dark eyes. "They heard, but they're not coming. People scream a lot in this room. And you don't like to have your rough play disturbed, do you, Señor Espeñosa?"

The visions that filled her mind confirmed it.

Heather studied the drug lord. The rate at which his nanite-infested bloodstream had repaired the damage to his body was amazing. Already he was able to stretch his arms and legs, rolling his neck from side to side as if recovering from no more than a bad crick. The muscles in his chest had worked the broken ribs back into some semblance of their original alignment, where they were rapidly being knit back together.

As incredible as that was, a glance at the mess in the room's center showed that even nanites had their limitations. It was a fact that the look in Don Espeñosa's eyes showed he was very much aware of.

"OK, enough recovery time," Mark said, yanking Espeñosa to his feet, the man's grimace giving evidence that he had not yet completely recovered.

Heather stepped closer. "Now you're going to take us directly to Jennifer. Believe me when I say I'll know if you even consider doing something different than what we tell you."

Espeñosa glanced at Mark, then nodded. "Then you're going to kill me?"

"You heard what I told Mark. We need you alive. You just make sure you keep it that way."

Don Espeñosa turned toward the inner door. "Walk with me. If we pass any servants, pay them no attention. They know better than to ask questions."

The Spanish opulence of the wide room into which Espeñosa led them made Heather feel as if she had just stepped into a luxury resort, the rich tile floor, high ceiling, and huge windows giving it an openness that, under other circumstances, would have made her reluctant to leave. A tiled staircase led up to the second floor, and along this Don Espeñosa led them. At the top of the stairs they entered a red-tiled hallway adorned with standing suits of armor and paintings of the conquistadors. Stopping just outside the third room on the left, Don Espeñosa rapped three times.

"Yes?" The familiar voice caused Heather's breath to catch in her throat.

"I've brought you some guests," Don Espeñosa said.

The sound of soft footsteps wafted out. Then the tall door opened inward.

"Guests?" Jennifer stood there frozen in shock, clad in a white peasant dress, looking pale and thin but incredibly beautiful.

Mark pushed Don Espeñosa into the wicker chair. "Don't move!"

As Mark closed the door behind them, Jennifer rushed forward, throwing her arms around Heather's neck, oblivious to the mess she was making of her beautiful white dress, great sobs shuddering through her body. Heather hugged back so tightly she felt they might become one. And as her own tears mixed with those of her lovely little friend, she felt Mark's powerful arms circle them both.

"My God, Jen! I thought I'd lost you." Mark's voice choked off, his own tears dripping down his cheeks onto their heads.

For the longest time, they just stood there, holding each other in an embrace they wished could last forever, experiencing a oneness Heather had feared they would never again share.

Jennifer was the first to release her hold, her eyes finally taking in the drying blood smears that caked Mark and Heather, along with Heather's towel-draped torso.

"Jesus! What happened to you?"

With Mark keeping a watchful eye on Don Espeñosa, Heather rapidly filled Jennifer in on the day's events, watching as shock turned to anger in her friend's gentle face.

Jennifer stepped toward Don Espeñosa. "You did that to my family?"

The don shrugged. "You know what I am."

Espeñosa stiffened as Jennifer's eyes locked with his.

"Jen? What're you doing?" The concern in Heather's voice caused Mark to step closer.

"Jen?" Heather repeated, reaching out to touch her friend's shoulder.

When Jennifer turned toward her, Heather released the breath she'd been holding. "It's OK. Just making sure he wasn't going to try anything like that again."

"So what's the plan?" Mark asked, also relaxing his stance. "We can't stay here."

Heather shrugged, a movement that almost caused the towel to slip from her shoulders.

"Actually, I think we are going to be staying here. We need to hear Jennifer's story. But first, we need a shower and some fresh clothes."

"I have a great shower and lots of clothes that will fit you," Jennifer said. "I even have a robe Mark can use."

"And then?" Mark continued.

"And then," said Heather, glancing toward Jennifer's laptop. "I think we need to reestablish contact with Jack and Janet."

Mark nodded, but Heather noticed his distant stare, and it didn't take one of her visions to imagine the blood and death on the movie screen behind those eyes.

CHAPTER 130

Music thundered in Raul's head, not that pussy stuff he'd been forced to endure in his former life either. This was pure Nickelback, Chad Kroeger screaming out his rage at the world. Why he hadn't thought of piping music into this prison, home, royal chamber, that was his section of the Rho Ship, Raul couldn't fathom. After all, he'd had Internet access for ages. He could scan all the satellite frequencies of television and radio, even decrypting the most classified communications.

Maybe that was it. He'd been so down in the weeds scanning data, he'd overlooked the simplest of things to make his life better. Understandable considering how hard he'd been driving himself.

He felt the door open before he saw it, just another of the mechanisms tied into his neural net, and he certainly didn't need to see Dr. Stephenson to know who had entered his inner sanctum.

"Good morning, Raul."

Letting the music fade from his mind, Raul waited, floating in the air just above the machine that had been the focus of his energies these last few weeks. Why Stephenson bothered to walk through the room was one of the mysteries that cloaked the scientist. After all, he'd shown he could override Raul's manipulation of the stasis field whenever he desired. But instead of floating effortlessly, the man wove his way through the alien conduits and machinery until he reached the open central area where Raul waited.

"Going to a party?" Raul asked. He'd never seen Stephenson wear a business suit in the lab, although he'd seen him in one on television. This was a navy-blue three-piece, a tangerine shirt, gold cuff links, a paisley tie, and chocolate Italian shoes.

Stephenson came to a stop before the machine. "The president's arriving for a briefing in an hour."

"Impressive."

"That's not what I came to talk about."

"Fine. Spit it out."

Dr. Stephenson's eyes flashed briefly, giving Raul the pleasure of knowing he had managed to annoy the man.

Stephenson returned his attention to the device, running his hand lovingly along the surface of the thick coils that snaked in and out of the thing, coils within which whirls of glowing energy flashed, growing in intensity and then fading out with no apparent rhythm to the pulses. In the dim grayness that filled the room, the strange luminance failed to seep beyond the coils that contained it, providing no point of light on Dr. Stephenson's hands, even when they touched a glow spot.

"You've done well."

The unexpected compliment caught Raul by surprise, sending a warm glow of pride through his entire body. Why the hell did he even care what Stephenson thought? After all, he hated the man.

"It's not finished yet."

"I know, but we're very, very close now. What about the power?"

Raul rubbed his hands together. As challenging as the repairs to the device had been, providing the huge increase in power that would be required to bring it online had proved the most daunting of his tasks.

"Eighty-three percent."

"We need at least ninety-five."

"You're not telling me anything I don't know."

"You need to pick up the pace."

"Why don't you get your ass in here and help me then?"

"I'm sure you can handle it. Besides, I have other pressing matters to attend to."

"Like the Bandelier Ship?"

Stephenson raised an eyebrow. "Among other things."

Raul had been monitoring the news about the Bandelier Ship, the one they had all believed stone-dead until it had unexpectedly come to life a few days ago.

"So that's why the president is visiting."

"Even I have to play tour guide sometimes." The annoyance in the deputy director's voice left little doubt what he thought about this interruption.

"You said I was doing well," Raul returned to the original subject. "You know I'm working around the clock. Why are you pushing me to up the pace?"

"There've been some complications with the nanite distribution."

"You mean the remotely programmable version you've been peddling around the world?"

Stephenson paused, as if considering what he would say. "You've been watching the news networks and spy satellite feeds. You know about our program at Henderson House."

Although the confirmation that Stephenson had been monitoring his activities annoyed him, he got the sense that something big was about to be revealed.

"Not going according to plan, is it?"

"Just a technical problem. But with the world so new to the challenges of complete health, it would be a bad time for anything about Henderson House to leak out."

Raul laughed. "I guess so. Lots of people are already upset about the total breakdown of birth control in the third world. Pill's not working. Normal abortion methods failing. Little sperms have gotten hardy. All the world for a condom, eh?"

Stephenson shrugged. "Which brings us back to Henderson House. We already had one leak, which we were lucky to plug."

"I don't get it. What's my work got to do with that?"

"All programs have leaks. Especially the most sensitive."

A light dawned in Raul's mind. "And you want to be able to instantly reach out and touch someone should that happen. By creating a gateway."

"I need you to stop surfing the Internet and focus every ounce of your attention on the task I assigned you."

"You know what I want."

"I've known for a long time now. You want the McFarland girl."

"Then you know why I've been searching the world's data feeds."

"You just focus on getting the machine working. You do that and I'll tell you where to go get her."

Raul was stunned. Was it possible that Stephenson could know where Heather was? He couldn't really put it beyond the man. He'd surprised Raul before.

"You'd let me bring her here?"

"She's a runaway known to be suffering from psychotic delusions. Nobody would ever know what became of her."

Raul stared into the deputy director's face. There was something else there, something Stephenson was hiding behind those cold eyes. Whatever it was, the scientist wouldn't be making him this promise if he couldn't deliver.

Raul shifted his concentration, and ten thousand tiny strands of force plunged into control panels around the room, the massive neural network directing the simultaneous repair work ramping up to full capacity.

Dr. Donald Stephenson grinned, then turned and strode from the room. His departure went entirely unnoticed.

CHAPTER 131

Garfield Kromly strolled nonchalantly through the crowds on the vast open lawns of the Washington Mall, enjoying the first really nice Sunday morning in weeks. Pam would have loved it. He could almost feel her delicate little hand in his, her shoulder pressed against him as they stared out at the great spire of the Washington Monument.

"Ah, my sweet little darling," he muttered under his breath. "I miss you."

Someone jostled him, but when he looked to his left, he couldn't tell who it might have been. All he knew was that the small brown paper-wrapped package he'd been holding in his left hand was gone.

Despite his best efforts and those of the few people he trusted in the CIA, Kromly had been unable to fully break the encryption on the data disk. But the one thing he had learned was enough to give him chills.

The network of Global Positioning System satellites, more commonly known as GPS, had been compromised by a super-secret US government program somehow connected to the Rho Project.

That it was using GPS was oddly fitting. When global positioning data had first been made broadly available, the US government had partially corrupted the downlinked time data using a process known as dithering, as part of what was called Selective Availability. The idea had been to provide the correct information only to classified subscribers so they would have much more accurate location data.

As was often the case with such schemes, civilian users immediately came up with ways to correct the data, allowing almost the same accuracy as was available to the US military and intelligence communities. Thus the huge sum of money aimed at Selective Availability was essentially a complete waste. Another hundred-million-dollar military toilet seat.

But now the GPS signal was being manipulated in a very subtle way, acting as a carrier signal for information transmitted worldwide. The data on the DVD disk had been extracted by the late Dr. Nancy Anatole from the personal laptop of Dr. Donald Stephenson. It was a disk she had hidden away with instructions that it be forwarded to a friend on the Senate intelligence committee should anything happen to her. And although the disk had eventually found its way into Kromly's hands, he had not been able to unscramble enough of the information to discover the true purpose underlying the GPS embedding.

As the soft breeze gently tousled his gray hair, Garfield returned his gaze to the Washington Monument and the small flock of birds settling into the grass near its base.

Well, the pass had been made. He could only hope that the Ripper's resources exceeded his own. The disk was Jack's problem now.

CHAPTER 132

"Prettiest pregnant lady I've ever seen."

The voice lifted Janet from her chair and whirled her toward the door. As fast as she moved, Jack was quicker, sweeping her up in an embrace that somehow managed to be both powerful and gentle, like being wrapped in warm velvet rebar. Then their lips met and parted, the gentle flick of his tongue barely touching her own, sending an electric thrill through her body that left her breathing ragged.

As she pulled her head back, she laughed. "Careful. That's how I got in this condition in the first place."

"Thought I'd taken care of that."

"Apparently, those nanites have been busy fixing what got snipped."

Jack stepped back, holding her out at arm's length, his eyes scanning her body from toe to head.

"So what do you think?" Janet asked, although a part of her feared the answer.

"I like it." Then Jack dropped to his knees, placed his ear right up against her belly, and tapped it twice with his finger. "Hey, you in there. What's your name?"

Janet laughed out loud. "I don't think he's going to talk back."

"You sure it's a he?" Jack asked, still listening for a response.

"Positive."

"Woman's intuition?"

"Tall Bear told me."

"And he would know?"

"Some sort of Navajo spiritual thing. He says he got it from his grandmother."

"Hmm," Jack said, rising to his feet and kissing her once again. "Well, I guess we can't argue with that. Jack Junior then."

"That's horrible."

"Jack Senior's taken."

"From the way he's been acting in there, I was thinking of an Indian name. Something like Kicking Donkey."

A broad grin spread across Jack's face, bringing a twinkle to his eyes. Lord, she'd missed him.

"Looks like we better keep his mom and dad alive long enough to hash all this out."

"Gonna disappoint a lot of people."

"Can't be helped." Jack paused. "You know we're going to have to get married for real now."

"Can't we just keep living in sin?"

"Nope. Can't have little Kicking Donkey getting teased at school."

Janet grabbed his hand and led him out onto the porch, pulling him into the swinging love seat. The warm rays of the afternoon sun felt nothing like November, but given this fleeting moment of comfort and happiness, she wasn't about to argue with the weatherman.

Jack's face grew more serious. "What have you got for me that you couldn't encrypt into a message?"

Janet sighed. The warmth of their moment had passed.

For the next forty-five minutes, she laid out the whole story as she knew it. How she'd finally pieced together the puzzle, how the whole time they'd been hunting their mysterious source in the Rho Project, it was right under their noses in the persons of Heather McFarland and Mark and Jennifer Smythe.

When she finished, Jack leaned sideways in the love seat, absently petting her stomach with his right hand.

"So they've made no contact since they disappeared?"

"None."

"And you think it has something to do with the second alien ship found in that canyon?"

"I've run a number of correlations. There are too many coincidences. That's not far from the cave where the Rag Man took Heather. You said that guy moved like no one on this planet. Mark showed incredible coordination, and we both suspected he was holding back from his true potential. Then the kids' project won the national science contest. Somehow, they just happen to be connected to a whole set of unusual happenings. Given that they disappeared right after that ship was discovered, if there's a better explanation, I'm listening."

"Not one I can think of. Whatever they stumbled upon has them running and hiding."

"Which is why they couldn't keep providing the hacker link we were using. They've been on the move."

Jack paused, stroking his chin with his hand. "Just because they can't keep that link up doesn't mean they haven't been checking in on us. Didn't our source say to leave a message on your laptop if we needed contact?"

Janet sat up. "I forgot all about that."

"I've got a disk full of data I need them to break for me."

"Got it on you?"

Jack pulled the DVD from his jacket pocket, holding it out to her.

Getting to her feet, Janet took it and headed for the laptop. "Then I guess we ought to put our message in the bottle."

CHAPTER 133

His face an unreadable mask, Don Espeñosa sat tied to a chair as Mark stood guard. They'd debated chaining him in the bathroom, but Heather had convinced them it was better to keep him under Mark's watchful eye, even if that meant letting the drug baron hear everything. It didn't matter. Heather had seen Espeñosa's future, and he no longer had any.

Don Espeñosa knew he'd only continue living as long as they needed him and had already gone out of his way to demonstrate the extent to which he could be useful. He'd placed a call to one of his cleanup crews, giving instructions to get rid of the human remains in the gym and to scrub it down so thoroughly no DNA samples remained. It was a risky thing, but far better than dealing with queries about the smell. This wasn't exactly the first bloody cleanup to have occurred on this property.

Jennifer wiped at her swollen eyes with the back of her hand, as if she could scrub away the memories that haunted her. For the last two and a half hours the story, begun haltingly, had spilled from her lips, sweeping Heather into a maelstrom of emotion.

Despite that she'd showered and changed into clean clothes, Heather felt sullied. A glance at Mark revealed a similar response. It wasn't just their fight for survival against Don Espeñosa and his guards. And they could live with the illegal activities Jennifer had performed for the cartel. But this Eduardo person was something altogether different. Jennifer's brief glimpse into his soul had been so horrifying it had left her at his mercy. Now he had both Jennifer's headset and the Rag Man's.

Halfway through Jennifer's description of the man, the visions that assaulted Heather left her hands shaking so badly she was forced to grip the table to steady herself. Eduardo had tried on the headsets. The thought of what he was now in the process of becoming filled her with a thick dread. When Eduardo found out that Jennifer had escaped, he would pay a visit to White Rock, and her and Mark's wonderful parents would die.

"Dear God!"

Jennifer only nodded, her voice finally having failed her.

Heather turned toward Don Espeñosa. "Eduardo. Where was he going?"

The drug lord shrugged. "He didn't say."

Mark's jaw tightened. "Bullshit! Just because we want you alive doesn't mean I won't hurt you."

Espeñosa stiffened. "El Chupacabra has many clients. Whoever called him had more pressing need of his services than I did."

"El Chupacabra?" Heather interrupted. "What is that?"

"A story mothers tell to scare their children. It's Eduardo Montenegro's favorite nickname. Most people know him as the Colombian."

"So he's a hit man?" Mark asked.

"The world's most feared assassin." Espeñosa grinned. "And the most expensive."

"Last time we checked, the headsets were in DC," Mark said. "What's he doing in Washington?"

Again, the drug lord shook his head. "No idea. Maybe you should ask your government?"

Heather leaned forward, spinning the laptop to face Jennifer.

"We can do better than that, can't we, Jen?"

A faint ray of hope dawning in her eyes, Jennifer licked her fingertips, then leaned forward and pressed the rectangular black power button. As the Windows logo splashed the welcome screen, Heather felt the first electrical pulse pass through the embedded special circuitry, a pulse instantly echoed in its quantum twin on the Mattaponi Indian Reservation, 2,300 miles to the north.

It took only minutes to discover the new message on Janet's laptop.

"To Heather, Mark, and Jennifer. Jack and I know you are our secret Rho Project source. We also know about your connection to the Bandelier Ship and how it has altered you. Don't be afraid. We need your help. I have placed the contents of an encrypted disk on my C: drive in a folder named Rho Project Data. The data was acquired from Dr. Donald Stephenson's personal laptop, but we have not been able to decrypt it. Please respond."

"Oh, shit!" Mark said, leaning over Jennifer's shoulder. "We're toast."

Heather scanned the text a second time. "I don't think so. It only makes sense they would figure it out. I think they need our help as badly as we need theirs."

Jennifer's fingers moved across the keyboard so fast that Heather had to concentrate to follow her. "Let's see what's on the Stephenson disk."

The monitor filled with binary data.

"It looks like a symmetric key block cipher," Heather said, leaning in close once more. "Can you make it auto-scroll?"

"No problem." Jennifer touched a sequence of keys, and the data began scrolling up from bottom to top.

There it was again, the same semirandom sequence Heather noticed earlier. "Faster, please."

"You've got it."

The data stopped scrolling. Now each page flashed onto the screen for a fraction of a second before being replaced by the next. Suddenly something clicked into place in Heather's mind, the encryption fading from her awareness as she read. And as she continued, the meaning became clear.

Stephenson had designed a new type of nanite that could be remotely reprogrammed via a broadcast signal, assuming that the signal contained the correct encoding scheme. It was this new type of nanite that was now being mass-produced and mass-distributed, starting with the world's poorest populations.

Even more shocking, an almost undetectable signal had been embedded in the worldwide GPS satellite broadcasts. And while the signal currently contained no reprogramming instructions, it was clearly intended to allow for rapid reprogramming of targeted populations.

Heather felt the future tilt on its axis, the shock pulling her into a vortex of competing realities. Something plucked at her shoulder, squeezing her arm so hard it hurt. But when she looked, there was nothing there.

Shift.

...She choked on the fetid smell of rotting vegetation. Campfires burned as seminude native dancers swayed in rhythm beneath the living bodies dangling from the trees above. With movements so precise that they seemed choreographed, the dancers sliced at their victims, the small cuts sending rich red rivulets running into pots below.

Shift.

...Screaming refugees pushed her to the ground in their frenzy to gather the few grains of rice that had leaked from the sacks at the distribution point. The sound of gunfire crackled overhead.

Shift.

...Clouds boiled overhead as she stared through the bars of a prison window.

Shift.

Shift.

Once again, the spectral hand gripped her, pulling her down into water so murky it felt like mud.

Heather struggled, but her strength was no match for the thing that held her, pulling her ever deeper into the blackness.

"Heather..."

The sound of someone calling her name came from such a great distance, she almost missed it. Like a whisper in the wind, she could almost believe she had imagined it.

"Heather! Snap out of it!"

The sting of the slap on her cheek brought with it a flash of light as Mark's face swam into view.

His hand moved to slap her again, but this time she caught it.

"Ouch! What are you doing?"

Relief flooded Mark's face. Beside him, Jennifer's face had gone so white it looked as if she'd seen a ghost.

"Jesus, you scared the hell out of us," Mark managed. "One minute you were scanning the data, and the next your eyes rolled back and you zoned into la-la land. That was fifteen minutes ago."

Heather rubbed her cheek. "So you decided it was a good idea to beat the crap out of me?"

Mark looked offended. "We tried shaking you first."

Heather started to give a sharp retort, but the memory of what she had seen brought her back to the moment. Moving closer to the laptop, Heather pointed at the screen.

"I broke the code. I know what Stephenson is doing."

"Which is?" Jennifer asked, recovering her voice.

"He's flooding the world with a carrier signal that can reprogram the nanites."

"Which nanites?"

"All of them. At least the ones that our government is busy pumping into people's veins all over the planet."

"That bastard! He's making a play for the world." Don Espeñosa tried to jump to his feet, but the ropes stopped him.

"Sit still!" Mark gripped the drug baron's arm and squeezed. "Move again and I'll break your legs."

"Easy, Mark," Heather placed her hand on his arm. "I get it. Don Espeñosa has a dose of those new nanites—don't you?"

The drug lord merely scowled back at her.

"So what are we going to do about it?" Jennifer asked.

Heather looked at her friend. "Anything that can be programmed can be shut down. We just need our little computer genius to figure out the shutdown command."

"That's not gonna help much," Mark responded. "Not unless you can broadcast it to the world."

"I can't, but we know someone who might be able to, if we supply the program."

"Jack!"

"And Janet." Heather turned back to Jennifer. "You think you're up to it?"

Jennifer nodded slowly. "If you help me with the decryption algorithm."

"Let's do it."

As Jennifer turned her attention back to the laptop, Heather's visions tugged at the drawstrings of her mind. If they were going to have any chance to put the dark genie back in the bottle, they'd better hurry.

Better hurry. Better hurry.

Heather forced herself to focus. But deep in her mind, the sound of distant laughter echoed.

CHAPTER 134

"Got it!" Janet scanned the new files on her laptop, marveling at what she was seeing. "Our wonder kids cracked the encryption."

Jack nodded. "So what's the bad news?"

"Dr. Stephenson's new nanites are remotely programmable."

"Let me guess. It's related to the weird GPS signal embedding."

"The GPS satellites are prepared to reprogram all the world's newly inoculated populations with one massive broadcast."

"So how do we stop it?"

"The kids uplinked their own reprogramming algorithm to my laptop. It's designed to send the nanites a shutdown command. Once the nanites shut down, they can't be restarted."

"How do they know it'll work?"

"They say they've already tested it on a subject."

Jack whistled softly. "That's still no good unless their program can be broadcast over the GPS link."

Janet nodded. "That's right. The note says we'll need to hardwire a link into the GPS control antenna so that the kids can spoof the control center."

"Why can't they just remotely override the commands going to the satellites, the same way they've been hacking into classified systems around the world?"

"According to the message, they can hack into just about anything, read encrypted data, insert new signals on existing lines, but they can't interrupt signals that are already on those networks. That means the new commands and the commands already being sent to the satellites would be going out on the same link. The control center would notice the status errors coming back on the downlink."

"Makes sense."

"So we have to physically cut the line and reroute it through my laptop. That way our young superhackers can send all the normal satellite responses back to the control center while we are uplinking the new commands."

"Where's the main antenna?"

"Global Positioning System Operations Center, Schriever Air Force Base, Colorado."

Jack stood up. "Grab your stuff. Let's get going."

Janet smiled as she clicked the shutdown button on the laptop. She'd almost forgotten how much she missed this.

"Give me five minutes."

Janet slid the laptop into its case, then turned toward her bedroom. It didn't take her long to pack. Being pregnant had already cut down on her clothes selection. And the Heckler & Koch 9mm Compact completed her outfit nicely. Giving her hair a quick twist, she slipped her special hairpin into place, glanced around one last time, then followed Jack out of the house.

By the time the private Learjet 35A reached thirty-five thousand feet over West Virginia, Janet had to admit Jack could still surprise her. She shifted in the copilot's seat to get a better view of his profile. Settled into the pilot's seat with his headset and microphone, he looked like a Greek god. No. Not Greek—Spartan. But if Jack had been among the three hundred Spartans in that Thermopylae pass in 480 BC, the Persians would have had their asses handed to them.

Looking through the windscreen toward their destination, Janet knew one thing for certain. Whoever got in Jack's way was about to get that same treatment.

CHAPTER 135

Garfield Kromly knelt at the graveside, his left hand resting on the grave marker as he gently placed a dozen long-stemmed red roses before it.

An inscription had been etched into the gray marble. Six simple lines.

Pamela Merideth Kromly
My Loving Wife and Best Friend

Long ago, I gave you my soul.
Take care of it for me,
until I find you again.
Garfield

Kromly blinked twice and then rose slowly to his feet. He'd chosen the Fairfax Memorial Park as Pam's resting place because of the cherry trees. On that April day when he'd laid her to rest, their lovely pink-and-white blossoms had been in full bloom. Now, shorn of their leaves by a November frost, they just looked dead.

As he watched, the sun sank beneath the western horizon, pulling whatever warmth and color remained of the day down with it. Garfield inhaled deeply, then turned toward the car, his steps taking him past a young man who leaned against a tree, face buried in his hands. Without pausing, Kromly passed him by, clicking the unlock button on his key fob, his own grief so intense he had nothing left to feel for the man.

Pulling open the car door, Kromly had only begun to slide into the driver's seat when a movement at the corner of his eye made him turn. The young man lunged at him, his hand striking Garfield in the nerve cluster at the base of his neck, sending a kaleidoscope of color blossoming across his vision…

He came to with pain worming its way through his head, a squirming snake of fire that started in his shoulders and crawled up his neck, dragging him reluctantly back to consciousness.

He tried to move, but his wrists were bound tightly behind his back. Higher up, near his armpits, his arms had been strapped together even tighter.

A memory clicked into place. The North Vietnamese army had used this particular method on captured US soldiers, airmen, and sailors. Bind the wrists behind them. Then tighten a second strap, forcing the upper arms together until both shoulders dislocated.

So it was to be death by torture. That was OK. It was something he'd prepared for his entire life. Pain. Whoever had taken him had no idea what that word meant.

The image of William Wallace leaped into his head. Drawn and quartered, disemboweled, his intestines roasted while he was still alive, but defiant to the end. Time for Kromly to give his own Mel Gibson imitation. Screaming held no shame.

"Ah, Mr. Kromly. So nice to see you awake."

The voice, so silky smooth, with a slight Spanish accent, seemed vaguely familiar. Kromly blinked again, a face swimming into focus before him. Recognition flooded his mind.

Shit! Eduardo Montenegro, aka the Colombian, aka El Chupacabra.

A thin smile spread across the Colombian's handsome face. "I see you recognize me. Good. That will save on introductions."

The killer turned away, walking out of Kromly's vision. Garfield tried to turn his head to see where the man had gone, but the pain in his shoulders stopped him.

He was in a single-room log cabin. The rough plank floors were covered with a layer of dirt, the deer heads mounted on the walls draped with cobwebs. A single filthy window let in a stream of daylight from the outside. Except for the chair to which he had been tied, the only other furniture in his field of view was a wooden cot pushed up against the far wall.

Kromly surprised himself with the steadiness of his voice. "You might as well go ahead and kill me."

Eduardo reappeared, setting a matching wooden chair in front of Kromly before sitting down.

"Now what would be the fun in that? Besides, I have some questions I want you to answer first."

"If you think pain will break me, then you're wasting your time."

Once again the Colombian smiled. "If you think my specialty is pain, then you've been misinformed."

Something in the assassin's voice sent a chill down Kromly's spine. He recalled everything he knew about El Chupacabra. One of the world's most feared assassins, Eduardo settled all his contracts with ultimate efficiency. But it was his personal killings that revealed the man's psychopathic underpinnings. Wildly violent, often sexual, orgies of blood. And with those victims, Eduardo took his time.

If his legs hadn't been tied to the chair, Kromly would have kicked himself. How had he failed to notice the resemblance of the young man in the graveyard to one of the world's most wanted killers? Admittedly, he'd been deep in grief for his lost wife, but there was nothing new about that.

Maybe his worry about the African nanite problems had provided the extra distraction.

Populations that had already been starving remained hungry, but were now strong and healthy. Violent food wars were breaking out all across sub-Saharan Africa. Roving death squads, which had once satisfied themselves with beheadings, had now become known as Torso Squads, hacking only the arms and legs from the victims, leaving their undying, limbless, nanite-infested bodies as burdens for their families.

Even more nasty blood cults had sprung up, their new religion based on nanite worship. Because they believed that immortality could be achieved by drinking the nanited blood from living bodies, their dark rituals involved hanging victims by their ankles and draining their blood into drinking vessels, which were then passed among the worshipers. Meanwhile, the nanites that remained in the victims' bodies worked their magic, keeping them alive throughout the festivities. At least until they were roasted for the final feast.

For problems to escalate this quickly, while worldwide nanite distribution was still ramping up, should have brought the program to a grinding halt. But it hadn't. Instead of being a show-stopper, the problems were regarded as the inevitable growing pains associated with a major breakthrough, a small inconvenience when compared to the amazing health benefits delivered to the treated populations. It certainly hadn't significantly muted the clamor in the UN to increase the nanite delivery rate. God only knew what would happen when distribution moved to the other continents, including Asia, Europe, and North America.

"Tell me about the Ripper."

The question surprised Kromly. As he refocused on the Colombian, a new question occurred to him. Was the assassin's mission somehow related to the Rho Project? Although it was well-known that Eduardo had a special fascination with Jack Gregory, that was strictly a personal matter.

"I can't tell you anything you don't already know."

"He was seen taking a packet from your pocket at the Washington Monument the day before yesterday. Tell me about that."

Kromly felt his chest tighten. How the hell did Eduardo have that information? Who had been watching him? A sick sense of betrayal churned his stomach. Someone he'd trusted in his efforts to crack the Stephenson disk must have turned. One of his own people.

Kromly took a deep breath. It appeared that lifetime of conditioning was about to be put to the ultimate test.

"I don't know what you're talking about. Sorry, I can't help."

Something moved in his head. *What the hell was that?* Not really a thought, something foreign. Weird.

"I told you." Eduardo's voice pulled Kromly's eyes to El Chupacabra's. "My specialty isn't pain. It's fear."

There it was again, a feeling so odd he couldn't place it. Even more disconcerting, Kromly found himself unable to break Eduardo's gaze.

"A little trick I picked up recently," Eduardo continued. "If this wasn't your death day, I wouldn't even be telling you about it."

Kromly struggled to speak but couldn't seem to make his lips respond.

"Don't worry. I can't read your thoughts. It's more of a feel-and-amplify-your-feelings thing." Once again, Eduardo smiled. "Now, let's find out what Garfield Kromly truly fears."

There was really only one thing that Kromly truly feared, and nobody else knew about it.

As Pam's breast cancer spread throughout her body, her other organs had begun to fail. At the end her lungs had filled with fluid, leaving her terrified, struggling for every little gulp of air. Garfield had sat beside her, holding her hand, hating himself for not being able to do something to help her. If only he could have breathed for her, just to ease her passage, but he couldn't. His lovely Pam had lingered for days before finally gasping out her last breath.

The terror Garfield had seen in her face those last terrible days haunted his dreams, leaving him gasping in rhythm with his wife when he awakened, as if he could unwind her fear by absorbing it into himself.

Suddenly, Garfield's world shifted. He was back in the Bethesda naval hospital, only this time he was lying in bed beside his wife. She looked at him hopefully, mouthing the words "Please help me."

Instinctively, he knew that his wish had been granted, that every lungful of air he inhaled would go directly to his wife.

Kromly struggled to inhale, but he couldn't. Pam was next to him, looking at him, counting on him, and he couldn't take a breath.

With panic rising in his chest, he worked his lungs. Nothing. It was as if he had stuck his head into a vacuum chamber. No amount of effort yielded the slightest amount of air intake. The hope that had shown in Pam's eyes only moments ago faded, leaving only a terror they both shared. Horror filled his soul.

Garfield Kromly screamed, the sound filling the hunting cabin and leaching out through the windowpane, through the crack beneath the door.

"What did the Ripper take?"

Disorientation made Kromly dizzy. "Screw you."

He was back in the hospital, but this time Pam was whimpering. Garfield reached for her hand, but something held him down. If only he could breathe, Pam would get air. He pulled with his lungs, but something covered his face. Someone was holding a plastic bag over his head. Eduardo's blurred face peered in at him, the thin smile crinkling his lips through the translucent plastic.

Can't breathe. God help me. Can't breathe.

Glancing to his left, Garfield could see Pam, her head now encased in another plastic bag, her wide eyes staring into his. Fear leached into his soul.

"What was in the packet?"

"Eat shit and die!" Kromly panted, struggling to rise despite the agony in his arms. *What the hell was Eduardo Montenegro?*

Back to dreamland. Again and again. Each time the hallucinations grew worse, his fear amplified until finally he found himself unable to stop shaking. The visions had morphed into an unearthly mixture of nightmare and reality. Pam was here in the cabin, lying on the cot across from the spot where he sat tied to the chair.

And, amid the rising liquid terror that threatened to drown him, Eduardo was there, asking his questions.

When Garfield Kromly finally began to talk, he told everything he knew about the disk. Where it came from. The strange code embedded into the GPS satellite signal. How he had arranged to pass the disk on the Washington Mall. Everything.

Pam disappeared and Garfield found he could breathe again, although tears had cut streaks down his cheeks and left his shirt collar damp.

Eduardo leaned in close. "One more question, then I'll release you from all the nightmares."

Kromly was numb. "Ask."

"You know the Ripper. Where is he going?"

If he could have managed it, Kromly would have smiled. If Eduardo wanted to meet the Ripper, then Garfield was happy to send him. Hell. He just wished he could be there to watch.

"He'll go to the place where the GPS signal is uplinked. The GPS master control station at Schriever Air Force Base, Colorado."

Eduardo nodded, then rose and walked out of Kromly's field of view.

Behind him, Garfield heard a familiar sound, Saran Wrap being pulled from a roll. Then, as Eduardo began methodically wrapping the clear plastic wrap around and around the CIA trainer's head, a new set of horrifying images writhed into Kromly's mind.

Only this time, his beloved Pamela was not there to slowly suffocate with him.

CHAPTER 136

Phil Rabin opened his front door, then paused, staring down at the DHL package propped against his step. He'd heard the doorbell, but he hadn't seen the truck. Funny. He normally noticed everything. He didn't even know they delivered on Thanksgiving Day.

Walking into his study, he examined the express-delivery package in his hand. About the size of an encyclopedia. But it didn't weigh enough to be a book. The ink of the handwritten return address had been smudged into illegibility. Oh well. If he wanted to find out who it was from, he was going to have to open the damn thing.

Tearing open the box's pull strip, Phil dumped the contents onto his desk: a sealed manila envelope and a Polaroid photo. Did they still make those cameras?

Picking up the photograph, Phil sat down. As editor of the *New York Post*, he didn't associate with anyone from the *Times*. But that didn't mean he didn't recognize their Pulitzer Prize winners, even a dead one. Freddy Hagerman.

Holding the photo up to the light, Phil examined it more closely.

It was Freddy Hagerman all right, sitting up in bed, clad only in a nightgown, the bedsheets thrown back to reveal his bare legs. The left one ended in a bandaged stump, just above where the knee should have been.

Across the back of the photo, a simple message had been scrawled in black marker.

"I can't trust my editor. Thought you might be interested in a story that cost me a leg. F. H."

The brown envelope drew his attention. Slitting the top with a letter opener, he removed an unlabeled compact disk. There was nothing else.

Sliding the disk into his computer, Phil scanned the contents. A text document labeled "Story," a sound file, and an images folder.

Curiosity thoroughly aroused, Phil played the sound file first. At first he thought he must have gotten a bad recording, with just some poor-quality background noise. Then the screaming began, first from a single voice, quickly joined by others. The horrible chorus grew in volume, barely recognizable as human, then wavered and died out. Perhaps a minute passed in relative silence before a new round of terrible howls filled the tape.

Even with no narrative on the tape to explain it, by the time he finished listening, every hair on Phil's body was standing at full attention, held in the grasp of tight little goose bumps that would not fade.

Opening the "Story" file, Phil began reading.

It was a full-blown report, complete with Freddy Hagerman's byline, already formatted for print. Before he had finished the first five paragraphs, Phil found himself flipping back and forth between the words and the photographs in the images directory.

Somehow, Freddy Hagerman had stumbled on a gallery of horrors worthy of Hitler's Germany. But this one was financed and operated by the United States government, a deep black program performing nanite experimentation on human subjects. And although Phil believed strongly in protecting legitimately classified information, his principal belief was in the importance of the First Amendment to the Constitution. It was no accident that the founders had placed it first in the Bill of Rights.

The experimentation in this report could not be explained as a noble attempt to cure children of terminal diseases, the explanation that had undercut Freddy's first Pulitzer-winning story.

In the tunnels below Henderson House, subjects had been collected from society's castaways. From the severely retarded and unwanted. From the homeless. From society's dregs, the disappearance of whom would go as unnoticed as their existences had. The only other requirement for admittance to the program was that the person be horribly disfigured or missing limbs, things that went beyond the capabilities of current nanite treatments to repair.

Not only had Freddy taken pictures inside the place, he had managed to get pictures of highly classified documents detailing the program objectives.

The program's goal was to reprogram the nanomachines to better understand human DNA, producing an upgrade that could understand the original blueprint, then fix any flaws, repairing anything that differed from the ideal. The very idea of such a master blueprint made Phil sick to his stomach. Unfortunately, the actual experimental results were far worse.

The new nanites were capable of being reprogrammed, an item which, by itself, would have been worthy of a front-page news story. Each nanite was a relatively simple machine, certainly lacking the sophisticated processing to understand human DNA. But the nanites didn't operate that way. Using a principal called swarm computing, the individuals passed information among themselves, much like colonies of ants or bees. When this was done correctly, the swarm acquired much greater computational capacity, something like a hive mind.

Efforts to train the Henderson House nanoswarms to understand human DNA had so far produced disastrous results. While the nanites had learned to regenerate new limbs and organs, their learning process was more complicated than that of a neural network. The objective was to make them understand the goal, then let them teach themselves to accomplish it.

The self-teaching process involved a complicated system of trial, error, and feedback. And despite numerous attempts at retraining, the nanoswarm view of making humans better by adding or replacing parts had produced things that bore little resemblance to humans.

In experiment after experiment, the human subjects had been turned into the stuff of nightmares, with extra internal and external organs, limbs where no limbs should be, extra mouths, eyes on stalklike appendages that could have been fingers.

Worse yet, the nanoswarms kept learning, changing their designs as they learned. The effect on the poor subjects was terrifying, producing mind-altering pain as the reconstruction process continued.

Phil finished examining the pictures, glancing down at the trash can into which he had just hurled the contents of his stomach. Suppressing a desire for two packets of Alka-Seltzer, Phil picked up his cell phone and pressed the first number on speed dial.

"Hello?"

"John. It's Phil. I want you to recall whoever you need. Tonight we're rolling out with a special edition."

"On Thanksgiving Day?" Annoyance crept into his production specialist's voice.

"Don't argue, just do it. And make it fast." Phil hung up without waiting for a response.

As he ejected the CD from his computer, Phil experienced something that most newspaper editors rarely experience: the feeling of having just been handed a story that was about to leap from the front page of his paper onto every broadcast news program in the country. Hell—in the world.

As he began to shut down his laptop, his eyes settled on the last photograph he had been viewing. On a pad just outside Henderson House, Dr. Donald Stephenson had just stepped out of a government helicopter.

Sliding the disk into his jacket pocket, Phil Rabin pointed at the screen and smiled.

"Gotcha."

CHAPTER 137

Military bases in the continental United States had never been this easy to penetrate, Janet knew, but alert forces had been stretched by an extended period of overdeployment. Wars in Iraq and Afghanistan had taken their toll on the US military. As great as the all-volunteer force had been under Ronald Reagan, that force had always been a mighty war ax, something designed to smite the country's opponents with overwhelming combat power, rapidly destroying all resistance before being returned to the shed to be sharpened and hung back on the wall to await its next use.

For years now, this awesome force had been used like a hatchet, thousands of small strokes steadily dulling its blade, no downtime allotted for resharpening. A new political philosophy for the use of America's military had emerged in Washington, a violation of the Powell Doctrine that Jack called the "Strategy of Underwhelming Combat Power," a term that yielded the unfortunate abbreviation "SUC Power."

Schriever Air Force Base had not escaped this drag on combat readiness. Although the gates were heavily guarded, with their ID checkpoints and random vehicle searches, the huge expanse of perimeter fencing was thinly patrolled. For that Janet was thankful. It kept some brave young American servicemen away from her Jack, allowing them to live to fight for their country another day. After all, this was Thanksgiving Day, an unusually warm one that should have them out on their porches visiting friends and family.

Jack cut out a two-foot-square section of the chain-link fencing, flapped it upward, and guided them through before dropping the section back into place. A thin crescent moon smiled upward, like the mouth of the Cheshire Cat, providing just enough illumination for Janet to see without the aid of the compact night-vision goggles in her backpack.

In front of her, Jack paused, examining what lay ahead with those strange eyes of his. Then he was moving again, down across the valley, toward the far line of trees.

Her baby kicked in her stomach, but Janet ignored it. Jack needed her attention on the here and now, not on the impetuous child in her belly, no matter how wonderful he was.

Each military base had its oddities, and those could be exploited. Command and control centers were always heavily guarded. But the antennas that performed the actual satellite uplinks were largely ignored. Manned facilities required guards, unmanned equipment didn't. It was an unchanted mantra.

The main GPS uplink antenna was an excellent example. It was hardwired to the GPS control center by a cable that ran adjacent to the metal maintenance building two hundred yards from the base of the dish.

Keeping to the deep shadows, they moved around the back side of the building, opposite the antenna, pausing at a padlocked door. With a quick twist of the pry bar, Jack jimmied the lock, then pushed the sliding door open along its track, revealing a forty-by-thirty-foot interior space. The twin beams from Janet's and Jack's LED flashlights sizzled into the darkness, illuminating a largely empty room that housed an assortment of tools and equipment, including four large spools of cable and a small forklift. Just to the left of the doorway, a steel-case desk snuggled up against the wall, its office chair tilting slightly to the right, missing one of its four rolling casters.

Janet scanned the room, quickly locating the electrical panel along the left wall. As Jack closed the door behind them, Janet walked to the panel, pressed downward on the latch, and popped open the cover.

The building was fused for both 220- and 110-volt circuits. She smiled. They had chosen wisely. This was the perfect spot to set up their wireless access point. The heavy-voltage circuitry drove the motors that directed the massive GPS antenna. With a door on the side opposite the GPS control antenna, the building gave excellent concealment for their computational needs. It allowed Janet to establish secure communications with Heather McFarland and the Smythe twins while Jack did the heavy lifting at the antenna itself.

Janet ripped the corner from a cardboard box, folded it three times, and slid it under the chair leg. Plugging her laptop's power supply into one of the 110-volt outlets, she set it on the desk and sat down. As the laptop struggled to wakefulness, she glanced over at Jack. He held a backpack that contained another laptop, just purchased at a Colorado Springs RadioShack, along with an assortment of electronic supplies that would soon be put to good use splicing into the GPS control cable.

Jack pulled out his walkie-talkie. "Commo check."

Janet extracted her own walkie-talkie from the laptop bag. It was amazing what you could pick up at RadioShack. A pair of 900-megahertz frequency-hopping walkie-talkies with over ten billion frequencies, all for just a couple hundred dollars. Certainly adequate for secure communications during the time she was going to be separated from Jack.

Thumbing the press-to-talk button on the side, she lifted her walkie-talkie to her lips. "Ground control to Major Tom."

"Very funny," Jack said into his radio, his words coming through her speaker loud and clear.

"Time to test our link to Mother."

Janet typed in her log-in password, letting the laptop finish loading its start-up programs. In their magical fashion, the McFarland and Smythe triumvirate had uploaded a new program to her computer along with instructions for its use. It was a chat program, very similar to the voice–over-Internet protocol, or VoIP, applications that were so common these days. Only this was voice-over-QT, the quantum twin components creating perfectly secure, delay-free conversation, irrespective of distance.

She launched the application, waiting as the image of a whirling maelstrom dissolved into the control panel. Janet had to admit it: even under extreme pressure, those kids had panache.

The user interface was elegant in its simplicity, an image of a speaker and microphone above a single large button marked SPEAKERPHONE. Janet clicked the SPEAKERPHONE button, its image sinking down and locking into position.

"Heather, Mark, Jennifer? This is Janet Johnson," she said, using the name they had known her by. "Can you hear me?"

After a short pause, Heather McFarland's voice played through the computer speakers. "We're all here."

"Mind if we ask where *here* is?"

A pause, some mumbling barely audible in the background. "Fair enough. We're in Colombia, at the hacienda of Don Espeñosa."

Janet glanced at Jack, whose left eyebrow had risen, crinkling his forehead.

"The drug lord?"

"That's right. At the moment, he's tied up in a chair across from Mark. He was our test subject for the nanite deprogramming."

Jack held up a finger.

"One second, Heather. Jack wants to say something."

Leaning in close, Jack's voice was serious. "Pay close attention. We don't have much time, but it's critical that you do exactly as I say. You listening?"

A brief pause on the line, then Heather spoke again. "We are."

"As soon as we're done with what we have to do in the next hour, I want you to get out of that house. Get to the Hotel Caribe in Cartagena as quickly as possible. A man named Juan Perdero works at the front desk. Tell him these exact words: 'Don't fear the Reaper.' He will reply, 'Agents of fortune?' to which you respond, 'Nineteen seventy-six.' Have you got that?"

"Yes," Heather replied.

"Good. He'll arrange to meet you in a more secure location. Once there, tell him I said to get you the papers and transportation you'll need to get to Santa Cruz, Bolivia."

"Bolivia?"

Jack ignored the question. "Once you get to Santa Cruz, hire a taxi to take you to the Mennonite community called Quatro Cañadas. It sits on the far side of the Rio Grande, a couple of hours northeast of Santa Cruz. The Robertson family will take you in. Ask for directions to their farm."

"I understand." Heather's voice carried a minor tremor, as if she dreaded what he might say next.

"There's one more thing. It's hard, but absolutely necessary. Before you leave the estate, you need to kill Don Espeñosa. If you don't, you'll have no chance of getting out of Colombia alive. Mark, do you understand me?"

Mark's voice sounded stressed, but steady. "I understand."

"Good. Remember, find the Robertsons' Mennonite farm. Stay with them until I come for you. Do what you can to fit in. They are good people." Jack leaned away, turning the microphone back to Janet.

Despite her curiosity, Janet returned the conversation to the job at hand. "As much as I'd love to chat with you all, we're a little tight on time. Jack and I have the supplies we're going to need to splice into the antenna's data cable.

"Right now we're in a maintenance building a couple hundred yards from the antenna. It's unoccupied and a good spot for me to set up this laptop. In a few minutes, Jack will take his kit and move on out to the antenna to make the splice. He'll wire in another laptop with a wireless network card that I can tie into from here. Once he's done that, I'll let you know we're ready."

Heather answered, her voice shaky. "OK. By then we'll have run a complete analysis on the data link so that we'll know the signals to feed back to the control center. We have to make them think the antenna and satellite downlinks are operating normally, even when Jack cuts the line."

"Then he'll get going."

"Wait. On second thought, there's no need for you to tell us when Jack's ready. We'll know as soon as he cuts the line. When we see that, we'll substitute our own signal through the QT on your laptop and out through the wireless card at the antenna."

"Anything else?"

"No."

"OK. Be strong. Talk to you later. Janet out."

Janet clicked off the SPEAKERPHONE button, briefly considering the possibility that the young savants were still listening. It didn't matter. They could do that any time they wanted.

Janet rose from the chair, stepping up beside Jack as he opened the door. Wrapping her arms around his neck, she kissed him deeply. "Watch yourself."

"Always do."

With that, Jack moved away around the side of the building and disappeared into the darkness. Janet closed the door behind her, set the Heckler & Koch 9mm Compact on the desk beside her laptop, and sat back down.

She wouldn't have long to wait.

CHAPTER 138

In the past, Eduardo would have needed the artificial enhancement provided by night-vision binoculars to see the dark landscape stretched out before him. But the growth of his abilities since he had first placed the artifact upon his head had changed all that. While it wasn't like daylight, this spectrum of illumination was almost as clear. Tonight the darkness shrouding Schriever Air Force Base would not help conceal its secrets.

It was almost as if he could see into the Ripper's head. The man had done exactly what he would have done, skirting the perimeter fencing of the air force base until he found the perfect spot, cutting a hole in the fencing and going through, directly toward the GPS antenna visible in the distance. As pleasurable as it was to kill guards, dead guards attracted more attention than live ones, failing to respond to radio queries, failing to check in at required intervals. Best to bypass them, letting them cluelessly continue their ineffective patrols.

The man was good. But tonight the Ripper was his.

Eduardo slid through the cut in the fence, the sniper rifle slung across his shoulders. In the distance he could see the GPS antenna silhouetted against a number of lighted buildings farther away. Closer at hand, perhaps two hundred yards away from the antenna, a steel building jutted up from the ground, obviously a maintenance building of some type.

As Eduardo began to move forward, the door to the building slid open, causing him to sink down to the ground. A man moved into the doorway, paused momentarily as a woman moved to embrace him. As they separated again, the man paused, like an animal sniffing the night air, his gaze sweeping outward. Then he moved away rapidly, rounding the building toward the antenna. The Ripper.

Eduardo's gaze refocused on the woman in the doorway, backlit by a dim glow from inside, something only he could see. Her extended belly told him all he needed to know. She was pregnant.

Why in the world would Jack Gregory bring a pregnant woman along on this mission? There could be only one reason. This was more than just a member of his team. This was his lover, and in her swollen stomach was his unborn child. Funny that Garfield Kromly hadn't mentioned that. Had he known? Was it possible that he had taken that secret with him to his grave? A last, small victory?

Eduardo smiled. He didn't think so, but it didn't really matter. He now knew. And it was perfect.

Stepping back inside, the woman pulled the door closed. Immediately El Chupacabra was up and moving again, covering the intervening distance in a ground-burning lope that kept the building between him and the antenna. Between him and the Ripper.

The metal building rose up before him like an ancient Sphinx rising out of the night, vainly trying to protect its pharaoh. Eduardo paused just outside the door, a grin of anticipation spreading across his face. There would be no protection from that which had been summoned. Not here. Not tonight.

In the darkness just outside the door, Eduardo stilled his breathing, allowing the sounds within the maintenance building to caress his enhanced hearing. Inside, fingers tapped a computer keyboard. He increased his focus. There it was. A lone heartbeat. Wait. Two heartbeats, one at a steady fifty-six beats per minute. The other, much less distinct, raced along at 110 beats per minute. And this second was at a higher pitch, the volume of blood pulsing through a much, much smaller aortic cavity.

The mother and her unborn child.

The woman was close, sitting at a computer not more than ten feet from the door. El Chupacabra couldn't have asked for anything better. What had started as a great night had suddenly gotten better. Much better.

With a pull that shot the door open along its track, El Chupacabra leaped into the room, racing across the intervening space with a speed that no mortal could match. Although surprised, the woman recovered immediately, her hand flying to the gun sitting beside the laptop. She was fast. But not nearly fast enough.

Eduardo's blow knocked her backward out of her chair, sending the weapon flying into the center of the room. Landing in a tuck roll that brought her back to her feet, the pregnant agent was too slow to deal with the onslaught that confronted her. Eduardo chopped the side of her neck with a precisely gauged blow.

She pitched forward, face-first, but before she could hit the concrete floor, Eduardo caught her, tossing her over his left shoulder as if she weighed no more than a child.

His eyes swept the room. Definitely not the spot where he wanted to take on the Ripper. Single exit, too enclosed. If the Ripper waited outside, Eduardo would be trapped here. Ignoring the laptop, his eyes moved to the walkie-talkie on the desk.

Picking it up, Eduardo paused in the doorway just long enough to ensure the path was clear. Then, backtracking along the way by which he'd entered the air base, he stuffed the woman's unconscious body beneath the fence flap, then ducked through. Once again, he lifted her onto his shoulder, the feel of the unborn heartbeat in her belly elevating his pulse with anticipation.

A quarter mile later he found what he'd been looking for: a draw that funneled into a perfect kill zone. Laying the woman down between two trees, he extracted his rape kit, pulling loose a precut strip of duct tape and placing it across her mouth. He didn't bother to bind her hands and feet. After all, he was a new god. Well beyond fear of any man, much less a woman.

Eduardo touched the woman's pregnant belly, looked back toward the air base, and smiled. In a few minutes he would press the button on the walkie-talkie to let Jack Gregory hear his girlfriend's screams.

A grin of anticipation split Eduardo's lips. The Ripper would come for him. And then El Chupacabra would show the Ripper the true meaning of fear.

CHAPTER 139

Janet struggled toward wakefulness, her lips so dry that they felt as if they'd been glued together. Then it came back to her.

Her eyes popped open, but her lips did not. A heavy strip of duct tape closed them as effectively as a padlock on a storage locker. She couldn't move her arms either. They were pinned to the ground by a pair of knees that straddled her stomach.

A face swam into her blurred vision, a startlingly handsome face. In her memory, it had a name attached to it, although in her current state of confusion, that name eluded her.

The night breeze was cold on her naked body, squeezing her skin into tight little goose bumps, puckering her nipples. She was completely naked. The realization brought her out of the haze. She moved her gaze to the man who straddled her. Although fully clothed, he was plainly excited.

Weighing her options, Janet looked again into that face, her eyes locking with her attacker's. Eduardo Montenegro.

She tried to scissor her legs, but they failed to respond. She was a cobra, locked in the snake charmer's gaze, her body frozen so that she could only stare up into those strangely active eyes.

Eduardo smiled as his hands caressed her body.

"Hello, Janet. It is Janet, isn't it?" The silky-smooth Latin voice creeped her out more than her inability to respond. "With this round body, it took me a while to recognize you from your file photos."

Eduardo leaned down and gently kissed her on the cheek, the feel of his lips sending a pulse of revulsion through her body. It felt as if she'd just been kissed by her mortician.

"Don't worry," he said, "I like pregnant ladies, especially ones as pretty as you. It excites me."

His breath on her cheek smelled faintly of cinnamon candy. Red Hots. Christ, she'd dated a boy in high school who had chugged down Red Hots. Janet had never liked him either.

"You know what makes me really hot?" Eduardo asked, opening the buttons on his shirt.

"Screw you," Janet mumbled behind the tape gag.

Eduardo smiled. "That too. But first, indulge me with a bit of fantasy. Tell me, young lady. What do you really fear?"

Suddenly, Janet found her gaze bound more tightly to his, and she was unable to move, unable to blink.

The night sky melted away, leaving her seated in a green, grassy park with a large sand playground. The sound of children laughing as they swung from the monkey bars tickled her ears. It was a perfect day. She didn't know why she should be uneasy, but she was.

Where was her Robby? He'd been right here just a minute ago, whirling round and round on the merry-go-round, but now he was gone.

"Robby?" she called, her voice barely rising above the children's laughter.

"Robby!" Her voice held an edge of the terror only a mother can know. "Where are you, baby?"

As she rose to her feet and took a step forward, she felt the sand shift between her bare toes, small fingers closing around them.

Looking down, she saw the familiar little hand slip away beneath the sand.

"No! Robby!" Janet screamed, dropping to her knees, desperately scooping at the sand.

Her fingers touched a headful of soft, curly hair, then a bare cheek. Another scoop revealed her baby boy's face.

"Mama! Help!" Robby's terrified scream was cut short by the sand as he once again slipped beneath the surface.

Suddenly she felt it. The tiny hand gripping her own. Janet redoubled her efforts, sending great scoops of sand arcing into the air behind her as she dug with her other hand.

Robby's head and left shoulder were now clear of the sand. Another few scoops and she should be able to pull him free.

Something metallic glinted in the sand just beyond her baby's shoulder, shimmering in a way that attracted his gaze. Mesmerized, Robby freed his other hand and reached for it, his small fingers closing around the shiny object with a surprising strength.

Janet felt the tug pull her child away from her as the object disappeared beneath the surface,

"Robby! Let go of that! Give me your other hand!"

But Robby didn't hear her. His little face turned away as he struggled to free himself from her tenuous grip in his efforts to retrieve the thing. With a sound almost like a slurp, the sand sucked him down, his tiny hand sliding from her grasp.

"Somebody! Help me!" she screamed. "My baby's under here."

But the other parents just sat on the nearby benches, pointing and laughing as if she were playing some sort of game.

There it was again, the touch of small fingers beneath the sand. Janet grabbed for the little hand, but she could only get the fingers, and those were slipping away, pulled downward by a suction she could not overcome.

As the little hand slipped away for the last time, her scream warbled out past the tape that gagged her mouth, carried away on the brisk night breeze.

Eduardo's face was back, his smile having widened since she last remembered seeing it. "Good girl. I think we've found it."

The Colombian grabbed her swollen belly in both hands, not exactly squeezing, but feeling very deeply. Janet coughed into her gag, her eyes watering so badly she could barely see. The vision of her unborn child filled her mind with more clarity than any sonogram could provide. And although it should have been a hallucination, she *knew* this was real.

Somehow El Chupacabra had formed a three-way loop, piping the feelings of her unborn child through his mind and into hers. Her stomach writhed, the child curling into a tight ball, kicking out with both feet.

A terror worse than any she could have imagined formed in her baby's mind, his small mouth working as if it were trying to form a scream. He rolled in the womb, twisting the umbilical cord around his throat, then again, tightening the fleshy noose.

"I'm gonna kill you, you sick bastard!" Janet screamed into the muffling duct tape, the white heat of hatred overriding her fear. "I swear to God!"

The baby rolled in her stomach again, twisting the umbilical so tightly that all blood supply was blocked off. Worse, his terror had risen to the point that his movements had become suicidal. But still, Eduardo increased his focus, steadily turning up the volume on her unborn child's fear.

As Janet screamed her terror and frustration, Eduardo thumbed the microphone on the walkie-talkie.

"Ripper. Do you hear your lover's muffled screams? If you hurry, she and your baby might still be alive when you get here. Come to me."

CHAPTER 140

Because of his dark suit and the rich, dark mahogany of his private office, the light from the laptop screen made Dr. Stephenson's face seem to float, disembodied, in the darkness. His normally impassive expression had tightened into a death's mask of anger.

The news could not have been worse. The story had broken less than an hour ago, in a special Thanksgiving-night edition of the *New York Post*, and had swept across the broadcast media like a Montezuma shit-storm.

If it hadn't been Thanksgiving night, with minimal staffing throughout the government, Dr. Stephenson would, no doubt, have already been escorted from the laboratory, his security clearance revoked pending investigation.

There it was on his computer screen, a reprint of the *Post* story with the hated byline: Freddy Hagerman...apparently not nearly as dead as they'd thought. An image of Dr. Stephenson stepping out of a helicopter onto the grounds at Henderson House filled the front page. The detail in the story proved to be some of the most impressive investigative reporting Stephenson had ever seen. He didn't have much time.

Dr. Stephenson pressed the key combinations that activated a special secure video link. Raul's strange face appeared on the screen, a look of annoyance scrunching his forehead beneath his Plexiglas-like braincap.

Without waiting for a question, Dr. Stephenson spoke across the link.

"I have coordinates for your girlfriend. I'll send it in just a few minutes. If you want her, you can go get her."

The transformation of Raul's face was remarkable, the harsh look melting into mad glee. Stephenson killed the link, letting the screen fade to black.

Ready or not, the fallback plan had been activated.

CHAPTER 141

"What's happening?"

The edge in Mark's voice relayed the stress produced by having to watch the two girls work. Jennifer's fingers danced across the keyboard as Heather talked her through the satellite downlink algorithms.

"I don't know," Heather said. "Jack finished the splice for the downlink, but we don't have our uplink connection."

"Which means?"

"It means we can spoof the control center to make them think they're still talking to the satellite, but we can't send any commands. We can't uplink the code."

"Maybe Jack is still working on that connection."

Heather turned toward him, her eyes just clearing from one of her trances. "I don't think Jack's going to finish the connection. I think something's gone terribly wrong."

"What?"

"I don't know."

Jennifer lifted her head to stare at them. "I started the fake downlink, but without that last connection we're dead in the water. And the control station will only be fooled for so long."

"Shit!" Mark began pacing back and forth across the room. "There has to be something we can do. Can we hack another system?"

Jennifer frowned. "That's just it. Jack cut the cable on the uplink side. Even if I could hack the control center to override their uplink, the commands wouldn't get to the satellite."

Heather leaned over the laptop and pressed the SPEAKERPHONE button on the QT chat program. "Janet. Something's wrong with Jack. Are you there?"

After several seconds of silence, she tried again. "Janet. We have an emergency. Please respond."

Silence.

"Shit!" Mark repeated, his level of anxiety rising with each passing moment.

"How much time do we have before they detect our spoof?" Jennifer asked.

"Twelve minutes, fourteen seconds or so," Heather responded.

"Or so?"

"It's just an approximation."

Mark stopped pacing. "What about a subspace hack?"

Jennifer shrugged. "I already told you, that won't do any good."

"Not on the control center. Can we get the coordinates on the uplink line at the antenna?"

Heather jumped up. "That's it. Mark, you're a genius. I should have thought of that."

The unexpected compliment brought a smile to Mark's lips. But before he could respond, Heather and Jennifer had turned their focus back to the laptop.

"There," Heather pointed at some numbers scrolling across Jennifer's display. "Those are the coordinates of Janet's laptop, and that other is the triangulation to the wireless signal Jack set up at the antenna."

"Got it." Jennifer's fingers increased their staccato pace. "Now I just have to search for nearby signals that match the downlink data signature."

"Nine minutes, twenty-three seconds."

Heather's countdown didn't help Mark's mood. He glanced at Don Espeñosa, sitting in the wicker chair to which they had tied him. The man's eyes showed no trace of the panic he should have felt, having heard Jack's instructions.

Looking into that face, Mark felt a sickness creep into his soul. He had no doubt that before this night was over he would have to kill the drug lord, if only because Jack was right: they wouldn't be safe otherwise. They wouldn't even get out of Colombia alive.

As he stared into that impassive face, Mark felt his resolve harden. He had once done a report on a quote from the Israeli military leader Yerucham Amitai.

"In the end, we may have to choose between actions that might pull down the Temple of Humanity itself rather than surrender even a single member of the family to the executioners."

He'd always thought the statement was over the top. But now he understood, though he didn't like it.

"I'm in," Jennifer said.

"What's the link status?" Heather asked.

"Good packets on the line. I'm receiving satellite downlink, which closely matches our spoofer signal."

"Try uplinking a test signal to the satellite."

"Already done. We have positive acknowledgment."

"OK. Start the program uplink."

Mark leaned in close. "Then what?"

"Then we wait. We've got to stay online long enough to ensure the commands get relayed through the military communications satellites to the entire fleet of GPS satellites. It's all or nothing."

"How long will that take?"

"It'll be close."

"How close?"

The tightness in Heather's face told him all he wanted to know.

As the minutes ticked away, the tightness increased, adding age to her face until it reminded him of their Las Vegas disguises. Something in that look told Mark that if they failed now, they weren't likely to get another chance.

A sudden sense of being watched nudged him, the intensity of the feeling making his scalp tingle. Moving away from the girls, he circled the room, his enhanced vision searching for the source of his discomfort.

There it was, suspended in the air. A tiny pinpoint of nothingness, ever so slightly twisting the light that passed through it. The same thing he had seen in his room, all those many weeks ago.

"Got it!" Jennifer breathed.

Heather reached down and hugged her friend. "You did it, Jen. Amazing!"

So intense was his concentration that Jennifer's exclamation and Heather's excited response barely registered on Mark's consciousness.

There it was again. That tiny pinprick in space. And on the other side, someone was watching. Who could have betrayed them?

Mark's eyes locked with those of Jorge Espeñosa.

"You son of a bitch!"

Mark moved so fast that the girls' heads had barely started to turn when he reached the drug lord. Grabbing Espeñosa's head between two palms, he twisted violently. A sharp crack echoed in the room, then the drug lord's lifeless body slumped forward in the chair, his head dangling at an odd angle.

At the corner of Mark's eye, the shock that registered in Heather's face matched Jennifer's. But as he felt his vision pulled back toward the anomaly, Mark thought he glimpsed something else he had never wanted to see in Heather's face—disgust.

CHAPTER 142

For a moment Raul thought he must be dreaming. By the time he had completely accepted Dr. Stephenson's statement as real, the deputy director of Los Alamos National Laboratory had broken the audio-video link. But a little while later, there they were in his neural network, coordinates accurate to within ten meters.

Medellín, Colombia?

What in hell had taken Heather there?

Not that it mattered. In a few seconds he would know whether she was really there or not. And if she was…well, he couldn't allow himself to think about that until he had confirmation.

Creating a worm-fiber viewer had become almost trivial to Raul. For the last several weeks, he had worked around the clock to repair as many of the Rho Ship's power cells as possible. And the more he fixed, the faster his repairs had gone. Even though he had only scratched the surface, according to his calculations he had achieved enough power to open a small gateway to any spot on the planet. Big enough for a person to walk through.

But Stephenson had insisted that he needed more power, enough to allow for redundant failure protection, to avoid any possibility of the gate closing prematurely. So, despite Raul's desperation to get to Heather, he had agreed to keep working, bringing online many times the power required for his purpose.

Apparently, his efforts to satisfy the deputy director had finally paid off. Tonight was the night.

As he watched, the worm-fiber opening stabilized, providing a clear view of a Spanish-style patio area, illuminated only by landscape lighting and light from inside the huge house.

Except for two guards lounging near an arched opening, no people appeared.

Raul manipulated the viewer, sending the worm fiber from room to room in the main house, starting with the first floor, then moving it upward to the second. With each empty room, his frustration grew. The occasional cleaning woman did nothing to alleviate this feeling.

Moving the fiber down a broad hallway, he passed through a wall and into another expansive bedroom.

Raul tensed. There was Heather, looking even more beautiful than he remembered, talking excitedly to Jennifer Smythe. Across the room, a man sat tied to a wicker chair, his lips locked in a sneer. What was going on here?

Just as Raul was about to turn his attention back to Heather, he saw the other occupant of the bedroom. Mark Smythe. And just as he had the last time Raul had looked in on that jerk, Smythe somehow detected the worm fiber's presence, moving forward until he was mere inches away from it.

"You son of a bitch!"

As soon as the words tumbled from his lips, Smythe moved toward the seated man. Fast. So fast, Raul had never seen anything like it.

Grabbing the tied man's head between his palms, Mark gave a quick and violent twist.

Crack.

The suddenness of the unprovoked attack and the volume from the neck bones snapping surprised Raul.

A glance at Heather's horror-filled face told him all he needed to know. Mark Smythe had somehow kidnapped her and taken her to Colombia, probably for some reason associated with whatever drugs he was on. Well, she wouldn't have to live in fear any longer. Raul was coming to the rescue. And if Smythe tried to stop him, he'd find out what it was like to be diced into centimeter cubes of jelly.

Raul's neural network reached out, manipulating the restored power-cell arrays and routing the energy into the gravitational distortion engine. At first it felt little different from the production of a new worm fiber. Then the power pulsed higher as one gravitational wave interfered with the next until they formed a standing gravitational wave packet of the next order of magnitude. Another pulse. Then another as more and more power cells came online.

Now the entire ship hummed with the strength of the growing distortion, each increase in magnitude accompanied by a brief pause as stability was reestablished. Raul monitored the energy production, letting the energy equations cascade through his mind. It was close now, another few seconds and he could damp the power output and activate the wormhole. After that, it would be a simple matter to extend the stasis field through that hole, grab Heather, and pull her through. And if Smythe tried to interfere, Raul would shield Heather from the splatter.

A mental countdown filled Raul's head.

Ten…

Nine…

Eight…

Another power pulse shook the ship, this one much larger than any so far. What the hell was that?

Raul shifted his attention to the problem, applying every bit of his massive parallel processing to finding the source of the power spike.

There it was again, another power spike. Every one of the repaired power cells was ramping up to peak power.

Damn it! If he didn't find out what was causing this, and soon, he was screwed.

Now another difficulty attracted his attention. The coordinate lock he had achieved on Heather's location had broken, a new three-dimensional setting taking its place. What the hell? Somehow, the thing had aimed itself somewhere in Switzerland.

The next pulse rumbled through the gravitational-distortion engine, sending a shudder through his equipment and dimming the uniform gray lighting in the room. To Raul's horror, the wormhole narrowed instead of expanding to human size, focusing all that power into a tinier and tinier spot.

Throwing the full weight of the neural network at regaining control of the ship's instruments, Raul suddenly became aware of a new issue. A large portion of the neural network had restricted his access, refusing to respond to any of his queries. And the level of neural activity within that section correlated perfectly to the rapidly growing gravitational distortion.

Raul tried to override the lock, but his attempt was blocked. He tried again, with the same result. Suddenly, a light dawned in his mind.

Stephenson! What had that bastard done?

A new analysis of the readings gave him an updated estimate of the magnitude of the wormhole being attempted. This was no intraplanetary doorway. Stephenson was trying to open a star gate.

Shit! Shit! Shit!

The ship didn't have anywhere close to enough working power to try something like that. And at the rate that power was being pulled from the working cells, some of which had already begun to fail, every bit of the Rho Ship's power would be sucked away, leaving it with no reserves to power his neural network. It would be rendered completely and irreparably disabled.

Another pulse rumbled through the gravitational engine, but this one was weaker than the others.

Raul redoubled his efforts. If he couldn't break the encryption on the protected section of the neural network, perhaps he could find another way in. The subnet was focused on controlling the distortion and on drawing all available power to support that effort. But what about a maintenance bypass, something that would switch the power cells into maintenance mode, forcing a power-down?

Another pulse sent a shudder through the dying ship.

There. As he'd hoped, the maintenance circuitry hadn't been included in the security system override.

Working as fast as he could, Raul began sequencing the commands to shut down all power cells that hadn't already burned out. A scan of the array status shocked him. Ninety-eight percent failure and rising.

Suddenly the stasis field gave out, sending him tumbling onto the equipment below. The force of the impact knocked the wind from him and opened a cut on his left eyebrow that dripped blood into his eye, a cut that his nanites closed almost as fast as it had opened. As Raul struggled to prop himself against one of the machines, the dim gray light that had always lit the room went out, taking his connection to the neural network along with it.

Raul froze. He was absolutely alone. Trapped in his former castle. Only now, that castle had been transformed into a dead, black cave.

"Stephenson!" Raul's yell echoed from the walls. "You hear me? You will be punished for this sin. By my father's name, I will find a way."

Then, as the weight of the darkness pressed in upon him, Raul dragged his legless body into a corner, curled himself into a tight ball, and wept.

CHAPTER 143

Eduardo confirmed that Janet's hands and ankles were tied securely behind her back, leaving her lying naked on her side. He reached over to rub his hand gently across her belly. The fire of hatred still reflected in those moonlit eyes. Good. He wouldn't be done with her until he'd erased all remnants of that strong spirit. And if that took a while, so much the better.

"I'm sorry I can't let you watch what I do to your lover, but I have to backtrack some. You might make a sound that would warn him. Can't have that, now can we?"

Picking up the sniper rifle, carrying it in the crook of his arm, Eduardo began moving back toward the hide location he had selected for the kill.

The clear night was unusually warm for this time of year, especially in Colorado. The moon was perfect, giving off just enough light for the Ripper to follow Eduardo's trail, but not enough for

Jack to spot him in the brush. Sliding into position, Eduardo nestled the stock of the rifle against his cheek, adjusting the focus on the sniper scope as his view swept the small draw leading up to his position. This was where the Ripper would come.

The slope was gentle, and there was no avoiding the clearing below without leaving the trail. He didn't think the Ripper would leave the trail and circle around to reacquire it. That would take time he didn't have.

In the distance, a movement attracted his attention. He centered the scope on it. There it was again, just a flash of movement within the concealment of the brush. Eduardo let the crosshairs slide along with the disturbance. It wouldn't be long now until the Ripper entered the clearing. Not long at all.

The man was being careless. It was almost as if he wanted to be seen. Eduardo would have expected him to suddenly appear, sprinting across the open space in some sort of zigzag fashion that would make the shot more difficult. If he entered at this pace, it was going to be like shooting a deer at the feeder.

The Ripper's next action was even stranger. He stepped into the clearing and stopped, his head in the air like a hunting animal sniffing the breeze.

The crosshairs moved across the Ripper's face, steadying on the spot where the bridge of his nose met his forehead. Right between the eyes.

A glint of red caught Eduardo's attention. Weird. It was almost as if the Ripper was staring directly at him. And both eyes flickered with that same crimson glow. It looked a little like animal eyeshine. Eduardo had seen it in the black leopards of the Amazon. But it reminded him of something else too, something he hadn't thought of in years.

Back in those horrible childhood days in the slums of Lima, his witch of a mother had locked him in a small, dark root cellar whenever she'd gone out. To keep him from crying out, she'd filled his head with tales of a demon that hunted such dark places, a demon with eye sockets filled with flame, a thing attracted by loud sounds. The being had a name.

Anchanchu. The Harvester of Souls.

Eduardo shifted his focus back to the crosshairs.

"What the hell?"

The Ripper was no longer in his sight. Eduardo's eyes swept the clearing. Nothing. How the hell had that happened? How long had he been distracted? Surely not more than a few seconds.

Rising to his feet, Eduardo shifted positions. Although it was unlikely that the Ripper had really seen him, there was no use taking any chances. He couldn't believe he'd hesitated on a shot. That had never happened to him before. Never.

Not that it mattered. He'd rather take the Ripper up close anyway. That desire to carve the Ripper up hand to hand must have caused his reluctance to shoot. That would be the only path to true satisfaction.

The brush to his left parted, and once again the Ripper stepped out, this time with a long knife in his right hand. Eduardo turned toward the other assassin, a smile spreading across his face. The Ripper was betting on what Eduardo wanted.

Perfect. Dropping the rifle, Eduardo slid his own blade from his pocket, the click of the stiletto loud in the semidarkness.

Then Eduardo moved, his newfound speed and strength eliminating the six feet that separated the two, driving the blade deep into the Ripper's throat.

But somehow, the thrust failed to find its target. His move precisely anticipated, his wrist was met with a twisting block, the pressure adding to his own forward momentum, sending him tumbling away.

Feeling the Ripper's blade graze his side, Eduardo twisted violently in the air, barely avoiding being impaled on the counterthrust. As he rolled back to his feet, a new thought dawned in his head. If he hadn't been remade by the artifact, he would now be very, very dead.

But he had been remade. And one lucky counterstrike was about to be repaid. Eduardo moved more cautiously now, circling his opponent as he watched for an opening. He thrust out in a lightning-quick motion that was met by a slight shift of the Ripper's knife hand, the blade slicing into the back of Eduardo's forearm.

It wasn't a deep wound, but it surprised him. Eduardo played back the sequence in his head. He was moving much faster than the Ripper, but somehow his opponent was anticipating his moves. Was it possible that Eduardo was subtly telegraphing his intentions?

El Chupacabra feinted left, then swooped in for an underhand strike at the midsection. Again, the cutting blade of his enemy awaited him, slashing across his thumb, deflecting his knife strike harmlessly to the side. Blood dripped from his hand, the red wetness making the knife handle slick in his palm.

Changing his grip to the left hand, Eduardo tried again, then again. The last stroke managed to partially penetrate the Ripper's defenses, inflicting a cut high up on his shoulder but missing the throat. Emboldened, Eduardo reversed the blade and came in hard toward the same area, but this time it backfired, the force of his blow impaling his left hand on the Ripper's blade, the assassin twisting it as Eduardo withdrew, breaking at least two bones and sending the stiletto spinning to the ground beneath the Ripper's feet.

The red eyeshine in the Ripper's eyes had grown brighter, adding another distraction to Eduardo's whirling consciousness.

As impossible as it seemed, he was being beaten. If he could just get his hands wrapped around the Ripper, he could squeeze until the killer's head popped like a squashed melon. But that was looking increasingly unlikely.

Fine, he had some new tricks of his own.

Staring into the other's face, he felt the Ripper's flaming eyes lock with his own. Eduardo smiled.

"Now, Ripper, let's see what you truly fear."

Eduardo pushed his mind through those red eyes and into the darkness beyond. The blackness closed in around him so thickly it muffled all sounds. He thought he heard a soft whimpering, but couldn't place it. Something pressed against the backs of his calves, the rough edges of broken cement steps. His hand reached out before him, but in this blackness he couldn't see anything. Where was he?

The damp smell of mildew seemed vaguely familiar, as did the whimpering, which had grown louder. His hand touched the wall to his left. Damp mud.

Lima! He was back in the cellar! But this time he wasn't alone. There in the darkness, two flaming eyes stared back at him with a demonic hunger that leached the strength from his legs, turning them to rubber. And those eyes were coming closer.

Eduardo suddenly identified the source of the whimpering. It was coming from his own throat.

He stepped backward, his hands thrust out before him, but his foot caught the edge of the step, sending him tumbling to the muddy floor. As he rolled back to his feet, Eduardo's terrified eyes searched the darkness. Something touched his shoulder.

"Anchanchu!"

The scream escaped his lips as he stumbled away from that touch.

CHAPTER 144

Face down, Janet felt her baby kick inside her, and that kick stoked her rage. That *thing* had reached inside her mind, had reached inside her baby's mind. Now he was going for Jack…and Jack would kill him. Janet couldn't allow that, wouldn't allow it. The bastard belonged to her and no one else.

Moving her arms, she tested the knots. They were tight, but the thing that prevented her from working herself free was the way the rope bound her upper arms behind her back, a painful technique favored by North Vietnamese interrogators during the Vietnam War.

Taking a deep breath, Janet held it for ten seconds as she readied herself. Exhaling, she twisted violently, dropping her left shoulder as she pulled up and forward with her right. The pain that exploded in her dislocating left shoulder might have robbed her of consciousness if not for the rage that it fed.

But now Janet had slack. It took her three agonizing minutes to free her hands, but the rest of the knots succumbed to her fingers in seconds. As the last of the ropes fell away, she arose, a vengeful, naked goddess. Walking to the nearest tree, Janet reached around it, grasping her left wrist with her right hand, and threw herself backward. Her shoulder popped back into its socket, unleashing a waterfall of pain that dropped her to her knees. But she didn't stay there.

No time to get her clothes, not with that monster out there. Janet turned to follow Eduardo's path, her long strides carrying her silently through the night. Soon the trees opened to reveal a clearing just ahead, and in that clearing Janet saw Jack, his knife held low and ready. Across from him, El Chupacabra stood frozen, his eyes locked on Jack's face.

Feeling her lips curl upward to expose her teeth, Janet lunged forward.

Janet's snarl spun Eduardo's head toward her as something long and pointed glittered in the moonlight, the force of her blow driving Janet's sharpened steel hairstick through his left eyeball and into his brain.

Eduardo's body pitched forward, but Janet hugged him close, twisting and turning the spike with all her might as she gently lowered him to the ground.

As Eduardo's body convulsed one final time, her mouth brushed his ear. "Like I told you...you're mine."

Sitting astride his body, Janet pulled the hairpin from the bloody eye socket, wiping it on Eduardo's shirt before returning it to her hair. Then Jack's strong arms encircled her naked body, lifting her into an embrace that threatened to crush the wind from her lungs. When finally he released her, Jack bent down to examine El Chupacabra's corpse.

"Damned fine work, young lady."

"He should have spent more time practicing his knot-tying."

Jack frisked the body, extracting a Beretta from the holster strapped to the small of Eduardo's back, and two shiny, horse-shoe-shaped metallic bands that reminded Janet of Alice head-bands. Something about the way they glinted in the moonlight gave her a déjà vu moment, but the memory slipped away before she could place it.

"What have you got there?" Janet asked.

"Don't know. But you can bet he wasn't carrying them for a bad hair day. We'll take a closer look later. Much as I like your current outfit, we'd better get you dressed and get the hell out of here."

"What about the satellites?"

Jack shrugged, "I cut the link, but didn't get to finish the con-nections. I don't know if it was enough to let those kids hack their way through a work-around or not. Too late to worry about that now."

By the time Janet had retrieved her clothes and dressed, alarm sirens had begun to warble across the air base. Going back for her laptop was out of the question.

With one final glance back toward the sirens, Janet took a deep breath, then turned and followed Jack into the darkness.

CHAPTER 145

Dr. Hanz Jorgen stared at the newspaper spread across his desk, the corners rippling in the wind that swept in through the cracks beneath the door of his temporary office, high on the cliff above the Bandelier Ship's cavern. The last two days had been filled with news, each story building on the last.

First had been the Freddy Hagerman bombshell that exposed the secret, and probably illegal, scientific experiments being conducted in the warrens beneath Henderson House. That had led to the arrest of Dr. Donald Stephenson, now currently on administrative leave pending the result of ongoing investigations.

Right behind that had come the news that a terrorist cell had somehow managed to uplink satellite commands that had shut down all the nanites the United States had spent the last several months working so hard to deliver. That was not quite true. Some people had been shielded from the GPS broadcast of the shut-down code, but those numbers were tiny when compared to the number of people who had been injected.

Now this. Just as the House of Representatives had begun impeachment proceedings against the president of the United States, President Gordon had been found dead in his quarters at Camp David, having apparently blown his head off with a twelve-gauge shotgun, a present from his former Naval Academy roommate, Admiral Jonathan Riles.

Hanz arose from his chair, walked to the door, and stepped outside. As unusually warm as the Thanksgiving Day weather had been, today had turned brutally cold. Wind howled down the east slope of the Continental Divide, whistling across the high canyon country of New Mexico as if trying to blast the earth's surface clean. It sucked Jorgen's breath away, instantly removing his desire for a short walk to stretch his legs. His legs didn't need that much stretching anyway.

As he ducked back inside, the strongest gust so far almost ripped the door from his grasp. Throwing his considerable weight into it, Dr. Jorgen slammed the door closed, then moved across the room to pour himself a cup of coffee.

The Channel 7 weatherman, Tom Karuzo—Hanz could never think of that name without chuckling—said the first blizzard of the year was less than six hours away. One good thing about that: the snowdrifts would fill the chinks beneath his door, helping his heater fight the good fight.

And if he got snowed in for a few days, no big deal. His work was his only family, and he had plenty of scientific papers to review, along with a report he was preparing for Congress. He had coffee, beanie-weenies, and crackers out the wazoo, three of his many weaknesses. Funny how most of those were food- or drink-related.

Dr. Jorgen lowered himself back onto his chair, careful not to spill the hot coffee on anything, and began methodically flipping through the pages of the *Albuquerque Journal*. A page-eighteen story caught his attention.

Among all the other Thanksgiving Day oddities, a group of scientists from CERN, the European Organization for Nuclear Research, had just completed correlating new data from testing being conducted at the Large Hadron Collider. The huge super-collider, commonly called LHC, occupied the center of a monstrous tunnel, its twenty-seven kilometer circumference crossing the Swiss-French border in several places. Physicists from around the world were counting on the LHC to accelerate protons so close to the speed of light that the energies produced by their collisions would rival those produced in the big bang, theoretically creating particles that had never before been observed. The granddaddy of home runs would be definitive validation of the physics standard model.

Unfortunately, the LHC had suffered a series of breakdowns and delays. The latest of these had occurred early in the morning of what was still Thanksgiving night in Los Alamos.

According to the article, LHC testing had gone well until a large number of instruments began reporting measurements well outside the expected norm. Program scientists had shut down the LHC, and it remained off-line indefinitely while they investigated the cause of this latest malfunction.

What made the article especially interesting to Hanz was a section concerning a group of independent scientists who had begun raising questions about the lack of public information on the malfunction. Despite vociferous protests, CERN had spurned all requests for external review, stating that the top experts in the field were already working on the problem.

Although Hanz didn't have any evidence upon which to base his suspicions, it smelled like a cover-up. Not that it really mattered what he thought. The problem would be sorted out during the LHC's winter shutdown. He'd leave those concerns to the thousands of scientists CERN already had working on the LHC.

Hanz pulled a big sip from his coffee cup. Crap. Already it had cooled almost to room temperature. And at the moment, this room wasn't all that warm.

Walking across to the pot, Dr. Jorgen poured the full cup into the sink and grabbed a refill. This time he decided he would remain standing until he had finished the whole thing. With his predilection for getting lost in thought, that was the only way to avoid a repeat of the coffee-cooling experiment.

His thoughts returned to the paper's headline story. Although it was never good for the nation to lose its president, he had a feeling this time was the exception. As for the arrest of that self-important bastard of a deputy director, well…

Dr. Jorgen raised his coffee cup in mock salute.

"Dr. Stephenson, this one's for you."

With a long, slow, satisfying sip, Dr. Jorgen let the hot liquid slide across his tongue and down his throat. The warm glow in his stomach felt very good indeed, although he had to admit not all of that feeling could be attributed to the coffee.

CHAPTER 146

Heather McFarland stared across the neatly lined rows of soy-beans that extended almost to the horizon, and smiled. She was so tired. And it felt *so* good.

The Robertson family farm had become her home away from home, the Mennonite family having taken them in, accepting them on nothing more than Jack's word. She didn't know what the mysterious killer had done for them, but it was clear that they loved him, completely and unconditionally. And Heather had grown to love them too. Norma and Colin treated them exactly as they treated their own kin.

The Canadian family had migrated to Bolivia over thirty years ago, along with a large number of their fellow Mennonites. And in loose cooperation with the Bolivian government, they had bought a large section of land northeast of Santa Cruz, a short distance from Quatro Cañadas, where they and other

Mennonites had built farming communities. Now they sold their soybeans to ConAgra and supported MEDA, Mennonite Economic Development Associates, helping the poorer members of their sect establish credit and buy their own land.

Life at Robertson Farm these last six weeks had been like stepping out of the modern world and being transported back in time 150 years. Although the Mennonites avoided modern technology, many families in the area used tractors to farm their lands. Not the Robertsons. Their love of the old ways allowed for nothing more than plowing the land with teams of oxen, driving to town in a horse-drawn carriage, and performing a good, hard day of physical labor.

By night, things changed in an almost magical way. The multigenerational family assembled around the candlelit dinner table, thanked the Lord for their abundance and for each other, and then dined in a spirit of appreciation that Heather thought truly wonderful. Something about coming in after a day of hard work made the shared repast even more special. In a sad-happy way, the Robertsons reminded her of her own family.

Heather glanced across the field at Jennifer and Mark as they worked their weeding hoes. Their run from the Espeñosa estate to Cartagena and then to Santa Cruz had resulted in two more deaths, both at Mark's hands, as they struggled to escape Don Espeñosa's grounds.

As Heather looked at Mark, a lump rose in her throat. When she had fallen in love with him she didn't know. Maybe she'd always been there. Sometimes she thought she should tell him. After all, his feelings for her were so clear they could have been stenciled on his forehead.

But somehow Heather couldn't bring herself to do it. As much as Mark thought she blamed him for the killings he'd done, she blamed herself. Everything Mark had done had been part of her visions. She had chosen the path they all walked. And while they were all still alive, the pain they had experienced could only be laid at one doorstep. She could have chosen differently. She could have chosen better.

If it hadn't been for the success of their operation to shut down the programmable nanites, Heather might have started questioning herself more harshly. While their success in that had been great, something about it worried her. Had she made her savant choices in a way that placed the good of the many over the welfare of her friends and family? She didn't think so, but until she knew for sure that she wasn't exercising some subconscious Joan of Arc agenda, her feelings for Mark would have to remain hidden.

Suddenly her attention was drawn to a plume of dust rising along the dirt road toward the farmhouse. A dusty black Ford Explorer pulled to a stop in front of the house, the sound of its engine dying as the driver's-side door opened. It had been six weeks since Heather had even seen a motor vehicle, and she found herself walking toward the house with an air of expectation.

A lean, handsome man in a brown leather bomber jacket and khaki slacks stepped out of the SUV and removed his sunglasses. Jack!

"Uncle Jack! Uncle Jack!" The excited yells of the two Robertson grandchildren drifted across the fields in an echo of Heather's own feelings. Jack grinned as he bent down to scoop them both up, laughing as the two girls wrapped their arms around his neck, covering his cheeks with kisses.

"What did you bring us?"

The universal question brought a smile to Heather's lips. Even with the Spartan self-discipline the Mennonite lifestyle taught, kids were kids. As she got closer, she could see Jack reach into his jacket and pull out two small bags of Hershey's Kisses, handing one to each child and then placing a conspiratorial finger to his lips. The chocolates immediately disappeared somewhere inside their skirt pockets. Then, with their chocolate treats calling them to a more private place, they raced off, each stopping for one last wave before disappearing around the largest of the barns.

Jack's eyes caught Heather as she stepped onto the gravel driveway, the warmth of his smile setting her at ease in a way that surprised her. Awkwardness usually came with reunions, but the bear hug with which he embraced her just felt right. Not exactly like family. More like the celebratory hug of a teammate after you scored the winning goal.

As he stepped back, his eyes swept her appraisingly.

"Let's see. Tan face. Strong, tan arms. Farm life seems to fit you well."

Heather nodded. "The Robertsons have been fabulous. They've treated us just like family."

Jack laughed. "Meaning they put you to work."

"Exactly," said Mark as he and Jennifer rounded the corner.

"Ah, I was wondering where the other two amigos had run off to," Jack said, hugging Jennifer, then gripping forearms with Mark in a way that reminded Heather of some old Viking movie.

"Can I help you with your bag?" Mark asked.

"Not necessary. As a matter of fact, you're the ones who need to start packing. After I visit with Norma and Colin for a bit, I'll be taking you all with me."

Heather asked the question before Mark and Jennifer could open their mouths. "Taking us? Where are we going?"

Once again, Jack smiled that devilish smile of his. Heather had a momentary flashback to the first night they had met Jack and Janet Johnson at her house. And although the memory was tinged with sadness, she had to admit, being around the man made you feel good to be alive.

"Oh, didn't I tell you? We're going to my ranch."

"You have a ranch? In Bolivia?"

"Long story. I'll tell you about it on the way. Don't worry. We'll have plenty of time for that on the world's crookedest straight road."

The front door of the house opened, and Norma Robertson leaned out, her gray hair elegantly pinned back beneath a small, round cap.

"Jack Frazier! Are you going to stand outside talking with your young friends or come in and have a proper visit?"

Jack winked at Heather and then strode to the door as they trailed along behind him.

"Never fear, Nana. I was just saying how we should step inside."

"Humph. I could see that." Despite her mock reprimand, the older woman hugged Jack like a long-lost son. "Please come in. I've sent Jonny to fetch Colin. Oh, and you are staying for dinner, so there will be no arguments."

"Wouldn't think of it," said Jack as they all moved inside the two-story farmhouse.

Dinner. Heather had taken a while to get accustomed to calling lunch *dinner* and dinner *supper*. Regardless, it passed too quickly: mutton, biscuits, and yucca, a fried potato-like Bolivian tuber that Heather loved. Then, as Jack, Colin, and Norma retired to the sitting room for their private conversation, Heather, Mark, and Jennifer returned to their rooms to pack.

Almost before they knew it, they had changed out of their Mennonite clothes and into jeans, tennis shoes, and T-shirts, had said their good-byes and thank-yous, and were turning off the Robertsons' dirt road and back onto the highway that led northeast, toward San Javier. Mark rode shotgun beside Jack while

Heather and Jennifer occupied the backseat, their bags filling the Explorer's rear.

It wasn't long before they understood why Jack had called it the world's crookedest straight road. For two hours Jack swerved across both lanes of the highway, dodging deep potholes that covered the straight two-lane highway. And he wasn't alone. As if in some sort of snake mating ritual, both directions of traffic swerved in and out as they moved toward and past each other, only straightening out at the last second to avoid head-on collisions.

"Were you serious about owning a ranch?" Mark asked.

Jack nodded. "I've owned it for the last eight years."

"How did you get it?"

"An acquaintance gave it to me."

"Gave it to you?" Jennifer interrupted.

"Well, I guess you could say he owed me. Anyway, he was a prominent member of the government, and when an elderly German with a somewhat soiled early life died suddenly, my friend discovered that I was the only heir. Down here people know me as Jack Frazier."

"Wow! Some acquaintance. What did he owe you?"

"His life."

Mark laughed. "Well, that explains a lot."

Jack grinned.

The straight part of the road ended as it began rising up through the foothills into the high cattle country surrounding San Javier. The soil in this part of Bolivia was old soil, capable of supporting an abundance of grass, several types of palm trees, and some tall, slender trees that reminded Heather of her high-country aspens, but it was ill suited to crop farming. This was the land that had called to Butch Cassidy and the Sundance Kid, a land of magical vistas and huge Bolivian haciendas.

"Is your ranch close to here?" Heather asked, leaning forward in her seat.

"It's in country just like this, but it's about an hour northeast of San Javier. I wish I could show you that town, but we don't have time. Sometime, though, Janet and I'll bring you down for a meal at our favorite German restaurant."

Just outside of San Javier, Jack turned off onto a bumpy dirt road, which became their new best friend for the last hour of the drive. By the time the Explorer pulled to a stop in front of the main house at the Frazier hacienda, Heather was sure her butt had flat spots in it.

As they piled out of the SUV, Mark's intake of breath brought her head up. The main house was a long one-story building with a high-peaked thatched roof, in the style of the indigenous peoples of the area. To the west, a number of smaller thatched huts stretched out toward the corrals. Beyond them the beautiful rolling countryside spread out in all directions, as far as the eye could see. Above this magnificent view, a spectacular sunset had just begun to bathe the western sky in fire.

Just then, a very pregnant woman stepped out on the front porch. It took Heather several seconds to recognize her.

Janet's greeting, while less strenuous than Jack's, held all the self-confident warmth that was this couple's defining characteristic.

"Janet! Oh my God, you're so pregnant!" Jennifer's exclamation brought a frown to Mark's face.

Janet laughed. "You think?"

As she recognized how she'd said it, Jennifer's face reddened. But as Janet slid her arm around Jen's shoulders, the color subsided.

"Come on, guys," Jack said. "Grab your bags, and I'll show you to your rooms."

He paused, looking slowly at each of them. "I wish I could say you'll all be going home soon, but the truth is, that's just not in the cards. Jennifer is wanted on a variety of charges associated with her actions for the Espeñosa cartel, and all of you are marked for death by Espeñosa's associates. To go home would be to put yourselves and your families in unacceptable danger."

Although Heather had discussed this very thing with Mark and Jen, hearing it from Jack's lips hit her with the force of a hammer. She could see that both Mark and Jennifer were also struggling with the shock of the blow.

"Jack," Janet said, moving up to put her arms around Jennifer's and Heather's shoulders. "We can chat about all this tomorrow. Things look much brighter in the morning. Besides, I have steaks in the fridge, just begging to go on the grill. I'm picturing a roaring fire, some marshmallows on sticks, and introducing these upstanding young people to a good bottle of Taquiña. After all, the world's best beer is Bolivian."

Heather shrugged off the depression that had settled on her shoulders like a wet scarf. Grabbing her suitcase, she followed Jack into the house, accompanied by her two friends.

A half hour later, her arms around Mark's and Jennifer's waists, they stood on the slope behind the house, looking out at the gathering twilight. They didn't have to say anything. Despite the horrific price they'd each paid, they had received compensation, a bond of friendship forged of steel.

As Heather hugged her friends close, she could feel it. A bond so strong she pitied anyone who might try to break it.

Janet leaned up against Jack as he turned the first steak, running her hand softly down his arm. Her gaze wandered down the slope toward their new wards.

"Those are three very dangerous young people."

"Yes," Jack replied, squeezing her hand. "They most certainly are."

ABOUT THE AUTHOR

Photograph © 2008

Richard Phillips was born in Roswell, New Mexico, in 1956. He graduated from the United States Military Academy at West Point in 1979 and qualified as an Army Ranger, going on to serve as an officer in the US Army. He earned a master's degree in physics from Naval Postgraduate School, completing his thesis work at Los Alamos National Laboratory. After working for three years as a research associate at Lawrence Livermore National Laboratory, he returned to the army to complete his tour of duty. Today he lives in Phoenix, Arizona, with his wife, Carol, dividing his time between developing simulation software for the US military and writing science fiction.